READY OR NOT

by

Chautona Havig

Copyright © 2010 by Chautona Havig

First Edition
ISBN 1450590497
EAN-13 9781450590495

Fonts- Book Antiqua, Times New roman, and Silverstien
Cover & Interior Photos- Dapetheape/iStockphoto.com
Gratje/iStockphoto.com
Matt_Benoit/iStockphoto.com
Edited by Barbara Coyle Editing

Many thanks also to Christy for her hours of labor in editing. You helped me make Barbara's job so much less painful!

The events and people in this book, aside from the caveats on the next page, are purely fictional, and any resemblance to actual people is purely coincidental and I'd love to meet them!

Visit me at **http://chautona.com** and **http://fairburytales.com**to meet more of my "imaginary friends."

For David — how did I write about you before I ever met you?

Imagine my surprise, when a year or so after I started writing this book, my daughter met one of the supporting characters at folk dance class! Luke showed up on our doorstep one day, and we've known him as David ever since. Their personalities are so similar that anyone who knows "our David" will automatically assume that Luke Sullivan was inspired by him. However, as much as I would love to say it's so, it isn't. Luke Sullivan is a composite of many men in my life— and now David is one of them. We couldn't be happier.

For a friend — you'll know who you are and why.

One scenario in this book is shamelessly ripped from the life of one of my high school friends and appears as I remember her telling it, but with a different "ending." It just fit, friend o'mine. It just fit.

For Crystal — thank you for all of your encouragement.

Every sentence of the original Aggie story was shared with my friend Crystal over instant messenger as I wrote it. One day, she popped onto the messenger with a story. It went something like, "I was driving down the road today and passed a sheriff. As I drove by, I found myself turning around to see if it was William."

Talk about a compliment! It made my day, and I promised myself I'd dedicate this book to her if I ever published it. Well, here we are. This book is for you Crystal. I can't wait to mail you a copy.

Chautona

HERE I COME

Chapter One

Thursday, February 28th

Aggie Milliken collapsed onto the disheveled bed, her energy sapped. With silent wicked glee, her alarm clock, "Sarge," taunted her with the approach of midnight. Stifling yet another yawn, she muttered to herself, "Two weeks ago, I had Grisham and Letterman. Now sleep is my best friend."

Aggie struggled to shift the tangled covers into some semblance of order. Fatigue won over comfort, and she kicked aside all but the stale top sheet. *"Lord, I can't pray, You know what's in my heart. I just can't..."*

Friday, March 1st

Aggie stirred restlessly as the wails of a hungry baby tugged at, then peeled away the cozy blankets of sleep that wrapped her like a cocoon. She squeezed her eyes shut tighter; she wished desperately that baby Ian would find his thumb. For the fifteenth morning in a row, Aggie struggled between guilt and frustration that her sister never taught the baby the satisfaction of sucking on a pacifier.

She risked a one-eyed glance at her archenemy. Sarge promptly announced the time of 4:34 a.m. as if Reveille played in the background. "Four hours? I've been asleep for four hours? I got more sleep than this during finals week!" She rolled over and covered her ears with her pillow, while groping, one-armed, for the silent commanding officer of her life. Swiping at Sarge, she knocked it off the headboard and toppled a glass of water in the process.

"Good. I hope you get electrocuted, you vile thing." With some satisfaction that the clock couldn't mock her while hanging from its cord in a puddle of water, Aggie sat up in bed. She fought to unwind the covers from her body, as Ian's wails grew more insistent. She focused every ounce of her will power on climbing from her warm comfortable bed. Each eye, gritty with sleep, strained to stay open as she rummaged for her slippers.

Shuffling down the dark hallway and past the baby's door, Aggie forced herself to hurry. Ian would wake the neighbors if she didn't hustle. She stumbled down the stairs, occasionally tripping over what she prayed were shoes and toys. Skidding through a pile of marbles made her thankful she'd found her slippers. *"Lord, is that where I left my brains? I knew I was hard headed but..."*

She felt blinded by the light as she snapped on the kitchen switch. Instantly, she flipped the switch off again and reached for the nightlight. Food encrusted dishes and unopened mail littered the counters, but Aggie found a clean bottle in the dishwasher. Deftly, she mixed the proper proportions of powder to warm water from the open can of formula on the counter and shook it thoroughly.

As she dragged her feet back up the stairs, Aggie considered the feasibility of a self-feeding crib. Her inventive thoughts came to a screeching halt once she reached Ian's door. His screams, now at an unbearable decibel level, spurred her to swifter movements. She changed his diaper, zipped his sleeper, and scooped him up in a football hold with the practiced confidence of someone with much more child-minding experience. Several steps later, she kicked off her slippers, shivered into the now cold sheets of her bed, and tried to resume a comfortable doze as Ian contentedly sucked his bottle.

Approximately thirty minutes later, bleary-eyed and cotton-headed, Aggie moaned and stirred, as she patted in the general direction of the baby's bouncing back. One sullen eye glanced at Sarge's usual post before she remembered that she'd sent him MIA. Ian rolled and tumbled like a gymnast and barely kept from bouncing off the bed. Aggie, certain that his high-pitched giggle was going to ensure her a nice, softly padded room in a lovely "house" with green grass and men in white coats, wrestled with the temptation to whine as she tried to quiet him. "What's gotten into you, kiddo?"

Ian responded with his one-toothed smirk and threw himself backwards, making the bed bounce again. Aggie pulled the cord of the clock until Sarge's face came into view. Five o'clock. She sighed. Seeing the wet spot Sarge made on the corner of the bed, Aggie jerked the cord from the wall. "It's a wonder that I didn't burn the house down or something."

She glanced back at her nephew. The enormity of her responsibilities seemed to smother her again. Ian probably had a better idea than she did of what she should do next. He usually slept until seven after his early morning bottle. This crazed energy was a new and unwelcome development. "Well, Ian, I suppose we'll get up."

With a sense of déjà vu, Aggie sighed and shuffled down-stairs with Ian, hoping his odd, yet gleeful, noises wouldn't wake his siblings. She wondered how she was going to survive another day without sufficient rest. As she dragged herself back into the kitchen to make a cup of her favorite flavored coffee, Aggie stopped and burst into tears. On the counter, where Ian's formula generally sat, was the still opened can of designer coffee — and the liners for his little bottles. "This child will *never* sleep again after this," the young woman groaned.

Aggie wondered, for what seemed to be the thousandth time in the past two weeks, if mothering was something she could learn or if it was infused somehow into women's neuro-wiring during pregnancy. Most mothers had children one or maybe two at a time and with at least nine months of careful preparation in between. Aggie, never one to do things the conventional way, inherited hers. She was now the mother of eight lively children. "Not bad for twenty-two and barely out of college," she sighed to herself in a weak attempt at humor. Aggie's tears overflowed, and Ian played with the streams coursing down her face. "Will I ever stop missing Allie, sport?"

Aggie sat the baby in his Bumbo and grabbed what was left of the clean Tupperware, wondering where she'd lost the rest.

"Ok, kiddo, I guess you'll be up for a while, so you play with these, umm, 'toys.'" Shaking her head, she handed the bowls and lids to the baby. Ian instantly began banging them together with vehemence that only drummers can appreciate. Glancing at the open coffee can, Aggie reached for a dirty cup, sniffed for the least-sour dish cloth, and turned the hot water on full blast.

As the water for her coffee bubbled merrily, Aggie took inventory of the kitchen. There was enough work to do to keep her busy for hours. The path of dirty laundry started at the back door and sprinkled itself across the house, all the way upstairs, and into each bedroom. Aggie had few pet peeves, but one of them was walking on dirty laundry. She had not yet learned that walking on clean laundry is even more obnoxious and irritating. The stress of the past two weeks stretched her in every direction until Aggie's nerves snapped.

She transferred the baby and his Tupperware into the playpen for safety, stormed into the well-equipped garage, and searched frantically for a screwdriver. With an exultant cry of victory, she punched the button to the garage door opener and waited impatiently for it to rise. Resolutely, Aggie charged out of the gaping hole left by the door only to return moments later for a ladder. This posed a bigger problem than she'd anticipated. There wasn't a ladder in sight. She searched corners and behind cabinets. In sheer exasperation, she threw her hands into the air and looked up as if to say, "I can't take much more, Lord," but the sight of a ladder hanging horizontally from the rafters halted her internal ranting. Now, she spoke aloud, her voice tinged with disgust. "Who would put a ladder up so high that you need a ladder to get the ladder down in the first place?"

After a moment's pause, she dashed into the kitchen and banged around the room, searching for the step stool. Ian squealed his slobbery encouragement as Aggie dragged the stool through the room, ruffling the few ruddy curls atop his bald little baby head. She teetered on the step stool, barely avoiding a collapse, and finally managed to jerk the ladder from its hooks. Hauling her prize out the garage door, Aggie surveyed the tattered basketball net she had remembered hanging deserted over the garage.

The uncooperative ladder fought her at every step. After several frustrating minutes, where every swear word she'd ever heard filled her brain and threatened to overtake her self-control, Aggie realized that the ladder was upside down. Righting it, she climbed to the mounting bracket, the ladder teetering with every step. She eventually managed to unscrew one side of the apparatus and then the other. With a few jerky movements, the backboard lay on the ground beneath the swaying ladder, hardly worse for the fall.

Aggie felt like a housekeeping genius as she wobbled through the house carrying her conquest upstairs to the wall above the hamper at the end of the hallway. The backboard was heavy and cumbersome; she found it difficult to hold in place and screw it into the wall at the same time, but several minutes later, she stood back and surveyed the results of her efforts. Though nearly satisfied, the lid on the hamper mocked her brilliant idea. Undaunted, she gave a swift jerk and ripped the cover off the offending hamper. "There. That'll work," she muttered as she trudged back downstairs, fighting the compulsion to pick up all the dirty laundry herself.

Allie, her obsessive-compulsive sister, would be horrified, could she see the effect of the dirty basketball hoop on her perfectly papered walls, but Aggie hardly noticed. At least she'd accomplished *something*. Surely, any child would feel compelled to put their dirty clothes in the hamper when they could make a bank shot in the process!

Aggie wondered if her sister's mother-in-law's objections to her being named the children's guardian were valid. Was she truly the best person to mother her sister's eight orphaned children? Could she really step into Allie's shoes? The confidence she'd originally felt was slowly melting into a puddle of despair. She had been certain that she was capable, but after a short time in her sister's home, she realized that she'd woefully underestimated the work involved in caring for a large family. Allie's shoes now felt enormous.

Once again, she wondered how she would ever learn how to get five children dressed, fed, groomed, paraphernalia gathered, on three different buses at the same time, and on time. Getting them home, fed, bathed, de-stressed, their energy exhausted, and then "home-worked" before it was too late to bother sleeping, was a seemingly impossible task, but mornings were much worse. Aggie keenly felt the lack of sleep this morning, drowsiness hovering and making itself a nuisance as she dragged through her still-unfamiliar duties.

She heard a voice call from the cavernous depths of the stairwell, "Aunt Aggie, I'll never be ready in time. Can't you drive us?"

Doubling her efforts to gather possessions and materials, she shouted her reply to no one in particular, "My car does *not* hold everyone illegally, much less *legally*. Hustle!"

Her sister's large van was a twisted pile of metal awaiting the final word from Allie's insurance adjuster. There was no doubt that the vehicle was totaled, but the insurance company seemed to be taking its time in coming to the obvious conclusion. Without a larger vehicle, Aggie could not take all the children anywhere at the same time. Her little VW convertible Beetle only held four passengers and even that was a squeeze. "That's it. If I do nothing else today, I'm buying a van. Forget insurance adjusters. I need transportation," she muttered to herself.

"Ten minutes and counting. Who is not ready? Ready or not, out you go!"

A suave young salesman hastened to meet Aggie as she climbed out of her little convertible. He was like a shark nearing his prey until he drew near enough to see Aggie. Her clothing was simple, yet feminine, and she wore no make-up to accentuate her features. Aggie was not a woman who intentionally drew attention to herself, and as a result, she often prevented undesirable attention. This young, self-proclaimed stud-muffin was a perfect example. Putting on his best salesman demeanor, he turned off his "wolf radar" and closed in for another kind of kill.

"May I help you? Are you looking for a new set of wheels? Perhaps something a little more sophisticated?" His eagerness to sell cars was glaringly apparent, and without bothering with introductions, or even asking what kind of vehicle Aggie needed, he steered her to a line of sports cars. "Surely, one of these beauties is just what you need. This cherry-red Miata, perhaps?"

Aggie, moving away from the line of shiny and brightly-colored cars, finally found her voice. She glanced at the man's nametag and tried to speak before he interrupted her again. "Hello. Jeff, is it? Actually, I am looking for something more substantial and roomier. Something that seats…"

The arrogant and smug salesman quickly interrupted her. "Oh, looking for an SUV, eh? Well, we have a nice selection of them right over here. Is there any particular color you are looking for?"

Before she had a chance to respond, Jeff said, "I see you in a nice blue sport SUV. You know, something to match those beautiful blue eyes." It was obvious to the flustered young woman that this salesman was uninterested in learning what she was shopping for and was quite proud of his smooth talk. It was also glaringly apparent that he was colorblind. Aggie's hazel eyes never looked blue.

Aggie sighed and spoke up, interrupting another of Jeff's self-centered, pushy monologues. "Excuse me, but are you interested in what *I* am looking for? If not, there *are* other dealers in town; maybe one of them would like to sell me a vehicle."

Without much of a pause, she continued. "I want a *van.* I want a twelve passenger, gas-guzzling vehicle that will hold my eight children and a friend or two on occasion. I don't see them, but do you have any available?"

Taken aback, the salesman expostulated, "You have eight children? Impossible!" Not even giving Aggie a chance to respond, he continued. "Don't you know what causes that?" Tact was obviously not Jeff's strong suit.

Aggie sighed and tried again. "I just inherited, for the lack of a better word, my sister's eight children, and I need transportation for all of them. Do you have a *van* that will hold all of us?" She was ready to concede defeat and leave, but the need for a vehicle overrode her burning desire to deny him a commission from her purchase.

"If you inherited all eight from your sister, why didn't she leave you her van too? You'd think it was the least—"

Sighing, she turned to leave. After taking a few steps from the bewildered and rude salesman, she looked over her shoulder and said, "If you want to sell cars, I'd suggest you learn how to listen to your potential customers and learn how *not* to insult them."

Hours later, Aggie sat in a dark, tacky, paneled office trailer at the last used car lot on her list. The previous car dealerships had offered no better help in her quest for adequate transportation than the first. She'd had her pick of pure junk or overloaded machines, sporting everything from DVD players to individual leather bucket seats. Her newest sales acquaintance, Zeke, listened intently as she tried to describe what she needed and why she needed it yesterday. Zeke found it difficult to pay attention to what she said. Her bright and lovely hazel eyes were overflowing with tears, and Zeke was always moved and helpless around a lady in tears.

Aggie liked Zeke's face. Deep lines etched around his eyes and white hair belied his youthful demeanor. He was a bit weathered, but his eyes were gentle and his voice low. He listened intently while stroking one side of an old-fashioned handlebar mustache. She noticed that the side he toyed with was slightly shorter than the other and wondered if it was due to his absentminded habit. Even sitting on the corner of his desk, Zeke was a large, imposing man. Instinctively, Aggie felt that he was a softie with a tender heart. His sympathetic demeanor and the understanding that shone in his eyes prompted her to confide in him, and she hoped he could give her the help she needed.

Aggie spoke almost incoherently through the threatening tears. "You see, I can't get all of them ready on time yet, and so they end up missing school because I can't take them all. I need at least a nine-passenger van, but really, with car seats and all, twelve would be much more comfortable. It's what my sister Allie had, and I think—" She sniffed and tried to continue her explanation.

Zeke cleared his throat and interrupted, "Ma'am, I see you need the van. I understand you have the money, but hon, we don't have one that size, unless you want that shiny new one out there, and it has all that fancy, schmancy stuff you said you don't want. Mighty wise financial decision, I might add."

He paused and smiled at Aggie, who continued to fight

tears. "Now, sweetie, we can get you a twelve-passenger van here in a week, at the most two, but I'd suggest, if you want cargo space for grocery shopping and such, that you buy yourself a nice fifteen-passenger vehicle. If we take out that back seat, you'd have lots of room for storing things. Now, if you need one before next week, and it sounds like you do, I'd suggest you shop in Rockland. There are more options in the city, and I see why you need one quickly."

The retired farmer-turned-used-car-salesman chuckled and snapped his suspenders against his chest. "But as for the school problem, maybe you could just teach those children at home for the rest of the year; that way, you don't even need to go anywhere for a while. It might work until you get a van anyway. Just tell them to bring their schoolbooks home, and then keep them going on their lessons until you get transportation at the least."

"I was trying to avoid Rockland. I actually live there now, but it's so overwhelming. If you find something, will you call? I'd rather wait for you, I think. At least you don't seem ready to talk me into something I don't want." She stood to leave, offering her hand.

Zeke walked to the door and opened it for her. "I'll be calling you when we get you a good one, and who knows, maybe it can be here before next Friday."

Aggie gave a half-hearted smile and thanked Zeke for his time. She gathered her purse and moved toward the door in a slight daze. As she left his office, Zeke shook his head, and the corners of his mouth turned up in his trademark grin. Zeke Sullivan was quite impressed with Aggie's determination. Her unique combination of grit and delicate femininity was a rare and lovely sight.

Zeke's words, "Just teach those children at home," played repeatedly in Aggie's mind as she started her little car and turned toward home. Before her sister's death, she'd intended to begin teaching the following fall. If she could teach a class of twenty to thirty children, surely she could teach five. Even if only for the last quarter of this school year, it might be a lifesaver.

Her education philosophy classes had debated whether the home schooling movement was a good thing. Aggie defended home education with the argument, "The proof is in the pudding." She now thought that home schooling might just be an answer to prayer, but she was clueless as to where to begin.

With those thoughts bouncing around in her brain, Aggie returned to find the older children home from school and diligently working on their homework, while their grandmotherly babysitter entertained the little ones. Five-year-old Kenzie carefully printed one-syllable words and colored matching pictures, while eight-year-old Elspeth hovered over a science worksheet. Elspeth's introverted twin, Tavish, was nowhere in sight. "Hey, guys, where is Tavish?"

The children rushed at her, as if she was an ice cream truck on a hot summer day. It seemed to Aggie that they acted as though she'd been gone for days. She hugged everyone as she tried to calm the mini-riot on her hands. She'd noticed that children tended to be overly enthusiastic with their greetings, but this seemed even more extreme than usual.

Mrs. Gansky, Allie's faithful babysitter, smiled and whispered to Aggie as she retrieved her purse from the hall table, "They aren't used to you leaving yet, and the last time that someone they loved left…"

Understanding dawned. She cleared the couch of jackets and stuffed animals and settled in the middle, gathering the children around her. Recent experience had taught her to let the children snuggle for a while after a meltdown of grief, until they felt comfortable going about their normal business. The tendency to be needy and then fiercely independent was surprising, and the resulting effect was both confusing and taxing on Aggie's physical and emotional resources.

By the time the last child wandered away from the impromptu group hug, it was dinnertime. She heard Vannie, the eldest of the little clan and second mother to them all, opening cupboards and peering into the refrigerator in an effort to find something for dinner. Aggie hurried to the kitchen and sent Vannie outdoors with Cari and Lorna. "Why don't you go push them on the swings? I'll see to dinner."

Aggie surveyed the chaos that threatened to overwhelm her again, and then issued orders to the remaining children. "Ok, Tavish— where *is* he anyway? Tavish and Ellie can go play laundry basketball. I mounted the rim in the hallway upstairs. Shoot some baskets. I don't want to see so much as a sock on the floor by the time dinner is done."

The twinkle in her eyes belied her stern tone. Ellie peeked in the little door under the stairs and called Tavish out of his sanctuary. Aggie almost smacked her forehead. She hadn't yet adjusted to Tavish's preference for hiding away in that tiny, confining space.

"Kenzie, you put everyone's school work back in their backpacks, and Laird, you come with me."

Aggie wondered what to feed everyone. The freezer and fridge were bare. Most of the boxed and fresh foods and the casseroles brought by the church were history. Digging through the back of the pantry, she found a jar of spaghetti sauce and a package of egg noodles. Grocery shopping was no longer optional. She shelved that thought for after dinner.

"Ok, Laird, looks like spanoodlie to me! You find or clean me a pan for the noodles, and I'll find one for this sauce. Is there any parmesan cheese in here?"

Aggie dug through the fridge. It was packed with unidentifiable containers full of even less recognizable food. Some containers were already sporting green, fuzzy hair-dos. Cleaning and de-junking the fridge was now a new priority. Triumphantly, she extracted a tall container of half-eaten parmesan cheese. "Eureka!"

Though it took a good half hour for everyone to scrub hands and faces and clear the table for dinner, the meal itself was relatively catastrophe-free. Ian ignored the excellent example of his elder siblings and cleared his place by dumping his sodden paper plate on the floor. Aggie, desperate to keep from becoming discouraged, chose to consider this a positive thing. With forced Pollyannaish gaiety, she shrouded herself in mock chipperness and attacked the neglected kitchen floor with a scrub brush and mop. There was nothing like spaghetti sauce and noodles on the bottoms of your shoes to inspire a cleaning frenzy, and she informed every child that passed by the kitchen of that little-known fact.

Her head spun once more with the enormity of her tasks. The moment she finished scrubbing the floor, the trash overflowed and spilled to the four corners of the room, spreading spaghetti sauce-coated paper plates everywhere. By the time she had that mess picked up and rescrubbed, Tavish tracked fresh mud across the floor as he returned from taking the trash to the dumpster outside. Aggie reached determinedly for the mop once more when Laird, carrying a filthy and wriggling Ian, stopped her. "Mom always saved the floor for last. She said that our floors were clean for one-third of the day— that third of the day when we're sleeping. I actually saw her just sitting in that chair once, looking at the clean floor, and drinking that nasty bedtime tea she loved." His voice cracked and tears spilled from his eyes at the memory of his mother.

Without another word, Laird carried Ian out of the kitchen and up the stairs. The sound of running bath water told her that he was bathing the baby. Aggie thanked the Lord, once again, that her sister had been such a type-A, perfectionist, first-born. She knew that when Laird finished bathing the baby, he would shower, then come down and rock Ian while Vannie took the little girls upstairs for their turn in the bathroom. Tomorrow night they would switch roles, and Vannie would go up first.

She once asked why they switched, and Laird nonchalantly quipped, "That way if things get too late, the same kids aren't always dirty."

It made sense to her, so she wisely kept quiet and let the

kids continue their routine. She also didn't want to admit that her ten-year-old nephew had more child-care experience than she did. Aggie had never bathed a child in her life, and right now, she had enough trouble trying to remember to take her own shower!

While Vannie readied the twins for their baths, Aggie attacked the counters ferociously. She jerked a large, decorative basket down from the cabinet tops, blew the dust out of it, and loaded it with the stacks and stacks of unopened mail that littered every surface of the downstairs. With that basket filled, she grabbed another. By the time she finished gathering up the mail, there were three overloaded baskets taking up the space she'd just cleared from the counters.

She looked around for another place to put the baskets but failed. Another sigh heavenward answered her unspoken prayer. "Excellent idea, Lord. Glad You shared it with me." Grasping the baskets, she heaved them back on top of the cabinets and surveyed the results. The counters were half-cleared, the mail mess hidden from sight, and no baskets took up any precious counter space. Success.

Aggie had a nebulous recollection of the children bidding her goodnight. If someone had mentioned Cari's screams or Ian's bottle spilling all over her freshly scrubbed counters, she would have remembered. As it was, the children put themselves to bed amid Aggie's third loading of the dishwasher. The fridge gleamed with empty purity, and the microwave was spatter-free. The pantry still sported a crumby appearance, but in general, the kitchen was now clean enough to ward off health inspectors. If nothing else, the scent of lemon cleanser, Murphy's Oil Soap, and dishwasher detergent hinted at a level of cleanliness that it hadn't sported since her sister left on her ill-fated date.

With a sigh of satisfaction, her eyes swept her now sparkling kitchen. Confidence bubbled inside her until she thought of the shopping, the laundry, the bathrooms... "Oh, my— the trash. I don't think I've taken it to the curb since I've been here!" All confidence gone, she flicked the light switch off and dragged herself up the stairs. She noticed the lack of laundry underfoot as she crawled over the mountainous pile at the end of the hallway, blocking the entrance to her room. "Mount Never-Rest," she muttered as she forced the door closed. She now understood what Allie meant by that phrase.

Aggie avoided a glance at Sarge. She knew it was late, but she chose to remain blissfully ignorant of just how late. Tonight, the formula was on a tray next to her bed, and with hot water in the bathroom, there would be no more going downstairs for her! The best news was that tomorrow was Saturday, and she planned to sleep until at *least* eight a.m.
Physically spent, but feeling a little more confident, she snuggled amidst the sheets with her laptop and a cup of chamomile tea that Tavish assured his frazzled aunt would calm her nerves and give her deep and restful sleep. The laptop booted slower than usual, nearly sending Aggie over the edge. However, moments later, she signed into her favorite instant messenger program, and her fingers flew as she conversed with her oldest and dearest friend, Tina Warden.

Aggie says: Tina
Tina says: How are you girl? I've imagined you taken hostage by a group of miniature savages!
Aggie says: LOL. Not yet.
Tina says: How is it really going? Are you doing ok? We're praying, but I feel so helpless!
Aggie says: Oh, Tina, this is so hard. Can I do this?
Tina says: Well, God sure seems to think that you can. He says that He won't give us more than we can endure…
Aggie says: Well, that's true, but how do I convince my heart that my mind is right? Besides, doesn't it end with something about a way of escape? Doesn't that imply that if I don't think I can hack it,

---

I can run away and whimper? How does a twenty-two year old child-illiterate make this work?

Tina says: I don't know. Probably, one day at a time.

Aggie says: Well, maybe in a few hundred more days things will seem more manageable. Right now, I just barely make it from day to day.

Tina says: I'd say that sounds Biblical. If His mercies are new every morning, then it only stands to reason that He'll help us make it from day to day.

Aggie says: Hmm. It's not very reassuring but it makes sense.

Tina says: That'll be one French Crème on the rocks.

Aggie says: Don't say that. Don't ever say that.

Tina says: Why? What?

Aggie says: French Crème. You'll never guess what I did with it the other morning…

Tina says: Do tell!

Aggie says: While sleep-deprived, I mixed Ian a bottle of it.

Tina says: NO WAY!

Aggie says: WAY… he was bouncing like Tigger on his tail, while the rest of the kids were snug in their beds. And the diapers that followed…

Tina says: tee hee…

Aggie says: Listen you; I know where you live, and I will come and find you…

Tina says: Like you dare leave the house for that long. Face it Aggie m'dear; I'm perfectly safe to enjoy your maternal escapades from this safe distance.

Aggie says: I'd love to tell you what I think about those escapades, but I hear a late night marauder wandering the hallway. I'm guessing Cari has finally discovered Ellie's candy stash. I'll bet she thinks she can snag some while Ellie sleeps. Bonsoir, my friend. I go to stop the natives from their plundering!

Tina says: Poofs then!

Aggie says: Poofs!

ALONG WITH THE HITS

Chapter Two

Saturday, March 2nd

Sarge's off-key bugle sounded the alarm promptly at six a.m. Aggie, through the thick fog of interrupted sleep, and determined not to allow another day of early morning chaos, jumped up, slammed her fist on Sarge's "head" and extricated herself from the tentacles of her covers. Without wasting time searching for her slippers, she tripped over the mountain of laundry that covered the hamper outside her door, creating a short trail behind her. She raced down the hallway, throwing doors open and calling, "Up and at 'em! We're not going to be late today. Every child on their bus and on time. Get up, get up, get up!"

She ran downstairs and turned on the TV to find out the day's forecast on the morning news. Channel after channel passed with a veritable smorgasbord of cartoon offerings. From *Power Puppies* to *Flutterby Days*, she had her choice of insipid and mind-numbing animation. "Arrrrrrrrrgggggghhhh!! I *forgot*! How could I *forget*?" Sighing, she jabbed the power button on

23

the remote and dragged herself back up the stairs calling, "Back to bed everyone, it's Saturday, and I need my beauty sleep."

Laird stuck his head out the door and said, "But, Aunt Aggie, you are beautiful enough as you are!"

The boy's impish grin wasn't lost on Aggie. "Who said anything about physical looks, bud? I am talking about beauty of temper. Go back to *sleep.*"

Once again, she scaled Mt. Washmore to enter her room and crawled back into bed. Aggie saw Ian's nearly finished bottle on her night table and sighed in relief. She hadn't woken the baby up with her maniacal shouts. Sleep consumed her, but much too soon, Ian's good morning coos beckoned her from his room. Almost immediately, infant giggles rang through the hallway, and she heard Vannie call, "I'll play with him, Aunt Aggie, and you sleep a bit more. Mama always..." Aggie heard a sniff as her young niece, too old for her years, tried to stifle her tears while she deftly changed the baby's diaper and descended the stairs.

She flung an arm over her eyes to shield them from the sunlight. In books, sunlight supposedly streamed gently through the curtains, illuminating the room with a warm glow. For Aggie, the sun blasted her face like a searchlight, blinding her with its sharp glare. Torn between the desire to comfort her niece and giving the girl space to grieve, she chose the latter. Dejected, she rolled out of bed, grabbed the last of the clothes peeking from her still unpacked suitcases, and moved toward the shower. After a day like the previous one, a shower was no longer optional.

Moments later, her "I'm overwhelmed" hymn wavered weakly from the depths of steam billowing from her half-closed bathroom door. Those who knew Aggie well could determine the state of her spirit by the songs she chose to sing. Some hymns were triumphant and cheerful; others she chose to bolster her spirits.

"My faith looks up to Thee..." Aggie always sang the dear old hymn when she felt weak or fearful. Usually, by the end of

the hymn, her voice rang out strong and sure. Aggie learned the habit of singing hymns as prayerful worship in the fifth grade, and years of singing had so ingrained the habit that her hymns became heartfelt prayers in times of rejoicing or distress.

"O, bear me safe above, a *raannsoommed soouuulll.*" Yes, Aggie was now ready to greet the day.

Aggie dashed to answer the doorbell, arms full of laundry and dropping socks and stray towels in her wake. Doris Gantry stood at the door, laden with plastic grocery sacks. "I noticed the fridge was looking kind of sparse in the raw materials department, so I picked up a few things while I did my shopping this morning."

Forcing her lower jaw to reconnect with the upper, Aggie stepped back, calling for Tavish and Laird to come help bring the bags into the kitchen. Doris watched as Aggie struggled downstairs to the basement with her laundry burden. "Laird, honey, you boys put the refrigerated things in the fridge. If it's frozen solid, should be, or can be, put it in the freezer."

Before she could return for a second load of clothes, the children filed downstairs, their arms full of dirty laundry. Doris shooed Aggie upstairs with strict instructions to stay out of her way. "But send Vannie down in a few hours with some water and a sandwich please. I think I'm going to get hungry."

Her protest died on her lips as the phone rang. Shaking her head as she thundered back upstairs, Aggie snatched up the kitchen phone with a breathless, "Hello?"

"Agathena, the proper way to answer a telephone is to let the caller know who is speaking. You must provide a proper example for the children."

"Well, I—" her heart sank as Geraldine Stuart cut her off.

"Do not interrupt me, young lady. I'd like to speak to each of the children."

Aggie, eager to get the children's grandmother appeased and off the phone, grabbed Tavish as he walked by with another armload of clothing and swapped clothing for telephone. "It's your grandmother."

She tossed the clothing to the foot of the basement stairs, feeling foolish that she hadn't thought of that idea earlier. "Guys, your grandmother is on the phone and wants to speak to you. Tavish is talking to her now."

Jumping out of the doorway, she fully expected the children to stampede to the phone as she remembered doing when she was young. All she heard, however, were a few nervous shuffles and stage whispers of, "You first," followed by, "No, you go!"

Shocked at their reticence, Aggie glanced anxiously at Tavish. Tears streamed down the young boy's face. He shook— with either rage or fear— which one, she could only guess. In a swift move, Aggie snatched the phone from Tavish's hand, gave his shoulder a squeeze, and listened as Geraldine continued her lecture. At the first pause for breath, she pounced.

"Geraldine, this is Aggie."

"I was speaking to my grandson, Agathena, and I don't appreciate being interrupted. I was surprised that you didn't send Vanora to the phone first. She *is* the eldest—"

"Mrs. Stuart! I've taken the phone from Tavish because he is visibly distraught. The other children are busy, so I'm afraid you'll have to speak to them some other time."

"I do not think you understand me, Agathena Milliken. I am the children's grandmother, and according to the law, I have the right to visit with them anytime I please. Now—"

Aggie interrupted for the last time. "Mrs. Stuart. Your so-called right to have visits with the children does not extend to unsupervised conversations that upset them."

For the next twenty minutes, she stared at the phone in her hand waiting for the irate voice to cease. She couldn't bring herself to hang up on an older woman, but neither was she willing to listen to the continuing tirade. When she heard Geraldine shouting her name, Aggie spoke. "I'm still here, Mrs. Stuart. Will there be anything else?"

Answered by sudden disconnection, she set the phone back on the receiver and sighed. Aggie rubbed her temple. A headache threatened to explode behind her eyes. In desperation, she reached for the coffee pot.

Once again, Aggie collapsed in bed physically sapped. Every muscle in her body ached, and she realized she hadn't been off her feet for more than ten minutes at a time all day. Her mind zipped from one thought to another at a dizzying speed. The silky cotton sheets smelled of fabric softener, and the open doors of her closet showed washed and pressed clothing hanging where Allie's clothes hung that morning.

Doris left just after nine-thirty. Every scrap of clothing in the house was stain-treated, washed, dried, pressed, and put in their proper places. The towels in the bathrooms were luxuriously soft and neatly folded. Stacks of fresh sheets sat in baskets on the washer awaiting a massive bed-changing event. Somehow, she knew that had Doris not run out of time, every bed in the house would be sporting newly washed and dried sheets.

Nestled in her freshly made bed, Aggie recalled the highs and lows of her day. The children seemed to be settling into the change of routine. Whereas their life had once been well-ordered and structured, now an incredibly loose routine was the best she could manage. "Geraldine would be appalled," Aggie muttered.

The thought of Geraldine Stuart brought a flush of anger to her face. Tavish, sobbing after the verbal assault by his grandmother over his inadequate mourning habits disturbed her so deeply that she'd called her lawyer and requested he return her call the first thing on Monday morning. This kind of emotional manipulation must cease.

Aggie recalled the antics of Cari and Lorna. She had always wondered why it was that no one ever mentioned the identical twins as "Lorna and Cari." Lorna was a full fifteen minutes older, yet Cari took definite precedence. However, they spoke of Lorna as an appendage and rarely mentioned her without both names linked together. Now, she knew why. Cari had enough personality and spunk for five toddlers. Lorna was often lost in her twin's shadow but was never absent from Cari's mischief. Somehow, the younger twin had learned to invent more kinds of mayhem than a young child should be capable of, and she was an expert at getting her less adventuresome twin to share the blame of her little escapades.

The past week had been a trial for her. She was learning how to balance sympathy and discipline, and by Saturday, the children had discovered that their young aunt knew nothing about children and were taking great advantage of that fact. Cari seemed to know exactly how to get her way without being outwardly resistant, but Aggie was certain that abject defiance was just around the corner. She thought she wouldn't care as long as she could learn to tell them apart. Anytime Cari wanted to exasperate her inexperienced new guardian, she suddenly became quiet and withdrawn, mimicking Lorna's demeanor and mannerisms perfectly. The result was a complete inability for anyone, even for most of the family, to tell the girls apart.

Five-year-old Kenzie was a sweet, impish darling. Apparently, everyone's favorite, Aggie had already lost her heart to the endearing little cutie. Thick red pigtails and a bridge of freckles across her nose set off her blue eyes. The result was an elfin beauty that called to mind County Kerry rather than Scotland's moors.

Little Elspeth concerned her, though. Ellie was quiet, reserved, and almost unnaturally unemotional. Such a definitively placid child seemed strange. However, she was fiercely loyal, especially and quite naturally to her twin brother, Tavish. She expressed her love and affection through her actions, though often with an expressionless demeanor.

Physically, Ellie was the odd child when compared to her siblings. Nearly black curls tumbled down her back on the rare occasions that she let it down from one thick braid. Her eyes were a deep emerald green, and her pale face blushed prettily. To Aggie, Ellie looked like the picture of a stereotypical Diana Barry from *Anne of Green Gables*. However, no one would call Elspeth a beauty. She was attractive enough but too ordinary to be called beautiful.

Her close relationship with Tavish made it easy for her to understand his unspoken thoughts and actions. When he disappeared into his little sanctuary under the stairs and their siblings teased him, Ellie defended him. She could make everyone leave him alone without a frown or a raised voice. Aggie was impressed.

Laird, however, was quite the opposite of his younger brother. He drove first-born, type-A, brand-X Vannie crazy and was entirely oblivious to it. While Vannie tried to pick up the living room that evening, Laird tossed his dirty socks into the ceiling fan to "dust it." Subsequently, dust flitted down to cover the freshly cleaned surfaces.

Vannie finally threw the dirty socks at Laird, trying to show her indignation. It didn't work. Laird promptly tossed them into the fan again. Before long, all the little ones raced around the room trying to catch the balled up socks so they could toss them into the fan and watch it hurl them across the room. The children were so engrossed in their play that no one but Aggie saw Vannie race upstairs in tears.

The scene played again through Aggie's mind, and her heart squeezed anew as she remembered it. She'd knocked gently and then opened Vannie's door. "Sweetie? Do you want to talk about it?"

Not sure how to handle her distraught niece, she'd kept talking, keeping her voice as light and conversational as she could manage. "What's bothering you?" Vannie didn't acknowledge the question. Instead, she sobbed and buried her face in her pillow. Aggie wasn't certain if Vannie's tears were from the frustration of her undone work, or if there was deeper pain surfacing. In desperation, Aggie finally said, "You just cry it out, and I'll sit here until you are ready to talk about it."

Vannie's response startled her. "He doesn't care about *anything*! He is so laid back and irresponsible! He's *just like Daddy*! If Daddy had been more careful and less immature they might be *alive* right now!" With that startling statement, Vannie dissolved into deeper and more heart wrenching sobs. Stunned, Aggie pulled Vannie to her and hugged her fiercely.

"Vannie, listen to me. Your father didn't do anything foolish or careless. The truck ahead of them had an accident. The most cautious driver couldn't have avoided hitting him." Looking deeply into the young girl's eyes, Aggie continued. "They would *not have died* if it weren't for the mix up at the hospital. They weren't even in critical condition. They just lost a lot of blood, and the doctors ordered a transfusion as a precaution.

She swallowed her rising need to deal with her own grief and focused on talking about the accident. "You see, a bus had a terrible accident in the rain and dozens of people were arriving, one ambulance after another. They were short staffed due to the storm, and the nurse just made a mistake."

"What kind of mistake?" Vannie's wails sounded almost panicked.

"Two nurses were there giving them blood, but when the ambulances started arriving, one went to help. The nurse that gave your parents their blood was tired, anxious to go help, and misread the bags or something. The hospital thinks the bags were actually mislabeled, but we don't know. Anyway, your dad got your mom's blood and vice versa. When you get the wrong kind of blood it can cause organ failure, and they'd lost so much blood already…"

Finally, Vannie's sobs quieted and she said, "No one ever really explained it. No one will talk about it. All we were told is that they died from complications from the accident."

She took a deep breath and continued, "I overheard Grandma Stuart say that Daddy had no business being out that late, and I thought she meant…"

As she comforted her niece, Aggie wondered how a woman who loved her son as much as Geraldine Stuart obviously did could never say anything kind to or about him. Why couldn't she simply keep silent when there *was* something unpleasant to say? A new resolve entered Aggie's heart at that moment. She would heed her sister's warnings. The children's paternal grandparents could forget unsupervised visitation and have extremely limited access to the children. Geraldine was already criticizing her grandchildren, and it wouldn't be long before they dreaded the sting of their grandmother's tongue just as their father had.

Remembering the discussion, Aggie snuggled deeper into her artificially sunshine-scented sheets, and the tears flowed. The grief she'd worked so hard to stifle with Vannie overwhelmed her, sending her into recurring waves of sobs. The line between consciousness and sleep blurred with each dropping tear until she finally sank into a deep and dreamless sleep.

Sunday, March 3rd

As she cuddled with Ian and his bottle the next morning, Aggie fantasized about sleeping in and skipping church services that morning. The fact that she couldn't fit everyone in her car tempted her to call the children and tell them not to dress for church. Just as she started to yell for the nearest child, the phone rang, startling both her and the baby. She soothed the baby with a quick hug and gave him back the bottle he'd dropped in his surprise, before snatching the phone from the charger.

Minutes later, she dashed down the hall shouting orders into each room. "Get your shoes on, find the brush, where are the socks, and what did you guys do with my can of coffee?"

As she rushed to button Kenzie's dress and then braid the twins' hair, Aggie felt like the proverbial chicken with its head cut off. Upon reconsideration, she changed her mind. "I'd imagine even half-dead chickens display more dignity than me in my current state."

Clutching four different shoes in one hand and a fist full of socks in the other, Aggie called up the stairs in desperation, "Does *anyone* have two *matching* shoes of the *same size*?" While she hurried to fill a bottle for the diaper bag, she muttered to herself, "Why Allie ever purchased identical shoes for identical twins is completely beyond comprehension! What am I supposed to do with two left white sandals and four feet?"

Somehow, she managed to find matching shoes for all the little girls. "Allie is probably getting dizzy from the spinning in her grave over these things," she muttered again. The ludicrous picture that her mind conjured as she spoke sent her off into a fit of giggles that rapidly melted into choking sobs.

Mrs. Gansky found the children and Aggie huddled around the bottom step in the entryway, wiping tears and looking miserable. Kenzie's nose ran, and Cari's face held a look of impending doom. Little Lorna seemed to have withdrawn further into herself, while Vannie looked several years older.

"We've had a bit of a sob fest, Mrs. Gansky. It's amazing how lost shoes can become such a big deal when you have bigger hurts wanting to be noticed, isn't it?"

Eyebrows rose as Aggie tore out of the parking lot from church and zipped down the road. She'd been so eager to be with the church and sing, listen to some encouraging teaching, and have a refreshing time of fellowship. After missing church the week before, she'd especially looked forward to the peaceful time of communion that always seemed to ground her and settle her spirit in ways that nothing else did.

Today, however, fellowship with the church had been stress personified. From the moment she stepped out of her car, until the moment she pealed out of the parking lot, people had flooded her with condolences, offers of help, and more advice than ten mothers could have tried to follow in a lifetime. The hugs, pats, and knowing-smiles were more than enough. When followed by announcements reminding the congregation of all the help Aggie was going to need, that was almost too much to bear. Guilt nearly smothered her until she realized that everyone was merely doing what the church should.

Aggie repeatedly p-mailed quick prayers, begging for patience and understanding with well-meaning people until she despaired of her prayers being little more than "vain repetitions." P-mail was Aggie's personal term for sending very quick, very short prayers. Aggie considered it her way to live out the Biblical admonition to "pray without ceasing." On days like today, she tended to feel like she'd abused her account, and that if she wasn't careful, her p-mails would bounce, or worse, be sent to God's spam filter.

After the first stoplight and a deep breath of relief, she drove home slowly, enjoying the chatter of the little girls and Ian's coos in the seat behind her. Remembering a drive-thru style convenience store, she drove out of the way, savoring the extra minutes before reaching home, and bought ice cream for the children's dessert. Dessert on Sunday was a Milliken tradition and one Aggie did not want her charges to miss.

Her car slowly puttered through elm-lined streets. Somehow, the Dutch elm disease hadn't yet touched the old stately trees in Allie's neighborhood. She snorted indelicately, amused at the idea of her little outdated Beetle hob-knobbing with the elegant homes of this proud and established neighborhood. As they reached the end of the street, through the tall junipers that lined the wrought iron fencing, she glimpsed a car. Pulling through the imposing (and in her opinion, pretentious) gates, Aggie managed to stifle an audible groan, although her mental mutterings were less self-controlled. Geraldine Stuart's late model Mercedes sat parked in the middle of the driveway, blocking her usual parking place. She was forced to pull into an awkward corner of the driveway far from the door and with little room to maneuver out of the vehicle. Forgetting earlier notions of an exceeded p-mail quota, she quickly sent another zinger heavenward. "Lord, am I in trouble or something? Why *today*?"

She rearranged her face into what felt like a pleasant smile and turned to greet her sister's mother-in-law. "Good morning, Mrs. Stuart! We didn't know you were coming, or we'd have invited you to church with us. I see you managed to get in just fine!"

Aggie jotted, "ensure all doors are always locked," on her continually running mental task list. Mrs. Gansky pulled up to the front of the house and diverted her attention for a moment as the older children spilled out of the Gansky's car and raced up the driveway to greet their grandmother. The look on Mrs. Stuart's face discouraged her from any more forced brightness. She stuffed down the feeling of impending doom that followed Geraldine Stuart like a cartoon cloud, and led the children into the house.

Any hope of a pleasant visit vanished. Mrs. Stuart took command from the second she crossed the threshold. She dispatched the older children to their quarters to change from their dress clothes and into "suitable Sunday afternoon attire." She narrowed her eyes and furrowed her brow at the sight of the mixed up shoe and sock situation. Ian's lack of shoes almost sent her into a tirade, but Kenzie's dress, now splotched with glue from a Sunday school project, distracted her.

She launched into a speech about appropriate attire and being neat and clean at all times. "Their filthy clothes show me that you are not taking your responsibilities seriously, Agathena." Aggie couldn't imagine calling a spot of glue on a five-year-old's dress dirty, but what could an inexperienced young whippersnapper like herself know about these things anyway?

34

The stalwart grandmother surveyed Aggie and the children with disdain. Aggie wore a broomstick skirt and a long sleeved peasant blouse. The simple outfit suited Aggie's taste and personality to perfection. Her hair hung past her shoulders, slightly tousled by Ian's curious hands. To Geraldine, she looked like a hippie.

"Agathena Milliken! Wearing combat boots to church? What kind of example do you think you're setting by doing something so outlandish?"

Aggie stared at her shoes and waited for the offending boots to materialize on her feet. She blinked. The shoes remained in place. Suddenly, her laughter rang through the entryway. Geraldine's eyes narrowed in anger.

"Oh, Mrs. Stuart! These aren't combat boots. These are Doc Martens! Absolutely everyone on campus wears them. They're the most comfortable things; you should try them!"

As Geraldine droned, eloquently but obnoxiously, about the importance of making a good impression with words, actions, and attire, Aggie did her own mental survey of the woman opposite her. Standing perfectly erect, and with excellent elocution, Geraldine's lecture was far from the awe-inspiring report she desired. She heard little of what Mrs. Stuart said. She didn't notice the expensive suit or her perfectly coiffed hair. The jewelry that spoke of old wealth went unnoticed. These things were clearly important to Geraldine Stuart. She saw only the lack of life and warmth in the older woman's eyes. They reminded her of the pictures of the British guard in front of Buckingham Palace, living, yet not alive.

"Aggie, we have a few things to discuss, and I intend to check on how the children are doing before I return home. However, they appear to be hungry. Please hurry with their lunch."

A quick rummage in the fridge and pantry showed the raw materials for lunchmeat sandwiches, chips, and fruit. Though certain to be inadequate by Mrs. Stuart's standards, she was happy that none of the ingredients were frozen or needed the use of the microwave for their preparation. While she slapped mayo and mustard on whole wheat bread, irritation showing with every swish of the knife, Vannie and Laird hustled out of their church clothes and into more comfortable and casual attire.

She grabbed for a clean washcloth to wipe the counter and found nothing. Empty drawers and baskets mocked her effort to clean up after herself. She thundered down the loud steps to the basement, hoping to find a basket of clean kitchen linens on or in the dryer. Freshly-laundered and outgrown clothing covered the floor of the basement in heaps. Aggie had forgotten about everything in her relief to have clean laundry. Mrs. Gantry would pick up what Aggie didn't want to save and take it to the thrift store on Wednesday. She shook her head slightly. "Stay on task, Aggie. Find a kitchen cloth and some dry towels."

With an arm full of towels and washcloths, Aggie moved toward the stairs. Mrs. Stuart stood at the foot of the steps, coldly surveying the room with obvious displeasure. "Agathena, this room alone should show you that caring for these children is much too much responsibility for you, and Alanna had no business requesting that you be the children's guardian. I am appalled that Douglas stood for it, but I can assure you I will not."

Mrs. Stuart stopped Aggie's attempt at a reply before she could utter a word. "Let me finish." Shoulders slumped, Aggie squeezed into a nearby child-sized rocking chair.

"My lawyer has the paperwork prepared and ready to submit to the court. Agathena, if you do not agree immediately to relinquish guardianship of these children to Douglas and me, then we will file the papers tomorrow. Furthermore, I want you out of this house before you do any more damage. This basement is littered with laundry, and you have ruined the hallway with your disgusting ball apparatus. You do not have the financial resources to fight us, regardless of the inheritance Douglas and Alanna left for you."

Geraldine Stuart's face looked as if chiseled in marble. Aggie considered a response but decided that it was foolish. Geraldine would not listen. The woman had no idea of the amount of insurance her son and Allie had left. She had no idea how strongly they had insisted that the children were to go into foster care rather than allowing Doug's parents to assume custody of them. One thing Aggie did know; she was going to have to move quickly.

Resigned to the ugliness that would follow, Aggie stood, shifted the towels, and moved past Geraldine on the stairs. "Do what you must, but I *will* honor my sister's and your son's wishes. I am sorry you feel obligated to disregard them. As to the house, we'll be out as soon as I can move us. Until then, I'll have to ask that you refrain from coming by or calling. I didn't want to do this; but if I have to, I'll get a restraining order."

Geraldine was stunned into silence by Aggie's uncharacteristic assertiveness. She seethed as she ascended the stairs, fiercely humming the hymn, "Angry Words." As she entered the kitchen, Tavish heard her almost biting out the line, *"May the heart's best impulse ever, check them e'er they soil the lip,"* and wondered at the reason. Moments later, he saw his grandmother climbing the stairs with a grim look on her face that told the young boy more than any child should understand.

Later that evening, Aggie decided to get some perspective. She turned on the computer and quickly signed into her instant messenger account. Her shoulders relaxed and tension began to ease even before clicking on Tina's name.

Aggie says: Oh, Tina, this is so hard. Are you *sure* I can do this?
Tina says: Déjà vu… didn't we discuss this yesterday? If I remember right, the Word says that He won't give us more than we can endure…
Aggie says: Well… I hope He handles Geraldine Stuart for me.

Eight children are enough work without adding in a temperamental, selfish, old woman!!!

Tina says: Uh oh… what happened?

Aggie says: Well, for starters, she hates me. Secondly, I hate her.

Tina says: Whoa there… Do you really? Do you really want to be guilty of murder?

Aggie says: Sigh. I guess not. I'm just scared. What if she can get custody of the children? Doug and Allie didn't want that, and here I am staring at that very possibility.

Tina says: Well, didn't your dad say that the court, prior to their deaths, approved the guardianship papers? I mean wasn't your sister pretty Type A about stuff like that?

Aggie says: Well, they are supposed to be settled… I just know that she's fighting me tooth and nail. This woman thinks I am completely incompetent.

Tina says: Oh, Aggie…

Aggie says: I am just afraid she might be right. And even if she isn't, I can't afford to fight her.

Tina says: I thought there was healthy life insurance and stuff.

Aggie says: I have to make this last for twenty years. Food, school, college, clothes, the works — times 8. That's a lot of kids and money.

Tina says: Hee hee… Aggie? Have you ever heard of INTEREST? You are going to be fine.

Aggie says: Things just aren't certain, and Allie trusted me. Can you believe it? She trusted ME. After years of me thinking that she considered me incompetent to do the simplest thing, she left me her children!

Tina says: But do you think she really thought that, or was it your insecurity seeing her as something more than she saw herself as?

Aggie says: What about my insecurities?

Tina says: Did your sister really think that you were

incompetent, or did you, due to some insecurity or something, assume that because you saw her as so over competent?

Aggie says: I don't know. I think you have a point. A strong point.

Tina says: That'll be one —

Aggie says: No coffee… chamomile. Trust me; it's tasty and not lethal to early morning slumber.

Tina says: Gotcha. Chamomile. I can't wait to tell the guys. Aggie without coffee. What next?

Aggie says: It won't last long. I'll get desperate before too long.

Tina says: Well, do it before I get there, will ya?

Aggie says: Will do. LOL.

Aggie says: Oh well, I better get back down there and find out what the munchkins are up to.

Tina says: Ok, take care… poofs!

Aggie says: Nighters.

Double Trouble

Chapter Three

Monday, March 4th

"Mr. Moss? This is Aggie Milliken. I am calling about the guardianship hearing. Can Geraldine Stuart gain custody of the children? She threatened to appeal yesterday. The temporary guardianship papers came so fast..." She listened for a moment and then protested, "But I thought I'd have to do all kinds of home studies and things—"

Mr. Moss heard the gentle tone of her voice strained with emotion and reassured her that everything was in order. "However, Aggie, I would recommend that you consider a new home for you and the children."

For the next few minutes, the lawyer explained his recommendation for the sale of the Stuart family home. She listened carefully and tried not to become overwhelmed at the realization of what moving would entail. Assured that there would be no custody problems, it was hard to concentrate on everything Mr. Moss discussed. The children were safe from Geraldine. That thought alone relaxed her features from the drawn, tense mask that had covered her face since she'd closed the door behind her sister's in-laws the previous afternoon.

Aggie's face was pleasant and appealing, yet few outside her family thought her beautiful. She had long, straight, silky hair, a delightful smile that brightened her face, and expressive hazel eyes. Her most distinctive characteristic was the tendency to wear her thoughts on her face like a billboard. Whether happy, angry, or sad, she couldn't hide it. Perplexing situations gave her the comical appearance of trying to read incomprehensible hieroglyphics. Nothing Aggie did in the attempt to mask her thoughts or emotions worked; her face simply refused to cooperate. Poker was not her forte.

"Thank you, Mr. Moss, I am very relieved. I'll be in touch with you if papers do happen to arrive, and in the meantime, I guess I'll look into finding another home."

Aggie groaned as she disconnected the call. She dreaded the thought of a move for an incalculable number of reasons. Staying meant stability for the children who had already lost so much. Moving eight children and everything in their large home was sure to be a nightmare, and she knew that the expenses incurred with a move and a large house purchase would be steep.

She stared at the phone, still in her hand, with glazed eyes for a moment before Aggie realized she was shaking. With a heavy sigh, she replaced the phone on its charging dock and moved toward the basement to start another load of laundry. The twins' squeals barely penetrated her consciousness as she mulled the lawyer's suggestion that Aggie put the house up for sale. His reminder to her that she had not only the right, but also the responsibility to the children to protect their inheritance pricked her conscience. Leaving the home empty would not be good for it, and if she decided to sell, the Stuarts would likely decide to purchase to "keep it in the family." Everyone would win.

Before she could reach the basement door, the phone rang. Aggie answered and was elated to hear that the car dealer had a van ready for her inspection. "Oh, Mr. Zeke! I will get there as soon as I can find someone to watch the little ones. It might take me a little while, but I'll be over ASAP."

Her face registered surprise, then relief, before she said, "Well, if it isn't too much trouble, you bringing it here would be wonderful. I can put the car seats in it and— Oh, I am sorry. I tend to talk to myself when I am thinking. Do you have my address? Oh, good, I'll see you when you get here then, and thanks, Mr. Zeke. Ok, Zeke it is. Bye!"

Aggie hurried the children into their jackets, shoes, and socks while waiting for Zeke to arrive. After what seemed like hours, a large white van eased into the driveway. With a squeal of excitement, she rushed out front with Ian on one hip and holding Cari's hand. Lorna followed dutifully behind her twin, as though conjoined by an invisible tether. "Ok, girls. Listen carefully. You may look for early flowers or play on the steps, but you may not step off the grass. Okay?" Somehow asking a child if it was "okay" when you weren't giving an option, sounded foolish, but Aggie didn't have time to think about it. The little girls sweetly nodded their heads and then skipped into the grass.

"Good morning, Zeke! Any trouble finding us?" She hustled to meet Zeke as he ambled up the walkway.

"Hello, missy. This is obviously the van. Let me show you what it has to offer, and then I'll put those baby seats in, and we can take it for a spin." Zeke smiled as he rubbed Ian's little head.

Tuesday, March 5th

The next morning, a sterile white van in the driveway replaced her beloved blue convertible. It had been a difficult decision, one Aggie hadn't wanted to make, but today her little convertible beetle sat on consignment at the dealership. The idea of having the van, the convertible, and Laird's inherited Jaguar seemed excessive for a one-driver family.

Aggie illogically hoped that the children would miss their bus to give her the opportunity to practice driving the new Stuartmobile. As she tied her shoes, she fought the rising panic that driving such an immense vehicle can bring. "If I never kill anyone, I'll be thrilled," she muttered under her breath as she stood, her shoes tied tightly enough to sever circulation in the top blood vessels of her feet.

"Aunt Aggie, I can't find my shoes. They're all gone."

"Come on, Kenzie, we have to hurry, the bus will be here any minute!" Vannie, voice muffled by the couch she was ransacking, was determined not to miss another bus.

"This is silly, guys. We have a van, I can drive you; let's not get worked up over things that aren't an issue anymore. Everyone, look for Kenzie's shoes. Any shoes will work; we just need shoes."

Twenty minutes later, a sheepish Kenzie found her shoes in the freezer and put the cold shoes on her feet before dashing out the door with the other children. Aggie weighed the cost, in time and gas, of driving the children to school each day with the extra time they'd have at home. The children spent almost an hour and a half every day sitting on the bus.

"Ok, Vannie and Laird, out you go! Come home on the bus. I'll see you then. Have a good day!" Aggie waved and watched as her eldest charges entered the throng of students flooding the entryway to Jefferson Middle School.

"Ok, you three," she called to Tavish, Ellie, and Kenzie. "Next stop, Westbury Elementary."

"Can you pick us up after school and take me to get the stuff for my science project, Aunt Aggie?" Tavish's eager voice melted Aggie's heart. She tried to think of any request he'd made of her in the last three weeks, with no success.

"I'll be here at two-thirty on the dot. Be ready."

Aggie mapped an alternate route home after ensuring her youngest scholars were safely delivered to their school. She had a list of a dozen possible houses and was determined to eliminate at least half of them before returning home. Aggie's concern was unfounded. After two hours of driving to each home on her list and peeking through the windows on several empty ones, her options were nil. Every house on her list was completely unsuitable.

"What a wash. That was an absolute waste of time and refined petroleum products," she muttered to Ian as she unbuckled him from his car seat. "Is *everyone* asking double the reasonable price for a house? Every one of those houses was tiny— and the bedrooms! They were ridiculously small!"

Aggie waited impatiently for Tina to answer her cell phone, but Tina's trademarked, "Hello, hello, hello!" relaxed her features into a characteristic smile. In a robotic, mechanical-sounding monotone Aggie responded, "Help me. I am in need of immense amounts of your wisdom. Teach me, Tina."

"It must be bad if you're resorting to *Riotous Robots*!"

Aggie laughed at the memory of the pathetic science fiction movie they'd been obsessed with as young teenagers. "Well, bad isn't quite right, but it is perplexing that there are no houses in the Rockland area that are realistically priced and large enough for all us."

Moments later, Aggie was zipping along the information super highway in search of a suitable home. She scoured several realtor websites, but to no avail. Grabbing the phone, she punched the "redial" button then hung up abruptly and clicked the instant messenger icon on her desktop instead.

Tina says: Broaden the area that you'll agree to live in. Change that to say within 5 miles, then 10, then 20 then 100 if necessary.
Aggie says: You think? Leave the town?
Tina says: If they are going to be uprooted, make it a place YOU want to live and are comfortable living in.

Aggie says: Even as far as say… closer to mom and dad?

Tina says: Now you are talking! Why don't you just say the whole state? Your parents are in the center, so pretty much anywhere would be the same distance you are now.

Aggie says: Well, now what about house size. I've been looking for houses that are about the same size as this place. The deed lists it as a 6523 sq. ft. But I am thinking… this is a lot of house to clean. I've seen three bedroom houses with about 1300-1500 sq. ft. and if I took the smallest room, gave the girls a master bedroom, and let the boys have the other bedroom… with them gone at school most of the time it'd be less work, don't you think?

Tina says: Well, hmm. There are a few things to consider. Lower sq. ft. is less to clean, but when summer comes, you'd have a lot of people in the house all day, which means a lot of messes and no room for them to disappear to. Not to mention they are only going to get BIGGER and take up more space just by existing.

Aggie says: True.

Tina says: But with a lower sq. ft., home taxes and insurance are usually cheaper and maintenance is easier…

Aggie says: Oh, boy. I have no idea what to do. I like less to worry about… with everyone close together, we wouldn't end up getting

"lost in our own little worlds" as much as they seem to here.

Tina says: Well, a smaller house would make that easier, but I think that's a matter of training and careful planning. It might even have something to do with how you arrange the house.

Aggie says: Well, I am glad I spoke to you… but you aren't helping me on size!

Tina says: Well, for what it's worth, I think I'd get something close to the same size. For one thing, the children are accustomed to the room, and I think you'd get less grief from Grandmother Dear if you don't put them in something "too

small."
Aggie says: OH, RIGHT. HER. You have a point. We'll stick with large and hire a "mother's helper" if I need to.
Tina says: Excellent idea!
Aggie says: Thanks girl, I'm off to find a house. See you later.

Aggie closed the messenger window and changed the search area to cover the entire state. Suddenly, she had the choice between hundreds of homes in various cities around the state. First, she narrowed those in the right size by price and then removed centrally located from possible search options. It was amazing how detailed the search could be. Horse property, swimming pool, and gas vs. electrical furnaces, stoves, and dryers were a few of the hundreds of options the site offered.

By the time Aggie weeded through fifty homes, she had two houses that looked somewhat promising. She was tempted to continue her treasure hunt, but she sensed something was wrong. A glance around the room proved unhelpful. Ian snoozed in his playpen surrounded by shredded paper, giving him the appearance of a guinea pig in a cage. Aggie smiled, until she realized what disturbed her. The silence was almost deafening. She'd never understood what that meant until she could hear every breath, rustle, click, and the steady hum of the refrigerator.

"Cari? Lorna?" Aggie called up the stairs and out the door. She charged down to the basement, and then up the stairs into forbidden rooms. A quick glance at Ian showed his downy head still nestled amid the colorful paper shreds, as his chest rose and fell in a soporific rhythmic cadence. Nearly frantic, Aggie dashed out the front door and around the side yard to the back corner where she was sure she'd find the twins climbing over the swing set. The play area was empty. The swings barely moved in the breeze. Just as Aggie thought it couldn't look any bleaker, the sun dipped behind the clouds, leaving an ominous feel to the air. The temperature dropped, and Aggie shivered.

The sound of a school bus rounding the corner caught Aggie's attention. Before the yellow loaf of bread on wheels stopped, Aggie saw two blonde girls climbing over a fence, fists full of tulips with the bulbs dangling from the bottoms. She started to call out to them, but several shrieks from several directions created a cacophony that struck her silent.

The twins, seeing Kenzie descending the steps of the bus, jumped up and down, their delighted squeals piercing the air. Kenzie, just old enough to realize that the twins should not be alone at the bus stop half a block from home, screeched, "What are you doing here?"

This would have been pandemonium enough, but the owner of the fenced yard recently exited by Cari and Lorna, dashed down her walkway screaming something about antique tulips and hooligans. Aggie bolted down the street. The twins wailed as the irate woman screamed at them and tried to take the flowers from their tight little fists.

Kenzie chased the little girls away from the angry horticulturist as Aggie tried to apologize. "Just get me my bulbs before they destroy them, and then keep them away from my garden. Those bulbs were over thirty-dollars apiece, and they have handfuls!"

As Aggie assured her that she'd make complete restitution for the twins' thievery, the twins showed Kenzie the "bowcakes" that they picked for her. Cari looked at the flowers with a critical eye. "These rocks are ugly. Take the rocks off, Worna!"

The three little girls tore the bulbs from the stems of the tulips and tossed them into the street. Aggie saw the movement from the corner of her eye and shouted "Nooooooooo," but it was too late. The bus, just pulling away from the curb after the last student stepped onto the sidewalk, crushed the bulbs beneath its massive wheels as it drove down the street and around the corner.

It took Aggie several minutes to assure the woman that she would replace the bulbs, to try to make Lorna and Cari apologize, and get back home before Ian awoke and chose that day to learn to climb from his playpen. Lorna cooperated and apologized with sincere penitence in her voice, but Aggie could do nothing to coax, bribe, or threaten Cari into an apology.

"I'll be back with a check, and she'll have to apologize at some point. I'm very sorry."

Lynn Wilston gave Aggie a disgusted look before returning to her house. At the door, she turned back and called after Aggie, "I know Alanna Stuart's lawyer, and I will call Robert Moss myself if I do not have a check for four hundred fifty dollars by Friday at noon. I wonder what Geraldine will have to say about this."

Aggie led the three children toward home with a dejected droop to her shoulders and her steps dragging in despair. She wasn't bothered by the twins' mischief. Being so young, they didn't understand the wrong they'd done. Even repentant Lorna was sorry only because she knew she'd upset Aggie. The idea that the girls could leave the house, walk over half a block away, climb over a fence, pick a dozen or more flowers, and hop the fence once more before Aggie noticed they were missing and found them, scared her.

"Aunt Aggie? Where is Ian?"

She'd ignored most of Kenzie's prattle about school as they shuffled home but the mention of Ian snapped Aggie to the present. "Run, girls!" In her struggle to extract an apology from Cari, she'd forgotten about the baby.

Grabbing the twins' hands, she pulled them along beside her, their feet barely touching the ground as they tried to keep up with their crazed aunt. Kenzie, seeing the look of panic on Aggie's face, dashed ahead, bursting through the front door and shouting for Ian. Pandemonium surfaced again as the baby, startled from his sleep, screamed in terror.

Aggie collapsed in an under-padded wing back chair, held

the wailing baby, and cried.

After over a week of diligent and exhausting house searching, things were looking dismal. It seemed as though there wasn't a house in existence to suit her unique family, and Aggie was beginning to feel desperate. Thus far, her shopping experiences, even for her convertible and the van, had been swift and painless. To Aggie, a week searching was tantamount to a lifetime. She'd understood that this motherhood experience was going to bring about the patience that her parents always encouraged her to cultivate. She'd always ignored the suggestion, but Aggie now saw the wisdom of it.

A look of excitement crossed her features, and Aggie dashed out to the back of her new van. Writing on her palm with a pink pen, she jogged back into the house and to the phone. Praying that Zeke was at work today, Aggie dialed the number for the car lot.

"May I speak to Zeke please?" Aggie's voice sounded much calmer than she felt. By the time Zeke came on the line, Aggie felt decidedly foolish. Zeke was a car salesman, not a realtor.

"Zeke, this is Aggie Milliken again. I have a silly question for you. Do you mind humoring me?" Zeke's familiar chuckle was music to her ears. "Yes, the van's running great, this is about a house. Do you know of any fairly large homes for sale?"

"Well, missy, I have to admit, I do know of a house that's big enough for your little clan. Do you know how to get to Brant's Corners? It's just across the highway from Brunswick, off Highway 32." Aggie shook her head and then realized Zeke was still waiting for an answer.

"No, actually, I don't, but I am very good with directions. Can you tell me how to get there? Do you know what the owners are asking for the house?"

"Well, the house hasn't been lived in for years. The county just put it on the market last week for back taxes. So far, there haven't been any bites that we've heard of, because it needs so much work."

Aggie demurred. "Oh, Zeke, I can't afford the time and expense of refurbishing a house. What if it wasn't safe? I have to think of the children."

"Oh, no, missy. The house is structurally sound. Our Luke went out there and looked it over when they listed it in the paper. He said it looks worse than it is. It just needs cosmetic changes and minor repairs. There isn't anything unsafe about it.

"My nephew, Luke, likes to flip houses. You know, when you fix up places and either rent them out or sell them at a profit? He wanted this one, but he's stretched a little thin right now. He bought another place on the other side of town just before the county put this one up. He was disappointed that he couldn't buy it— such a nice place and all."

Still unconvinced, Aggie hesitated. "I don't know Zeke. I mean, I have eight children to care for, and the last thing I need right now is more work. Any house I buy needs to be safe and practical for our family. I'm not sure I am prepared for the time, expense, and hassle of a 'fixer-upper.'"

Zeke tried again. "Missy, how about you and I go out there? I'll show you around and give you an idea what the place would need to be livable. You might be able to get it before spring is over, and you'd have all summer to get it refurbished. I think you could have it all fixed up and be settled by winter if you found the right handy man."

She felt bad about being difficult when she'd asked for the elderly man's help, so Aggie agreed to see the house. She arranged for a sitter with one of the names on her volunteer list, and a couple of hours later, Aggie and Zeke zipped down the highway between Brant's Corners and Rockland. Before long, they pulled into an overgrown circular dirt driveway.

"Here we are, missy. Pretty place, isn't it? Those trees are a

51

hundred years old, but the house is near about fifty. They had a nasty fire back in the forties and didn't rebuild for almost ten years. Those oaks made it through the fire beautifully, though; didn't they?"

Aggie sat, hands wrapped around the steering wheel, and stared in silence. Before her, in all its decrepit glory, was the house of her dreams. Built like a cross between an old farmhouse and a Victorian mausoleum, it had a "turret" on one side and a lovely bay window on the other. A railed porch curved around the front of the turret, wrapping it gently like a blanket. Broken lattice ran along the front of the house, below the porch, and left the effect of broken teeth in a much-neglected mouth. The picture tugged at Aggie's heart and reminded her of her English classes where they'd dissected Edgar Allen Poe and his poems. She wanted to restore the home's dignity and beauty and hear her children's laughter ring from its windows.

The oaks Zeke spoke of were huge sprawling trees that almost completely hid the house from the road. On one side, an orchard of fruit trees, covered in buds, almost entirely blocked the view of the highway. With a tall fence running along the road, the children would be safe from passing cars. The back of the property showed both the most neglect and the most promise. There was room for a huge garden, a massive play area, and beyond that, a meadow for horses.

Dilapidated stalls and an abandoned barn stood in the far corner of the property, waiting to house new equine friends.

The back door was unlocked, much to their delight, and it took very little time for Zeke and Aggie to explore the basement, the attic, full of exciting treasures, and all the bedrooms. Skepticism filled her heart at the dank odor that permeated every room. Although Zeke assured her that the plumbing was sound, the wiring, although inadequate, was safe, and the foundation secure, she wondered if paint could kill the scents of age and decay. He admitted that he hadn't inspected the roof but said he remembered his nephew saying that it wouldn't need replacing for a few years.

Aggie, having kept a mental tally running as she examined the property, was certain she could not afford both the house and the repairs it would require. Prepared to admit it was beyond her budget, she asked for the amount in back taxes. Zeke's reply astounded her. For one-third the cost of comparable houses near the current Stuart home, Aggie could purchase this one. The sale of their house could finance the repairs and furnishing of the new home. She could do this!

Aggie returned home and phoned Mr. Moss with the details. "Can you take care of the purchase of that house and submit a reasonable offer to sell this house to the Stuarts?"

Cari and Lorna dashed through the room, decorating it with toilet paper. Aggie took up the chase, trying to prevent the TP'ing of the house. Exasperated, Aggie called "Stop," and both little girls paused — stunned at Aggie's tone. Desperate for a little order, Aggie called all the children into the house and explained that for safety and sanity, she was instituting her first hard and fast rule. Anytime they heard the Aggie say the word "stop," they were to freeze as if they were playing freeze tag.

Following the incident with the toilet paper, Aggie decided to have one of the twins' hair styled in a nice pixie, so she could tell the difference between the girls. After weeks of trying daily, and years of visits, she still hadn't been able to differentiate between the two, very identical, twins. It was time to change all that.

With Vannie's help, Aggie figured out which girl was Lorna and drove them all to Allie's favorite hair salon. Lorna was getting a pretty pixie cut, and Aggie was going to regain at least a small fraction of her former sanity. Cari cried and wailed as Lorna's snipped curls fell to the floor. Aggie tried to comfort her, but keeping seven children from taking up all the waiting space and creating mayhem at the same time was more than enough for her abilities.

Aggie awoke to a mess. She spied wisps of hair scattered from here to there and everywhere in between. Groggily, she followed the trail and to her dismay, found a very scraggily looking Cari. The now shaggy twin wandered aimlessly through the house whacking off hair as her hand found uncut patches on her head. Aggie stole quietly behind the child and tried not to scare her into an unfortunate whack that would surely make things worse.

"I'll take those," Aggie said, as she pulled the scissors from Cari's overly creative hands. "What do you think you are doing?" Aggie's words were stern and low.

It took every ounce of self-control not to scream at the child. Cari's beautiful curls were gone. Her hair looked like one of those freakish teen styles that fill parents' hearts with dread. She also didn't know what to do. If she took the child to get the mess corrected, she'd not know how to tell the two girls apart again. Regardless of the quandary, she had to do something! The child looked frightful!

"I wook wike Worna." Cari's voice broke through to Aggie's thoughts.

"What, honey?"

"Wins 'posed to wook a same. I *wook wike Worna*." Cari's tone was both defiant and emphatic.

"Aunt Aggie?" Vannie's voice interrupted Aggie's attempt to extricate logic from Cari's announcement.

"Yes, Vannie? What is it?" Resignation crept into Aggie's voice. She was clueless about how to handle this situation. Clearly, Cari knew it was wrong to cut her hair. The child's face scowling up at her, the piles of hair, and the scissors in her hand were a silent, glaring testimony of Cari's defiance.

"Can I talk to you?" Vannie sounded hesitant, yet serious. Aggie left Cari with stern instructions not to move and followed Vannie to the bathroom.

"Do you know something I should know?"

Vannie, after a hesitant start, shared her concerns at the amount of defiance that Cari, and even Kenzie, had shown in recent weeks. "Aunt Aggie, Cari *knows*! I know she's little, but she knows. Momma made it *very* plain that they are *not* to touch scissors *ever*. She would not have done this if Momma were here." Vannie's voice caught, but she forced herself to continue. "I think Cari knows that you don't know they're not allowed to touch the scissors, and that's why she did it anyway. I overheard her tell Lorna that she'd 'fix her hair' last night, but I didn't understand what she meant."

Vannie paused, and then spoke before Aggie could respond. "Aunt Aggie, I really think she needs you to give her a spanking. I don't mean to tell you what to do or anything. I'm not trying to be disrespectful, honest, but I know Cari. I think she thinks she can push you around." Aggie started to speak but Vannie wasn't finished. "She tried it with Grandma Millie a few months ago, and Mom had Grandma spank her for it. She hasn't given Grandma any trouble since. Cari's just one of those children who needs to know who is in charge, or she'll take over."

Vannie's eyes pleaded for understanding. After reassuring the girl that she'd done the right thing, Aggie sent Vannie downstairs to play with Ian. Minutes later, a weeping and penitent Cari hugged her and apologized. "I be'ave. I pwomise!"

Aggie gave the child an extra squeeze and sent her downstairs. She returned to her room, closed the door, flung herself across the bed as she'd done so many times when she was a teen, and sobbed. She wasn't prepared for the heartbreak of parenting any more than she'd been prepared for the work of running a home. She remembered the tearful eyes of her father as he assured her, "This will hurt me more than it hurts you." As a child, she'd been insulted. She wasn't stupid. She knew it didn't hurt him at all! How wrong she was. Aggie added another mental note to her ever-growing "to-do list." *"Call Dad, thank him, and apologize for doubting him."*

Aggie says: I quit.

Tina says: Yeah right.

Aggie says: Ok. Well… I SHOULD QUIT.

Tina says: Now you're talking. Just kidding! So what now?

Aggie says: Cari cut her hair.

Tina says: Well… You can tell them apart now.

Aggie says: I had Lorna's cut the day before. Cari has an overdeveloped sense of twinness.

Tina says: How funny. So… how bad is it?

Aggie says: I had to cut her bangs completely off. It looked best that way. Now she looks like she started a flat top but gave up and quit.

Tina says: Oh, how funny!

Aggie says: I'll send pics when I find my camera and my cord. Remind me to buy a laptop with a built in card reader next time.

Tina says: Doesn't Allie have a camera? I thought she was into all that scrapbooking stuff.

Aggie says: Well, duh. Of course she does. I didn't think to get it out. I'll do that today. Allie's is better than mine too. One of those crazy things with different lenses and words that sound like allergies and racial slurs.

Tina says: So how goes the house hunt?

Aggie says: I found one. Oh, Tina… it's like every one we've ever stopped and drooled over.

Tina says: Does it have a "turret?"

Aggie says: YEP! And no gingerbread!!!

Tina says: Victorian?

Aggie says: Sort of a mix… part Victorian, part country farmhouse. It has siding like farmhouse but the shape of a Victorian.

Tina says: If it has a porch...

Aggie says: A southern belle would sit on the "verandah" and serve mint juleps.

Tina says: WOW! And you can afford this paragon of homes?

Aggie says: It's a dump right now. Broken windows... cracked paint... UGLY carpeting and it's FILTHY. The kitchen is left over from a bad '70's remodel including avocado and harvest gold everything.

Tina says: Ick. I don't think I would have liked those when they were IN!

Aggie says: It looks like a retro nightmare. But... it's going to be beautiful.

Tina says: But, how can you afford to buy and fix?

Aggie says: This house is being sold for peanuts. I'm just whipping it into peanut butter and adding jelly for the perfect sandwich.

Tina says: That's it. Go to bed. You're getting loopy.

Aggie says: Nah... it's just my subject matter these days. I have made more PBJ sandwiches in the last MONTH than I have in my whole life!

Tina says: Nighters. You need your sleep. Poof

Aggie says: GRRRRRRr ok. Poofs. Thanks...

Hullaba<small>loo</small>

Chapter Four

Saturday, March 23rd

The Stuart Clan was celebrating the toddler twins' birthday. The girls were dressed as little farmer girls in matching overall jumpers with red gingham shirts and a mini-pony tail on opposite sides of their heads. When the little girls stood side by side, they looked like Siamese twins, joined at the head and with one continuous hairstyle. The result was completely adorable. Aggie had also gotten into the theme and had thrown on a denim skirt and red t-shirt. The rest of the children, eager to feel festive, quickly followed suit. The result was the appearance of an all-American family.

Aggie's parents were expected at any time, and Aggie dashed throughout the house, stashing things in odd places to cover the remnants of the mess she'd been fighting to conquer for the past few days. Grabbing a pile of schoolbooks left by Vannie on the floor beside the couch, Aggie stumbled downstairs, looking for a safe, *dry* place to put them. All she needed, after her exhausting week, was a cup of punch to get dumped on the detailed report that Vannie had spent the past three weeks perfecting.

Dry— that was a thought. Aggie opened the dryer and carefully set the books inside. Half-way back up the stairs, she decided to unplug the dryer— just in case. The second to last thing she wanted to do was replace a stack of schoolbooks.

Aggie arranged paper plates and cups on the table while smiling to herself. *"No dishes to wash,"* she mused. *"You can't help but love birthdays!"*

Vannie carried in two beautifully wrapped packages, and Aggie exclaimed over the young girl's handiwork. "How did you get them so pretty? Mine always look like something done by someone about Ian's age!"

"I love wrapping presents, Aunt Aggie! That's my favorite part of Christmas. All of the pretty packages under the tree…" Vannie's voice grew wistful before continuing hesitantly. "Aunt Aggie? Will Christmas be fun this year? Will we get to have a tree, and presents, and eggnog without the nog, and sing carols, and be happy?"

Aggie sighed and hugged the girl. "We will have the *best* Christmas we can possibly have. Just because your parents aren't here, doesn't mean that we have to refuse to have fun ever again. We miss them. I know that I miss Allie, and I didn't see her very often. I *want* you guys to miss your parents. I would think that there was something wrong with you, or them, if you didn't. But, I think we need to just live a normal life until the pain is more like emptiness when we think of them. Like a little piece of us that isn't there anymore, and we wish still was."

Vannie nodded and Aggie continued. "I think what we need to remember is, they were finished with this world. They had accomplished all that God wanted them to. And I must say; you were quite an accomplishment!"

A sad face lifted wet lashes and a droopy mouth, trying not to cry. "I just think, Aunt Aggie, I think we weren't finished with *them*." The girl turned and went to find the twins, while

Aggie looked around the room as though she were a lost child in a museum. She had no idea how to answer a statement like that.

Choosing the twins' birthday to talk about this had not been a good idea. "Mental note: Don't speak of sad subjects on happy days." With a whispery wavering voice, Aggie started singing as she rounded up the children to go out front and wait for Gramma and Grampa. *"Then to life I turn again... learning all the worth of pain..."*

Aggie saw a familiar, silver Mercedes drive into the driveway, and her heart sank. Now what should she do? The last thing Aggie wanted to deal with on the twins' birthday was an ugly scene, but lately, encounters with Geraldine Stuart had been anything but pleasant.

With a forced smile, Aggie turned to Vannie and said, "Sweetie, will you and Laird go check on the punch?" Aggie knew that drama was probably coming. With Geraldine Stuart around, it seemed unavoidable, but Aggie wanted Laird and Vannie out of earshot if at all possible.

Vannie had helped the children make tissue paper flowers, so Aggie told everyone to gather some to give to their grandmother, and then went to meet Geraldine and her husband at the car. She tried to come up with an honest excuse for not having thought to invite them and couldn't. If her mother hadn't called to remind her of the girls' birthday and tell her that they were coming to celebrate, this party wouldn't have happened.

"Hello! How are you today? We are having a party for the twins, and my parents are arriving soon. I would like to invite you to stay; honestly, I have been so busy getting used to life in the Stuart house that I didn't think to call you." Geraldine made an indelicate snort, but before she could speak, Aggie continued. "However, if you cause a scene, or in any way mar the joy of this day for them, you will be asked to leave. Do you understand?"

Geraldine glared at Aggie with the eyes of a haunted and

angry woman. "Aggie. There is no way that you will *ever* get me out of anywhere unless I choose to leave. Do *you* understand *me*?"

Aggie sighed as she realized Geraldine Stuart must be one of the world's most unhappy women. "I'm not an unreasonable woman, Mrs. Stuart, but I will call the police and have you removed if you create a scene that causes pain to these children. It's the girls' birthday. Please remember that."

Aggie turned before the woman could shoot anymore of her verbal arrows in her direction. "Come on everyone! Give Gramma your flowers! Ooh, Lorna, your bouquet is beautiful. Cari, I love the pansies. How sweet! I'm sure she'll love them."

Aggie saw her parents arrive and flew across the yard to greet them, hugging her mother fiercely. She'd missed them more than she'd realized. In an undertone she said, "Dad, I think I blew it. After Mrs. Stuart's ugly scene the other day, I warned her not to make one today, and she's already looking for anything to criticize. I should have kept my mouth shut and just prayed."

Ron Milliken and his wife Martha wanted to spend more time with Aggie and the children, but Martha's health kept them home most of the time. Ron was a gentle man and a quiet one, but behind a meek demeanor was a man with hidden strengths. Since Allie's death, Aggie thought he had aged considerably and wondered how a parent processed outliving their child.

Martha smiled up at her daughter and said, "Get the cake out, honey, will you? I'll see what I can do with Geraldine. She seems to think I'm harmless enough."

With tact and a bit of pleasant manipulation, Aggie watched her mother steer Geraldine from the yard already littered with broken flowers and destroyed streamers. Party decorations had never been Aggie's forte. She now realized that she should have let Vannie and Ellie decorate to their heart's content. Perhaps the childish overuse of tape in any given situation would have given the décor a longer life.

Aggie was amazed at her mother's grace and patience as Martha kept Geraldine talking while they entered the house. Disgusted, she watched as the fastidious older woman pulled a large handkerchief out of her purse and set it on a chair before sitting down. P-mails flew heavenward faster than Aggie could have ever articulated the simplest request.

Thinking it best to find a quick diversion for the children, Aggie chose to let the girls open their gifts before eating, and Geraldine immediately sent Douglas outside to bring in their gifts. Laird followed to help his grandfather when Aggie indicated that he should go. "Douglas isn't an invalid, Aggie, and Laird isn't your personal servant. Let the boy stay."

Laird followed quietly as if he hadn't heard, while Aggie exclaimed over the little dolls that the girls opened from "Grandma Millie," choosing to ignore the woman's spiteful words. What pleasure Geraldine Stuart got out of being unpleasant wasn't worth ruining the little girls' party.

Aggie almost groaned when she saw the piles of gifts that Laird and Douglas carried in. She first thought that they were trying to have Christmas in March! It was soon apparent that Geraldine didn't believe in buying gifts for just one child. She felt obligated to get them *all* something equally important, impressive, and expensive.

For the next twenty minutes, Aggie worked diligently to distract the twins from realizing that the other children were opening gifts too. Every time Cari saw someone touch a package, she'd shriek and wail over her "pwetty fings." Aggie worked very hard not to let the child continue to be unpleasant without having to remove her from her own party.

Things went rapidly downhill when Cari saw Ian playing with his box. In typical baby style, the infant was happier to chew on the corner of the box, than he was trying to tear off the paper. At five months old, it was silly to assume he would do much of anything else. A squeal of fury erupted from the little girl, and she plowed across legs and feet to reach Gramma Milliken's side. Reaching the drooling infant, the angry girl snatched the box from the baby and slapped his face and hands repeatedly. Aggie had reached her limit. Picking up the furious toddler, she attempted to remove Cari from the room.

Geraldine protested, softly at first and then quite vehemently. "It's her birthday, Aggie. You are being quite cruel. I insist that you put Cari down. The child didn't understand." Looking at the screaming kicking little girl Geraldine said, "You thought he was hurting your present, didn't you, darling? That box was for him, honey."

Cari screamed, "Nooooo! My birthday. *My* pwesents! Ian not have *my* pweasants!"

Aggie gave Geraldine a pointed look and continued her journey upstairs to deal with little Cari. Aggie suspected that this outburst had more to do with Cari sensing the underlying tension in the room and being overwhelmed with the sheer volume of *stuff* than anything, but her remaining in the room was only making things worse. She also wondered why Mrs. Stuart couldn't see it and keep quiet. At the very least, the woman could keep calm so as not to make a bad situation worse.

"Aggie, let her have the present. For heaven's sake, he's a baby and won't know. I'll buy him something later. You can't ruin her birthday over something so insignificant."

Ron stood and nodded to Aggie, who escaped into her room to try to calm Cari. "Geraldine. My daughter was right. Cari was out of control and needed to be removed from the room."

"I'll thank you to keep your opinions to yourself, Ronald Milliken. Your daughter obviously has no idea how to handle a high-spirited child."

Martha Milliken had tried to keep calm and silent, but this was too much. With a quiet but firm voice, she spoke. "Geraldine Stuart, sit down. You are making things worse. Cari was overwhelmed with all of these gifts." Her eyes flashed with uncustomary rage. "You know Doug and Allie didn't allow you to bring very many gifts, but you deliberately chose to override it this time because you *knew* Aggie wouldn't be prepared for it. You've hurt Cari, Aggie, and the rest of this family with your ostentatious display, and I think you'd better leave now. The girls' birthday is ruined."

The strain was too much for Martha, and she slumped back into her chair weakly. A look of alarm crossed Ron's face, and he quickly found his wife's medication. "That's it. Douglas, Geraldine, you have the choice to leave, or I'll call the police. Either way, you *will* go *now*."

"You do not have the authority to throw us out, as you well know." Geraldine was unfazed.

"Geraldine..." Douglas seemed ready to acquiesce, but the irate woman shot her husband a look that silenced him.

"I may not, but if I call the police, Aggie *will* tell the officers that she wants you off of the premises. Do you understand me? Shall I call now, or are you leaving?" It broke Ron's heart to hear the children sniffling and see them beginning to huddle together, but due to previous experiences with Geraldine, he knew that this was only going to escalate.

"I am not leaving. I am going upstairs and bringing that poor child down here to enjoy her party."

Aggie's voice interrupted. "Mrs. Stuart, you are doing nothing of the kind. If necessary, I will bodily stop you from moving up these stairs."

Turning to the children Aggie said, "Go out back — all of you. *Now!*"

"You will not raise your voice to my grandchildren. The court will hear about the verbal and emotional abuse of these poor mother and fatherless children —"

"Parentless or not, these children are in my care, and I have not and would never hurt them in any way. I have called the police to report a domestic disturbance and a trespasser. I'd suggest you leave my house immediately." Aggie worked hard to remain firm, when all she wanted to do was escape into her room and collapse. The woman's histrionics were enough to drive even a stronger person to despair.

65

"Your house! *Your* house," she repeated livid. "This house has been in the Stuart family for three generations! It's an historical landmark, not that you'd know or care with the way that you treat it! I refuse to set foot out of this house without seeing that Cari is all right."

Geraldine sat in the nearest chair without bothering with a handkerchief. Aggie almost laughed at the look on the irate woman's face. It was identical to the look given to her by Cari just moments ago. Aggie went into the kitchen and grabbed a black trash bag. Slowly, she stuffed each piece of the discarded wrappings now littering the living room into the bag and tied the top when it was full.

Ron Milliken came to her side, put his arm around her, and spoke low into her ear. "Aggie, your mother isn't feeling well. I can see her trying not to let her hands shake, and I know her heart is pounding. I can hear it. This isn't safe for her, and I refuse to leave you alone with Geraldine, but the second the police arrive, I am going to put your mother in the car, make my statement, and get her home. It's been too much for her."

Aggie glanced at her mother and then sighed. She should have known better than to try to have a party at the house. They should have gone north to her parents' house. They would have missed the Stuarts, and the party would have been calm and pleasant. Aggie sometimes felt that she could do nothing right. She was in a boxing match, and she'd never have a chance to win. Geraldine Stuart knew how to, not only ruin a beautiful day, but also how to make others accept the guilt for it.

The scene was emotional and ugly when the officers arrived. Aggie had a file folder full of court documents and other legal papers naming her as guardian and legal occupant of the house. While it hurt him to do it, Ron Milliken spoke to the officer, gave his statement and a cell phone number, and then drove away as quickly as possible.

The older officer, with a firm tone and a no-nonsense stance, stood before the irate woman and said, "Mrs. Stuart, according to these papers, this young lady has the right to evict you from her property. You will leave immediately, or I will have to arrest you for trespassing."

The woman screamed and actually swore at one point. Aggie thought for a moment she would throw herself on the floor and pound it with her fists like an out of control two-year-old. Geraldine argued every step of the way, as Douglas Stuart and the officer escorted her to their vehicle. She demanded to see that Cari was all right, claiming that Aggie had beaten the child for wanting to open a gift. The officer turned to speak to Aggie about the claim and found the young woman standing there, holding the prettiest little girl he'd ever seen.

"That your granddaughter, ma'am?" The officer had obviously lost all patience with the situation.

"I don't know!" the woman spat. "She has an identical twin. They are almost 'super-identical,' whatever that means. There isn't a single physical identifying mark to tell them apart, and they pretend to be each other all of the time. That's probably Lorna."

"Miss," the officer turned to Aggie with sympathetic eyes, "I hate to do this, but to save us all a lot of trouble, and me more paperwork than you can imagine, would you *please* go get the other twin. As much as I don't want to give this woman the satisfaction, I think it'd be best."

Aggie walked Cari around to the side of the house where a female officer talked to and comforted the other children. "I need Lorna — the little one that looks like Cari." Aggie pointed to the child in her arms. "The other officer wants to see them both so their grandmother will feel better about going."

She was careful with her words so as not to alarm the children. Moments later, Aggie, Cari, Lorna, and the sweating officer watched the Stuart's Mercedes peal out of the driveway. The man swore under his breath and then sheepishly apologized.

"I oughtta take after 'em and give 'em a ticket! She's got an angry foot that one."

"And an angry tongue," Aggie muttered to herself as she turned to send the children out back.

"Miss, I suggest you consider a restraining order. There is something very ugly about that woman. I've seen a lot in my years on the force, and I gotta tell you: this one is only going to get worse." The officer shook his head, gathered the proper information that he needed for his report, and then circled the house looking for his partner.

He found her entertaining the children with her badge, uniform, nightstick, and all of the other fascinating trappings of police activity. The children were disappointed that neither officer would draw their gun from its holster and let them see it. Aggie, on the other hand, was relieved. The last thing she needed was for the children to start building guns out of household items and creating a war zone.

The officers asked a few subtle questions to gather information on the tone of the home and how the children were handling the situation. It would have to go in their report. They seemed relieved to find nothing negative in the children's situation outside the obvious antagonism of their grandmother.

Hours later, the day's celebration seemed like a nightmare that was mercifully over. The streamers were gone, the wrappings tossed, and the cake devoured. The children were subdued, but appeared to be happy; however, Aggie was brokenhearted. She had tried hard, perhaps too hard, to make this first birthday as the mother of her "clan," as she had begun to call her family, something to help brighten their pain-laced days.

Tina says: Aggie?? You there yet?? How'd the party go?
Aggie says: You don't want to know. Those poor girls.
Tina says: What happened?
Aggie says: Well…

Tina says: No wait

Tina says: The Dragon Lady showed up?

Aggie says: Be nice, she IS their grandmother.

Tina says: I'm sorry, you're right. So what'd she do this time? Didn't you say she used to be nice?

Aggie says: She was before I got the kids. Then everything went downhill. She is like another person. Dad says she's always caused trouble in Allie's marriage, but it was little things. I don't think even Doug knew how bad it could get. It seems to be a control thing.

Tina says: She's obsessed with overcoming her past or something. It's so weird. Like she hasn't had 40 years of redemption time to overcome that need.

Aggie says: I think it's the fear of being alone. She has no faith to lean on, her husband is detached… as if that's a shocker, and now the one person she was close to is gone, his wife is gone, and she's lost their children. Doug just didn't want them to be so emotionally stripped and guilted into "correct behavior."

Tina says: I feel kind of sorry for her, but she makes me so mad!

Aggie says: The appeal was denied, and the paperwork is signed by the judge. Just waiting for my copy. Everyone told me it would take six months, but between Allie's forethought and Mr. Moss' staying on top of everything, it's been great. I think he has a friend in the courthouse though.

Tina says: GOOD. You need it. Think now that it's final, Dragon Lady will withdraw into her lair and return as the ever prim and proper Grandmother again?

Aggie says: We can only hope. After today's demonstration I assume she'll be ashamed of herself and resolve to keep communication open. I can't imagine her not wanting to have a relationship with the children. They are all she has left.

Tina says: Which is why she needs to return to her "correct behavior" before she loses these children all together.

Aggie says: One can only hope and pray.
Tina says: Go sing your helpful hymns. I'll be praying.
Aggie says: How well you know me. Nighters.
Tina says: Poof!

From the Beginning

Chapter Five

Saturday, March 23rd

Aggie's bed lacked the comfort of previous nights. She struggled restlessly with the covers, trying to settle down for a good night's rest. The house seemed loud with the quiet noise of nighttime. She could hear a gate slam shut across the street, and a car zoomed down the road until it melded into the other sounds of the dark. A faint snore from Tavish's room felt somehow reassuring. The children were, as the famous Christmas poem describes, "All snug in their beds," but Aggie wondered if they dreamt of sugarplums, or if their dreams were tormented by the loss of something precious.

She resisted the intrusion of Geraldine into her thoughts. Like the invasion of her carefully planned party, every instinct fought her presence. Relentlessly, with predictable aggressiveness, the intimidating grandmother assaulted her mind, forcing her to relive painful memories.

As the children slept, Aggie reflected on her first real encounter with Geraldine Stuart. The memories were still raw, and Aggie didn't want to remember, but somehow she found herself reliving those first terrible days after Allie and Doug's deaths. The more she remembered, the more vivid the images in her mind seemed to grow until eventually, she felt like the present *was* the past.

Friday, February 15th

Aggie trailed behind her parents up the steps to Allie's home. She looked at the immaculate, snow-covered lawn, the valentine wreath on the beautiful oak front door, and the tall evergreens that stood like stalwart soldiers protecting the castle. Somehow, Aggie had never been to Allie's house. They always seemed to meet at the Milliken home a few hours north of Allie's home in Rockland. The house was immense— and extravagantly beautiful.

"Ronald, Martha, Aggie, how thoughtful of you to come." Geraldine Stuart was the epitome of elegance. Wearing a suit in the style of former First Lady Nancy Reagan, the woman was perfectly poised and in control of the situation. "I'll call the children in. They are watching home movies and looking at Alanna's scrapbooks."

It was thoughtful of them to come? To Aggie, this sounded so morose. Was the woman trying to devote some kind of shrine to Allie and Doug? "That's all right, Mrs. Stuart, why don't I go see them and talk to them in there? Mom needs to rest a moment. The trip was hard, and with the loss…"

Geraldine nodded and led Aggie to the family room. The children all sat together, huddled in the middle of the room, surrounding a scrapbook and listlessly turning the pages. "Children, your Aunt Agathena is here to sit with you for a while. Now you must be very strong for her. If you give way to tears and emotion, you will bring disgrace on your parents, and I know you don't want to do that."

With those terrible words, Mrs. Stuart walked from the room, nearly floating to the front door to welcome yet another visitor. Aggie's shocked face wasn't lost on Vannie, the oldest. "Hello, Aunt Aggie. Would you like to sit down?" Aggie's heart broke as the girl wiped a tear from her already red eyes.

Aggie started to take the next chair when she heard a baby's cry. "Is that Ian? Where is he?" Aggie looked around the room but saw no evidence of the child.

"He's up in— in—" Vannie choked up and willed herself not to cry.

"He's in Momma's room." Laird stood and led Aggie out of the room. Walking through the living room, the boy answered his grandmother's inquiry with, "We heard Ian; he's probably hungry. I'll get him a bottle after I show Aunt Aggie how to find him."

Geraldine nodded proudly at the boy and patted his back. "That is very thoughtful, Laird. You are behaving like quite a gentleman. I'm proud of you."

Aggie noticed that Laird didn't smile with pleasure at the compliment. The boy almost seemed bothered by it. Shrugging off a feeling that something terrible was happening, Aggie climbed the stairs. The baby's wails grew louder as Aggie and Laird stood over the crib. "Aunt Aggie?"

"Yeah?" Aggie was distracted with the baby. Looking at Ian's chubby little baby cheeks, and thinking about Allie never holding this sweet little bundle of baby was tearing her up. She blinked back tears for Laird's sake, but they still continued to fall.

"I'm going to go get his bottle. Grandmother hasn't said that you can't cry, but I think she'd prefer not to see it. I hope you understand." The boy didn't wait for an answer.

Aggie felt the baby's diaper grow warm and looked around for changing supplies. Seeing nothing in sight, she tried the bathroom and then the closet. "Eureka!" she whispered to the downy little head. "Wow! What a closet! No wonder the changing table and your little dresser and everything are in here! I had no idea that Allie lived in such a mansion."

"It's been in our family for three generations. We gave this house to Douglas and Alanna for a wedding gift. Do you remember?" Geraldine's voice was sad but deliberately strong.

Aggie, startled by the sudden appearance of Mrs. Stuart tried to change the baby's diaper, as she listened to Geraldine talk about the people who had lived in the home, and how Allie had been such a good housekeeper. It seemed that Allie had even restored the home's woodwork all by herself before having her first child. Aggie wondered how her sister had managed to do it. Her first child was born exactly ten months and five days after her wedding day.

Aggie peeled the soggy diaper off of the now cooing baby and chucked him under the chin in the process. She found a diaper pail next to the table and dropped the five-pound, super soaked diaper inside. "Don't forget to wipe him thoroughly, dear. Too many mothers don't wash their babies with just a wet diaper, but I insist on it. They must be clean."

Aggie nodded at the woman and reached for the wipe container. Allie had always been so organized. A little rack of clean clothes hung in front of her, along with the wipes, powder, rash ointment, and every other thing a mother could want for changing or dressing her baby there. As Aggie disposed of the used wipe, she reached for a fresh diaper. Before she could get the diaper under the baby, he sprayed the front of Aggie's dress.

"Uggh! I forgot that little boys were supposed to do this!" Aggie laughed and finished fastening the diaper before grabbing a few wipes and trying to mop up her dress with one hand. "I'll have to get Dad to go out to the car and get me my suitcase, so I can grab a change of clothes. I can't wear this thing." Aggie tried to be lighthearted about the whole situation, hoping that Geraldine wouldn't think she was too flighty.

"Were you and your parents planning to stay here?" Geraldine's tone was not one of approval, and Aggie hastened to reassure her.

"We would never presume. Mom needs the quiet that a

good hotel offers anyway. She's already overdone. We'll stay with the children until they're in bed, and then we'll go. We wouldn't dream of leaving the care of all of them to you and Mr. Stuart. We're just here to help where we can." She paused to gain some self-control. "I'm sorry, Mrs. Stuart. It's just hard. Allie and I were very close. We spoke on messenger or by phone almost every day."

"I understand, my dear. You are much more mature than I had imagined. You are in your last year of college I understand?"

Aggie picked up Ian and gestured towards the stairs while speaking. "Actually, I graduated mid-term. I had mono the fall that I was supposed to start college, so it set me behind a semester. I could have taken it easy and graduated with the rest of the kids this year, but I just wanted to finish, take a few extra classes and relax before I began teaching."

Descending the stairs ahead of Aggie, Geraldine asked, "And what do you plan to teach?"

"History— high school level history. I have a few offers already, but I haven't accepted any as of yet. I am hoping that my high school will have an opening. The man who taught me is considering an early retirement." Aggie followed as Geraldine walked into the living room and sat down.

"Here, let me hold him for a few minutes. Poor motherless boy." Geraldine cooed and made gurgling noises at baby Ian, but he immediately began to fuss. Aggie had to give the woman credit. She jostled him and rocked him, before finally turning to Martha and asking what could be the matter.

Martha Milliken smiled through eyes filled with pain and tears and said, "I think Laird has a bottle ready for him. He says that Ian slept through his last feeding."

Geraldine held the baby out to Aggie. "Would you mind feeding him, dear? Your dress is already dirty— well, you should probably put a towel over your chest before you feed him. We wouldn't want him to touch— Do you mind?"

Aggie smiled at the baby as she took him. Laird silently

brought her a burp cloth and a bottle before returning to where his siblings were sequestered. As Aggie sat between her parents on the couch and fed the baby, she watched Geraldine flawlessly control the conversation. There were no uncomfortable pauses and no awkward moments.

Ian downed the bottle in no time. Aggie laid the baby against her chest and patted his back and bottom. Moments later, the baby let out a loud burp. Aggie couldn't help but think that an Amish mother would be proud of such a hearty belch. The baby spit up just a little, but a bib got most of it.

"I always find it amazing how uncivilized babies are when they are born. Think of the work that must be put into them to teach them proper manners. Alanna was an excellent mother. The children are so poised and well-mannered. I've always been so pleased that we could have her as a member of our family." A delicate, well-timed tear was dabbed away from Geraldine's impeccable make-up. Aggie wanted to scream. Was this woman for real?

The woman continued on another vein without a pause. "I was thankful that you weren't here last night, Martha. With your heart condition, it wouldn't have been good idea." Aggie wondered if it was *ever* a good idea to sit around waiting for word that a loved one had died. The impulse to chuckle at herself felt overwhelming for a moment. My, she was being sarcastic tonight.

"We are also thankful that we were here when the officers came. What if it had just been that teenager that Alanna and Douglas hired? If I hadn't come to visit and sent the girl home, those poor children could have been placed…" Geraldine's voice lowered to a stage whisper. "In foster care." The woman shuddered.

"When the officers told me what happened, I just didn't believe it. I am still suspicious. How can you die from a blood transfusion? People get them to *save* lives. The idea is preposterous. My husband has requested a copy of the medical charts, and they'll be reviewed by our lawyer and his medical counsel."

"Accidents do happen. I feel badly for the nurse. It was clearly an accident. The officer that we spoke to said that the ER turned into bedlam when a six car accident, with multiple fatalities, flooded them unexpectedly. She'll probably lose her license." Martha's quiet voice was so filled with pain that Aggie stood to make room for her father to comfort his wife. She wanted to hug her mother, but it was difficult while holding the baby.

Aggie, seeing the expression on Geraldine's face, tried to divert her attention with the first thought that came to mind. "What I don't understand is why they were driving the van. I mean, it's a good thing, the impact in a little car like the Jaguar might have killed them immediately."

Geraldine's eyes grew cold, her voice hard and icy. "I beg your pardon, but due to that woman's negligence, there are eight children in this house who are motherless and fatherless. I have lost my only child; you have lost your eldest daughter. I cannot believe that you could be so callous, Martha Milliken." Geraldine drew herself up, left the room to gather coffee for everyone, then turned back. "And as to the Jag, the car is being repaired. I told Douglas that it was a foolish gift when he gave it. Classic or not, an old car is an old car."

Aggie was furious. Allie had called Aggie while she got ready for their Valentine date. Allie had not wanted to go. Kenzie seemed to be coming down with a cold, and Doug was just home from a business trip. Geraldine was a very persistent woman however, and in the end, Doug and Allie had chosen to be pleasant and go. It seemed wasteful to refuse concert tickets. *"Why she doesn't learn that we like being home with the children, I'll never know."* Allie's words rang through Aggie's mind as she fought to hold her tongue.

Ron Milliken whispered something to his wife and then turned to Aggie. "I'm going to take your mother to the hotel. Would you like to come with us, or perhaps you might hire a cab?"

Aggie said she'd call a cab and bade her parents goodbye. Geraldine's change from genteel pleasantness to almost venomous was startling. Aggie chalked it up to suppressed grief and said, when Mrs. Stuart came back into the room, "I'm sorry, Mrs. Stuart, Mom started feeling weak, so Dad had to take her to the hotel. I'll call a cab later, but I thought you might like help putting the children to bed."

"Why, thank you. Your mother's health is so delicate, isn't it? Perhaps she should not have attempted the trip." Geraldine sipped her coffee and set a cup for Aggie on the coffee table.

"Yes, we're very cautious of her health, but at a time like this, she would have worried about the children and the arrangements and everything if she would have stayed home."

Geraldine gave an enigmatic smile and sipped her coffee. Aggie realized that, while Mr. Stuart was sitting in the room throughout her parent's visit, she hadn't heard him speak or be spoken to. "Mr. Stuart, would you like a cup of coffee? You are welcome to mine; I can't drink and hold little Mr. Squirmy here."

Douglas Stuart shook his head as he flipped through papers in a briefcase on his lap. "Thank you, Aggie, but I am fine. Do you need Vanora to come in and take him? I am sure she would be happy to." The man smiled as he started to rise to get the girl.

"No, thank you. I have only seen Ian once. I'm enjoying him." Aggie laughed at the baby's antics.

"Aggie, I am thinking that if it's convenient for you, I would like to invite you to stay here tonight. With my sleeping pills, I don't know if I'll hear the baby should he awake. I think Vanora had to get up with him several times last night. He is," her voice lowered with affected discretion, "unused to drinking from bottles."

"Well, Allie nursed him exclusively I presume. She did the others." Poor baby, no wonder he'd been so hungry. It was obvious that he had been refusing the bottle most of last night.

"Would you mind holding him, Mrs. Stuart? I think that

he might still be hungry. He seems to be seeking something, but I'm afraid my plumbing won't help him. The works aren't turned on yet." Aggie tried to joke as she handed the baby to his grandmother, but she realized, too late, that she'd only managed to offend the proper woman. Talking about bodily functions, even something as natural as feeding a baby, was probably a huge social faux pas.

Aggie carefully read the instructions on the little baggie box and the can of formula. Hoping she was getting the water warm enough and the formula shook up well, Aggie mixed her first bottle. She had no idea that this would be the first of many. Shaking vigorously, she squirted the mixture on her wrist. It was warm but didn't hurt. She hoped that was the goal. One sniff killed the fleeting notion of taste testing it. The "milk" smelled vile. "How do babies drink this stuff?"

Monday, February 18th

The next two days followed a similar pattern. Geraldine sat on her "throne," directing everyone's moves in expressionless grief. One of the first things she did was to send Aggie shopping for funeral dresses for the little girls. "'Nautical would be lovely, Agathena. A true navy looks black, you know, but it's not quite so stark on a child. The children must look their best,'" Aggie muttered to herself as she headed through yet another upscale boutique on Geraldine's list. Seeing the prices, Aggie was glad that Geraldine had insisted she take along the Stuart's credit card.

She found a rack of gorgeous dresses. The color was perfect and the style was impeccable. They carried the dresses in every size she needed, but at over one hundred dollars per dress, Aggie was in sticker shock. After looking further, she found a clearance rack with similar dresses and debated within herself. The first dresses were gorgeous; however, the discounted dresses were also very nice and appropriate. Hearing Geraldine's voice in her head, Aggie returned to the first rack and picked out the proper sizes.

Before she could pay for the dresses, Aggie heard her purse ringing. "What now?" she muttered to herself as she flipped open her phone.

"Agathena, I have been looking at the boys' clothing, and they also have nothing appropriate. Do you have a pen and paper handy? I have measurements for you..." Aggie grabbed a shopping bag from the rack behind the customer counter and began taking notes. Geraldine was now sending her in search of suits for the boys. Three piece suits, white shirts, and red ties. Aggie wondered why red ties were so important, but she returned to her now expanded shopping excursion. Aggie learned to despise shopping that afternoon.

Tuesday, February 19th

The day of the funeral dawned in typical storybook fashion. The sky was gray and drizzled in sporadic spurts. The snow that had been so pretty and picturesque was now slushy, dirty, mush. The children were squeaky clean in their somber navy clothing with the little touch of red on the boys. They all had a white rose on their collars and lapels and had strict instructions as to when to remove them and place them on the double casket.

Geraldine had wanted a military funeral, in memory of her son's short stint in the navy, but the ever-organized Allie had even planned their funerals. It was to be informal, which chafed Geraldine's need for being "correct" in form. The couple's wishes were honored, and songs of praise and rejoicing were sung about entering heaven, while anyone who wanted to could say something in remembrance of Douglas and Allie.

Wednesday, February 20th

Aggie left the law office of Moss and Younger with a stack

of papers and in complete shock. Still in the offices, a very upset Geraldine argued with the lawyer. Aggie's parents, the only ones not surprised at the contents of Doug and Allie's will, had left nearly an hour earlier. Seated on a bench at a bus stop, she waited for her taxi to arrive. "Guardianship. Of eight children. I'm only twenty-two! What was she thinking?"

"What?" Aggie hadn't noticed the elderly woman sitting on the bench next to her.

"Hello. I'm sorry; I was talking to myself." Aggie opened the manila folder and flipped through the pages.

"Did you say you were guardian of eight children?" The woman was pleasant but curious.

"Yes. My sister died last week. She had my name on the title to the house to avoid probate problems, she had signed and notarized temporary guardianship papers— the works. Power of attorney for the estate… and I'm beneficiary of a very large life insurance policy. *What* possessed her to give me this responsibility?" The fact that she was dumping her shock on a stranger didn't even register.

"Do you have parents that can help you?"

"My mother has a serious heart condition. She can't handle stress or excitement for long. There is no way she could help. I expected that Allie would leave the children to her mother-in-law, but I have a letter to read from them that should explain why they didn't."

"Are you ready for this? It's quite a responsibility. What about *your* plans for your life?"

She didn't know it yet, but the woman's question would become one she heard repeatedly over the coming months. "You know what? I prayed years ago that if I was going to make a decision for my life that was wrong for me, that God would radically change my direction. It appears that He has. I think my dreams must have been just that. Dreams. I don't want them if they're not what He wants for me, now do I?" Aggie realized that her words to the woman were really just a self-pep talk. She turned to look at her companion, but the

81

woman just smiled, stood, and walked away.

Aggie reached her hotel room and flipped through the papers, while carefully avoiding Doug's letter. Eventually, she gathered her emotions and opened the letter.

November 11

Dearest Naggie Aggie,

Well, I won't be calling you that again this side of Glory, but never fear, if Jesus will let me continue on the other side, I won't callously drop your special name. I know how sorry you would be to lose it.

I know you are wondering why I left you the responsibility of our children, and I want to share the story with you so that you will understand and fight for them like no one else can.

My mother was born on what she would call the "wrong side of the tracks." Her father left the family when she was an infant, and she grew up in an era where the combination of a working mother, bad neighborhood, and no father meant that she was essentially a social outcast. By high school, she vowed never to live alone or in poverty again. Just picture her as a twentieth century Scarlett O'Hara.

Upon graduation, she researched businesses, found a position with Delta Advertising, and worked her way to secretary of the most up and coming vice president in the building. I know it sounds like a pathetic B movie, but it's the truth. Before that vice president knew what hit him, they were married. Enter, Douglass Stuart, nephew of Weston Lyman, Rockland's great advertising mogul. He had everything she was looking for. Family connections – boy that sounds like something from 19th century England – money, and social status were her ticket to never being hurt, poor or alone again.

My father quickly learned that my mother was determined to control every aspect of their lives in order to accomplish her purposes. Now don't get me wrong, Aggie, Dad and I love Mother. What she does is always because of her love for us, and her fear of the past repeating itself.

Aggie, I cannot allow her to try to raise my children. She would be determined to control the children's lives the same way she's controlled my father and me. Though she puts all her time and energy into controlling the family, she's lazy, Aggie. She doesn't believe she should have to work. Can you imagine how much of the burden of the children's care would be left to Vannie and Laird? The children would feel like they'd already raised a family before they graduated from high school. The baby would be neglected. I know it's a lot to ask, Aggie, but the children need someone young enough to have the time and energy for them.

She'll smother the children. You know that we've tried to shelter our children as much as possible, but she will completely smother them. They will be sent to the doctor for the slightest sniffle. If they want to have a friend over, there will always be an excuse not to do it "just this time." If they want to learn the piano, she'll send them to lessons daily and insist that they practice three times a day. She'll send them to boarding schools and then bring them home days later. She professes love for the children, and she does love them in her way, but they will be alternately smothered and then neglected. I know I keep using the word smother but it's the one that really fits.

Aggie, imagine a life where you must constantly keep up appearances. The family must appear to be the epitome of taste, education, and class. There can never be a mistake. If you drop a spoon at the dinner table, it is equivalent to dropping a bowl of hot food into the president's lap. If you have the nerve to sneeze inappropriately, it's a crisis.

Making our home perfect was hard enough with just me, can you imagine how tormented everyone would be with eight? We can't have a meal, without milk spilling, or a child opening their mouth while chewing, or needing to be reminded to say, "excuse me" after a burp. The whole mental picture is enough to ensure a mental breakdown for everyone involved. I can't do that to the children.

Aggie, my childhood is a long series of different schools, psychologists, medical appointments, vacations, cancelled parties, and ostentatious displays. She didn't know how to relate to a child. Whenever I showed a preference for cartoons over Shakespeare or French fries over caviar, I was packed off for yet another evaluation.

Emotions are forbidden in her home. If there is a problem, you don't talk it out, work it out, or forgive. Instead, you pretend that it's not there and hold a grudge about it. Forever. I am not exaggerating. If you want to test me on this, just mention the cabin up at the lake. I guarantee you'll hear about how, when I was eight, I dropped a frog inside her swimsuit, and she "couldn't sleep for a week in fear of what else that boy might do."

You cannot imagine the guilt-driven manipulation. If they don't say "I love you" every day, several times a day, she'll be hurt. If they do something wrong, she'll bury them in guilt on how they've hurt her until they **beg** for forgiveness, and then she'll smother them with things. They'll be the world's most spoiled, immature children ever. She will try to buy their affection, and you know what that does to children.

Aggie, please understand what we are asking you to do, so you'll never doubt if the decision you make is correct. Do not let our children EVER be alone with her. Do not let them spend the night, go shopping, or even speak for a long time on the phone with her. We have made it quite clear in our documentation to the courts (my six inches of medical records with only four pages since the day I graduated from college will help, I am sure) that we would rather the children be sent to foster care than to be given to her.

Honestly, I don't know how she will respond. She may take it as relief but feel it's her duty to care for them. She may give a token fight and then leave you alone. I don't think so, though. I have almost been her life since I was born. With me gone, and Dad still in his own world, she will probably latch onto them harder than ever. Be careful, Aggie. All I know for certain is that with mother, there are no certainties.

Thank you, Aggie. I know I can thank you in advance, because I know you. You'll handle this beautifully. The children love you, and with your training at college you should be ready for a challenge like this. You'll be graduating soon. I hope you don't have to quit your dream job or anything like that.

We forgot to update this letter after the twins. I pray that you never have to read it. I have written three since you turned eighteen, and each time, I hope I can convey how seriously I want you to take my warnings and how thankful I am that I have a little sister whom I can entrust my children to. I love my mother, Aggie. I love my children. I love you, and I pray that you will find fulfillment in this new step in your life and that you never resent us for putting you in this position. Love, teach and train our children. Enjoy them. Weave their lives into yours; don't just enter theirs.

Waiting on the other side,
Douglas

Aggie sighed as she finished the letter. Tears streamed down her cheeks, but she found herself crying as much for Geraldine Stuart as she did for the loss of her family. She recalled the reading of the will with perfect clarity. It appeared that every time a purchase over five hundred dollars was acquired, it was immediately assigned ownership to Aggie, her parents, one of the children or Doug's parents. Aggie would be responsible for passing out these things or holding them in trust for the children.

Aggie was in shock to see how much was entrusted to her. She had no idea that Allie and Doug had such wealth. There were two insurance policies that both listed Aggie as the secondary beneficiary. There were investments that had to be controlled, and all of the bank accounts, including several CDs, had her name on them in order to avoid trouble with the transfer of property.

As she picked up the papers and put them back in the folder, Aggie spied a note on Mr. Moss' letterhead that she'd overlooked.

Aggie,
At the request of Doug and Allie, I hired a locksmith to change the locks on their home while we had our meeting this morning. They wanted to be certain that Mrs. Stuart could not lock you out of the home. The locksmith will leave the key at the front desk of your hotel as soon as he has finished.

If you have any questions, or if I can assist you in any way, please don't hesitate to call me at home or at the office.

Respectfully,

Aggie called down to the front desk and learned that the key was indeed waiting for her. She phoned the law office and found that Geraldine was still in conference with the lawyers. Reluctantly, she decided that perhaps it would be better to go now, get inside the house, and talk to the children before Mrs. Stuart arrived.

At the house, Aggie found bedlam. The children sobbed nearly uncontrollably, the baby screamed, and Vannie was visibly distraught, trying to keep everyone calm. It took Aggie a while to comfort everyone, and reheat one of the many casseroles in the kitchen for the children's dinner. As she worked, she discovered that Geraldine had not hired a sitter to watch the children and had left them alone during the afternoon meeting with the lawyers. Aggie's face showed her anger, and at first, poor Vannie thought she was in trouble.

"I'm so sorry. I really tried. When no one came back right away, Kenzie flipped. She was sure that you and Grandmother were dead too—"

"Vannie, honey, this is not your fault. You did nothing wrong. I had no idea that you would be left here alone. I don't think your grandmother was thinking clearly. She must be hurting more than she lets on." Aggie prayed that she was telling the truth, but Doug's words in the letter she'd just read troubled her. *"Can you imagine how much of the burden of the children's care would be left to Vannie and Laird?"* Oh, how was she to know what to do or what to say?

Aggie led the children into the living room and sat them all down. "Well, guys, it looks like we are going to be together for a long time."

The children looked at her with huge questions in their eyes and hearts. Vannie started to speak, but Aggie didn't notice and continued. "You see, your parents worked things out with the lawyers and the courts and everything, so that I would be the one to take care of you from now on. I'm not going to try to be your mom. We are so different, that I couldn't if I wanted to. But, I promise you guys; I will do everything I can to be the best Aunt Aggie I can be."

Before Aggie could continue, the doorbell blared. Looking out of the window, Aggie found that Geraldine was there already. She glanced around frantically and then said, "Vannie. I need your help. Please take everyone downstairs and stay there— no matter what happens. Take a bottle for the baby, just in case this takes a while. Laird, I really need you to help her."

The children nodded somberly and trooped downstairs like little soldiers. It was incredible how quickly they had adapted to Geraldine's expectations and terrible to see them so nervous. She hated to put so much on Vannie again so quickly but honestly didn't know how to avoid it.

The doorbell rang again, followed quickly by a sharp knock. Aggie looked at the door, then picked up the phone and dialed the office of Mr. Moss. He advised that she not open the door without witnesses, for Aggie's legal and personal safety. He assured her that he was on the way. "She can't know you are there, so she's just getting angry at the children. She is probably trying to figure out why they can't hear her. Don't walk in front of any windows, though. I'd prefer to just walk up with a key and open the door without her knowing that you are inside."

Geraldine was in her car using her car phone when Robert Moss arrived. He quickly let himself in the house, locking the door behind him. "What do you want to do, Aggie? I'm afraid if you let her in, she'll refuse to leave without police escort. If you don't let her in, she'll call them anyway. She seems near the breaking point. I've always known her to be very self-controlled, but she lost it for a second today. I saw a face I don't hope to see again anytime soon."

Aggie decided that she would go outside, with a copy of Doug's letter that Mr. Moss had brought with him, and speak to Geraldine at her car. If necessary, she could run around to the back of the house and Robert Moss could let her inside again. It sounded so childish, but the fact was, if it had to happen she would do it.

Thirty minutes later, Geraldine coldly announced to an officer that Aggie was holding her grandchildren hostage in *her* house. Aggie sat silently on the porch furniture, waiting to be questioned. A young officer stood nearby, trying not to look like the guard that he really was. Aggie couldn't believe the nerve of the woman. Doug's letter was in her hands, and she read the words repeatedly to give her strength.

People always saw Aggie as a very strong person, but it would take a will of iron to endure the strain that Aggie bore. She knew she was close to tears, and that would only add to the problem. Mrs. Stuart didn't handle people who emoted, and she didn't want to antagonize the woman any further.

"Now young lady, can you tell me why you have the house locked up and won't let this woman in to see her grandchildren?"

Aggie asked the officer to step inside, speak with her lawyer, and review the documents that showed her as temporary guardian and legal owner of the home. The lawyer explained the process that Allie and Doug had gone through to avoid Geraldine being named guardian of the children. "They were so bothered by the idea that they held practically nothing in their names. Everything was used in trust for someone else."

Finally, Aggie handed over Doug's letter. She hated to do it. It seemed so wrong to share personal information about another person to a stranger, but she felt like it was necessary. "Would you like to go downstairs and see the children? I sent them to play in the basement. I found them home alone here when I arrived this afternoon. Geraldine had just left them here. I didn't know how bad it was going to get and didn't want them caught in the crossfire."

The officer accepted the offer, took down pertinent information for his report, and then exited the house leaving them with instructions to keep the doors locked until they knew the woman wouldn't be any trouble. "I'd keep a sharp eye for a week or two. If nothing seems amiss, then things are probably all right." He glanced at the young woman, remembered why she was now guardian of so many children, and added, "I'm very sorry for your loss."

Aggie thanked the officer, and asked him to deliver a note to Geraldine. Quickly she wrote a short, pleasant, note, offering to meet the woman for lunch to discuss when a good time to visit the children would be. With instructions to make arrangements with Mr. Moss, Aggie folded the note and handed it to the waiting officer. "Thank you for being so kind. I appreciate it."

"Not a problem, ma'am. I just hope that everything works out just fine. I'll escort her off of the property if necessary."

Aggie had never been as exhausted as she was that night when she went to bed in her new home. She didn't know how she was going to cope with being a mother to eight children, but she knew that regardless of whatever else she'd need, she would definitely need sleep. Her last thought before drifting off to sleep was to wonder if she would hear the baby when he awoke for his mid-night bottle. Several months later, she'd laugh when she recalled the thought.

Aggie says: Tina, are you there?
Tina says: I was just logging off… I was doing more research. I couldn't sleep thinking about Dragon Lady — er well…
Aggie says: Me either. I kept remembering how pleasant she used to be. I think something is up with her. I think it's more than missing the children. She's has some issues that go deeper than not liking me.
Tina says: Well, I have to sleep. What are you doing up so late?
Aggie says: Jr. Muffin needed a mid-night snack. So, enter Aggie's Snack Bar.

Tina says: Remind me to adopt children older than nine months. I love sleep. I really love my nice, long, uninterrupted nights...

Aggie says: BYE you ... you... you evil tormentor!

Tina says: * poofs*

Pests & Pains

Chapter Six

Monday, March 24th

Aggie's children were inordinately late for school. As they tried to load into the van, Vannie became frantic, running from room to room, opening odd doors and cupboards, looking under furniture and behind doors, unable to find any of her schoolbooks. Eventually, Aggie put her foot down. "I'll speak to your teachers; I'll throw myself on the mercy of the principal, but all of the children can't be any later than they already are."

With Vannie in tears over a writing assignment due that day, Aggie spoke individually to each teacher, trying to get the girl a twenty-four hour extension on any of the assignments that were due. Finally, Aggie got approval from all of the teachers. She chuckled to herself as she loaded up the little children in the van and drove away. "Small children are a huge asset when you want your way and don't want it to take a long time."

Aggie spent the next hour searching for the books, keeping Cari out of mischief and Lorna from following in her wake, and answering the ever-ringing phone. Thanks to the crazy escapades that Cari consistently contrived, Aggie had dubbed the twins "Lucy and Ethel" when no one was listening.

Finally, Aggie sat down to feed the baby. After he finished, Aggie tried to burp him and ended up with baby formula all over her. "Little guy," she choked as the stench of partially digested bottle reached her nostrils, "That is what I call 'fountains of formula.'"

Frustration mounted as Aggie dug through her suitcase, the closet, and glanced around the room in search of clean clothes. She dashed downstairs wearing her stinky shirt, opened the dryer, and prayed that there'd be a clean shirt in there for her, yet knowing that there couldn't be. She hadn't washed in days. Just that morning, Kenzie had been forced to wear a "church" dress to school.

Aggie didn't know whether to laugh or cry. "Well, at least I know where her books are! Drat it all!"

Aggie found a clean shirt folded on top of the dryer and changed quickly. Upstairs, she went into the changing area, grabbed a fistful of wipes, and scrubbed herself with the new shirt still on, trying to remove some of the stench of regurgitated baby breakfast. She pulled sleeping Ian from his crib and buckled him into his little carrier. There's nothing like walking the halls of an American middle school, twice in one day, to give you an appreciation for toddlers who prefer to use macaroni and cheese for finger paints instead of food.

"How do mothers do it all?" She muttered to herself as she drove back to the house.

As Aggie rewashed the now soured clothes that were almost crusty in the washer, she made one of her trademarked "mental notes." "Never start a load that you can't finish."

While the clothes were freshening in a new wash, Aggie went upstairs to call Mr. Moss. She felt obligated to give the Stuarts first dibs on the family home. Based on what she assumed the house was worth, Aggie instructed the lawyer to offer it to the Stuarts at a minor reduction from market value.

"I'll sign any paperwork when we meet over the appeal slash finalization papers. Meanwhile, do you have any information on the place in Brant's Corners? Oh, wonderful! I am so excited. Tell me when I have to sign for that too. I can't believe they accepted my offer so easily. Did we offer too much?"

Aggie's lawyer explained that no one had bid against her, and since she found the property at the end of the closing date, she didn't have to counter any bids that were made. Aggie became concerned at the condition of the house. "Why didn't anyone else want it?"

"Well, Aggie, I went and checked it out myself with a property inspector. Nothing against your friend Zeke, but sometimes, big problems aren't obvious to the untrained eye. The inspector says it'll be expensive to fix, but that all it needs is cosmetic work. Remodeling, not restoration. You can afford the repairs because of the proceeds from the Stuart House sale, but the average family can't buy the house *and* afford to renovate like you can."

Aggie hung up with a goofy smile on her face. A house. First, she had purchased a twenty thousand dollar vehicle, and now she had purchased a house! My, she was living large these days.

When the children came home, they all started the routines Allie instituted and that Aggie had continued. Vannie went downstairs to do a laundry "switch," while Laird took out the trash in every room and Tavish swept the porches. Ellie wiped down all counters, and Aggie ran around trying to keep everyone on track and the mess from growing worse with the work.

"Aunt Aggie, I can't get the dryer to work! Something's wrong with it! Do I just hang the clothes on hangers?" Vannie's voice came up the stairs in a panicked wail.

"Go ahead and do that, Vannie. I'll send Kenzie down with more hangers and call the appliance guy." Aggie picked up the phone and dialed the first appliance repair place listed in the phone book. The man on the other end was trying to help her troubleshoot when Aggie groaned.

"Is something wrong, ma'am?" The deep voice sounded even more concerned now.

"No. You don't need to come out. I just remembered. I unplugged it the other day when I put my niece's schoolbooks in there. It just has to be plugged in again." Aggie thanked the very confused man and hung up.

"All right, Vannie, try plugging in the dryer, I bet it'll work better that way!" Aggie decided that if anything else went wrong, she'd send everyone to bed and call it a day.

Monday, April 15th

For the first time in a long time, that she could remember anyway, Aggie woke up feeling positive. She finally had the house completely clean; the baby had slept through the night and was still sleeping peacefully. The estate taxes had been filed days ago, thanks to the fast footwork of Mr. Moss' financial consultant at Franklin Financial Services, and it looked like a hefty return was headed their way. Aggie was excited about that. Thus far, she'd always had to pay at tax time.

That thought registered and then assaulted her mind causing her to wail, "Oh, noooooooooooo! My *taxes*! I forgot my *taxes*!" Aggie screamed to no one in particular.

After the children left for school, and after half an hour of frantic searching, she found the large box of mail that she'd neglected to look through since her dorm mate had shipped it all to her. Flipping feverishly through the stacks of paper in the box, she found the booklets, forms, and her W-2 forms. The children were instructed to eat standing at the counter while Aggie spread her forms across the table.

As Aggie was tallying up her totals, she heard Ian's cry. "Hey, bub, your timing is lousy," the overwrought "mother" said to the little boy as she picked him up from the crib. Ian felt a little warm, but with a heavy blanket sleeper and a warm baby quilt, Aggie assumed that he was just over dressed.

She bounced downstairs and into the kitchen, jostling the baby as she went, trying to keep him happy as she mixed and shook a bottle like a pro. The young woman was now so accustomed to her routine; her movements were automatic — almost rote. Taking a napkin she wiped a mouth full of drool from little Ian's face. "Oh, dear, you drool like your grandpa Milliken. Why that man when he snores — Ohhh, nooo! Girls *stop!*"

Aggie watched as both little girls froze in the middle of scribbling all over her almost completed tax forms. She had no spares. She hadn't remembered that she needed to file, much less get extra forms! She fed the baby, found the twins' shoes, and packed everyone in the van.

Three post offices later, she was growing frantic. All of the EZ forms appeared to be gone. Either almost no one needed them this year or *everyone* did. Out of desperation, Aggie drove over to Brant's Corners to see if maybe a smaller town's post office would still have some.

Aggie backed into a sheriff's deputy as she pushed the post office door open with her rear and tried to get the rambunctious children inside. "Excuse me, officer." Aggie hardly made eye contact. If she took her eyes off the children for more than a second, Cari was sure to make a best friend with someone in the room and drive off with them. The child knew no strangers.

The deputy saw a woman coming at him backwards and thought of holding the door for her but realized that she'd probably end up sitting down rather hard. Instead, he stood still and took the jolt to protect the woman and her baby from sprawling across the entryway. Beautiful identical twin girls smiled at him and one spoke. "You are a nice powice man. I like you. I am C—"

"Come along, Cari. We need to hurry and get those forms, and this officer has criminals to catch." Aggie led the girls to the boxes of tax forms and tried to do a mini-jig as she found a box full of them.

The deputy sat in his cruiser, watching, as the woman came out with a handful of forms. The man shook his head at his partner. "Why is it that people wait until the last second to do their taxes? That baby is sick. I know it. I felt his little head as she bumped into me. He has a fever." The deputies talked about how parents seemed to just drag their children everywhere, unless it cramped their style. Only then, a babysitter was called in— the children always the ones to suffer.

Aggie stood in line at the post office hours later and minutes before they closed. Eight children stood in line behind her like little ducks in a row. Aggie was determined to *watch* them postmark her check for $132.58 made payable to good old Uncle Sam. From now on, she would schedule this to be done by February fifteenth. It wouldn't hurt to have a budget either. Tacking "make budget" onto the ever-growing mental list, Aggie wondered if she'd ever be able to cross any of her planned "Aggie-dos" off that list.

Tuesday, April 16th

"*Aunt Aggie*! Help! My ant farm is broken, and they're all gone! They've vanished…. Oh, wait! There's one… two…" Tavish's voice trailed off as he tried to rescue his little pets.

Aggie stumbled into his room and shivered as she felt the critters crawling under her feet. "It's my science project. I'm supposed to see if I can force them to go in a particular path by where I put their food, and now…" he looked around him. "It's ruined. I'll *fail*!" The boy was completely distraught.

Moments later, Aggie saw a bedraggled kitten dash from behind the dresser and out the door. Forcing her voice to remain pleasant, she spoke in deliberately measured tones, "Um, where did that filthy fur ball come from?"

Sanity vanished as it disappeared down the hall, Aggie dashed after the kitten. The other children noticed and took up the chase as well. Aggie tried to calm the frenzied race, but it was all for naught. Chairs were toppled, a glass broken, and one pair of curtains were shredded before Aggie nabbed the kitten. The poor kitty's heart raced, and she mewed pitifully.

Aggie picked up the phone and called animal control before demanding to know who had brought the kitten into the house. "I want to know how this kitten got in here, and I want to know now!"

Laird spoke up. "I did, Aunt Aggie. I found her on the way home from the bus stop yesterday, but I couldn't tell you about her with going to the post office and everything, and then I just forgot about her until last night, but you were on the phone, and I'm really sorry." Aggie was glad that she wasn't that boy's grammar teacher. She'd never seen nor heard a worse run-on sentence in her life!

Tavish mourned his science experiment all the way to school. There were only three weeks until he had to turn in his project, and the best Aggie could come up with was the standard electric potatoes or volcanoes. Tavish was insulted at the thought. He was hoping for a spot in the science fair, and he couldn't make it with "snow job" experiments.

Just before he jumped from the van, the boy had an idea. "Hey! Aunt Aggie? Can I get two mice? I could record which breed learns to find his food the fastest and through the most complex mazes. Please, Aunt Aggie... I'd give them to the science lab after I was done..." The singsong pleas of the boy were extremely out of character.

Aggie promised to think about it, and once the children were on the school grounds, drove towards home. Thinking about the boy's forlorn face, Aggie made a U-turn and zipped across town to the mall. School was school. It was time to step up as "mom" and do the difficult things that mothers have to do.

Going with the twins and Ian, however, was not the wisest move Aggie had made to date. Cari and Lorna made a beeline for the bunnies and guinea pigs with Aggie stumbling behind, trying to keep Ian's pudgy hands from grabbing things off the shelves and toppling birdcages. The sales assistant, panic rising in her voice as each second dragged by, grabbed the cardboard carriers, and tried to engage the twins in picking out the perfect rats for Tavish, but the girls would have nothing to do with it. They raced to the fish tanks, drumming their fingers on the glass trying gain the attention of swimming fish, crabs, or turtles.

"See the fwoggie!" Cari's delighted voice caused Aggie's head to whip around in alarm. Before she could protest, the child dipped her hand into an aquarium and pulled out a frog to show her enraptured little sister. The result was pandemonium.

Mr. Frog wisely sensed danger and leapt from Cari's hands. Unfortunately for him, Lorna was fast, and when he paused to determine his next step, the excited little girl wasn't able to halt before squishing him. Screams of horror erupted from both girls, startling Ian into joining their wails of terror. Puppies barked, birds screeched, and the harried sales assistant grabbed the rats and dumped them on the counter before rushing to clean up the remains of the frog.

Trying to purchase rats, a cage, a book, get basic instructions, and keep the twins and the baby from eating or otherwise killing the rest of the fish and mammals was the most harrowing maternal experience Aggie had yet faced. Her bill was atrocious once she paid for the squished frog, not to mention the three fish that were scooped out of the tank without benefit of a nice bag of water as temporary housing.

Hours later, Aggie watched as Laird and Tavish built an elaborate maze of empty toilet paper rolls and hollow-ended Velveeta boxes. The time and care that the two boys put into the endeavor astonished her. She had a hard time believing that these were the same boys that balked at hanging up towels in the bathroom. The rats were sequestered in Doug's old study; Aggie hoped she hadn't made a mistake in getting rid of that kitten...

Friday, April 19th

Laird slipped into Aggie's room with a miserable expression on his face as she was dressing Ian for the day. "Aunt Aggie?" His feet shuffled awkwardly. "I didn't want to tell you because Tavish was so upset and everything, but I have to— see these bites?" Laird lifted his pant leg and pulled down his sock. Aggie stared in disbelief at the welts up and down his legs.

"I'm slightly allergic to ant bites, but Tavish is *really* allergic. His legs are covered, and I think the ants are now in the bathroom too."

Aggie groaned and handed Ian to Laird. She went to the locked cupboard where Allie kept the medicines and found children's Benadryl. Ant bites were one thing that Aggie understood. After giving a very miserable Tavish a dose of the medicine, Aggie went in search of ant spray.

Monday, April 22nd

Once the children left for school, Aggie took Ian, the cordless phone, the phonebook, and went out on the patio table to call an exterminator. She gave the twins bottles of bubbles and taught them to blow them while she begged every extermination company in town to come immediately.

"I'll pay for an emergency visit, I don't care what it costs, but we can't go upstairs in our own house. Ants are *everywhere*. I have children here who are allergic to ants, and these guys are vicious. I don't know how to get rid of them without exterminating us in the process." Eventually, a small company promised to send someone immediately.

When the man knocked at the door, Aggie practically grabbed him and pulled him up the stairs. "In here. They're in here. They're everywhere. *The floor moves.* How did one little ant farm create an invasion like this?"

The poor exterminator backed away slowly looking

frantically from Aggie to the floor. He half-stumbled, half-walked back down the stairs and brought a hand held can of pesticide with a spray nozzle and worked quickly to kill the ants and find the source. He acted suspicious of Aggie as if he was certain that she'd pull a knife, or some other dangerous object, and threaten him with bodily harm if he didn't kill every single ant inside the house. He was closer to truth than either of them wanted to consider.

"All right, guys. We've got a problem." Aggie spoke with deliberate calm to a table of chewing children. She'd learned quickly, in her on-the-job-training in Mothering 101, that some things require a captive audience. "The exterminator found food in just about every corner of this house. All bedrooms, the bathrooms, the dining corners, cabinets... and ants were covering it all. We are talking about two different kinds of ants causing the problem."

Aggie scanned the children's faces. "The ants that were biting are the ones from Tavish's ant farm, but the rest—those came in from outside, and they came because there was food everywhere for them to find." Aggie's voice grew serious. "I am sorry to make more rules, but we have to have a new one. *No food* may be taken from the kitchen area. Period. *No* exceptions. If anyone sees someone with food upstairs or in the living areas, *someone* needs remind him or her that it's not allowed. Do you understand?" Aggie smiled, rose, and put her plate in the sink.

While the children silently finished their food, Aggie made a list of things to inspect and or clean on a weekly/biweekly basis. Closet corners were top of the list. Next, she began a list of things she needed to do to pack them up for moving. That would be an entirely different and challenging project.

Saturday, May 4ᵗʰ

"Vannie? Are you ready? Let's go room by room, starting here at the door." Aunt and niece walked through the house cataloging what would stay behind, what would be sold, and what would move with them.

Aggie had gotten mixed reactions to the move. Vannie and Ellie seemed too attached to their home to want to leave, but the boys seemed to consider it an adventure. The little children had no opinions—only questions. Was it big? Where would everyone go to school? Would they have the same Sunday school teachers? Aggie answered to the best of her ability and prayed that this move would be a blessing.

"Aunt Aggie! I had an idea!" Laird was excited. "Remember how that shoe organizer thing ripped up right away and you wanted something else?"

Aggie nodded. "Why? What's up?"

"Well, what if Tavish and I took that old apothecary's chest and converted it into one? I know we can do it. Those drawers are so *big* and there are sixteen of them!"

Aggie gave the go-ahead and turned back to her list making. "Ok, what pieces of furniture do you know you guys would like to have with you? Were any of these your mother's favorites, or are there any with personal sentimental value?" Aggie surveyed the room with dismay. "You know, Vannie; I think your mom and I had opposite tastes. I'm only taking the beds, your toys, the books, and a few pieces of furniture that you *want* to have with you. The attic at the other house has a lot of furniture and things in it, and if we have to, we'll buy some."

"Momma didn't like most of our furniture. She couldn't stand the couches. She thought that white couches in a family full of children were ridiculous. Oh, and those dining room chairs with the fabric seats, Mom spent every night covering and scrubbing those. She hated them."

While not surprised to discover that Geraldine Stuart's idea of proper furniture dictated much of the décor of her home, Aggie was relieved to find that almost none of the furniture meant anything to the children. It was easy to decide what would come and what would stay. The gold plated silverware set would not come along, but the lovely stainless steel set would. They'd keep most of the books, all of the beds, the casual dishes, the children's toys, the scrapbooks, and the photo albums. Things like the grandfather clock, couches, chairs, sideboards, credenzas, desks, curio cabinets, and any oil paintings they intended to leave behind. Aggie added, "Buy sheets at the thrift store to cover furniture," to the to do list clipped to her clipboard.

Vannie packed boxes of books as Aggie packed family pictures, the children's keepsakes, and boxed up Doug's coin collection to be added to their safe deposit box. The little children created huge toy messes in every room, which sent Aggie's clutter tolerance into the danger zone. Instead of making the children clean up their messes, Aggie had Ellie and Kenzie pack them and set them in the rapidly filling garage. The children didn't need so many toys all the time anyway. "Children all over the world live without very many toys," she muttered to herself. "The Stuart children can live with limited toys for a few weeks."

Aggie was about to wind down for dinner when Laird called to her from the entryway. Walking around the corner, she saw the boy standing next to the apothecary's chest beaming with pride, but Aggie had no clue why. She felt like a very small child had handed her a page of scribbles, and she was supposed to know what they represented. Cautiously, Aggie asked, "Well, are you going to show me how it works?"

Laird glowed. "See, we took all of the drawers out and took the fronts off of them. Then we took the fronts and screwed these hinges to them." Laird demonstrated by lifting one of the drawer fronts upward. Inside was a pair of shoes. The boy was almost dancing with excitement. "Now, the doors lift up so no one hangs on them or leaves them down so they get bent off. And the little kids can put two pairs in one spot!"

Aggie was excited. She complimented the boys on their work and called Vannie in to see. "This is so well-done boys! Everything is lined up perfectly. I am very impressed."

Aggie was truly amazed at how beautifully the boys had lined up the drawer fronts. No one would ever imagine that the drawers didn't slide outward. Aggie's enthusiasm diminished when, as she carried boxes to the garage, she tripped over the leftover drawers scattered about the floor. Aggie's foot caught inside one of the drawers, and she went down at an extremely awkward angle.

Aggie's cry brought all of the children running. Laird took one look at the mess of boxes, drawers, Aggie, and then turned and ran out the side door. Just as Vannie stooped to help Aggie stand, the baby cried. Aggie sent Vannie to get him and begged the rest of the children to clear a path to the couch.

She felt nauseated. It took every ounce of self-control to prevent herself from crying and vomiting simultaneously, and when her head began to swim, she wondered if she'd make it to the couch. Each movement was torture. The horrible pains in her ankle felt like repeated stab wounds, and by the time she reached the couch, Aggie was exhausted. Moments later, she was sleeping soundly.

When Aggie awoke, the house was quiet; too quiet. She sat quickly upright with both legs still extended on the couch. One glance at her ankle sent a wash of relief over her; it wasn't swollen. Turning it sideways, she gasped. All of the swelling was concentrated on the side of her ankle. It looked like a tennis ball had grown out of the bone. Where were the children, and how was she going to get to a doctor for x-rays?

Aggie called and called, but silence was the only answer. Frantic for the children's safety, she crawled across the floor until she found the phone, tears of pain streaming down her face. Quickly, she dialed Tina's phone number. "Tina, *help!*"

Tina's voice was soothing, and her normal, unruffled, matter-of-fact, words calmed Aggie immediately. "Sit down, Aggie, and tell me what is wrong."

"I either badly sprained or broke my ankle this afternoon. It hurt so much that I got sick. The next thing I knew, I woke up on the couch—I barely remember crawling there—and Tina, *the kids are gone*! I keep calling, but no one answers. Cemeteries are louder than this house!"

"Are they outside? If you are really quiet can you hear *any* noise outside?"

"*None*! What if Vannie got scared and called Mrs. Stuart? I have no idea how long I slept. How irresponsible can I *be*!"

"Aggie, hush! Mrs. Dragon Lady does not have your children. They are safe. We just don't know where yet. You are going to get off the phone, call anyone you can think of who can come look, and then call me right back."

Aggie agreed and hung up. Grabbing the phone book, she called Mrs. Gansky, the minister's family, and every woman who had watched the children in the last three months. No one was home. Aggie nearly screamed in frustration. Out of desperation, she flipped through the yellow pages until she found the used car section. Feeling foolish, she dialed Zeke's work number and caught the man on his way out the door.

Aggie prayed like she had never prayed before. Tears were streaming down her face, and she was audibly crying out petitions for safety and wisdom when Zeke came through the door. "Oh, Zeke. What can I do? I don't know how I can find where they've gone!"

"Well, missy, did you look upstairs? Oh, no, you couldn't do that could you? Let me do some searchin' and then we can figure out what to do next."

Zeke slowly climbed the stairs and wandered around the upstairs. Next, he went through the kitchen and checked the backyard. On his way back through, Zeke noticed a note on the refrigerator door. "Well, here's the mystery all solved. They're walking up and down the street to keep things quiet so you can rest."

Aggie was so relieved the tears started again. "Now, don't cry, honey. It'll be just fine. You call a cab—that ankle looks bad—might be broken even. I'll go get the kids and bring 'em back in so you can see that they're fine. I'll stay until you are ready to come home, and then call me, and I'll come get you in your van."

Four hours later, Zeke helped Aggie manipulate her new crutches in order to get inside the house. The children swarmed her and nearly toppled her over. Laughing, Aggie insisted that they back away and give her room to maneuver through the house. Zeke helped situate her on the family room couch, brought her baby supplies, a stack of books, the phone, and a jug of ice water. With promises of an intercom by ten the next morning, Zeke left the Stuart house and drove home.

Aggie groaned. She couldn't get the children up, ready for school, make lunches, drive them anywhere, and the idea of chasing toddlers made her cringe. Those twins were going to drive her up the wall. Aggie just knew it. Meanwhile, with Vannie's help, she fed and changed Ian. Vannie put the baby in his portable playpen, and the children went to bed.

Aggie stared at the ceiling. She looked at the stack of books but didn't pick up any. She drank a glass of water. She regretted it. The water only created a need to use the bathroom. Not a simple thing when you can only put weight on one leg. Aggie almost wished she *had* broken the ankle. A cast would certainly be preferable. There was something pathetic about taking thirty minutes to use the restroom because you couldn't easily dress and undress yourself.

Hobbling back to the couch, Aggie spotted something she hadn't noticed in the two months she had lived there. Doug had a laptop. All Aggie needed to do was figure out how to get the laptop to the couch and she could talk to Tina.

Tina says: What are you doing online?
Aggie says: Laptop! Isn't it great!
Tina says: Only you would find a laptop and get online

---

while

hobbling around with an injured ankle. Speaking of which, what's wrong with it?

Aggie says: Sprained. I'm on complete bed rest for 3-5 days and limited motion for two weeks. They all think I'm nuts.

Tina says: Why is that?

Aggie says: Well, they told me to take it easy and do as little possible.

Tina says: ROFLOL

Aggie says: I was under the influence of pain and partially effective Tylenol. What more do you expect?

Tina says: Aggie. What are you going to do? I can't leave right now. I've got finals in a week.

Aggie says: Well, Zeke is coming first thing tomorrow to put in an intercom system.

Tina says: The car sales guy?

Aggie says: Yep. I couldn't find anyone else home, so I tried him. He's always been so nice to me.

Tina says: How old is Zeke again?

Aggie says: Over sixty for sure. Knock it off Tina; he's just a nice old man.

Tina says: Making sure. Ok. What about meals? School? That field trip next week? The baby?

Aggie says: I have no idea. I'm working on a plan but hoped that you would possibly give me some ideas?

Tina says: Hire a cleaning service to come in twice a week. You can't do it alone. See if you can't find a college student who wants some extra cash for watching the kiddos at the house with you. Then… STAY OFF THAT FOOT! Remember that bad sprain I had? I can tell you. You have to do as little as is humanly possible until setting the foot down does not hurt at all. Trust me on this!

Aggie says: Oh, but Tina!

Tina says: If you say one word about the money, I'll shoot you.

If you don't spend it here, those children will come home from school, do their homework, and then try to clean up the house — it's too much. They can do their part on the weekends.

Aggie says: What about my part? I can't do anything!

Tina says: You are working hard to get well. Order pizzas, buy macaroni and cheese, Ramen noodles, canned soups, fish sticks, whatever — have someone go get them so that food is fast and easy. It won't hurt them for a couple of weeks.

Aggie says: What do you think they're eating now? Add in pot pies, a few leftover casseroles that came after the funeral, frozen burritos, and this is their dinner. I've taken to cereal and a bag of apples for breakfast every day.

Tina says: You're not cooking?

Aggie says: Since when can I cook? I don't know how to shop, make the food, and make enough to feed everyone. Every recipe says it serves 4-6. If I double it, that's 8-12. We need 9 and those are adult servings. So, do I need to make 4-6?

Tina says: Ok, ok. I get it. Consider this training time. I'm going to overnight a couple of basic cookbooks. Read them. I'll also send some regular recipes that you can make from that gal at our church. You know, Priscilla, the lady with like 5 kids under 6? She should know what you should do. You've got three more kids, but no husband to feed and guys eat a lot.

Aggie says: OH, BOY. Wouldn't that be awful?

Tina says: What would?

Aggie says: A HUSBAND! Eeeeeeekkkkkkkkkk.

Tina says: It would be helpful, dear. Most mothers like husbands.

Aggie says: No self-respecting husband would put up with the frozen stuff I've been feeding these guys, the condition of the house, and you haven't heard my ANT story!

Tina says: I don't want to know. You know how I hate mice, cockroaches, and ants.

Aggie says: I guess I won't tell you about Bonaparte and

Wellington then.

Tina says: Not mice. Tell me that they are not mice.

Aggie says: They are not mice.

Tina says: A lie?

Aggie says: No really… they are not mice. They're RATS!

Tina says: You are a sick, demented woman. Where'd you get the names?

Aggie says: Well, Bonaparte was so named so that his cage could be named "Bonaparte's Retreat"…

Tina says: GROAN. Wellington?

Aggie says: Well, Laird's trying to figure out a neat way to make something "Wellington's Beef." I'm not sure how he'll do that unless he builds a cage that looks like a cow!

Tina says: What about a gargoyle on the cage… but instead it's one of those little plastic cows?

Aggie says: I'll go get one tomorrow! That's cute!

Tina says: You will NOT! You will sit there and figure out how to get housekeeping service for Tuesdays and Thursdays through the month of May. You can use the move in June as an excuse not to continue after that.

Aggie says: The move!!!!!!!!!!!!!!!!!!

Tina says: I'd be there if I could. You know that, right?

Aggie says: I know.

Tina says: Meanwhile, it's late. I'm tired; you're rebuilding tissue, GO TO SLEEP!

Aggie says: Nighters Tina…

Tina says: Poofs!

Help Unwanted

Chapter Seven

Sunday, May 5th

Aggie woke for what seemed like the millionth time. This time, it was Ian squirming on her chest. She sighed. After almost dropping the little tyke as she pulled him from his playpen, she had decided that he could just sleep on her chest. Ian slept wonderfully, but Aggie thought the whole cuddling with your baby thing was definitely overrated. Well, least it was when you're snuggling *all night*.

Tavish was up early and came tumbling downstairs. Within seconds, Aggie saw him sprawled out at the bottom of the stairs with an antique book broken at his feet. "Oh, noooooo!"

Aggie fought to sit up, concerned that the boy was hurt. "You all right?" Tavish's sobs were heartbreaking, but they didn't sound like cries of pain.

"I ruined Dad's book. I wasn't watching where I was going, and I dropped it."

"Well, Tavish, I know it was your dad's, but it is just a

109

book. Perhaps we can try to fix it?"

"It's a first edition Oliver Optic that belonged to Dad's granddad. It was very special to Dad, and I ruined it." Tavish was almost inconsolable.

Aggie sat on the couch trying to get Ian safely put down to go comfort the boy. Before she could get to her crutches, Ellie came down the stairs and gathered up the book. Looking carefully at the pages, the spine, and the cover, Ellie set the book aside and comforted Tavish. Aggie hadn't seen the twin aspect of these two very often, but Ellie seemed to know just what to do and say to console her brother. A moment later, the book was put away, Tavish was playing with Ian, and Ellie was mixing a new bottle for the baby as though the earlier histrionics hadn't happened.

When Zeke arrived, the children were eating their breakfast. Excited children rushed from the table and surrounded the elderly man. "Awww, now, kiddos, you go back and finish your breakfast. There'll be time enough to talk after you're done with the food.

"So, missy, how is that ankle feeling today?" Zeke's smile always reached the corner of his eyes and made them wrinkle up like a department store Santa Claus.

"I haven't tried to stand on it yet, but it hurts—badly. I think I need to rewrap it. This wrap thing makes it itch!"

"Don't you be trying to stand on it yet, young lady! It's too soon!" Zeke shook his head in disapproval. "I've sprained my ankles many times, stickin' 'em in snake holes when I wasn't looking, and I'm telling you girl, you don't want to mess with pushing yourself."

Aggie laughed and asked how much she owed for the intercom. Zeke assured her that he hadn't spent a dime yet. "I just realized that you might need a good nap, and the children might like to go to Sunday school with us, so I came by to see if you would let me take them to church for you. I didn't think you should try to get in that big old van again. Driving home last night wasn't exactly legal you know."

Aggie remembered sitting wedged between the rows of bench seats and the van's doors, praying that the doors wouldn't fly open and spill her into the road. "I don't know if the kids can be ready…"

Vannie piped up, "Oh, can he drop me off? Our class is having a special collection, and we're boxing up care packages and having chips and salsa for Cinco de Mayo. The high schoolers are going to take the boxes to Mexico the week after school lets out."

Aggie looked into the face of her eager niece and thought about how the child never asked for anything for herself. Acting like it was a huge imposition, Aggie groaned and moaned and sighed, then said, "Oh, all right!"

A cheer rose from the children while Aggie sent them packing. "Get shoes from the new ankle wren— er— shoe box! Girls, clean dresses! Boys, no *jeans*! Come on! Let's get some buttoned up shirts, or at the very least, polos without holes!"

"Now, missy, my Martha is working in the nursery, and she'll take care of the little tyke here, the little girlies can go to their class, and you can just lay here on the couch and rest. After church, we'll take everyone to that new hamburger place over by the freeway that has all the gizmos. They can play 'til they're half dead, come home, and take a nap."

"I really appreciate this, Zeke. I shouldn't let you do it— you've been so good to me already, but I really need a nap!"

"After church, my nephew is going to come over and put in that intercom. It's pretty easy, I think— shouldn't take him long. I'll leave the door unlocked, so you don't have to get up to let him in."

Though she felt funny about it, Aggie decided that there was nothing else she could do, short of locking up the children until she could walk. She really was at everyone's mercy, and she didn't like it. She barely moved her foot, and it screamed in pain. Yes, everyone needed to go. She needed to *breathe* again.

Aggie didn't rest while the family was gone as intended. First, she surfed the Internet, perusing every site she could find on the subject of sprains and the best way to heal them. Aggie hoped that there was some vitamin C in the house — it was supposed to help heal tissue.

She tried to ding Tina on the messenger, but her friend was obviously at church. Knowing Tina, she'd invite the entire Mullins family out to dinner, so she could pick Priscilla Mullins' brain on recipes and food preparation.

Lastly, Aggie searched furniture sites, hoping to find a style that would fit her, the kind of family she had, *and* be sturdy. What she discovered was that she did *not* like the showroom type furniture groups. She found rooms decorated in only one style to be too sterile. She really liked the rooms that showed a lovely mixture of different periods, giving an eclectic aesthetic. A new thought occurred to her as she remembered the furniture she'd seen in the attic of the "new" house.

With no regard for day or time, Aggie picked up the phone and dialed Mr. Moss. Getting an answering machine at his office, she contorted until she could reach her purse and grabbed Mr. Moss' card from her wallet. "May I speak to Robert Moss, please?" Aggie hoped she wasn't interrupting anything important.

"Hi, Mr. Moss, sorry to bother you, but I just had a thought, and I wanted to know when I can look over the new house. There was a bunch of old furniture in the attic, and I'm curious to know if it's salvageable."

"If it wasn't Sunday, I'd say to come in and get the key now. However, I don't have it at home, so you'll have to pick it up next week if you like. It was delivered to my office on Thursday."

"Sunday. I called you at your home on a Sunday. I'm so sorry. I forgot what day it is." Aggie's voice was flat. She was so excited; she'd called her lawyer on his day off!

"Aggie, are you ok?" Mr. Moss' voice seemed concerned.

"I sprained my ankle yesterday and am on bed rest for several days. I'm going stir crazy already. I'm sorry. I'll bother you next week. I can't drive out there anyway. *I can't drive!* What was I thinking?"

Aggie said goodbye and hung up abruptly. The strain and pain of the last two days caught up to her, until she finally collapsed on the couch sobbing. Aggie wasn't an overly emotional woman, but she'd held onto the frayed end of her rope for weeks now. She finally let go and cried. In minutes, Aggie slept.

Luke Sullivan walked through the door, knocking gently as he entered. "Aggie? Helloooooooo?" Entering the room, Luke saw that the young woman was sleeping, albeit fitfully. Her face appeared tearstained, and the silence of the house was occasionally broken by her muffled sobs. A glance at her feet deepened his sympathy. Luke knew just how painful a sprained ankle could be. Wait until she started feeling antsy! The poor girl would drive everyone around her crazy. Luke was very experienced in that department.

"Poor little momma. She's having it rough. Help her, Lord. Please heal her ankle quickly and be Aaron's arms to her, Lord. Hold her up when she's ready to fall. I'm sure she'd love to sense Your help." Luke whispered his prayer as he began installing the intercom system his uncle had requested. He felt foolish. The children could have installed it in minutes. It was wireless and needed only a place to mount and a nearby outlet. His uncle had been adamant. He was to "install that system," and Luke had wondered if Uncle Zeke was growing senile.

Aggie heard his prayer. In her exhausted state, she thought she was seeing things. She thought she saw the physician Luke, of the New Testament, hovering over her couch and praying for her healing. A fleeting question ran across her mind as she wondered if she was hallucinating, but Aggie drifted into a perfectly peaceful sleep before she could make sense of her thoughts.

Luke thought he saw the woman visibly relax as he finished setting up the intercom next to the couch. Answered prayer was a wonderful thing, but he marveled at *observing* it answered so quickly and so visibly. Whistling "Sweet Hour of Prayer," Luke marched up the stairs to install the second unit. He found an outlet in the middle of the hallway, and in moments, had the intercom mounted to the wall.

He started to leave, when he noticed Aggie's crutches by the couch. She'd be hungry when she awoke from her nap. Luke put down his things and walked to the kitchen; smiling, he opened a refrigerator covered with pictures inscribed to "Aunt Aggie." Pulling out condiments, lunchmeat, and vegetables, Luke made a whopper of a sandwich and put it on a plate. He rummaged through the pantry and found some crackers and a small bag of chips. Grabbing a banana from the fruit basket on the counter, he brought the food and set it near her on the coffee table.

A thought occurred to him, and he went back into the kitchen. At the back of the pantry, he found what he was looking for. A good quality thermos would work beautifully. Luke boiled water and mixed a thermos full of the "imported coffee stuff" mix that he'd seen sitting on the counter. He grabbed a paper towel and scribbled a note on it.

Aggie (Sorry, I don't know your last name),
The intercom system is up and running. I thought you might wake up and be hungry before Uncle Zeke got back, so I left you a sandwich. I hope that ankle feels better soon. Having had a couple myself, I can attest to the fact that the longer you rest in the beginning, the sooner you can really move around.
Praying for you,
Zeke's Nephew

Wednesday, May 8th

Aggie pressed the intercom buzzer for what seemed like the fiftieth time. "Girls, come downstairs, *now*." Aggie didn't know why she bothered. She was getting the hang of the crutches, but going up and down stairs was still impossible —

and the twins knew it. Lorna would likely have come had Cari not been in one of her moods. Getting Lorna to go against Cari's wishes was like getting a mule to volunteer to carry heavy packs up a steep mountain in the rain — wearing heels.

Aggie nearly screamed in frustration. After three days of having the twins run wild all over the house, she realized that Tina had been right. She would have to call for help. Picking up the phone, Aggie swallowed her pride and called Zeke. Again. This was becoming a terrible habit of hers. "Zeke? This is Aggie. I'm so sorry to keep bothering you, but you've lived here a while, and I thought maybe you might know where I could get some help."

Zeke chuckled. "What kind of help do you need, missy?"

Aggie realized that she was not making sense. "I need to hire two people for the next two weeks. I need a mother's helper type person. Someone who can come in and take care of the twins and Ian for two weeks, so they don't run wild. I can't control them!"

"And the other person? What is this other person going to do?"

"I need a cleaning service or something. My friend Tina told me to call someone, but I forgot and the house is already a mess. Please, if you can think of anyone who can do either of these, I really could use the help. It's so hard to get the baby in and out of his playpen. I re-injured my ankle last night when I was getting him up for an impromptu midnight feeding. I whacked it on the coffee table." The defeat in Aggie's voice showed the strain this enforced bed rest was causing her.

Zeke was silent for a moment before speaking. "Oh, I know! There is a lovely woman in our church. Her husband just got laid off, and they're cutting it pretty close these days. Why don't I call her and see if she's available? If she is, I'll give her your phone number."

Aggie sagged in relief. "What could she do? Cleaning or watching?" Aggie was praying that it would be watching as she heard yet another *loud* thump upstairs.

"Why, I imagine she'd be doing both. I'll give her a call."

Aggie says: Mom? Are you there?
Martha says: I'll get her.
Aggie says: Hi, Dad!
Martha says: She's coming. How is that ankle?
Aggie says: Healing, but slowly.
Martha says: I'll bet. Here's mom. If I don't talk to you later, take care.
Aggie says: Night, Dad.
Martha says: Hi Aggie! How are you? Are you sick of that question yet?
Aggie says: Yep, but I'll live.
Martha says: What is wrong, young lady? I can tell something isn't right.
Aggie says: I can't do it.
Martha says: Can't do what? Last I read, Paul promised we could do all things through Jesus.
Aggie says: humph
Martha says: I'm waiting.
Aggie says: The twins won't listen, I can't lift Ian, and I've had to give up and hire help to do what Doug and Allie thought I could handle. I'm a failure.
Martha says: Hogwash. If you don't quit this pity party, I'm going to drive down there myself and spank you.
Aggie says: As if.
Martha says: Do not sass me!
Martha says: Listen to your mother. I don't need her up fretting half the night.
Aggie says: Yes ma'am/sir.
Martha says: That's better. Now, let me get this straight. You're pretty much stuck on the couch all day, is that right?
Aggie says: bingo
Martha says: Furthermore, you have small children that need attention, but you are physically incapable of providing it. Do I have the situation described correctly?

Aggie says: Yes, Mother.

Martha says: Well, when Allie was unable to move around at the end of her pregnancy with Cari and Lorna, if you'll remember, she hired an assistant to do the housework and keep the children from killing themselves and each other.

Aggie says: How did I miss that? When—

Martha says: I think it was your second semester at college. You were probably sleep-deprived and didn't remember. I remember you spent the whole trip to see the babies in the hospital studying child psychology or something and drove us all insane with your new-found knowledge.

Aggie says: Oh, yeah, I think a woman brought the kids to the hospital that day. Was that her?

Martha says: Yep.

Aggie says: Why do I feel like such a failure?

Martha says: Because when you're curled on the couch, it's much easier to stare into your own navel than it is to see reality.

Aggie says: Gross, Mom.

Martha says: I call them like I see them. Did you find someone to hire, or did you just realize you'd have to?

Aggie says: Zeke says he knows someone. Sigh.

Martha says: We're proud of you, Aggie. You know that, right?

Aggie says: I know, Mom. Thanks

Aggie says: Am I crazy not to move to Yorktown?

Martha says: I know your dad thinks he's being sneaky about suggesting you keep far enough away that I can't drive, but as much as I don't want to admit it, he's right. I'd try to come, it'd be too much for me, and you'd have nine kids to take care of until he could rescue me. Staying close to Rockland gives you a broader support base, and even though you'll have a new church, the old church will be close enough to help out if necessary. It's a good decision, Aggie.

Aggie says: I guess.

Martha says: Aggie?

Aggie says: hmm?

Martha says: Is Jesus big enough to handle this?

Aggie says: yeah

Martha says: Then give it to Him. Your dad is giving me slicing motions across his neck. I'd better go before he grabs a knife. Night.

Aggie says: Night, mom. Love you.

Martha says: Night, Aggie. Love you too.

DISCOVERY

Chapter Eight

Thursday, May 9ᵗʰ

The children rushed out the door the next morning, just as a car drove into the driveway. Vannie looked curiously at the woman but rushed past, trying not to miss the bus. The woman counted the children as they dashed out the door. Kenzie tripped over her shoelace but was up and running again before the startled woman could try to help.

Aggie called out with a welcoming, "Come in," as she heard a knock at the door. A smiling woman, with beautiful russet hair piled on her head in a bun and jolly green eyes, hesitantly entered the room. "Are you Aggie? Zeke didn't give me any other name, just Aggie."

Aggie noticed that the woman looked ready to work. She wore an old hand painted t-shirt that said, "East or West, our mom's best" and bleach stained jeans. "My name is Iris Landry. It's nice to meet you." The slightly plump woman extended her hand to Aggie.

"Hello, Mrs. Landry, I'm Aggie. As you can see..." she gave the rooms an embarrassed glance.

119

"Now, never mind, Aggie, I'll get this place ship-shape in no time." Mrs. Landry smiled at the younger woman. "Where are the other children? I thought Zeke said I would be looking after three?" She smiled at Ian. "Is this Ian? Zeke is taken with him."

"The twins, Cari and Lorna, are hiding upstairs. They're being the epitome of "terrible three" right now. I can't get them to obey me at all since I've been laid up. They just do their own thing, knowing I can't stop them." Aggie sounded even more defeated than she looked. "Only three months, and I'm already a failure as a mother. Oh, and don't ask which is which. I can only tell when one of them does something especially naughty. Then I know it's probably Cari."

Mrs. Landry laughed and suggested that she bring the twins downstairs for the morning. "I'll have enough to do down here without worrying about what they are into upstairs."

Aggie tried to stand and hobble over to the stairs when she heard the woman laughing above her. "Aggie," Mrs. Landry called downstairs. "Aggie, I have to show you this. You won't believe me unless you see it."

Iris held Bonaparte up for Aggie to see as she carried the rat to where the "invalid" stood, staring at the sight in disbelief. She sat on the stairs, collapsed in helpless laughter, and her guffaws brought the twins running to the top of the stairs. Aggie held Bonaparte and tried not to drop him between bursts of giggles. The poor rat had a pink, butterfly, snap-style barrette pinned to the bottom of his tail. "This is one of those times I wish I had a camcorder on. This would be perfect for that ridiculous show on TV where they show you blooper clips from home movies."

Mrs. Landry picked up the rat, and as she carried him back to his cage, she removed the little clip. The poor critter seemed relieved, and it was obvious to the woman that he had been in some pain from the experience. Looking at the rest of the upstairs, Iris tried not to chuckle. The girls were watching her warily. They weren't exactly sure how to react to an adult being upstairs again.

"Ok, girls. We're going to go downstairs now, so let's gather a few books and some toys for you to play with down there." Mrs. Landry's tone was confident and matter-of-fact. Aggie cringed as she heard the little girls arguing and becoming a little petulant. Mrs. Landry didn't seem to hear them. She simply gathered what she decided to let them play with and herded the girls toward the stairs.

Aggie hobbled back to the recliner next to the couch and put her feet up. She considered offering to read to the girls but realized that this was a chance to watch someone else interact with the children. Maybe she could learn something from Iris. Aggie hoped that the woman wouldn't mind being under close scrutiny.

"All right, girls. This is how things are going to be. You will stay downstairs. Do you understand? I can't be running upstairs to check on you while I'm trying to clean up, so you have to be down here. Do you understand?"

Iris Landry sounded more confident than she felt. She wasn't sure how the children would react to a stranger telling them what to do. She wasn't left wondering for long. Cari piped up with an, "I don't want to," the minute Iris was finished speaking. However, Lorna was hesitant. She looked at Aggie, then at Mrs. Landry, over to Cari, and then back at Aggie again.

Trusting Aggie's instincts on which child would defy, Iris replied calmly, "Well now, Cari, I don't think I asked what you wanted to do. This is what we *are* going to do. Now you can be pleasant about it— you can have fun with your sister and baby brother— or you can sit in his playpen all by yourself, but you *will* stay downstairs."

Cari seemed ready to do battle but surprisingly picked a book out of the laundry basket of toys and books. Settling as far away from everyone as she could, Cari acted like she was reading intently. Lorna seemed at a loss. Finally, Lorna sat next to the baby playing on the floor and began trying to engage him in a game of peek-a-boo.

Satisfied that things were working smoothly, Iris went to her car to get her caddy of cleaning supplies. Walking back into the house, she saw Cari scrambling up the stairs. Aggie sat in the recliner with eyes shut, apparently napping. Mrs. Landry didn't want to wake the young woman but knew that the line had been drawn, and Cari fully intended to determine who controlled the territory. She set her caddy of supplies down and walked swiftly to the stairs. When Cari saw that she'd been discovered, she tried to climb more quickly.

Aggie woke from her short nap as Cari's screams pierced the air. Opening her eyes just in time, she saw Iris scoop the girl up and carry her back down the stairs. Sighing, Aggie telegraphed her apology to Mrs. Landry, but the woman shook her head. Aggie expected to see a stern disapproving look on Iris' face as she spoke to the disobedient girl but was surprised to see her smiling.

Without a trace of sarcasm, and with that same smile on her face, Mrs. Landry deposited Cari in the playpen saying, "Well, it seems like you prefer to stay in here. That's fine with me." The woman didn't miss a beat. Picking up trash around the room, the sharp woman kept a close eye on Cari's movements. The second the girl rose to escape, Mrs. Landry would quickly sit her back down in the pen.

After the fourth or fifth return to sitting position, Mrs. Landry sweetly remarked, "When you think you can sit here like you're told, I'll be happy to let you sit on the couch for a while."

Cari's face clouded over. "I don't want to sit on the couch. I want to go *play*."

"Oh, you do? Now, that is funny. I thought you wanted to sit in the playpen. You act like you want to sit in the playpen." Mrs. Landry had the room cleared of all trash and dirty plates and was working on watering and dusting the plants.

"I want *out*!" Cari was angry. Aggie was certain that the

child would lose it completely. "I want out, now, now, *now*!"

"Well, Cari, it's pretty simple. If you want out, you have to *act* like you want out. That's all it takes. Right now, you are acting like you want to be *in*."

Aggie was extremely impressed. By that point, she would have sent the girl off to play, with admonitions to behave now and enough p-mail requests in that department to overload the Lord's inbox. This woman wasn't angry and didn't act stern or foreboding; she simply smiled and waited for the child to be obedient. This was different anyway. She wondered how it would work.

In no time, the room looked presentable again. The furniture shone, and the room smelled clean and seemed bright as the morning sunlight shone through the south and east windows. Iris opened the windows and fresh air blew through the sheers, causing them to billow gently around the sills. Ian started crying when the vacuum started up, but Aggie was able to comfort him before he became too distraught. She watched Cari as Iris helped Lorna move the vacuum back and forth across the floor. Lorna was having the time of her life making the carpet fluff up in neat little rows. Cari quite obviously wanted in on this new "game."

Aggie was certain that Cari would demand a chance to try but was surprised when the child sat down with her legs crossed and folded her hands in her lap. The scene was almost comical. Cari clearly wanted to be noticed, but Iris was just as clearly *not* noticing her. It was readily apparent that Iris knew exactly what Cari was doing but was not jumping to free her captive. When the room was finished, Mrs. Landry turned the vacuum off and stowed it in the next room.

"Cari! You look like you want out of the pen! I think you're ready to sit on the couch now." Without another word, Mrs. Landry sat Cari on the couch and placed a stack of books beside her. "I'll check on you in a minute, but Lorna and I are going to work in the living room now. Come along, Lorna, and I'll show you how to polish a table. It's really fun to do. If you do your very best job, you should be able to see yourself in the table."

Aggie barely stifled a giggle. Cari's despondent face was comical. She wanted so badly to join them and knew the only chance she had was to do as she was told. She waited for one of the child's characteristic outbursts, but Cari exhibited admirable self-control. Several minutes after she would have sent the child off to play, Iris came back into the room. "Cari, would you like to try to polish the other table? Lorna did a *great* job! I bet you can do it too!"

Eagerly, Cari jumped off the couch and ran to catch the older woman's hand and join her. Aggie barely heard Cari's "I'm sowwy. I'll be nice now."

Picking up Ian, she patted his hands together as she recited patty-cake. The baby's hearty chuckles filled the room as she helped him "roooollll it up and throw it in the pan." Once finished with another round, and a few tugs to his "piggies," the little tyke dropped a sleepy head to Aggie's chest and popped his thumb into his mouth. Seconds later, she saw his eyes growing droopy. Covering his ear with her hand, she called to Mrs. Landry for help in putting him down for his nap and hoped that Cari wouldn't see the occupation of the playpen as license to return to her defiant behavior.

When the older children arrived home, Aggie lined them up "Sound of Music style" and introduced them. "This is Vannie… she's twelve. Next is Laird who is ten—"

"And a half, Aunt Aggie!"

"And a half," she agreed before continuing. Elspeth and Tavish are eight, and little Miss Kenzie is five."

"Well, it's nice to meet everyone. I think I've got your names down… Vannie, Laird, Elspeth—"

"You can call me Ellie. Everyone else does."

"Ellie, Tavish, and Kenzie."

"My real name is MacKenzie, but everyone just calls me Kenzie," the little russet-haired girl explained.

A hot meal was in the oven, the downstairs shone, and the

twins napped on the family room floor. The tired housekeeper/nanny pulled Vannie aside as she left and said, "I see the girls have been busy upstairs."

Vannie nodded slowly. "I didn't tell Aunt Aggie. I didn't know how. If I tell her, it's like I'm tattling, and it's not like she can stop them. I tried to clean it up but…"

"I know, sweetie. I'll take care of it tomorrow, and I'll tell your aunt. She won't blame you, though. I want you to know that." Mrs. Landry smiled at the young girl.

"I've tried, but the children don't mind me anymore." Vannie was obviously trying to bear more of the burden of the family than Aggie intended.

"Well, what I think your aunt needs right now is help getting the food on the table and the children washed up and in bed. I can handle the rest. Don't worry about the girls. They're just testing the waters." Mrs. Landry turned to leave but came back. "And don't let those little ones sleep too much longer. They need to sleep tonight too."

Friday, May 10th

Iris Landry surveyed the damage. Up and down the upstairs hallway were flowers, smiley faces, and many undistinguishable objects. It appeared that the twins had used wet toilet paper to decorate the hallway with pictures made of sodden balls of the stuff. Someone, Vannie most likely, had tried to pull them off of the walls in places, but the result was even worse. The wallpaper in the upstairs hallway was old. It appeared new, but it was definitely vintage paper. With each ball removed from the wall, huge portions of paper were torn away as well.

In between the pictures, sometimes almost in a dot-to-dot pattern, were drawings created with some kind of cosmetics. Cari and Lorna stood nearby, looking up at her as she surveyed the damage. "Well, girls, it appears that you were being awfully creative while your aunt was downstairs, weren't

125

you?"

Cari grinned. "It was fun! We made pictures. Like wallpaper!"

Mrs. Landry smiled. "I am kind of curious, girls; would you have made these pictures if your aunt could walk?"

Lorna began sobbing. "I am sorry. I am sorry."

Cari looked at Lorna as if she were a traitor. "I am not sowwy. It's pwetty!"

Iris Landry looked at the two girls. They were a study in opposites. Lorna looked dejected and forlorn, while Cari was determined to be right. Mrs. Landry looked upward as she petitioned for help. The sight almost pushed her over the edge. The ceiling was completely covered in toilet paper wads. It looked like a seventies style cottage cheese ceiling gone wrong.

Aggie saw her "helper" dashing down the stairs like something was chasing her. "Aggie, do you have a camera, camcorder— anything? I have *got* to show you this. You will not believe it unless you see it. This is *too* funny."

Aggie's reaction alternated between tears and giggles. She knew exactly when the girls had enjoyed their TP spree. The splats were quite audible, and the girls had giggled with glee for quite a long time. Soon, the utter destruction of the hallway was obvious to her, though.

"My sister searched every online vintage wallpaper site she could find. She poured through page after page of paper on eBay. The woman was almost obsessed with matching the original wallpaper. Now look at it." Aggie sighed.

"Well, Aggie, she put a basketball hoop over the hamper right through the wallpaper. I doubt she'd be that upset about this. Ingenious idea too! I wish I had thought of that. My kids would have *loved* to make sock baskets!"

Aggie blushed. "I did that. I was walking through the house one day after a rough early morning with Jr. Muffin and lost it. I had that basketball net up and the screwdriver put who-knows-where before I knew what hit me."

"Well, it's obvious that you have the mind of a mother! I

126

am quite impressed. I will have to take all the paper off of the walls. With the lipstick and eyeliner pencils… it's gone. I can't even try to salvage any of it. Sorry."

"Well, it'll just be one more thing that Mrs. Stuart can be mad at me about. It'll do her good." Aggie's grimace belied her words.

Tina says: Well… so tell me.
Aggie says: Well I forgot to call for help around here until Wed. Monday and Tuesday were ridiculous! The girls…
Tina says: Cari and Ethel? Er… I mean Lorna?
Aggie says: You know those old acoustic ceilings that look like they are leaking cottage cheese?
Tina says: Dare I ask?
Aggie says: Well, the girls decided to texture the ceiling in the upstairs hallway. Iris Landry video recorded the entire thing. It was amazing. LARGE CURD though. It was very LARGE curd…
Tina says: And the medium used?
Aggie says: Ummmmm how does wet, wadded…
Tina says: SPILL IT GIRL!
Aggie says: TOILET PAPER sound to you???
Tina says: NO WAY!
Aggie says: WAY! The wallpaper upstairs is ruined. Sigh.
Tina says: So is this woman helping at all— besides discovering the ruined hallway?
Aggie says: And the decorated rats…
Tina says: Ohhh, this I gotta hear!
Aggie says: Well… it seems that Cari was a bit incensed to find that both rats were boys, so she put one of those plastic bendy kindergarten hair barrette things on their tails!
Tina says: Are you sending these into Readers Digest? Maybe they'll hire you as the new Erma Bombeck.

Aggie says: Oh, and this woman is incredible! Cari pitched one of her stubborn fits and the gal never broke a sweat. She smiled the entire time that she kept Cari exactly where she wanted her. I think Cari is secretly happy not to be in control anymore.

Tina says: Have you asked her secret???

Aggie says: Not yet but I intend to! I am going to figure out how she knows EXACTLY what to do. Kenzie was sassing her yesterday and the woman marched her upstairs and shut her in my room. Told her that when she could speak respectfully she could come out. Cari would have been in there for HOURS but Kenzie stayed maybe three minutes max before coming out and apologizing.

Tina says: WOW!

Aggie says: How do I know which to use when? This is what I want to ask!!!

Tina says: Well, I'm sending you a meal card system that I made with Celia Mullins.

Aggie says: Celia?

Tina says: If your name ended up being Priscilla Mullins… of Longfellow fame, would YOU go by Priscilla?

Aggie says: Point taken. Well, according to Mrs. Landry, she will have the upstairs cleaned up by tomorrow.

Tina says: HOW! With those three mess makers, how can she get so much DONE!?

Aggie says: Well, it appears that she puts the girls to work with her…and they LIKE it!

Tina says: I want to sit at this woman's feet!

Aggie says: Me too… uh oh… Ian just bonked his head again. He's pulling up on everything, and it's just awful! Everyone says it's too early, but he's doing it so early or not, here I come. I better go.

Tina says: Keep me up on the latest!

Aggie says: Poof!

Tina says: Poof de de poof poof!

LESSONS & PLANS

Chapter Nine

Saturday, May 11th

Aggie gave work orders to the children and had everyone working on them by the time Mrs. Landry appeared. All of their bedding was on the floor in front of the washer, and their rooms were devoid of trash. As they gathered dirty clothes, Aggie's voice rang out through the upper floors telling them to put clean clothes away and not back into the laundry.

"Mrs. Landry…"

The smiling woman interrupted her. "Please call me Iris. I feel like we are becoming good friends, and my friends don't call me Mrs."

"Iris it is, thank you. I need all the help I can get, and after watching how you interact with the children for the last two days, and seeing how you have managed to make these children mind—" she stumbled over the right word, "cheerfully, I want to know your secrets. Teach me, oh wise one!"

Mrs. Landry laughed as she moved the armchair a little closer to Aggie. "I think I can offer you some suggestions. I'm no expert, but I do have a bit of experience with children, and my grown kids aren't criminals— yet."

Aggie sat up eagerly. She knew she had been too lenient with all of the children, allowing them to do pretty much what they wanted until it became dangerous, annoying, or destructive. Even when she did put her foot down, Aggie had a sinking feeling that if the children really pressed her, they would win. Having already faced facts, the truth was glaringly obvious. She was outnumbered. "Stop" was the only hard, fast rule that Aggie knew would be obeyed no matter what, and training them to obey that simple command had been torture.

"How do you know what to do to get the children to *choose* to obey you? I mean, the way you handled Cari and Kenzie—"

"Ok. Let's start with a simple premise. If you don't want a child to do something, you have to make the behavior counterproductive. They must want to avoid the consequences and never do it again."

"You've never raised your voice or even looked sideways at them."

"You don't need to. I believe it's very important to teach children to obey you the first time and without unpleasantness. Can you imagine a police officer pulling someone over every three minutes saying, "I thought I told you to slow down! If you don't slow down and stay slowed down, I'm going to *have* to give you a ticket."

Aggie chuckled. "I can't see the speeder pulling over again after the second or third time!"

Iris laughed. "Exactly!"

For the next hour, Iris told— and showed when the occasion arose— Aggie how to anticipate behavior problems and how to prevent them. She would have to know her "suspect." If the child was social and wanted to be with people, removing them from what they wanted would possibly deter them. Conversely, if they liked being alone, sitting in a chair next to her would likely deter them even more.

"Be careful using time outs in another room. It tends to just give children an opportunity to pout and seethe. Occasionally, it's good for helping them settle down when they're out of sorts, but if they've been disobedient, or even defiant, it rarely works in the long run."

Iris continued to think of how to explain things. "Ok. Here's the quick and dirty. If they complain about working, give them more work, for practice in doing it pleasantly. Every time they complain, give them another small job. Don't get sarcastic or unpleasant yourself. You'll just reinforce what you don't want them to learn. If they speak unkindly to a sibling, make them say five nice things about their sibling. Make whatever they did, not worth doing again." She smiled. "Basically, make the wrong behavior too much trouble to go through."

Aggie was thoughtful. "What if they refuse to obey me all together?"

Iris smiled. "Aggie, it's obvious that your sister trained these children well. They are accustomed to being obedient, and that's good for children. It's good that they learn to obey, and at a young age, obey without question. We don't always know why God requires this or that from us; we just have to obey. We learn to say 'Yes, Lord' from saying 'Yes, Ma'am' to our mom.

"If they had never been trained, they wouldn't have a respect for authority and this would be harder. But, your children respond to me because they *do* respect authority. I established authority immediately, and the children naturally responded to that. You just have to move from being 'fun buddy, Aunt Aggie' to authority figure Aunt Aggie— their second mother."

Iris got up, and with a pat on Aggie's shoulder, got to work. Soon, the house seemed to buzz with activity. Aggie watched as the toddlers became cranky, and she expected that Iris would settle their hash. She was surprised when Iris gathered the girls in her arms and whispered in their ears. The two girls smiled and got busy pulling out chips, bread, peanut butter, and jelly. Thirty minutes later, the girls slept on exercise mats on the family room floor.

"Iris?" Aggie's voice was quiet, but she was curious. "Iris, why did you feed the girls when they were whining? They were being difficult, and it looks like they got rewarded."

"I told them to stop their whining, and they did. Then, I told them what they could do to help me. I just made sure the help that I requested was something that they needed too. Small children have a hard time controlling themselves when they're hungry. If they hadn't stopped their fussing when I told them, I'd have had to deal with that first, but there was no reason to exasperate the girls. That's unnecessary punishment rather than good training and discipline."

When Iris left that day, Aggie had a new understanding of motherhood. Her frustration and disappointment in her lack of skills had dissolved into a full-blown pity party until Iris put a stop to it. "Aggie, I know women who have given birth to three, four, and even five children, who still don't know how to train and rear children. They spend their days just going from one thing to the next and from one day to the next... and then to the next. A success is when they don't have huge disobedience problems *all* of the time."

Iris thought carefully and continued. "The best mother is one who is always learning, not the one who thinks she has arrived. You need to remember that you aren't going to 'finish' these children. They won't be 'done' at ten, sixteen, eighteen, twenty-two, or even forty! Your job as mother is to equip them to turn themselves completely over to the Lord for the perfecting that He does in each of us— every one of us— every day."

With that, Iris, check in hand, left with promises to return on Monday. Aggie watched her drive away and fought the desire to cry. She hadn't felt this alone since the day she learned that, with no training, experience, or even desire to be a mother yet, she was now responsible for eight children and everything that came with them. She now had the tools to parent; the question was, would she know when to use them?

"All right, guys, front and center." Aggie sounded determined. The children gathered around her, but Aggie waited until she had their full attention before she spoke.

"I owe you an apology. I've watched Mrs. Landry, and I have talked to her. I see that I really blew it when I moved in here. I came in as the 'buddy,' Aunt Aggie, and that's not who I need to be anymore. We can still have fun and enjoy each other, but I need to put on a mom's hat. It's not just that I need to keep you guys out of trouble; I need to teach you to do things that are right too— even if you don't like it."

All the children looked solemnly at her with odd expressions on their faces. To lighten the mood, Aggie whipped around and made a goofy look with her face and turned back. The children's laughter broke the tension that had stolen over the room. Vannie took a deep breath and asked, "So you're going to be a mom-type but stay goofy enough to still be Aunt Aggie?"

"That's about right. Now let's eat that casserole Mrs. Landry made. It smells heavenly."

Sunday, May 12th

On Sunday, Aggie decided thirty-three seconds after the twins awoke that they were not attempting a trip to church. Cari, usually quite annoyingly chipper in the mornings, woke up with a nasty disposition, and Aggie, who had banged her ankle during an attempt to crawl up the stairs into her bed, hadn't slept well herself.

She sent everyone but Cari downstairs for canned cinnamon rolls and pulled the grumpy girl into bed with her for a little chat. "Do you still feel sleepy?"

Cari's vehement "No!" was unmistakable. "I's wide 'wake."

"Then do you feel sick? Does your head or your stomach

ache?"

A surly look crossed her face. "I's not sick!" Cari moved as far away from Aggie as she could get without actually leaving the bed.

Careful not to jar her ankle again, Aggie scooted next to Cari, making it impossible for the little girl to move without falling off the bed. "I'm glad to hear that. Did you know, that I can tell something is wrong?"

"What's wrong?"

"I don't know what it is, but I know there is something wrong. If you're not sick and you're not sleepy, I am not sure what it might be." She wrapped arms around the little girl and pulled her closer. "I wonder if maybe you just need someone to hold you and tell you that they love you."

Cari's eyes widened in surprise. "Mommy did that."

"Aunt Aggies can do it too."

How long they lay curled against the numerous pillows on Aggie's bed, she never knew. By the time she'd hobbled downstairs, with Cari leading the way giving advice on nearly every step... "Don't hit it 'gain! Cariful! Oh, you's going to huwt it!" the remaining cinnamon rolls were cold and looked singularly unappetizing.

"Maybe we should heat them up while I make me some coffee."

"I have coffee too?"

Against her better judgment, Aggie poured a swallow or two in Cari's cup and watched the child's face as she swallowed her first drink. Contrary to expectation, the girl loved it and begged for more. "I'm sorry, Cari. A sip now and then is an ok treat, but coffee is a grown-up drink. How about we find you some milk."

For a moment, Aggie was sure Cari would protest. The little girl's face scowled in anger, and then, as though a light switched on, disappeared and a smile replaced it. "I likes milk with cinnyman wolls!"

The simple tasks of making coffee, heating cinnamon rolls,

and pouring Cari a glass of milk took twice as long as she'd ever imagined it could, and through that entire time, she hadn't heard a peep from the other children. "Where are they?"

"Outside. Vannie takes them outside so's you can sweep." The child paused looking confused. "Sleep." She tried out the first word again. "Sweep." With a strange look at Aggie, she quipped. "I said sleep wrong, but it's right too."

Tina says: Hey!

Aggie says: Well, I got my first parenting lesson yesterday.

Tina says: Oh? Do tell!

Aggie says: Already there's a different attitude from the children.

Tina says: But WHY?

Aggie says: The best way to describe it is that I expect there to be. It's like they picked up on my expectations, and they are "living up" to them. Is that too weird?

Tina says: Well, what did you expect of them when you moved in?

Aggie says: I knew Vannie and Laird wouldn't give me any trouble. I didn't expect much from Ellie and Tavish either way, but I was pretty sure that the baby would be sweet and that Cari, Lorna and Kenzie would give me a run for my money; all kids that age do right?

Tina says: hmm…

Aggie says: You think I'm crazy?

Tina says: Well no, but look at what you just said. You said you didn't expect trouble from the oldest four and the baby. Who didn't give you trouble?

Aggie says: You have a point. I expected trouble from the little ones and got it. Had I expected obedience, they might still have been some trouble, but not as much?

Tina says: Exactly! All children, including Vannie, Laird, Ellie,

---

Tavish, Kenzie, Cari, Lorna, Ian... and a couple billion other children will push the envelope from time to time. But if you expect decent behavior, it's natural that you'll get more!

Aggie says: OOOhhh, like in my psychology class. The teacher talked about those teachers and coaches that always try to drive kids to do better by telling them how they'll never amount to anything. They think the kid will want to prove them wrong, but most kids won't. They'll do exactly what is expected of them. It was like 80% or more!

Tina says: Exactly!

Aggie says: Anyway, things were better tonight. I told Cari and Lorna to go brush their teeth and then come show me, and they were so happy. Before, I almost begged them to do it, and usually it took me having to get the toothbrushes and almost hold them still.

Tina says: You know they'll test you. You don't expect things to be smooth forever do you?

Aggie says: No, I think I can see the reality. I'm just excited because I can feel the whole shift in tone around here.

Tina says: So off topic, how's your foot?

Aggie says: Well... I can hobble on one crutch with no pain and if I have to let the crutch go I can walk if I go really slow and put almost no weight on it, but everyone says that if I re-injure it I'll be laid up twice as long the next time.

Tina says: And Iris is keeping things going?

Aggie says: Yep. I'm thinking about hiring her and her husband to do the packing and moving. I can't move us now, and it's just a couple of weeks away! Mrs. Stuart will want us out the day that we close escrow.

Tina says: That is smarter anyway. Your sister left you the money to be used for the children's upkeep— that includes helping you so that you can do your job. You'll be a better mother to those children if you will use the resources that you have coming in to cover it.

Aggie says: I guess.

Tina says: Don't you get benefits from Social Security?

Aggie says: Yeah, I am supposed to start getting around 3k.

Tina says: With no mortgage, no car payment— that's plenty to live on, so let yourself spend some of the interest money to do things like hire a housekeeper from time to time. Buy organizer things if it helps. Go to the movies with the children if Hollywood ever decides to make something worth seeing. Have the van serviced and washed. Pay for movers and for someone to help you fix up that house.

Aggie says: I don't want to waste money, though.

Tina says: Aggie, if there is one thing I've learned from my father it is that money is for spending.

Aggie says: What! Your father never spends any money!

Tina says: He has definite financial goals. He wants mom to spend whatever will keep her out of his hair, and to have plenty to cover retirement and leave something to his grandchildren.

Aggie says: What about savings?

Tina says: Dad says, "Money is for spending, Tina. You can spend it now, or save it and spend it later. But, if you are just hoarding it, you are wasting it. Money is for spending. That's its purpose."

Aggie says: I have to think about that one.

Tina says: Remember. Dad doesn't say that you should blow your money. He just says that cash in hand does you no good if are unwilling to use it if you need it. The point is to spend it now if you need it, save some for later when you need it but never just 'hoard' it.

Aggie says: Well, that's really more like what I am doing. I am saving it for them to spend later. I don't want them coming back and saying, "Why did you spend all of that money on things to make your life easier? Why didn't you save it for when we'd need it?"

Tina says: I'd shoot them with my iciest squirt gun! How ungrateful can you get?

Aggie says: It's fear isn't it? I'm afraid of running out of money. I'm afraid of what people will think if I spend it on me.

Tina says: You are afraid of what GERALDINE STUART will say.

Aggie says: I am, aren't I? Tina! I have a mother-in-law and I'm not even MARRIED!

Tina says: Yep. And why you care about the opinion of someone like her, I will never understand!

Aggie says: You're right. I need to pray about this. I'm sorry, but I think I need to go now. Ian is teething again and not sleeping well.

Tina says: Hug the little tyke for me. I'm praying for you too. This is a big responsibility, but I think Allie picked the best person for the job.

Aggie says: Thanks. Nighters.

Tina says: Poof!

$\mathcal{G}$RADGIGATION

Chapter Ten

Friday, May 17th

Aggie hobbled clumsily from the closet to the bathroom and back to the closet again, as she tried to dress for the day. She'd volunteered to accompany Tavish and Ellie's class to the Children's Museum before her accident and hadn't remembered to withdraw her offer when she was injured. Though she'd managed to walk without much difficulty for the past few days, this morning she chose to get dressed and ready for the day without using her ankle any more than necessary, in hopes she could save it for the long morning ahead of her. Her eyes glanced at the crutches a few times before she finally sighed in defeat. She needed them today.

After dropping all the younger children off at the babysitter's house and their respective schools, she drove to the museum, parked the "Stuartmobile" and gingerly climbed down from the driver's seat. So far, so good. The class should arrive in just over an hour — plenty of time to have breakfast at the diner next door.

Over a perfectly cooked omelet, a cup of simply delicious coffee, and the most moist blueberry muffin in the greater Rockland area, Aggie relaxed and made notes for the upcoming move. She wrote, ate, and sipped three cups of coffee before she realized she'd hogged a prime booth for the better part of the busiest time of morning. Apologetically, Aggie left an extra-large tip and walked back to the museum just as she saw the big yellow buses arrive.

Two hours later, Aggie followed Tavish from one thing to the next. It fascinated her to watch the way he immersed himself into whatever he did. The boy seemed nearly obsessed with working with the tools and building things and then rapidly switched to papermaking. With a uniform, foam nightstick, and whistle, he directed traffic as a policeman, and then quickly dropped it all to plant seeds. Aggie watched him walk through a large, clear maze until she saw Ellie across the room and wove her way through a different kind of maze—one of short bodies, racing to get to where they wanted to go.

Ellie sat on a tall stool in an art center, surrounded by art medium of all kinds. Some children worked with clay, sculpting oddly shaped animals or people, while others assembled sculptures from junk or made mock stained glass. Ellie painted. While most of the children at easels painted the predictable pictures of eight-year-olds the world over, Ellie had carefully drawn an extremely realistic tree with a single cluster of daisies beneath it. The effect was beautifully serene.

Aggie stood astounded at the sight of it. She didn't know much about children's drawings, but she did know that after two college art classes, she still couldn't begin to produce the kind of proper perspective and accuracy of a real tree that Ellie had managed. Then again, Aggie had also learned in those classes that she didn't have the patience to try.

"Is she your daughter?" Aggie dragged her eyes away from Ellie's work to a man leaning against a nearby pole. His badge identified him as an employee of the museum's art department.

"She's my niece. I had no idea she could draw so accurately and yet not sterilize it." Ellie had taken tempera paints and watered them down like watercolors. The effect was bold color, yet soft and gentle. Aggie watched as Ellie carefully tore her newsprint picture off the easel pad and hung it on the line to dry.

"She has definite talent. Most people can be trained to draw accurately, but you said it well when you called it sterilization. Few people put their soul and real talent into their drawings. She does both." The man sounded a little bohemian, but Aggie knew what he meant.

Again, they watched Ellie as she tried to draw chubby baby arms and hands holding a ball. No matter how many times she erased or tore off the page, the child never showed any signs of frustration. She simply tried again. Eventually, the man, who introduced himself as Dave, strolled to her side, hunkered on his heels, and showed Ellie how to look at one of the other children's arms for perspective. The picture that resulted was endearing. The baby's profile was very like Ian, and the ball was perfectly proportioned in his little hands.

She painted the ball a bright red but left the rest of the picture in pencil. Aggie asked the girl why she hadn't painted the child. Based upon Ellie's natural talent and understanding of art, she expected there was some kind of deep meaning or reason. She laughed when Ellie confessed, "I don't know if I can get the color right, and I don't want to ruin it. I'll color it in later if I find the perfect shade. Do you like it?"

Aggie tried hard to show her enthusiasm without being excessively effusive. Ellie was very nonchalant about her talent. It was obvious that she'd been drawing for years, but Allie had never mentioned a particular talent. Aggie wondered if her sister had ever known.

On the way home, with Ellie's pictures carefully rolled in a cardboard tube, Aggie asked Tavish, riding shotgun and out of earshot of Ellie, how long his sister had been drawing. "She's always drawn, Aunt Aggie. She's really good too. Momma always bought her new drawing books, but Ellie doesn't usually let people see her pictures, just me."

"What did your mom do about her art?" Aggie was thinking about how to get the child more training or something.

"I don't think Momma really knew how good Ellie is. Ellie just found books that show how to draw eyes or something, and Momma would buy it. I heard her tell Daddy that it wouldn't hurt to let Ellie try."

Aggie was still thinking about it when she arrived home with the children. After sending them to do their homework, Aggie laid the pictures out on the desk in the study and showed Iris what Ellie had drawn. "Iris? Can I show you something? Should I get her an art teacher? I mean, I think these are really good!"

Iris examined the pictures carefully. Aggie was right; the child was obviously talented, but Iris thought that people pushed children into developing their talents much too young. Praying for wisdom in how to word her thoughts, Iris agreed cautiously.

"Well, she *is* very good, but she's just a child. I would keep her supplied with pencils, markers, different paints, videos and books. That will be sufficient for a few years. I think parents try to direct their children's talents so young that, by the time the children really would be enjoying them fully, they are burned out. I think at eight years old, Ellie should just be allowed to be a child."

Aggie thought about that. "You have a point. I have a friend who won't pick up her violin anymore. She spent so many hours in student orchestras and recitals that she simply can't stand to play anymore."

Iris had another thought. "Oh, Aggie? Try to help her develop interest in something less mental and more active. It's good to balance your time with different activities."

142

The simple harmony of the congregation's voices swelled as they prepared their hearts for communion. Sunlight streamed through the tall narrow windows, the children sat quietly, Ian sleeping on the pew between Aggie and Laird. The bread and "wine" passed from person to person until Aggie too was refreshed as she "sat at the Lord's Table" during worship. Reflecting on the work of Christ on the cross always humbled the young woman. The words to the old hymn flowed through her mind and her heart as she focused on the memorial.

> *When I survey the wondrous cross*
> *On which the Prince of Glory died,*
> *My richest gain I count but loss,*
> *And pour contempt on all my pride*
> *See from His head, His hands, His feet*
> *Sorrow and love flow mingled down*
> *Did e'er such love and sorrow meet*
> *Or thorns compose so rich a crown.*

The minister stood and smiled at the end of the memorial feast. Aggie liked this congregation. Somehow, without making it overtly formal, they had restored a stronger meaning to the Lord's Supper. Actual cups of juice or wine were brought to the members, and the "loaf" was about the size of a small piece of bread. You had time to chew and reflect on Christ's sacrifice as you feasted. The supper wasn't rushed, nor did it drag. As she added her cup to the tray at the end of the memorial meal, Aggie realized that she had really missed this last Sunday.

"I'm reading from Galatians chapter six in the NASB this morning. Turn with me; let us reason together and see what great things the Lord will encourage us with this morning."

Aggie listened attentively to the lesson. When the words "let us not lose heart in doing good" were read, Aggie's mind strayed. Those words were powerful words. She was doing "good," and she had lost heart for a time. Those times would come again and Aggie knew that she had to not "grow weary." This new direction that the Lord had taken her life into was exciting as well as exhausting. Many women her age were starting a career, or at the *most* they were *starting* a family. Aggie's family was handed to her ready-made, and when she hadn't known what to do, she'd grown weary.

The closing hymn was "My Faith Looks up to Thee." Aggie thought the words were fitting, and they encouraged her more than she ever could have imagined. Throughout the day, she found herself humming the tune, and her spirit was refreshed. As she went to sleep that evening, back upstairs in her own bed, Aggie prayed a simple heartfelt prayer. "Lord, remind me Who is the Potter and who is the clay. I tend to try to model myself and hope that You'll just kind of keep me from cracking in the fire of life. Please, Lord, teach me to simply be a lump of clay." Aggie slept better that night than she had in weeks. Perhaps it was her prayer already being answered, or perhaps it was simply that her bed was much more comfortable than the couch.

Friday, May 31st

The children were hyper, and the house was a perfect set for a disaster movie. Aggie tore up and down the stairs in search of socks, barrettes, and baby Ian's shoes. Between groans of frustration, gasps for air, and wiping beads of perspiration from her upper lip and forehead, Aggie realized that people who said mothers at home didn't get enough exercise were more than ignorant; they were foolish!

"If women need more exercise at home, they should have another child or two. Twins would help," Aggie muttered to herself.

"What did you say, Aunt Aggie?" Laird eyed his aunt warily. He thought he had heard her correctly, but she sounded a little insane to him.

"I was just muttering to myself over the idiotic comments that people make about mothers. Ignore me."

Aggie dashed back upstairs one last time and finally found a brush under her dresser. Frustrated with the amount of time it took to find simple household staples like pens, pencils, scissors, a hairbrush, and similarly unexciting items, she decided to make a kit for emergencies. She would buy a lockable tool box and fill it with things like, barrettes, hair brushes, socks for everyone, spare keys (note to self: don't use a keyed lock) pencils, pens, checkbook, cash— anything that she might need and can't find in an emergency—or at least a hurry.

"Aunt Aggie, we have to hurry! I'll be late to my gradgigation!" Kenzie was near tears as she stood in the entryway wearing her nautical dress, her hair in a ribbon, holding her little purse and a present for her teacher.

"We're about ready, sweetie. I just have to brush Cari's hair, and we'll be out the door. Everybody load up!"

The Stuart children and Aggie almost filled the front row. Ian bounced, giggled, and squirmed, Cari and Lorna sat in rapt attention, mesmerized by exciting things like water fountains, microphone testing, and the elementary school band warming up with its discordant squeaks and ill-timed twangs. When the little kindergarteners filed out on stage in their little white caps and gowns, the baby clapped and clapped. Aggie had to stifle a laugh when Kenzie clapped with him. The children led the auditorium in the *Pledge of Allegiance* and in singing the national anthem. Aggie choked and sputtered when she heard one little boy nearest the edge of the stage singing, "What so proudly we *bailed* at the twilight's last gleaming..."

The kindergartners were all given a rolled "diploma," and each made a speech. Some speeches were long and rambling, while others were, considering the fifty-two that year, mercifully short and sweet. Kenzie looked adorable, and very serious, as she stood at the child-sized podium.

"Thank you for coming. My big sister Vannie helped me

145

write my speech. We worked hard this year. We learned to read, and we got to draw pictures, and our teacher was very nice. I am good at pluses and take-aways now, and that is because Miss Williams is so nice. My Aunt Aggie is my mommy now, and I want to thank her for that too. Vannie didn't help me with that part. Thank you." Kenzie gave a little bow and took her place in line.

She smiled over at Vannie, but the frown on the girl's face unnerved her. Aggie telegraphed a question to her, but Vannie refused to respond. Something was amiss. She would have to talk with her later, but for now, she had a graduate to congratulate.

The cafeteria reverberated with chattering voices. Aggie, fighting a headache sparked by the constant drone, worked hard to keep her eyes on the children as they laughed and wove between the people trying to find their classmates. For the first time, she realized that moving would also mean leaving their friends. The children must not realize this yet.

Aggie was trying to clean marshmallow off Ian's face when she heard a voice a little too close to her ear; she jumped. "Excuse me?" She took a step back instinctively. A man, taller than most in the room, and a little too suave in his attire and demeanor, stood before her with a lazy smile on his face.

"Do you have a child here? Well, except for the little mister..." The man obviously thought his line was clever.

"Actually, I have eight here today. And you— do you have any children present?" The look on Aggie's face would have daunted someone less arrogant, and the frost in her voice was not that of cookies and cakes.

"Yes," his smile was perfectly timed. He must have perfected his approach either by practice in front of a mirror or "on the job training." "My daughter Emi was one of the graduates. She's... oh, right over there— talking to the little girl with the sailor dress." Her words finally pierced his self-filled consciousness. "Did you say *eight* children?"

Aggie followed his line of vision. "Yes, eight, and the little

146

girl she is talking to is my Kenzie." Aggie's tone should have warned the man, but he seemed oblivious to her irritation.

"Wow! Eight children—" he glanced at her hand. "And no wedding ring. You look good for having so many. Hasn't anyone told you what causes that?"

Aggie's jaw dropped. Before she could answer, an arm took hers and led her away. Aggie, after one last astounded glance at the insulting man, tried to thank her rescuer. "I— I—" She was still speechless.

"I know about your family, Miss Milliken. I'm the assistant vice-principal here at Lincoln Elementary, and if I could slug that man, trust me, I would. What you are doing for these children is remarkable. I am just sorry to hear that they won't be back next year."

With that, the man left her and hurried to where a group of boys were attacking the refreshment table. Aggie watched as he handed them each one cookie and sent them packing. He turned as if to come back to talk with her, but another parent stopped him.

The assistant vice principal watched as the young woman herded her charges out the door and to the parking lot. He saw her laugh at something Kenzie said and ruffle Tavish's hair. Those children were going to be all right. It was much too bad all the children in his school weren't as fortunate.

Aggie says: HELP TINA!!!

Tina says: What!

Aggie says: We have a situation.

Tina says: Oh, well, a situation. That's helpful.

Aggie says: Ok. Tonight, Kenzie gave a little speech at her "gradgigation."

Tina says: How cute!

Aggie says: It was. She obviously idolizes Vannie a bit, but she said something that made Vannie upset. I need to know how seriously to take this.

Tina says: Well… what did she say?

Aggie says: She said something about me being her "mommy" now, and Vannie is upset about it.

Tina says: I can see why.

Aggie says: Well, so can I, but how do I help her. I am not trying to be THEIR mom. Allie was given that role first; I want the children to keep her in their memory as their mother.

Tina says: But the little ones are going to see you as mom. Kenzie is already transferring her "loyalty" if you will.

Aggie says: I didn't expect that.

Tina says: You know, you have to prepare Vannie for this. The baby will call you mom most likely. Explain to Vannie that you are not trying to take the place of her mother, but the little children won't remember as much. Allie is probably fading already in their memories. She's going to be a "feeling" and a picture someday. It's how things are going to be. No one prepared Vannie for that.

Aggie says: You have a point there. Sigh. Guess that'll be my job. I'll add it to my "to do" list for the next YEAR!

Tina says: So, how are you going to be able to do that whole list and move? Aren't the Landrys coming to help you move tomorrow?

Aggie says: Well…

Tina says: Don't put it off too long, Aggie. I know you. You'll let the move, the settling, the fixing up this house… everything will crowd it out, and you won't ever resolve this. Talk to her, Aggie. Don't forget.

Aggie says: Yes, oh wise Tina. I will not forget. Bug me until I say it's all settled ok?

Tina says: Will do. So, Kenzie is all "graduated" huh?

Aggie says: It was an interesting evening, that's for sure.

Tina says: Spill it.

Aggie says: Well… I learned that we proudly BAILED in the

Star Spangled Banner. Better to bail with pride than in shame right?

Tina says: Too funny. Anything else?

Aggie says: Yep… and then this creep asks me if I know what causes "that" yet when he finds out I have EIGHT children.

Tina says: WHAT?

Aggie says: Yep. The assistant VP rescued me. I wanted to deck him.

Tina says: Glad I wasn't there. I would have!

Aggie says: Oh, blech. I have to go upstairs. Ian is crying.

Tina says: You can get upstairs now?

Aggie says: Yep. It's a slow process, but I do it. No crutches too!

Tina says: Ok, then… Poofs

Aggie says: Poof!

THE SHAMBLES

Chapter Eleven

Saturday, June 1st

Pandemonium reigned in the Stuart household the Saturday they moved. While Aggie attempted to keep Kenzie and the twins out of the packed boxes, and Ian from screaming, Vannie and Laird filled other boxes with the remaining kitchen items and packed suitcases with the final loads of laundry from the washer and dryer. Mark Landry expertly filled a rental moving van as Aggie directed Iris with what to pack and what would stay. All the while, Iris' ten-year-old son, Jonathan, raced from one room to the next, helping everyone and thoroughly enjoying a house full of playmates.

Seeing the frustration that the boys felt in their inability to get to know each other, Aggie obtained permission to take Jonathan with them as they drove over to the new house. She still hadn't shown the children the home she had found for them to live in but had high hopes that they'd love it. The adventure, the room— what child wouldn't be thrilled? There was even a ramshackle old summerhouse-type building. With a little repair and a thorough cleaning, the children could use it for a playhouse!

After one last look over their old house, Aggie drove away from the historic Stuart home, onto the Rockland loop, and took the Fairbury/Highway 32 exit. Mark and Iris followed behind them caravan style; Iris in their vehicle, Mark driving the moving van. The younger children bounced in their seats and sang silly songs from a CD that Aggie now promised herself she'd destroy the moment she found it. Meanwhile, Vannie questioned Aggie about schools and neighbors. Laird and Jonathan played "Slug Bug," laughing uproariously at their improvised "Clunker Junker" version.

The drive around Lake Danube resulted in begs to have a picnic, but Aggie made no promises. She had much she wanted to accomplish in the two and a half months until school started again, and didn't know how much leisure time there'd be. Thirty minutes later, they drove past the road to Brunswick and down the road that led into the little town of Brant's Corners. There was a small pizza parlor, a lovely park, three churches, and a small combination grocery and hardware store along the main street. Aggie pointed them out, as well as the road to the school complex down a side street from the park. At the edge of town, she drove down the last street and turned into the first driveway. They were home.

"Ok, guys. This is the place." A collective garden of necks stretched and swayed in the motion of the van as the children all tried to see the house behind the massive oak trees. She watched anxiously for their reactions in the rearview mirror. The little ones were excited and bounced up and down with glee before the house was completely in view. Vannie and Laird, however, were more apprehensive and reserved.

When the three story house was in full view, Vannie gasped, "Aunt Aggie! This place is *falling apart*! We can't live here!" The distraught girl burst into wails and sobs about danger, filth, and what their grandmother would say about such a ramshackle place.

Stunned by Vannie's reaction, Aggie looked quickly at

Laird. While she had expected Vannie to find it ugly, she'd assumed the girl would see the house's potential. The idea of the children seeing it as unsafe had never entered her mind. On the other hand, she had definitely expected that Laird wouldn't like the inconvenience of so much work, but she saw a completely different light in Laird's eyes. The laid-back boy usually showed little interest in anything but the computer, a good movie, or goofing off outdoors, but Aggie saw wheels turning in his ten-year-old mind.

"Hey, Vannie, look at that old fashioned swing there on that oak. I bet we could put new ropes on that board, and it would be just like that swing that they had in that old *Pride and Prejudice* movie. You know— the one with Greer Garson that Momma loved so much?" Vannie didn't look impressed. "Oh, and *look*, there is a turret-looking thing over there! That is sooo cool!"

Interest momentarily sparked in Vannie's eyes and then fizzled. "Aunt Aggie? You said this house needed work. Just how much work were you talking about? Can we *afford* the work this place will take? How long—"

"Vannie, cool it! Aunt Aggie is doing her best. Don't attack her until you have seen *everything* you want to complain about!"

Vannie started to retort, but Aggie called out her trademarked *"stop."* Aggie's child training lessons had definitely paid off. The children respected her position as ad-hock mom, but the thing that had made the most difference in the house, Aggie had come up with on her own. The "stop" training sessions were almost hysterical to the onlooker, but they'd worked. Safety wasn't an issue anymore. She could simply say "Stop," and the children froze in place.

Parking in the circular gravel driveway, she turned off the engine and spoke to the children in the rearview mirror. "Listen, guys. This is how it is going to be. First, you will look *all over* the house. Then, you can check out the back yard. After that, report to the living room. Does everyone understand me?"

Nods of agreement came from all the children, even little Ian. The goofy baby had no idea what he was agreeing to, but being the amiable boy that he was, he nodded anyway. The children, now much more accustomed to Aggie "laying down the law" from time to time, responded positively to simple directions.

All assembled in the living room inside half an hour. While Mark and Iris unloaded the truck into the yard and onto the porch, Aggie addressed her troops. "Ok, guys. Hear me out." All heads nodded, but a look of distrust had entered Vannie's eyes. "I bought this house because it was a steal. This house cost us less than half what other houses this size were going for, and none of them had the amount of land this one does. Even if we spend the savings on fixing it up, we will have a better house than we otherwise could have afforded. Does everyone understand what I just said?" Heads bobbed once more, but Kenzie seemed confused. "Kenzie, this means that this is *going* to be the best house we could have bought, it's just not there yet." Kenzie smiled and nodded more emphatically. Distrust lingered on Vannie's features.

"I had the house inspected and this is what I learned. First, the foundation is strong; that's a most important point as you all remember from your Bible classes. The electricity is modern, but we need to have some of it rewired; in addition, the plumbing is all copper, which means it's the best you can get. Other than the electricity, all we need is to scrub it up, a lot of paint, a new kitchen, and in some rooms, flooring. We are going to make this place just how we want it. The basement downstairs is wonderful! The contractor I spoke to said that we could hang swings from the ceiling and have a slide and everything."

The toddler twins squealed in delight. "So, do you want to hear how I plan to do things?"

As Aggie laid out plans for improvements, the vote was unanimous, even though the younger children didn't understand the benefits and negatives, to attack the upstairs rooms first. With that decision made, Aggie directed the boys

154

to help carry in the beds to the dining room, while the girls grabbed the brooms and scrub buckets and hurried to sweep and mop the dining room floor, making mud soup in the process, thanks to an insufficient job of sweeping by Ellie. Meanwhile, she threw open every window in the house, trying to blow out the staleness of the rooms.

Within minutes, it was clear that they'd need to expand their improvised dormitory into the living room. As she swept and scrubbed that room, Aggie prayed that they could get the upstairs finished before Mrs. Stuart had a chance to stop by and see the sleeping arrangements. Somehow, Aggie knew the woman would arrive within the week, insisting on inspecting where Aggie dragged "those poor motherless children."

Aggie sent the children to play while she and the Landrys assembled the beds. As she dug through boxes for fresh sheets, the children began an intense game of hide and seek in the yard. Aggie heard cries of "olly, olly, oxen-free" and the impatient counts of the "it" child. The younger twins almost gave away hiding places faster than the hiders could find new ones. Jonathan proved to be a brilliant diversion for the children, allowing Aggie and the Landrys to accomplish a great deal of unpacking and mess transference.

The afternoon whizzed by after the crowd devoured the pizzas that Aggie had delivered for lunch. One room, filled with wall to wall bookcases that Tavish immediately dubbed "the library," was used as a central storage for boxes. As fast as the Landrys carried in the boxes, Aggie sorted them into rooms and put the ones she expected to need soonest into the front of the tall piles. At Iris' recommendation, Aggie carried anything for kitchens and bathrooms into their appropriate rooms and unpacked them. It'd be a while before those rooms were remodeled, and they'd need to live normally until then.

Near six o'clock, she jumped in the van, drove back to town, and made her acquaintance with the grocery store. She'd expected to buy lunchmeat and rolls, but the sight of several rotisserie chickens sitting hot at a deli counter changed that. To the clerk's astonishment, she ordered four of the five chickens, three quarts of potato salad, four bags of green salad from the produce section, and bought six half-gallons of ice cream. As a last minute thought, though feeling quite extravagant, Aggie added a large bunch of mixed cut flowers to her cart and hurried to pay for their meal.

Just as the woman began ringing up the first item, Aggie groaned. "Please let them go ahead of me, I forgot cereal. There's nothing in the house to eat."

Talking her through the aisles to find milk, cereal, bread, peanut butter, jelly, and some juice, the cashier rang up the purchases of a deputy who watched the proceedings curiously. His small basket of food that would make any health-conscious person proud, was scanned, bagged, and paid for before Aggie arrived back at the counter, her last minute purchases almost spilling from her arms.

"Thank you," she gasped as the checker began to scan her items. To the officer, she hardly gave a glance but did give an effusive, "I am so sorry about that." As she apologized, she dug through her purse looking for her debit card, and in frustration, dragged out the credit card Mr. Moss had insisted she carry.

Deputy Sheriff William Markensen watched, a frown forming, as the young woman dug through her purse for her money. Seeing her dismay at the sight of her credit card sent his mind into mental calisthenics of the conclusion variety. *"Great — another dussie. The girl's living on credit,"* he thought to himself as she finally slid it across the counter. Something about her was familiar though, and not knowing what it was, he observed without attempting to disguise it.

Tessa Braun kept a running dialogue of questions and observations as she checked ID, accepted the signed slip, and wished the woman a good day. He was tempted to offer to help, but something in her demeanor held him back. This woman didn't want anyone's help if she could avoid it. As she pushed her way through the doors, Tessa glanced at him. "What's someone so young doing driving that monster?"

"I don't know, but I intend to find out."

"Oh, William, she seems nice enough. You see a criminal behind every tree. Maybe she's going to run a day care."

"She'd better have her licenses in order, or I'll haul her in so fast she'll wish she'd never tried it."

"You," Tessa said as she reached for the next item at her counter, "are the most suspicious person I've ever met. I'll bet you one of my pies against one of your steaks that she's just a nice girl who needs a friend. No criminal record and doesn't do anything to get one in the first month she's here."

"You're on. Make that pie your caramel apple pie."

"I want my steak medium rare with that seasoned salt you always use. Mushrooms on top."

"Better not forget the nuts!" William called, laughing as he exited the store and hurried to his car. Shift was over. It was time to clock out mentally as well as physically.

The officer's scrutiny wasn't lost on Aggie. The more he watched, the more flustered she got until she'd felt ready to scream. Tossing the bags a little roughly behind the passenger seat in the van, she backed out as slowly and carefully as she could bring herself to move and drove toward home. "Lord, I don't know what that man thinks of me, and on the one hand, I really don't care. However, I didn't like the look on his face, so if you could just take care of it for me, I'd be obliged. I have a house to renovate."

As she retraced her route home, Aggie's voice wavered as she tried to sing something to bolster her spirits. *"I've seen the lightning flashing..."* By the time she turned on Last Street, her voice was stronger and more confident. *"He promised never to leave me, never to leave me alone!"*

Children raced to the porch at the sight of the van in the driveway shouting, "Dinner, dinner, dinner!"

"Well, if you want it, you'd better come and help me carry it in!"

Despite the incredulity of the store clerks, Aggie, the Stuart children, and the Landrys managed to consume every scrap of chicken, three bags of the salad, two of the quarts of potato salad, and all the ice cream. As Aggie rinsed plates and cleaned up two puddles of milk, she glanced at the flowers she'd stuck unceremoniously in a juice pitcher, and smiled. Extravagant or not, it had been a good purchase. They took a dingy and very dirty room and made it feel like a home. Iris tried to help scrub down the kitchen, but Aggie, against her own wishes and better judgment, shooed them out the door with a generous check and heartfelt thanks for all their work.

Beds and bunk beds cluttered the dining and living rooms, making a quick pick-up impossible. As much as she'd tried to keep the beds along the perimeter of the walls, she'd failed. She shooed the children upstairs to choose their rooms while she finished dragging wads of packing paper from beneath every surface. Six rooms and two bathrooms were on the second floor with a seventh room and bath on the top floor. She'd claimed that top floor room for herself at Tina's suggestion. Tina had convinced Aggie that she would need the privacy at the end of a long day. There was a little sitting room directly off of the master bedroom, so Aggie reserved that for Ian until he was old enough to sleep through the night.

All the children agreed unanimously that Vannie should take the "turret" room. Aggie insisted that Laird have his own room as well, while Tavish and Ian (once that sleeping through the night thing finally occurred) shared a room, and Kenzie and Elspeth paired up. They all begged for Cari and Lorna to have their own shared room as well, instead of putting two sets of bunk beds in Kenzie and Ellie's room. It seemed so sweet and thoughtful until she saw the relief and glee on the children's faces when Aggie agreed.

158

Everyone, including Aggie, had difficulty settling that evening; Vannie seemed distant, and the other children were excitable. After several futile attempts to engage them in anything that calmed them, Aggie sent them to bed. A chorus of groans and wails followed, but she remained firm. Once everyone had clean teeth, hands, feet, and faces, and were laying in their beds, she sat in a chair between the two rooms and led the children in singing choruses and hymns until she noticed their voices growing weaker— quieter. Then she told them all to be quiet and carried Ian and her chair back to the kitchen. Once Ian slept soundly in his crib at the far corner of the living room, Aggie made a cup of French Crème coffee, sat on the porch steps, and watched the stars put the world to sleep.

Sunday, June 2nd

Aggie had not adequately prepared for church assembly the next morning. As the children searched for their clothes and tried, with utterly futile attempts, to get ready, Aggie decided that they weren't going. Disappointment filled their faces, but they changed clothes again and eventually wandered outside to do some more playing and exploring— all but Vannie. Before long, squeals of excitement and play were heard all around the house.

She and Vannie walked all over the house exploring, making plans, and talking. With a few well-chosen words, Aggie broke through the wall Vannie had constructed at Kenzie's graduation. She appealed to the girl's reason and asked for help in finding ways to keep Allie and Doug in the hearts of all of their children. After a long talk, the breach that had made Vannie so miserable and kept Aggie awake longer each night was mended and the bridge stronger than ever.

When they reached the dusty attic, it was as though they'd entered a neglected antique paradise. They discovered boxes of old books under one dormer window, and Tavish was called in to "rescue" them. He disappeared downstairs with one box containing several first editions of *The Rover Boys*, muttering something like, "They don't make mindless fictional drivel like they used to."

Aggie and Vannie found wonderful pieces of furniture and began making plans for them. It nearly killed Aggie to watch her niece finger this piece or that saying, "Momma would have loved this." After a while, the girl found a dainty vanity table. One leg was broken, but the mirror was intact, and when Aggie rubbed it with her t-shirt, she saw beautiful birds-eye maple under the layers of dirt and dust.

"Oh, Vannie, it's beautiful! We have to remember it's up here when your room is done. This would look so pretty between those two windows on that funny shaped wall."

Vannie looked up startled. "You mean that you don't want it? Can I really have it in my room?"

Aggie smiled and assured Vannie that the vanity was hers. "I'll see if Laird thinks he knows how to fix that leg though. I would hate to break that mirror with a bad "fix-it" job."

Later, Aggie unpacked a stack of decorating magazines and catalogs that Tina had mailed them and encouraged the Vannie to see if she could find something that appealed to her. "Maybe it'll give us a place to start. There are so many things that would look good in there, but I don't know anything about decorating, and I don't know what you like.

After half a dozen magazines that either showed rooms that looked like hotel suites or overly themed rooms that promised everything from a beach hut look to a disco nightmare, Vannie said, "You know what I think I want? I don't like the themes— they'd be good for the little girls or the boys, but I want something I'll like for a long time. I don't like change."

"So, what do you want?" Aggie realized that with the words, "I don't like change," she'd been given a priceless look into Vannie's thoughts.

"I read a series of books at Grandmother's last summer

that she'd read when she was little. In the first book, there was this girl who visited her four aunts one year, and one of the aunts created such a beautiful room." The girl sighed. "It would be silly though. There were a lot of white and light colors. It would get very dirty with all the little hands."

"Vannie, this is *your* room. There won't be that many little hands in there, unless you invite them in. So, if you like, you can decide who you want in and if they need to wash their hands or even take off their shoes before they come in. It'll be your decision."

"But what about when I am at school? The twins will come in anyway, and they'll ruin everything. I had better stick to something more Victorian or something. The big flowers will hide the dirt."

Aggie's heart broke for the young girl who wanted something she was convinced she couldn't have. "Vannie, we have three months to teach them to stay out of the room. If necessary, we'll put a chain on there so that they can't get inside." With a rueful smile, she added, "And I consider it a personal challenge to teach them better respect for my word and my rules."

The change in Vannie was tremendous. All the weights and cares that she had put on her shoulders seemed to roll off, much like Christian's burden in *Pilgrim's Progress*. Eagerly, the girl described a room with white trim, robin's egg blue walls, and apple green accents. "I don't think it would be expensive. I think we could even use that old white eyelet comforter that Momma gave us when we were sick. We could dye it apple green couldn't we?"

Aggie laughed and assured the girl that they could afford to buy her a few pillows and a new bedspread without too much expense. They would go shopping for paint and accessories the next morning. "The only thing is…"

"What is it, Aunt Aggie?" Vannie put a guarded look on her face. Her face screamed her thoughts — she knew that this was too good to be true.

"Well, I wonder if I should see about getting some new outlets put into the rooms before we paint. I think you only have one in your room; I know that Laird only has one. While we get the paint and things, I might want to find an electrician to add some outlets."

"I can still have the room, though?"

Aggie laughed. "Get those catalogs out and find the comforter or bedspread you want. We're doing the room, and we're starting first thing tomorrow."

Wednesday, June 5th

By Wednesday, the house was littered with items that had no assigned place to rest. From shoes to purses, books to toys, and everything else in between, just keeping the two huge dormitories picked up when there was no place to store things was difficult. The trip to the store for paint and bedding had been pushed back one day, and then another. Aggie was determined to get to the store that Wednesday morning, regardless of any further obstacles.

As the children ate their cold cereal, the reality of their food choices pressed on Aggie again. They were back to paper plates and macaroni and cheese. She knew that they were going to miss the "real" food that Mrs. Landry had provided for the last few weeks. When the potpies, canned soups, and frozen burritos were brought back to the table, the children were likely to revolt! Well, they would, unless the children were too weak from rickets or some other terrible deficiency. Even if the children didn't, her stomach would. Two days back on the convenience food menu, and already, Aggie had had it. A trip to town was an immediate necessity.

After forty minutes of searching for shoes, socks, and hair accessories designed to hide the fact that no one had bathed in four days, Aggie loaded her charges into the van and drove to town. They piled out of the van and into a hardware store, but the absence of shopping carts killed that idea. Immediately, she

162

sent them back to the van, getting directions to Brunswick in the process.

The whole gang waded through the paint department of Brunswick's Wal-Mart store. Aggie allowed each child to choose three paint chip cards and the children had a grand time picking out which colors they wanted. When Laird chose three cards of all blue paints, she decided that Vannie's nautical theme suggestion might be a good one. Aggie pulled her favorites from the rack as well, though she knew that she wouldn't get to use them for a while. The children's rooms must come first.

Vannie found the bedspread and throw pillows that she wanted and the color matched her paint swatches perfectly. "Let's go have them mix that paint. This is going to look beautiful!" Aggie found a rocking white wicker chair from a mismatched set that was on sale in the garden department and got an idea. "Vannie, go back and get that really big pillow that we saw, remember? It'll make a perfect cushion for this chair!"

She'd planned to shop the Brant's Corners' market, so she'd know what they had available, but the ease of purchasing everything at once and not having to load and unload four children in car seats trumped that idea. They strolled through the produce aisles looking for carrots, apples, celery, strawberries, and any other quick to fix and easy to eat fruit. She bought bread, lunchmeat, frozen lasagnas and eggs. They'd eat a lot more eggs. Aggie wasn't much of a cook, but she could make a mean omelet and quiche. At the last minute, she added a bottle of multi-vitamins to her cart. Surely, whatever she failed to provide nutritionally could be augmented by a nice chewable vitamin.

The children chattered excitedly about their rooms, the croquet set she'd purchased, and lunch all the way home. Aggie groaned audibly when she drove into the driveway and parked behind the Stuart's Mercedes. The children gave her odd looks, but Vannie seemed to understand. "Aunt Aggie, can I show Grandma the playhouse out back?" The look of horror on Aggie's face was hidden to Vannie as she continued, "We swept it out, scrubbed the floor, got rid of the glass and all the bugs. It looks pretty neat, and maybe she'll forget what she saw in the kitchen?" Aggie saw the wisdom of the plan and nodded her appreciation.

Vannie was out of the van and running to the house before Aggie was out of her seat. As usual, Laird unbuckled Ian and handed him to Aggie before reaching back to help Kenzie unbuckle the twins. To say that Aggie was moving slowly would be an understatement; snails have moved swifter than Aggie's dragging steps. Tavish looked over at his tired and discouraged aunt and said, "Aunt Aggie, are you in trouble?"

Aggie's laughter could be heard out in the playhouse. Saying that Geraldine Stuart frowned would be the epitome of understatement. "Why do you ask a question like that, Tavish?" Aggie was afraid of the answer. "'Cause you look like Cari does when she's about to get a spanking," was the observant child's innocent response.

Aggie decided she needed to look more confident than she felt, so she went directly to the bathroom, splashed water on her face, pulled her hair up into a loose bun, and tucked her shirt in. Stepping out of the door, she found Geraldine Stuart standing there. "What have you done to these children?" The woman was beyond livid; she was irrationally furious. "You uproot them from the home that some of them were *born* in, move them to this unsafe, filthy pile of rubble, dump them into dormitories, and expect that I won't have a problem with this?" Aggie was certain she could see steam coming from the woman's nose. "I demand that you send the children home with me, or my lawyer will serve you with papers before morning."

Aggie sighed and then said the one thing she'd hoped never to have to say. "Mrs. Stuart, I have been more than patient. You know that you can't legally take these children from me. My lawyer will express a handwritten letter that Doug wrote to you tomorrow. When I read it, I hoped to never have to give it to you." Taking a deep breath, Aggie continued, interrupting Geraldine before she could get her next sentence formed. "I now have to ask that you leave my property."

Shock registered on the bitter grandmother's face and then anger overtook every fiber of her being. *"I will not leave this house without my grandchildren!"* As Geraldine began an ugly tirade, Aggie shooed the children out into the back yard with strict instructions to stay there. She walked to the telephone and shakily pressed the proper speed dial button for the sheriff's office. Reporting an unwanted trespasser and a domestic dispute, Aggie turned to the overwrought woman to request again that she leave— preferably *before* the sheriff or one of his deputies arrived. Before Aggie could speak, Geraldine slapped her. The force was so strong that it spun her into the door jam. Who would have thought such an elderly lady could produce such force!

Between the huge red welt of a handprint and the tears streaming down her face, Aggie was a sight when the deputies arrived. Deputy William Markenson pulled up to the house and exited his vehicle with a female deputy close behind. They found Aggie sitting on the couch, head in her hands and eyes on the back door. Occasionally, a head would peek through the window, and Aggie would give a small shake of her head. The officer introduced himself and his co-worker, Meg Reese. Aggie stood to shake their hands and explain the situation, but Mrs. Stuart interrupted with obvious disdain. "I arrived today to visit my grandchildren, who are temporarily in this woman's care. This is what I found. This living room has a couch and three beds, and the dining room has a table and six beds! I defy you to tell me that these are proper living conditions. I insist that these children be released into my care."

The deputies looked around, back at each other and then Deputy Reese led Aggie out the back door. The two women could still hear the ranting of Mrs. Stuart. "Ms...?"

"Milliken. Agathena Milliken, but just call me Aggie." The defeated tone in Aggie's voice was evident even to the nearby children. Kenzie whimpered and moved closer. "Do we have to go live with Grandmother, Aunt Aggie?"

"Shhhhh, honey, of course you don't. The judge has said that you will live with me, just like Momma and Daddy wanted." The frightened little girl began the silent weeping Aggie knew so well. Kenzie's little "I want my mommy," almost broke her heart.

Deputy Reese took Aggie's statement and then suggested that she wait outside. After a few whispered words with Deputy Markenson, the two officers escorted Geraldine Stuart to her car. The woman appeared subdued, but the look that she shot Aggie told the younger woman that this was only the warm up to round one.

Both officers went back to speak again with Aggie. She'd just stated that she didn't want to press assault charges against Mrs. Stuart, when a call came in for the officers. Deputy Reese took the call, gave Aggie her cell number in case she wanted to talk, and left.

Deputy Markenson seemed almost at a loss for words. Kenzie, her face contorted in concern, came inside and edged close to him. "Are you going to 'rest my Auntie Aggie?"

The terror behind her words was heart rending. Aggie just shook her head, as the tears ran down her face, while Deputy Markenson lifted the child on his lap and spoke very carefully to her and the other children, who had drifted nervously into the room. "Your Aunt hasn't done anything wrong." He paused, searching for just the right words. "You see, your grandmother just loves you all so much that she wants to have you with her all the time. Do you know how sometimes you want something so badly that you forget to do what is right? Like taking a cookie before asking permission?" Several heads nodded. He mentally counted six children who visibly relaxed at his assurance that he wasn't there to haul Aggie off to jail. "This is what your grandmother has done. She has forgotten what is right, because she loves you so much."

Kenzie stopped crying and ran her fingers over the

deputy's badge. William Markenson lost his heart to the child at that moment. Some at work called him heartless because of the detachment that characterized his demeanor; they certainly wouldn't recognize him at this moment.

Markenson, the oldest of three children, learned to resolve disputes long before becoming an officer, and, of course, had no trouble attracting female attention everywhere he went. Physically speaking, he fit the old stereotype of tall, dark and handsome perfectly. "What is your name?" William smiled at the child who promptly spoke up. "Kenzie Stuart."

"Kenzie, do you pray with Aunt Aggie? At bedtime or at dinner?" William Markenson was treading on precarious ground with this line of "questioning," but he hoped he had read the young woman across from him correctly. At the little girl's smile and the nods around the room, William continued. "I want you all to pray for your aunt, and for your grandmother. Can you all do that? Can you pray that your aunt can be strong for you, and that your grandmother can find a better way to show you that she loves you?"

The children made affirmative assurances of their eagerness to pray. Aggie, after sending them to bring in the groceries and purchases from the van, followed William outside. "Thank you, Deputy Markenson, for being understanding. I know the place is a mess and the sleeping arrangements aren't... *normal*, but I'm working—" William held up his hand. The gesture made Aggie smile. How often must this man have to deal with incoherent emotional females?

"Ms. Milliken."

Aggie shook her head and said, "I'm just Aggie."

William tried again. "Aggie, you'll get things cleaned up. You've only been here four days, and you have a lot to deal with, just being a guardian to these children."

Aggie interrupted. "How do you know how long I've been here? I didn't tell you that. I am certain Geraldine didn't tell you—" William smiled. Aggie noticed that the smile reached the corners of his eyes, creating slight wrinkles that, had she still been a carefree college student, would have sent her senses reeling. The man was tall — at the least, six foot two.

"Aggie, this is Brant's Corners. We know when someone comes in, moves out or sneezes after eight p.m. Welcome, and if you'd like, we would be happy to see you at *The Church* next Sunday."

Aggie frowned. "Knowing which church might be helpful..." She had a twinkle in her eyes, as she raised her eyebrows at the officer.

"*The Church.* That's the name. It's on the corner of Third Street and Main. Services start at ten-thirty; Sunday school is at nine o'clock. It's a very nice congregation — more like family than a social club, if you know what I mean." William's deep bass voice carried across the street to where an elderly lady made a poor attempt at trimming her shrubs as she tried to figure out why the sheriff's deputies were at her new neighbor's house. William had noticed the woman's ruse and decided to introduce the women.

"Aggie, do you have a moment to meet your neighbor? Would the children be ok?" It seemed as though that William had no real experience with children but was conscientious about their welfare; how wrong perceptions can be.

Aggie called to Vannie and Laird. "Keep your eyes on the girls and Ian. Everyone, stay *in the yard.* I'll be right back." Turning to William, "I'm ready to meet my neighbor, Deputy Markenson. Let's shake up the place! She doesn't look like someone I'd like to TP, so maybe next May Day, we can leave flowers and run."

Stunned, and unable to formulate an appropriate response, William insisted she call him by his first name and led her across the street to where the elderly widow was pruning with a destructive vengeance. "Mrs. Dyke, this is your new neighbor, Aggie Milliken. Aggie, I'd like to introduce one of the dearest ladies in town, and also of *The Church.* I know you'll be friends before long." William also knew that if he didn't explain his presence, the elderly lady could have heart trouble from wondering about his arrival. "Mrs. Dyke, please keep Aggie in your prayers. She has just taken guardianship of her late sister's seven—" Aggie held up eight fingers, to correct him. "— make that eight children, and the paternal grandmother is being a little difficult about it."

Aggie looked startled that the officer would divulge private information so freely but wisely held her tongue and offered her hand. "Hello, Mrs. Dyke, I hope we'll be good neighbors. I'll try to keep the children away from your beautiful plants and pray we don't break any windows with stray baseballs! Bill has been most helpful already."

Both Mrs. Dyke and Deputy Markenson suddenly looked uncomfortable. After an awkward silence, Mrs. Dyke smiled and leaned conspiratorially near Aggie. "Miss—um, Aggie, our William doesn't go by nicknames. They just don't seem to fit him. I'm sure you understand." William looked visibly relieved, while Aggie stammered an apology. They talked for a few minutes, until Aggie heard Laird calling her. She quickly excused herself and jogged across the road.

Mrs. Dyke looked at William and gave a small smile. "She's a pretty little thing isn't she? Not flashy like most girls these days, and isn't that a relief? Quite the responsibility she has taken on. Eight children... My, I remember when Herbert and I had four, and we were worn out with them!" William nodded absently. The wise older woman grinned to herself and went back to her pruning. "I imagine we'll see a lot of you around here until all is settled up with that grandmother. You come see me when you are around. I still keep a jar of snickerdoodles for visitors."

William slowly walked back to his cruiser. He wasn't sure he agreed with Mrs. Dyke. Aggie wasn't homely by any means, but William had always been attracted to women with a little more shape and sparkle. Whatever Aggie didn't have in physical attractiveness; however, she sure made up for in personality. He didn't know how to take her comments, but then people often said odd things to him.

Tina says: Well?? What is going on these days?

Aggie says: Well…

Tina says: C'mon girl, is the house painted? Ready to move in?

Aggie says: We are technically moved in, but a lot of work needs to be done.

Tina says: You still starting in Vannie's room?

Aggie says: Yep.

Tina says: All right… something isn't "right." Spill it

Aggie says: Hee hee… just had another run in with the GIL

Tina says: The gil?

Aggie says: I'm calling her the GIL. Grandma-in-law, or for short, Geraldine is livid.

Tina says: That bad huh?

Aggie says: I'll say.

Tina says: Well, what now? Spit it out.

Aggie says: Well, between her yelling, slapping me, getting escorted off the property by the sheriff's department, I think our family has made an impact on this community already.

Tina says: OH, nooooooooooooo, she didn't!

Aggie says: I've still got the imprint on my face. The kids were scared that the officer was going to take me away.

Tina says: I wish I could come.

Aggie says: Me too. Think you'll get down this way before the new term?

Tina says: I thought I might come for two weeks before I have to register, and then I can just drive straight to school.

Aggie says: Sounds good to me! I miss you.

Tina says: Sounds like you are busy enough without me.

Aggie says: Why do you think I want you? I NEED HELP!

Tina says: Well, mid to late August, I'll be there.

Aggie says: I have to get outside. I hear havoc building. Bye!!!

Tina says: Well, I'm glad I convinced you to have internet set up before you got there! Poof!

ENTER: LUKE

Chapter Twelve

Thursday, June 13th

Chaos was an understatement. The children squealed with delighted hysterics, while Aggie tried not to cry as she dashed from room to room trying to identify which room's lights were coming on from which switch. As she jotted down notes, she decided that she would kill Deputy William Markenson. There was no doubt about it. As an aside, she wondered if they made jail cells with mother's quarters.

He'd asked her about her house renovations after church on Sunday, and when he heard that she was looking for an electrician to add outlets, William had given her the name and phone number of an electrician that he recommended. Too busy to do the work himself, the electrician sent his brother-in-law to install the new outlets, and the result was scary! The concept was simple. He would add new outlets to every wall of every room that didn't have one, add an extra breaker or two to the box to handle the new load, and arrange for each room to have its own circuit on the breaker in order to shut off power to each room of the house.

However, after the ad-hock electrical genius disappeared down her driveway with a substantially larger check than he'd earned, they'd discovered that flipping on a light switch in one room did nothing. At first, she thought maybe he'd forgotten to turn the breaker box back on but on her way to check it, found the hall light burning. Undaunted, she started to flip the switch off and found it already in the off position. Assuming he'd installed it upside down, Aggie flipped it on and nothing happened, or so she thought.

"Aunt Aggie, the light just came on in the kitchen, but no one turned it on!" Ellie sounded both indignant and a little frightened.

"What! Turn on the light in there."

The bathroom light shone brightly. "How is this even possible?" she'd muttered and began a hunt for switch patterns that looked like a stunt out of a reality TV show. Not knowing where to find her pathetic electrician, Aggie poured her frustrations into the absent and oblivious officer.

"If that man was here I'd give him a piece of my mind. What kind of electrician did he recommend anyway? This guy would fail standing in line in kindergarten!"

Aggie's ranting carried through the open window and across the yard to where Mrs. Dyke weeded around her driveway. Though she couldn't hear all of what her neighbor said, at the sound of William's name, she wisely went inside and called the sheriff dispatch to send out Deputy Markenson. When William arrived, the children, sent outside by Aggie, were playing tag in the front yard as she systematically switched each room's lights on and off, making notes and trying to see if there was any kind of discernible pattern.

William cautiously entered the house after waving hello to the children, calling Aggie's name. "I'm in here, *Mr. Markenson.*"

Something in her tone unnerved him. Angry females weren't his specialty, but when William reached the upstairs landing, his laughter boomed loud enough to be heard across the street. The sight was beyond funny, but Aggie had lost her sense of humor. "If you want to laugh, you go right ahead, but *you* can pay this incompetent bozo. Do you see this? I can't figure out if this room's switches really do turn on the one right behind it or if there is a mix up at the breaker box."

Not familiar with electrical wiring, he pulled out his cell phone to call the electrician to come fix the error, but, Aggie shook her head. "William, I appreciate you trying to help me, really I do; but I can't do this."

The young woman looked ready to collapse with frustration and exhaustion. "If that man shows up at my home, I am liable to say or do something that I shouldn't. I'll call Zeke. Somehow, I think he'll know what to do; he's always been so good to me and known exactly what to do when I didn't." Aggie slumped on the couch downstairs and picked up the phone. The local pizza delivery had already been added to speed dial, and Aggie needed to feed this crew — *fast.*

She looked up at the officer standing on her last step and sighed. "William, thank you for trying to help. I know this isn't your fault, but right now, it *feels* like it is. I know that's irrational, but right now I *want* to be irrational. It makes me feel better."

Her ridiculous words showed how bothered Aggie really was by the situation, and Mr. Take-Charge Markenson did something that the officer normally wouldn't do. He excused himself and drove away. Strains of a fierce rendition of "Angry Words" were playing repeatedly in his head as he headed back to the sheriff's station. Absent mindedly, the man hummed the chorus, filling in the words now and then. *"Love one another… thus saith the Savior… mmm…mmm…mmm"*

Friday, June 14*th*

A hammer banged in her dream-filled mind. Still lost in what she thought was a dream, Aggie decided the sound was her heart hammering at some horrible thing the twins escaped from at the last second. She struggled to awaken, but her eyes refused to budge. Finally, one eye peeked open as a second round of bangs pierced her burgeoning consciousness. That wasn't a hammer or her heart. It was the door.

Stumbling from the dining room, Aggie prayed that it wouldn't be the Sheriff with legal papers. She'd waited, a constant knot in her stomach, for over a week, to be served with some kind of court documents. While she had little concern that the Stuarts could do anything to change the court order, she did dread the idea of the children being dragged into an ugly custody battle, and selfishly, dreaded the time away from work on the house. They'd been there almost two weeks, and all that was accomplished was adding wonky wiring and a little cleaning.

At the door, toolbox in hand, wearing an old ARMY t-shirt and half worn-out jeans, was a man. His eyes were kind, and the smile on his face was oddly familiar for someone she'd never met. His eyes seemed to laugh at an inside joke as the man introduced himself. "Miss Milliken? I'm Luke, my Uncle Zeke sent me to fix your power."

Aggie knew she looked as startled and discomfited as she felt, so she gave up the idea of trying to hide it. "Isn't it a bit early? It can't be past seven..." Aggie added acting lessons to her list of things to do someday when she had a spare second.

Luke grinned broadly before replying, "Well, actually it's just after eight. I meant to be here on the dot, but there was a line at the gas station this morning. If you'll just give me that list you talked about with Uncle Zeke, I'll get to work on it, and you can go back to bed. From what Uncle Zeke tells me, you need all the rest you can get." As an afterthought, he added, "Oh, and how is the ankle?"

"Ankle? How'd you know about that?" Aggie was rarely coherent before her first cup of coffee.

He shuffled his feet uncomfortably, making Aggie even more suspicious. "Uncle Zeke told me about it. That must have been pretty stressful." Luke smiled again as he waited for

Aggie to step aside so he could enter and get to work.

Aggie wanted to be angry with him, but at that particular moment, anyone who could fix her electrical nightmare was on par with a knight on a white charger— or at least a great substitute for a battery charger. She dug the list out of her purse, making a mental note to find her clipboard for these kinds of things, unwrinkled it, and handed it to Luke. As the handyman took it, Aggie noticed how strong his forearms appeared to be.

Luke wasn't a large man. Average height, weight, and build implied a common, everyday Joe. Luke, however, was remarkably strong for someone his size. Though not classically handsome, he had a firm jaw line and incredible blue eyes that seemed to light up his whole face when he smiled. To the delight of most single females of his acquaintance, he smiled often. Aggie, lost in her sleep and java-deprived stupor, noticed nothing but his forearms, the tool belt around the man's waist, and a lingering scent of shaving cream once he turned to leave.

As Luke strolled outside to check the breaker box and turn it off, Aggie snatched up her rumpled clothes from the previous day and hurried to the shower. The children were stirring around her, and if she didn't make a dash for it now, she'd find another day over and another layer of grime on her unwashed body. The piles of laundry in the corner of the room caught her eye on her way up the stairs, so Aggie made another mental note to ask Luke to hook up the washer and dryer while he was here. She could pay him for both things at once, and surely, that wasn't an expensive or time-consuming job.

Although Zeke had encouraged her to make a list of everything she needed to do and give the Luke the most difficult of the jobs, Aggie hadn't intended to do it. She was already rethinking her plans. She turned on the shower and stepped into the tub, the water pouring over her body like a torrential rain. She missed a daily shower but just didn't have time— That was it. If he'd walk her through the house and help her make lists of what he could and couldn't do, she'd hire him to do all the coulds. Maybe she could even pay him to hire out the other jobs so that they'd get done right—that is, *if* he did manage to fix the major gaffe of the last guy.

Just before lunchtime, Aggie decided that it was time for real food— not thrown together real ingredients like carrot sticks now and then, or an apple when she realized that their entire menu for a day was out of a can or box, but *real* meals out of *real* food. She thought of calling her mother, but the thought of the worry she'd cause stopped her. For two weeks, she'd picked up a bag or two of groceries here and there, but there had been few meals that weren't thrown together, or borderline junk food. It was better than it had been, at least there were vegetables and fruit on the snack list, but she needed more. If she only knew where Celia Mullins' menu plan was hiding...

Why she picked this day, when she needed to be home and supervise an electrical repair job that she had no idea how to supervise in the first place, to go to the store, Aggie didn't know. However, she brushed hair, washed little faces and hands, and ordered all the children into the van. She found Luke unscrewing every wire from every outlet and switch in the house and informed him she had to make a trip to town.

"Do you need anything while I'm there? Bolts, wire, circuits, duct tape? Doesn't that stuff fix anything?" Her eyes twinkled as she laughed at herself and her silliness.

"I'm good. Happy shopping."

"Yeah, right," she muttered as she hurried down the stairs and out to her van. "I've got a certifiable nut case working on my electrical. *Happy shopping.*" Had Luke heard the harrumph that followed, he'd have howled with laughter.

For reasons unfathomable to Aggie, the children were excited about their grocery shopping excursion, and all the way there, they sang silly songs about hunting for food in the store. Aggie couldn't decide if it was some game Allie had taught her children, or their keen, collective, and wacky imaginations. She would later learn that Allie never took her children grocery

176

shopping with her, and she would soon understand why.

Suffice it to say, three children desperately needed to ride in the front seat of a shopping cart. This meant Aggie, Vannie, and Laird all had to push a cart. Thanks to injury, helpful church members, and a wonderful mother's helper, Aggie had yet to do a full shopping trip for the family. Today would be her debut into the world of family nutritional procurement. Halfway through her shopping trip, she was livid. How she'd managed to make it through high school and college without a basic understanding of how much food each person needed per day, she didn't know. Furthermore, how to multiply that by people and days, all while sticking to whatever food guidelines were popular this week, and keeping her sanity, eluded her. She could explain the intricacies of the Battle of Ticonderoga, but she couldn't predict how much she needed in grains vs. proteins, or how to balance that knowledge with fruits and vegetables. Furthermore, from her observations, the children didn't eat a consistent amount from day to day anyway. Vannie was helpful, as were Ellie and Laird, but they simply knew some of the foods their mother often bought— not how she used them once they arrived home, or how she balanced them in the family's meals.

Feeling like an incompetent fool, but knowing that food was food (even if it didn't seem to have rhyme or reason), Aggie bought almost an entire cart of meat, half a cart of frozen veggies, and the other half of fresh vegetables for salads and snacking, an entire case of apples, several bags of other fresh fruit, canned soups, lunchmeats, bread, boxed cereals and ten gallons of milk. With all three shopping carts filled, she then filled another one. By the fifth cart, Aggie was getting desperate.

As she tried to keep the little children from climbing from their seats, she realized that other than the fruit, there were no snack foods. She also realized that tuna, peanut butter, and jelly would be helpful and sent the other children in different directions, while trying to keep the twins and Ian occupied and quiet. Only three displays and two jars were demolished in the process, and Aggie thought surely that was good!

Several hundred dollars, two box helpers, and a half an hour later, the food was bagged and stored in the van. The children held bags on their laps, under their seats, and between their feet. All the way home, she tried to compare the large trip with her near daily rushes into stores for basic staples and wondered just how long the food would last. Surely, it'd be a week or two— maybe even three if she was careful.

Luke jogged out to the van as Aggie drove up the drive. Before Aggie and Vannie could climb from the front seats, he had the twins on the ground with bags of bread in their hands to carry into the house. Smiling, he passed Ian to her and urged her to go rest while he and the children brought in the food. Aggie was amazed at how that one small act of courtesy could mean so much, and, not knowing how to express her gratitude, she gave him a weak but heart-felt smile and said, "Thank you, Luke, I appreciate the help."

Luke felt her thanks as well as heard them, and it was apparent that they were partially the result of overwork and under-appreciation. He determined, as he loaded his arms with nearly a dozen plastic bags, to make sure he found many opportunities to help her, and especially compliment her, in the coming weeks. Some said Luke's spiritual gift was service, and his specialty was observation. He was a fixer.

Before long, all the bags of groceries were piled around the living room and kitchen. Every table, counter, and most of the floor was covered with bags upon bags of food. Aggie had the daunting task of quickly putting away the perishables, while trying to come up with some organizational system of knowing what was in there and where to find it again. As he piled meat in an empty laundry basket, Luke commented on the need for a deep freeze, so Aggie snatched a crayon from the floor under the table and began a list of needs. It took some creative rearranging, but all the food was safely stored away forty minutes later. Luke promised to return in the morning with a freezer for the meat that was sitting on shelves in the refrigerator.

"You won't have time to cook it all before it goes bad."

Collapsing on the couch, Aggie realized that she had just bought enough food to feed them all and now had no energy with which to *make* any of it. Tears formed in Aggie's eyes as she wondered, for what seemed the millionth time, how her sister had ever managed to keep things running so smoothly without wearing out. Ian crawled up to her and lifted his arms to be held. Within seconds of settling in Aggie's arms, Ian slept soundly. He'd missed his morning nap, causing him to enter a deep sleep quite quickly.

A short while later, Luke came in and sat across from her. "Miss Milliken?"

Aggie interrupted. "It's Aggie. I am going to call you Luke. Partly, because I don't even *know* your last name, but mostly because I am hoping that you'll consider me a friend."

Luke started over using her first name. He told her that the children were making peanut butter and jelly sandwiches and having chips with them. "I brought a jug of juice with me to bribe the kids into liking me, so they are guzzling that as well." Luke winked and continued.

"I have the wires fixed. It really didn't take long. If it makes you feel better, the other guy may not have known what he was doing, but he managed to get the boxes in right, without destroying the walls, and just mixed the wires in a way that I can't even imagine. Not exactly a good thing, but not the end of the world either, you know?" Aggie smiled and nodded, too tired to answer.

"I think that the little roundish room you asked me about just needs the old carpeting removed, floors refinished, and a good coat of paint. I already checked, and there are beautiful hardwood floors under that green, shaggy monstrosity. All in all, I think I can have it ready for her to move into by next Thursday or Friday night, if you want me to do it. I'll go get the paint tonight on my way home, but with your ok, I can pull out

179

that carpeting right after I eat my lunch." Luke seemed to hesitate. Aggie couldn't decide if he had another question or if there was something else.

"Thank you, Luke. I'd appreciate you taking out that carpeting. I am so tired; I doubt I can do anything more right now. I was hoping to do most of the work around here myself. Save money, you know? Well, I see that I am going to need more help than I thought." She paused a moment, trying to read his face. She wondered why other people didn't have open book faces like hers. "So, if you'll tell me how much time you have to work on this place, I have a feeling that I can fill it up. On the other hand, the good news is that we have the paint for that room. I bought it last week."

Luke excused himself and went into the kitchen. Taken aback, Aggie slowly became afraid she had overwhelmed him with too much work already. Mentally, she began writing a "help wanted" ad for the local classifieds and prayed that the Lord would protect her from people like her first electrician.

When Luke returned, he held two paper plates piled with salad and lasagna. Setting them on the makeshift coffee table, Luke lifted sleeping Ian from her lap and laid him in the nearby playpen. Something about the take-charge actions irritated her and blessed her at the same time. Luke offered to pray for the meal once he'd returned to his seat. Still stunned, Aggie nodded and bowed her head. "Lord, thank you for Mom's great leftover lasagna. Thank you for new friends to share it with, and a wonderful old home to restore to Your glory. In the name of Jesus, Amen."

Aggie raised her head and smiled. "I can tell you are going to be a very difficult person to stay irritated with." Taking a bite of the delicious lunch, Aggie added, "And please thank your mother for this. I love lasagna, and the frozen ones just don't quite cut it."

Luke smiled, started to speak again, and then hesitated. Aggie smiled, and nodded her encouragement, but it was several minutes before he spoke. "Aggie, I like to help. I always have— I, well— I see a need, and I want to fill it."

Long, silent pauses, where he clearly had more to say, almost drove Aggie to distraction, but she tried to hold her tongue. She couldn't decide if she was that nerve-wracking or if it was something peculiar to Luke. As the minutes ticked by, Aggie, ready to scream with frustration, kept chewing so she wouldn't prematurely open her mouth.

"Sometimes this means I overstep my place. So, if it looks like I'm trying to take over, number one, I am not." Luke appeared to be choosing his words carefully. "Number two; all you have to do is tell me to back off. I can handle it."

All reservations about Luke disappeared with his reassurances. In their place, discouragement arrived and moved into her heart. Any moment, she was certain that he'd decide this job was so *not* worth it.

"Well, Luke, if you haven't noticed already, I can't hide my thoughts. If it's in my head, it's on my face. So, if I look irritated, back off. If you keep that in mind, you and I will do just fine." Aggie smiled to soften her words, and stretched. "I feel refreshed after a rest and the excellent food. Let's go tackle that carpet! I'll put the twins down for their naps and be right up."

Two hours later, they shoved the carpet out of the window and watched it roll down the roof and onto the ground. Aggie realized it would never fit in the trashcan, and was about to have Laird start cutting it into small pieces to be tossed into whatever space was left in the garbage cans on trash day. Luke read her thoughts on her face, grabbed the phone from the hallway, and headed downstairs. He turned to Aggie on the second step, "I'll call for a trailer can. They just roll it up to the driveway, and when you tell them you are done, they roll it away. You won't need to call for trash service until you have it taken away either."

While he ordered the can, Aggie began sweeping the room of years of dirt that had sifted through the old fibers, nearly choking on the dust, dirt, and the revolting scent of eau de cat urine. An hour later, they were still pulling up tack strips and preparing the floor for sanding and sealing. Hearing a knock at the door, Aggie sprinted down the stairs to see a very concerned Deputy Markenson standing behind the screen "at ease."

"Hey, William! Nice to see you; come on in!" Aggie started to apologize for her curt words the last time she saw him, but she was interrupted.

"Aggie, who called us, and why?" Aggie's startled face, and the sight of baby Ian chewing on the phone, answered the question for her.

"Oh, *no!*" Her horrified cry was heard upstairs, outdoors, and at the mailbox where the carrier was inserting the daily barrage of junk mail and legal documents. In record time, Luke clamored down the stairs, the mail carrier ran up the drive and opened the door uninvited, and all the children came screaming in the house from the back yard where they had been playing. Even Tavish crawled out of his hideaway that he had created for himself under the day bed.

The result was the instant chaos that she felt trademarked her life these days. The twins woke up crying, and Ian, frightened by Aggie's squeal, began to whimper. The three men looked around for some way to calm the din, but none of them knew just how to do it. With tears running down her face, Aggie mustered all the vocal strength she could and shouted, "*Stop!*" Even little Ian hushed his whimpers for a few seconds.

Handing Ian to Laird, Aggie walked up two stair steps, turned, and spoke. "Everything is fine. The phone was left on that table next to the playpen, and Ian must have picked it up to play with it. I guess he just hit the right buttons or something; I don't know. No one is hurt; nothing is wrong." Her voice caught as she tried to control herself. "I am sorry you came out here for nothing, William. I assure you that everyone here is fine."

Turning, Aggie ran back upstairs and locked herself in the bathroom. Luke heard her sobs as he climbed the stairs a short while later. He'd introduced himself to the stern officer and assured the mail guy that all was fine. The twins, now awake and wanting snacks, were comforted and the baby moved to the play area that Aggie had corralled off as a safe place. Tavish sat *on* the daybed this time; book in hand, with strict instructions to keep an eye on the little one. Kenzie and Laird were sent to make peanut butter cracker sandwiches for an afternoon snack, and the rest of the children went back outside to play a game of tag.

Luke's gentle knock was almost inaudible over the deep sobs from within. "Aggie, please come out. Everything is fine now, really. The deputy is gone, the mail guy left your mail on that funny table with all the drawers in the hallway, and the kids are all settled. I put the phone back on the charger." The sobbing slowly ceased, but the door remained shut. "Aggie, I am sorry; it was my fault. I left the phone there and should have put it away." The silence continued. Finally, Luke tried a new tactic. "Aggie, I don't care if you are mad at me; you have that right, but those children need to know that *you* are all right. Please go down there and reassure them, ok? I am going to finish up the floor."

A good five minutes later, Luke heard the door open and footsteps descending down the stairs. Faint strains of a wobbly hymn drifted up the stairs. *"When for deeper faith I seek… hill of Calvary I gooooooooooo…"* The handyman had never felt *less* handy in his life. He had no idea how to help her.

Near dinnertime, the room needed only a coat of paint on its walls, and polyurethane on the floor to make it habitable. If this dry spell lasted, they would be able to move Vannie in by the middle to the end of next week. As children raced into the room to see the progress, he glanced at the doorknob and tested it. He'd have to replace that first. Somehow, he could just see little Cari and Lorna-sized shoe prints permanently etched into his freshly sealed floors.

Aggie's heart dropped into her stomach when she saw the phone in Ian's hands. The local sheriff's office must think she was the most inept and irresponsible guardian in the greater Rockland area — possibly the entire United States. How had Ian called them anyway? What were the odds that he could get just the right combinations of numbers? Her wail created pandemonium, and the ensuing chaos was more than Aggie could handle. It had been a rough night, followed by a rotten morning, and what had seemed like a somewhat redeemed afternoon just flushed itself away down her toilet. Aggie knew she was acting like an over-emotional teenager as she ran back up the stairs, but right then, she didn't care. Once the flood of tears began, Aggie couldn't seem to stop them. All the pain, frustration, and loss of the last four months flooded to the surface and spilled over until she was a quivering mass of sobs and wails.

Aggie missed her sister. Over the past several years, their time together had been limited to Allie's visits to the Milliken home in Yorktown, but late night chats on the messenger were common, as well as long phone calls. Allie had been so wise and practical, and anytime Aggie needed advice, she turned first to her mother, and then to Allie.

Luke knocked on the door at just the wrong time. Aggie had begun to calm herself down when she heard him ask if she was all right. Somehow, the concern and understanding in his voice was enough to send her into a fresh round of tears. The depth of her emotional response surprised her, but although she tried, she couldn't handle the mental gymnastics necessary to analyze it.

His last plea, on behalf of the children, eventually gave her the strength to stop her emotional roller coaster. He was right; she had to get downstairs and show them that she was just fine. A minute passed before she stood. A glance at the mirror sent her eyes rolling and her hands wiping away the residue of tears. Humming her "buck up" hymn, Aggie washed her face, brushed her hair, and forced herself to smile. Somehow, it looked more like a grimace to her, but she figured something was better than nothing.

She forced her eyes away from Vannie's room as she passed it. The wavering hymn grew stronger and louder as she descended the stairs. *"Then to life I turn again... learning all the worth of pain..."xi* Aggie wasn't sure how her pain would help, but she was determined not to let it hinder the relationship with her children. They needed her to be strong. Not knowing what she was going to find when she found the children, Aggie stopped singing and yelled, "Come out come out wherever you are..."

The house looked and felt deserted. Cracker crumbs and peanut butter smears covered one corner of the newly cleared counter. An empty jug of juice sat nearby, with plastic cups littering the counters, floor, and wastebasket. Looking out the kitchen window, Aggie saw a game of duck, duck, goose, in progress. As was becoming her habit, Aggie started counting heads. "Three...five...six. Where are Tavish and Ian?" Aggie wondered aloud.

"Over here, Aunt Aggie. I gave Ian one of those baby biscuits— I hope that was ok." Tavish was in his usual horizontal position, with a book in one hand and a peanut butter cracker in the other.

"Tavish, why don't you go get Cari and Lorna for me. I promised them a story when they woke up, and if I don't do it now, it won't happen." Picking up the filthy baby, Aggie peeled the clothes off of him and rinsed off his face and hands in the sink. Five minutes later, a clean, happy baby sat on her lap while pixie haired twins leaned against her on each side as Aggie read one of Beatrix Potter's tales.

Vannie came into the room as she finished the story and pulled Aggie aside. "While you were upstairs, I was hanging the calendar, and I noticed the date!" She shook her head as though to clear it. "My days are all mixed up since the move and school is out and everything."

Aggie looked confused. "So, what is today's date?"

185

"It's the fourteenth, Aunt Aggie. It's Kenzie's birthday! I thought it was next week, but it's today!"

Where had the month gone? Two weeks had already passed in this house. "Kenzie's birthday. We have to do something *now*. You go ask Luke if you and I can go into town. We'll buy a cake and get her a present and be back for a 'surprise' party."

Vannie giggled excitedly and tore up the stairs two at a time. Luke's answer must have been in the affirmative, because she sailed back downstairs almost as quickly as she had ascended. In minutes, they zipped toward town discussing their options for celebrating Kenzie's birthday.

"We could buy her favorite ice cream— and a cake from the store... Or, maybe we should buy a mix and a thing of frosting, some candles, sprinkles and a tube of that writing icing. We could let her bake her cake— of course, it'd probably be kind of messy and taste funny. She would really like that, though." Vannie's ramblings were evidence of her convoluted thought processes.

Aggie agreed. She was willing to go with just about anything, as long as it was reasonable. They discussed every present under the sun. Craft supplies, games, puzzles, and dolls were all discarded in the interest of clutter control. Vannie suggested a new comforter and pillow like hers, but Aggie ruled it out. "We'll all get new ones anyway. It wouldn't be much of a gift if she's getting one anyway."

Vannie pumped her fist, as if she'd managed some amazing feat. "I just realized what we should get! She has *always* wanted one of those *big* stuffed bears. You know, the ones that you can almost use for a chair, they are so big..." Vannie showed Aggie with her arms what she was talking about. "They are only about twenty dollars over at Wal-Mart, but can you see her excitement over the *big* box and then the *big* bear..."

Vannie's voice was almost as excited, as if the impromptu party was for *her*, and it showed in her excessively italicized speech. They found an enormous purple bear holding a pink and white polka dotted smaller one. It'd match their new room perfectly, and the bear's quirky expression was exactly the kind of thing to keep it from being just another stuffed animal. They purchased silly party hats and cheap kazoos to add to the celebration. Behind the store, they found a large empty TV box and used the paper and tape they'd purchased to wrap the box in the van.

When they arrived home, Aggie called everyone out front. Luke heard her voice and watched from the window as Aggie presented the present to Kenzie. Quietly, to himself, he joined in as they all sang "Happy Birthday" to her. Vannie showed the excited Kenzie the cake mix and took her inside to make the cake.

He continued watching as Aggie chased the twins around the yard until she tripped over her skirt and went rolling across the grass. The twins jumped her, and a fierce tickle fest ensued. Amused, Luke observed as she struggled in vain and then begged for mercy. Her insecurities in mothering her children were evident, but watching her now, he wished he could help her step outside herself and see what the rest of the world must see. Aggie was doing wonderfully. Regretfully, Luke turned back to the room, stuffing more broken tack strips in a large box as he did.

Just after five o'clock, Luke descended the stairs, his arms laden with tools, trash, and other indistinguishable paraphernalia. "Well, Aggie, the room is ready for a good coat of paint." Luke's grin was infectious. "I can't do much more up there tonight without my rollers and drop cloths, but maybe you can show me where to find her furniture and stuff? I can at least carry it upstairs and into the room next to it, so we can move it in as soon as the floor is dry."

Aggie grimaced. She had no idea what furniture was going in Vannie's room. She didn't even have a separate bed for the girl. Vannie had slept at the top of a triple bunk bed before the move. A look crossed the girl's face, and she realized that Vannie wasn't looking forward to bringing the large bed into her dainty little room.

"I decided to give Vannie my daybed. That will have to go up there later because we haven't set up Allie and Doug's old bed— it's too big for in here, but Vannie knows which boxes are hers. They are all on the east wall of the study in there." The look of surprise and thankfulness on Vannie's face was worth the loss of Aggie's childhood bed.

"Meanwhile," she continued, unwilling to think about what she'd just given away, "we need to decide which dresser she can have and get her some shelves for her personal things and such. Oh, she'll need a night table as well." Her mental list grew before her eyes.

Luke looked thoughtful for a moment and then said, "You know, for furniture, there are great garage sales around here this time of year. I bet you could find some good bargains on Saturday." She started to reply, but then Aggie noticed that he wasn't quite finished. After what seemed like an hour but was truthfully *only* a minute or two, he turned to Vannie. "Do you have things you'd rather keep out of reach of little hands? Something you'd like to protect?"

When Vannie nodded emphatically, Luke continued. "What if I made a shelf that runs across the wall with the window and along the top of it. With a step stool in there, you could easily reach your things, but the little guys couldn't."

Vannie squealed and threw her arms around his neck. "Oh, thank you! That is just the best—" Without another word, she dashed upstairs to plan exactly where she'd put everything.

A look crossed Luke's face that unnerved Aggie. While she moved into the kitchen to stuff a pan of chicken in the oven, she asked, "What is it? I can see something is bothering you."

To her surprise and annoyance, Luke went outside without answering her question. Just as she was about to storm after him and demand that he stop leaving her so confused and frustrated, he reappeared, arms empty and his clothes dust-free. "Sorry, I was sifting dust all over the floor." He hurried to wash his hands and arms. "You're right, something is bothering me. I just realized that you have a teen—"

"Near teen. She's not quite there yet— almost, but not quite."

"Anyway, I remember my father being very careful to give his daughters plenty of time and attention. When all their friend's fathers were pulling back and feeling awkward about showing affection to their daughters, Pop got more affectionate than ever. It was different, but he was determined to try to prevent them seeking unhealthy attention."

"You think Vannie seeks unhealthy male attention?" It didn't make any sense to Aggie. While she pulled lettuce, tomatoes, cucumbers, and other veggies from the fridge, she waited for Luke to explain himself.

"No, I don't—"

"Is this about her hugging you? If it makes you uncomfortable—"

Shaking his head emphatically, Luke tried again. "It's not the hug, really. It's more about the realization that it's not going to get any better. You don't have a brother, your father-in-law isn't much of an option, and your parents don't live close."

The extended pause that followed irritated Aggie enough that she began shredding the lettuce with unnecessary force. She chopped cucumbers within an inch of their existence, and the tomatoes were nearly sauce, but still Luke stood, silently thinking, and cracking his knuckles systematically. The sound seemed to echo her knife chops, almost a percussionist accompaniment to her rhythm.

After much longer than Aggie had ever imagined she could wait, he spoke again. "I think you need to find men that you can trust to invest in these children's lives—Maybe William..."

She thought she understood. "Are you hinting that you'd rather not have the job as a male influence around her? I can handle that."

189

It was a lie. She couldn't. Just as the idea of yet another need in the children's lives had dawned, she'd realized that Zeke and Luke were excellent options. Now she was being warned not to count on them. "Great. How do I give the girl male attention? I can't! I am not a male. I remember Allie talking about how Doug had ways of being affectionate without making Ellie uncomfortable..." Aggie sighed in frustration. "I wonder if they didn't make a huge mistake when they named me guardian. I can't be a mother and a father. Children need both. This was a huge mistake. At least the Stuarts could give them male and female role models." Aggie started to continue her rant when Luke placed his hand on her shoulder.

"Aggie, from what I have heard of the Stuarts, your sister and her husband made the best decision. If Doug had been the only one to die in that accident, your sister would have been doing this alone too. I think God knew what He was doing when He prompted them to choose you. We'll just have to figure out how to get all of those little girls some healthy male attention before they get old enough to seek unhealthy attention."

Aggie didn't realize it, but the use of the pronoun "we" was very comforting. "You're not trying to tell me not to count on you for help?"

"Of course, I'll help. Uncle Zeke, my cousins, my uncles — we'll all help if you'll let us. We're family, Aggie." At the odd look on her face, he rephrased. "No, you're not a Sullivan or a Tesdall, but we're all Christians, and for us, that means we help just as if you were my sister and Laird was my brother. We're here to help, if you want us, no matter what."

For the first time in a long time, her spirit was at peace. She wasn't alone in this daunting journey of hers. She had the Lord on her side; she had friends. Everything was going to be just fine. She just knew it. "Thank you." She wanted to show her full appreciation but didn't know how. Instead, she decided to invite him to stay for Kenzie's party. "Hey, if you want to be family, you need to join in family festivities. We're about to have a semi-impromptu birthday party. Would you like to join us?"

With a face full of regret, Luke tried to demur. "I'm filthy, I don't have a gift, and—"

"Gifts aren't necessary, I can probably find a generic T-shirt big enough for you, and dinner will be filling, if not exciting, and if I can find that box of potatoes. What did I do with those things anyway?"

Tina says: Aggie?? You around??
Tina says: Aggie…….. where areeeeeeeee youuuu?????
Tina says: Ding ding?? I saw you sign in…
Tina says: Wooooooohoooooooooooo
Aggie says: Back. Sorry. I got on and Ian decided he wanted to change his diaper habits, so I had to change him.
Tina says: Tee hee…
Aggie says: Easy for you to say… you don't smell him! Toxic waste dump. I call him Chernobyl on really bad ones. Think I'll warp his psyche?
Tina says: In that house, if that's the worst that happens to him he'll be fine.
Aggie says: "If that ain't the truth," as Granny would say…
Tina says: So, what chaos are you in the midst of this week?
Aggie says: Well, actually no chaos to speak of. Just the baby called 9-1-1, the electricity was wired backwards, we're working night and day to get Vannie's room done, and oh yeah, Luke thinks Vannie is starved for male attention. Oh… and I forgot Kenzie's birthday. Not bad for a week's work, huh?
Tina says: Wooooaaaaahhh. One at a time. Ian did WHAT?
Aggie says: Somehow, he called the sheriff.
Tina says: 9-1-1?
Aggie says: Dunno, your guess is as good as mine.

Tina says: So what happened?

Aggie says: Deputy Markenson showed up. First I chewed him out, because the electricity was messed up, and then he shows up thinking he's saving the day, only to find a baby chewing on the phone.

Tina says: I'm trying not to laugh here...

Aggie says: Why stop yourself? I'll be laughing later, I am sure.

Tina says: So what's up with the electricity?

Aggie says: Well, you see, William talked someone into doing the wiring for a reasonable price. Yep, got it free even. Well, free, after the guy wired my house backwards, so when I turned a light on in one room, it came on in another! Luke says he did a good job putting in the boxes, but he didn't know how to connect it right.

Tina says: Who's Luke?

Aggie says: Zeke's nephew. Remember when I was looking for this place, and Zeke said his nephew really wanted it, but he'd already extended himself?

Tina says: So... what's he like?

Aggie says: Well... he is really helpful. Knows lots about kids. He has Vannie's room almost done.

Tina says: Details girl!!! Age, appearance... I want the works!

Aggie says: Hmmm, I am guessing here. I haven't paid that much attention. He's kind of average, umm probably mid to late twenties. His eyes are kind. That I noticed. He's a Christian. What are the chances of that? Two Christians in my life right off the bat. I am so thankful.

Tina says: That tells me a lot. :P

Aggie says: Sorry, I'm just so busy that I don't have time to notice these things. He'll be around a while, so I'll try to get a better run down for you later.

Tina says: You better. So what's this about Vannie and men?

Aggie says: Oh, wait— he has amazingly strong looking forearms. There. I noticed something.

Aggie says: Vannie hugged Luke today.

Tina says: And that's significant how?

Aggie says: He told me we have to make sure the girls get enough male attention too. Like I can do that in between keeping Cari out of trouble and getting through to Ellie on her withdrawn days. Oh, and there's that little matter of us all sleeping in the living and dining rooms because our bedrooms need work. I'll tack that on at the end of a rough day maybe.

Tina says: I don't know. Maybe Luke's uncle would adopt them as a surrogate grandpa?

Aggie says: That's what Luke said. It was really sweet. He said that we're all Christians, all family, and he has cousins, uncles, and they'd all help. I think I'll see if Dad can come up for a week too.

Tina says: That's a good idea too. And what about Kenzie's birthday?

Aggie says: Well, we totally missed Kenzie's birthday. I have never been able to keep the birthdays straight and just assumed that the kids would be talking about them for weeks before hand. Well... she didn't! Vannie noticed that today was the 14th, or she would have been completely forgotten.

Tina says: Uh oh... well, did she have fun?

Aggie says: She was thrilled. We let her make her own cake and decorate it anyway she wanted and we bought her this HUGE bear. She's sleeping with the bear, but I swear it'll knock her onto the floor before the night is over

Tina says: How funny. I'll have to drop a card into the mail. It'll make her happy. Well... looks like they're going to cut us off. Just got one of those maintenance boxes. SEE you soon!

Tina says: Bye.

Aggie says: Thanks, Tina.

Tina says: What for?

Aggie says: For being you.

Tina says: Love you girl, bye.

Aggie says: *Poof*

ONE FINE DAY

Chapter Thirteen

Saturday, June 15th

By eight-thirty, Luke was busy working in Vannie's room. While Aggie placed the baby gate at the bottom of the stairs and ordered everyone to stay away from it, he taped off the trim, taped down the drop cloth, and started cutting in as he prepared for the roller. He'd started to wash the walls, but Aggie pointed to a box of TSP and a scrub bucket in the bathroom and assured him she'd scrubbed it down twice before bedtime the previous night. In her opinion, his prep work took an obscene amount of time; she was itching to get her fingers on a paintbrush and do something constructive in the renovation process. She hadn't painted anything since her elementary school art classes, but just how hard could it be to paint a windowsill?

An hour later, she still waited. Between trips up and down stairs to check on Luke's progress, she made beds, washed dishes, bandaged three scrapes, and kissed a bruise. Furthermore, she'd broken up two fights, changed a diaper, and realized that the dishes she'd washed were done without soap, necessitating another run through the sink. She'd accomplished that and more while waiting for Luke to finish a wall for her to start painting. Her clipboard now had a new page.

Kitchen Needs—
2 dishwashers

Sometime around ten-thirty, Luke called for her. She'd held off the baby's nap in order to be able to put him down the minute she had to go upstairs, so now she handed him his favorite little silky blanket, patted his back, and crept out of the library. The baby's wail slowly rose from a faint cry to a screeching wail and fell abruptly. After she hurried outside to remind the older children to keep an eye on the twins' whereabouts, she peeked in on the baby once more before she went upstairs. A soft snore sent her out of the room with a peaceful heart. Ian would sleep through lunch.

To her immense surprise, the "easy" job of painting window trim and baseboards wasn't nearly as easy or exciting as she'd expected. Luke showed her how to use a guide, make slow steady strokes, and how to load her brush without overloading it. Kneeling next to her on the floor, he dipped, brushed across the bumpy surface of the paint tray, and then holding the trim guide in place, brushed with careful strokes until that incredibly small section was perfect.

Unlike his perfect eight-inch strip, hers was streaked. When she moved the guide, it dripped paint along the area of the wall that he'd just cut in, and the result was a mess. Stricken, she looked up at him with an apology on her lips. Laughing, Luke wiped their trim guides with a rag, and then, using a fresh one, wiped off the paint drip from the wall. "You didn't expect it to be perfect, did you? You'll get the hang of it."

"Yeah, after you have to redo all your work," she muttered, dipping the brush into the paint tray and trying again. With each swish of the brush and each push of the roller, it seemed as if the filth, grime, and even the stench of the old house were being replaced with a freshness that restored her spirit.

Lunchtime arrived before they expected it, and, once again, Aggie was at a loss as to what to serve. She was used to bagels with a cup of coffee for breakfast, salad for lunch and a simple dinner. The children were accustomed to three squares and two snacks a day, all nutritionally balanced, and with a variety that taught them to appreciate different tastes and textures. On the other hand, Aggie ate what she could procure quickly and didn't worry about silly things like nutrition and health. It couldn't happen anymore, and it was up to her to make the change.

Frustration welled as she realized this was at least the third time she'd made that resolution. Every other week, she planned to make more wholesome and nutritious meals, and a week or so later, she found herself pulling out pot pies, frozen pizzas, frozen burritos, and canned ravioli. Again. It had to stop, but regardless of her brilliant system for meals, she felt helpless to implement it.

Luke sensed her hesitation and began pulling out sandwich fixings and one of the watermelons she had purchased. Upon cutting open the melon, Luke sent it to the trashcan via Laird, carried another one to the counter, and knocked on it. Aggie was confused at his actions, but when she saw his smile before cutting open the second one, she knew that there must be a secret to good watermelons.

"Luke, what was wrong with the other one?"

Seconds ticked by into a minute as Luke continued to cut. It took every ounce of Aggie's self-control not to scream, *"Just answer! This isn't a trick question! I did not ask for a dissertation on quantum physics!"* Instead, she reached into the freezer and pulled out a roll of ground beef.

"Well, Aggie, it was over-ripe. Actually, I think it was on its way to fermentation. Or, maybe it was already Watermelon Wine. So, unless you want to be hauled in for intoxicating a minor, I think we'll just leave it where it is."

"I don't get you. You brought juice yesterday and today instead of Kool-Aid. If I hadn't heard Allie complaining about the stuff at Mom's a few times, I would have loaded the kids up on that colored sugar-water without thinking twice. Kids drink Kool-Aid, right? You also look as comfortable in this kitchen as you do up there with your tools and paint." She was determined to ascertain exactly how Luke seemed more at home doing her job than she was. Meanwhile, she started slapping mayo and mustard on bread as quickly as she could. "Most of the guys I know wouldn't have had a clue."

"Well, I have four sisters, and Mom kept us equally busy with every aspect of housework. She told me one day I'd have to keep things running for a pregnant wife, and she was going to make sure that I knew how to do it." Luke paused and chuckled. "My sister says that she's sending Scott to stay with Mom for three months before she gets pregnant again. That poor guy is worthless in the kitchen."

Aggie giggled nervously. At Luke's raised eyebrow she confessed quite sheepishly, "Well, I can't make anything that requires more than one or two ingredients. And even then, I've really never tried that often. Boxes and frozen and I get along very well." She was obviously embarrassed at her lack of homemaking experience.

Luke looked thoughtful and then replied, "Let's start with what we have in here, ok?" Without waiting for agreement, he opened the freezer and continued. "Well, you have chicken chests and lemon pepper. Do you know if you have any rice?" Aggie shook her head and chuckled.

"Chicken *chests*?" she queried incredulously. Luke grinned and replied, "Well, you see, my mother always said that it was less intimate to call them chicken chests, and since the poor chicken was already plucked and stripped, the least we could do is give him the dignity of a less embarrassing name." Aggie's laughter could be heard across the street. It was a pity that Mrs. Dyke was indoors baking snickerdoodles for William.

The curious neighbor needed more fodder for her next gossip fest with the quilt guild.

Luke tried again, "Noodles? Chips? Something?" Aggie shook her head again, and this time a look of defeat lingered around her eyes.

He opened and closed cupboards, taking stock of what was in the house. Picking up a stray crayon and one of the envelopes that Aggie had emptied from the previous day's mail, Luke began a list of what he thought needed to be bought. "You have great main ingredients, you just need fillers. Rice, beans, noodles, potatoes, oats, and things like that. You bought spaghetti sauce, but it's kind of hard to eat without something to put it on." The twinkle in his eyes took away the sting that might come if he'd truly tried to mock her. When she protested that she'd just spent over eight hundred dollars on food, Luke assured her that with another sixty dollars or so, there would be enough food to last more than a month, barring milk, bread, and fresh fruits and veggies. Aggie's relief left her speechless, until he was finally able to persuade her to admit that she assumed she'd be spending that much every week or two!

By four o'clock that afternoon, the first coat of urethane was drying. The baby gate was installed in the doorway of Vannie's room, and the young girl leaned against it while looking at the lovely effect of robin's egg blue, apple green and ivory. Aggie eased next to the girl and said, "Your colors turned out so pretty. With that green on the shelves, and curtains at the window, this will be a room to dream wonderful dreams in."

Vannie smiled and looked wistful. "I've always wanted dotted Swiss curtains. Do you think we can find some anywhere? Momma tried every store and catalog, but she always thought they were too expensive on the rare times she found them." The longing in the girl's voice was evident, even to Luke, who was washing up his brushes in the bathroom.

Calling from his brush-washing, Luke said, "You know

Vannie, I could look on eBay and see if maybe someone has some old ones that they are trying to get rid of. That's a standard window size." Her answering smile was lovely. "I'll look tonight after I take Meggie for her walk."

Sunday, June 16th

Aggie's clan filled a back pew, and Aggie had her hands full just trying to keep everyone quiet. By the end of the service, Aggie sorely missed the less formal service in Rockland. She debated making the weekly trek to the other congregation but knew that a local church family would be important.

The people were welcoming and friendly. More than one person asked if they were "all hers." Aggie couldn't wait until her family was no longer a novelty and could just be another family who happened to have a few more people than most. Aggie graciously refused half a dozen invitations to dinner knowing that there was no way someone was really prepared to feed all of them.

Ellie asked if they could buy lunch somewhere and walk over to the park to eat. Aggie, with no regard for how quickly Ian would become heavy, readily agreed. With every child carrying a bag of something, Aggie and the children almost ran to the park.

"Aunt Aggie, may I go play now?" Kenzie's little face was covered in lunch, but Aggie had, unfortunately, forgotten to buy napkins.

"Go to the drinking fountain first, and try to wash your face. Try to keep the food from getting in the little basin though!" Aggie ended up calling out her instructions as the excited girl ran for the water.

Time passed slowly, as though too lazy to keep up with the day. After several minutes laying on Aggie's chest as she swung gently in the swing, Ian drifted to sleep. She shrugged awkwardly out of the bolero she wore to cover her sundress and dropped it on the grass. While not as convenient as a blanket, and sure to be covered in grass stains before the afternoon was over, the jacket protected the baby's face from the prickliness of the grass blades. He slept soundly, for which Aggie was grateful. The children were having much too much fun to drag them all away for Ian's nap.

Aggie watched her little clan play all the games that she and Tina had played over the years. Freeze Tag, Hide and Seek, Mother May I— all the games that punctuate childhood rang out across the grass and through the trees. When the twins grew tired, Laird ran to the van to retrieve a blanket he remembered seeing that morning. While the younger children slept, Aggie played every game she could remember, and even taught them a few that they didn't know. It seemed to her that they were healing. Routines were developing into a new norm for all of them. It was going to be all right.

Meg Reese watched as William drove away from the church, trying to hide her amusement with his interest in the latest residents of Brant's Corners. As she watched Aggie and her children walk towards the park carrying hot dogs and sodas, Meg saw William's car make a U-turn and follow them. She knew it wasn't any of her business, knew she should mind her own, but she ignored her conscience and followed William.

An hour later, Meg's stomach growled, demanding lunch, but William hadn't moved from his spot under a large maple tree. She bought two hot dogs from the nearby stand and loaded one with William's favorite condiments. Taking a deep breath and praying for divine protection from the wrath of Markenson, Meg walked over to William's car and opened the passenger side door, sliding into the passenger's seat. "Here, eat."

William didn't try to hide his surprise. As much as he disliked them, he took the hot dog and took a large bite.

"How'd you know I was here?" He grimaced as the scent of frankfurter and mustard flooded his nostrils.

Meg laughed. "I saw you do a U-turn and follow them. I thought it was odd, so I followed you."

"And you've been watching ever since?" William's voice was curious, and Meg sagged in relief. She'd been certain that he would be furious and lecture her on privacy.

"I wasn't sure what to make of it. As far as I know, you don't sit around watching pretty ladies and their eight children every day."

"You think she's pretty? So does Mrs. Dyke." Wiping his chin with the napkin she passed him, he added, "I don't see it myself." William sounded perplexed.

Meg was thoughtful. William rarely offered an opinion on anything unrelated to work. "I don't think she'll ever win any beauty contests, but then again, most women wouldn't. She just has that sweet all-American look about her."

William nodded. "I can see that. She sure is good with those children. You wouldn't know she didn't have them six months ago."

"I noticed that the other day. Too bad all mothers don't put as much care and effort into their children as she obviously does."

William's emphatic "amen" startled Meg. Before she could question him, William spoke again. "You know, Meg, I don't want to be rude, but I came out here to be alone."

William's voice was uncharacteristically apologetic. Usually he spoke his mind quite bluntly. Meg smiled and opened the door. "I'm going. I just had to make sure you were ok. See you in the morning, and don't scare our new citizen. They pay our salaries you know!"

William watched Meg walk away and was thankful she seemed fine. Irritated partners made for miserable workdays. A squeal from the park tore his eyes away from Meg. Something about the children, their innocence, the carefree air that surrounded them like a protective bubble, even their laughter as it reached him, soothed his spirit. Watching Aggie was almost like watching one of the children. She laughed and played as hard as the rest of them.

Later, she sat between the twins as they slept, stroking their hair, and it looked like she was singing to them. Something about the way the breeze flicked at her hair and ruffled her dress created a picture of beautiful young womanhood, and at last, William saw the beauty in her that others had mentioned. He was moved in a way he didn't understand, and it bothered him. What about this woman affected him so strongly? He knew he wasn't physically or emotionally attracted to her — or was he?

Aggie says: You'd better be there.

Aggie says: I mean it, woman. Show thyself.

Tina says: I'm here, I'm here. Have a good Sunday?

Aggie says: The best. Seriously, it was just one of those perfect days where nothing could go wrong if it tried.

Tina says: You fell in love.

Aggie says: You're right, I did. How exciting.

Tina says: Which one is it?

Aggie says: I can't make up my mind. I think all of them, but tonight, I'd have to say Ian. He was just so stinkin' cute!

Tina says: *rolls eyes* You're certifiable, you know that right?

Aggie says: Yeah, but it's a wonderful life.

Tina says: I'm going to ask something you don't want me to but as your friend, I have to.

Aggie says: I'm not dating and have no intention of starting now.

Tina says: That's not my question. I want you to be completely honest with me.

Aggie says: Ok. Why do I feel like I just put a stink bomb in Mr. Haley's class?

Tina says: Residual guilt. Now listen, and don't reply until I

---

tell you.

Aggie says: Ok! You're so bossy!

Tina says: I said no replying.

Tina says: Now, I'm worried about you. You graduated, planned to live in Yorktown, meet a great guy, or at least marry Mark Sakimo...

Aggie says: Oh, puhleeze!

Tina says: I'll come and sit on you! Shut up and listen. Instead you graduate, bury your sister, become an overnight mother with a GIL to boot, and then started renovating a house. All your dreams are sitting on a shelf getting very dusty. How are you handling that?

Tina says: That was a question. You can answer it.

Aggie says: I don't know how I'm handling it. I doubt that I am. I'm too busy worrying about diapers, Kenzie's new loose tooth, if I can afford the kitchen I want to put in, and if it's a waste, since I don't know how to cook anyway, if the GIL is going to show up tomorrow and create new havoc, or if I'm just tired and paranoid.

Tina says: How's the Bible?

Aggie says: It's an excellent book. I highly recommend regular and liberal infusions of it in any person's life. Imperative for Christians.

Tina says: Getting any of that stuff infused in you lately?

Aggie says: Would I still be sane if I wasn't?

Tina says: Are you still sane?

Aggie says: LOL. I may not be able to carry on a semi-adult conversation anymore, but I think I'm still sane — today.

Tina says: Prayer? How's your p-mail outbox?

Aggie says: Sigh. Overloaded. I think they're going to start bouncing back soon.

Tina says: God's server is big enough to handle it. You keep sending them and He'll keep answering. How are the hymns?

Aggie says: I think I sing "Angry Words" too much.

Tina says: Why do you say that?

Aggie says: I heard Kenzie singing it the other day. She sang all three verses AND imitated my exact tone when I grind out that "Love one another, THUS saith the SaviOR..." Ahem. It's not pretty.

Tina says: Can you do this Aggie?

Aggie says: I have to, Tina. Mom and Dad can't, and there just isn't anyone else.

Tina says: If there was someone else, would you want to keep going like this?

Aggie says: I know it sounds crazy, but this is kind of my life now. I really can't imagine doing anything else. I'd feel naked without someone pulling on my skirts.

Tina says: LOL... um, that just came out wrong.

Aggie says: You're telling me. You know what I mean though. It's not what I would have chosen, but it's what I have and thinking about "what ifs" isn't going to help.

Tina says: You always wanted to get married, have a house down the street from your parents, and run the History department at the High School. How can you possibly—

Aggie says: I can because I have to. Remember when I asked God to give me a 180 and make me know, without a doubt, if my goals took me out of what God's will for me? Well, I'd say this was a 180 if I've ever seen one. I have to trust that God knows what He's doing.

Tina says: I worry about you. It's a lot of work and responsibility.

Aggie says: Allie did it.

Tina says: And she had years to prepare.

Aggie says: Which makes me even more qualified to take over. I'm younger and have more energy. I'm not worn out from having eight children.

Tina says: Allie wasn't worn out and you know it.

Aggie says: Yeah, but I think sometimes she was. She had a lot to prove to people. I find myself doing the same thing. If you're tired, you don't want it to show. Someone is sure to make a comment on how hard it must be. Yeah, it's hard, but it gets old being reminded of it—especially when you've made yourself vulnerable and admitted it.

Tina says: Just take care of yourself. You won't be any good to those kids if you're worn out and in need of a padded room.

Aggie says: I'll remember.

Tina says: My pizza is here. I'd better go. See you later and don't stay up too late.

Aggie says: Nighters.

Tina says: Poofs.

9-1-1

Chapter Fourteen

Monday, June 17th

"Morning." Aggie jumped at the sound of his voice as Luke stepped around her, deposited a jar of grape juice in the fridge, and then climbed the stairs to Vannie's room without another word.

She shrugged and went back to filling bowls of cold cereal and adding slices of leftover watermelon to their plates. The children carried their meal to the far corners of the downstairs and out onto the porches. She knew she shouldn't allow it. If she wasn't careful, the children were going to lose every dish and utensil they owned. However, she was tired, anxious to finish the rooms upstairs, and ready for her morning cup of coffee, so she let it slide.

Half an hour after his arrival, Aggie hollered for the kids to bring back their dishes, grabbed two hot mugs of coffee and a plate of bagels, and climbed the stairs to see the progress in Vannie's room. Luke took the coffee gratefully, and a strange look crossed his face as he took his first sip.

"Is something wrong with it?"

"I was expecting coffee, not one of those imports from

Seattle. Whew!"

Aggie chuckled and handed over a cream cheese-slathered onion bagel. "I'll get some regular coffee next time I am in town. Meanwhile, have a bagel." Aggie surveyed the room and tried to ignore the question in her mind. "Looks like if things go as planned we can put one more coat on this tonight, and it's ready for moving in the day after tomorrow."

"Actually, you need to wait until Friday at the earliest. We really want these floors to cure well."

She ran her hand along the floor, feeling the glossy finish under her fingertips. "I really hoped—" Clamping her mouth shut, she stood abruptly.

"Aggie," Luke knew something was on her mind, "what's up? You have something to say, I can tell. Just talk to me." Luke had a sickening feeling that he was being fired. While the job wasn't going to pay well, he was eager to keep working on the old house. The money was better than nothing, and the personal satisfaction in seeing the house restored was invaluable to him. He remembered the children. Luke loved being around the children. How often did a job include a houseful of children to enjoy?

"I hate that!" Aggie's frustration replaced the thoughtful, contemplative expression previously shown on her face.

"What? What did I say?" Luke actually started putting the lids back on the paint and gathering his tools, but Aggie didn't notice.

"The way everyone always knows what I'm going to say before I say it. It's so maddening!"

Luke's laughter was infectious. Gasping between giggles, Aggie asked why they were laughing. Luke couldn't answer. Just as she regained some of her composure, Luke admitted he'd expected to be fired, sending her into fresh waves of giggles. "Who would have thought the proverbial pink slip could be so funny!"

While Luke applied the final coat of urethane to the floor, Aggie went back downstairs to find the scattered dishes. "All right, guys, I see four bowls, five plates, and two spoons! I want every dish in the house, yard, van, and anywhere else I haven't thought of, in five minutes. Spread the word and hustle!"

Kenzie and Tavish looked at her with odd expressions and took tentative steps toward the door. "You heard me! Find dishes," Aggie insisted.

She grabbed Ian from the playpen and carried him upstairs for a bath. The little boy hadn't been cleaned up after dinner the previous evening, and dirt seemed caked onto his face, hands, and knees. It dawned on her that the careful routines she'd kept in place at the Stuart home had dissolved like Jell-o in water the moment they'd moved to the Shambles.

Thanks to half a dozen interruptions, the water overfilled the tub, soaking the carpeting as she undressed Ian, and, seconds later, her voice wavered in obvious distress as she mopped up the soggy mess. "Shall we gather at the riiiiveerrr..." a tearful giggle escaped, "where the bathtub overfloooooowwws..."

"Aggie, have you considered that the bathroom up here might need to be the next thing you do?"

"I have," she called, flinging tears away from her eyes as she knelt, her knees squishing into the soggy carpet, "but I really think we need to get the kids in their rooms first. If nothing else, it'll quiet the GIL."

"GIL?"

"Geraldine Stuart. The grandmother-in-law. She'll be happier if she can walk in the house and not see beds everywhere." At Luke's face in the doorway, she smiled. "I have to try to make peace where I can."

"Why don't we plan what you want to do, so we can order anything we'll need and have it ready? If everything is here and ready to go, we won't have as many delays."

Aggie agreed, and pointed down the hallway. "I was wondering what you thought of a half bath down there in that linen closet. I think there's room for one of those little pedestal sinks, a toilet, and a shower stall. The kids could get ready for school much more quickly if we had more bathrooms."

True to his character, Luke disappeared down the hallway to inspect her idea. It wouldn't be easy, and it would be a little expensive, but with a piece of Laird's closet bumped out, they could put a full bathtub in there. He measured, played around some more, and measured again. It could be done.

"We'd have to get permits for that, but we can do it."

Aggie jumped at his voice in the bathroom door. "Oh! You scared me. Good. Are we talking dirt cheap, reasonable but a dent in the checking account, or pray we win the lottery expensive?"

"I think you're looking at a small dent, but a discernible one."

Wrapping Ian in a towel, Aggie stood and carried the boy out of the bathroom and started downstairs. "Good. Whatever has to be done to make it happen, let's do it."

"Aggie?" Luke waited for her to look back at him before he continued. "If Laird can handle a smaller closet, you could have a tub in there if you wanted."

"Even better. Do that."

He watched as she carried Ian downstairs, babbling to him about baths in rooms with tile floors and no more soggy carpets. Her admission that paying closer attention to the tub filling might make a difference brought a smile to his face. Just as he was about to call down to tease her, Aggie's voice rang out clearly. "I still only see six bowls! One of those is mine! How do I have seven forks and nine spoons? Where did all these glasses come from?"

He smiled and stepped into the bathroom to take measurements and saw the towels soaking up the water on the floor. The last inch of water trickled out of the tub, as if reluctant to leave. He'd have to snake that. Luke grabbed the towels and hung them over the shower rod, and then went into the twins' room to retrieve his large fan. There was no reason to leave that carpet soaked if he didn't have to.

By the time he left that night, Vannie's door was open, with the baby gate installed to keep little feet off the curing floor. The pungent scent of urethane hung in the air, and Aggie tried not to think about the effects of the fumes on the children's developing brains and prayed they wouldn't get "high" on them. The vanity stood polished and repaired in the twins' room, waiting for Friday as moving day. A new mattress, still wrapped in its plastic, leaned up against the wall. Vannie's boxes stood against the other wall with a "bed-in-a-bag" sitting on the floor, as though not quite a part of the group yet. The young girl had spent much of the afternoon carrying her things upstairs, leaning into the room, planning her layout, and wishing the days away until Friday.

Friday, June 21st

The house was in a state of excited confusion. After a long list of jobs to keep the smaller children occupied, Aggie, Vannie, and Luke climbed the stairs after breakfast to begin moving Vannie into her room. While the young girl carried her clothes and hung them in the closet, Aggie and Luke maneuvered the vanity out of the room next door and onto the wall between the two bay windows. It looked as though it'd been made for that spot.

Aggie tied a new cushion she'd purchased onto the bench, and shrugged at the unsatisfactory result. "Well, that looks terrible."

"If you tell me what kind of fabric you want, I'll have Mom get it and some foam, and we'll recover the bench for you." Luke spoke quietly as he examined the underside.

"You sew too?"

Laughing, Luke shook his head and pointed to the screws on the underside. "You just staple it down, screw it to the bench, and no one sees the staples."

Vannie and Luke exchanged amused glances as Aggie whipped out her ever-present pad of post it notes and scribbled something on one. She passed it to Luke and went downstairs to dismantle her bed. Laughing, Luke passed the note to Vannie before he folded it carefully and tucked it into his wallet. *"Buy some light green or blue fabric. Think blue like eggs or green like Granny Smith. Now I'm hungry. Thanks."*

"Aunt Aggie is one of a kind, isn't she, Luke?"

Nodding, Luke agreed. "Definitely. While I help your aunt with her bed, why don't you drag your rug in here and get it rolled out? It'll be easier to assemble the bed again without scratching the floor if that rug is down."

Luke arrived in the living room just in time to see the back of Aggie's wrought iron daybed fall and whack her on the head. Before he could ask if she was ok, another hymn burst forth as though propelled by sheer willpower. *"Oh, what peace we often forfeit, oh, what needless pain we bear..."xiii*

"All because you do not tarry, and wait for me to help you there." The filler was pathetic, and he knew it, but Aggie smiled regardless.

"I'm pretty sure that's not how it goes."

"You have a hymn for everything, don't you?" Luke pulled the back of the daybed away from her and started toward the stairs.

"Old Sunday school habit," she muttered as she grabbed the end pieces and hefted them clumsily.

Without a glance back, Luke called down the stairs, "Leave those for me, and grab the springs or the hardware. If you leave that hardware there, someone is going to help themselves to it, and we'll be in a pickle."

It irritated her that he was right. Why, she wasn't sure. Was it because she couldn't trust the children to leave things alone? Was it because he thought her too wimpy to handle the work? Was it because Ian had been up half the night wanting something to chew on, and nothing had satisfied him except for her knuckle? "Yeah, probably that," she muttered, and scooped the hardware into an empty box.

Upstairs, they reassembled the bed, finding it harder to

accomplish than Aggie's swift, but not quite painless, demolition. Several trips back and forth, looking for stray parts, were needed before they were ready to carry the mattress into the room. While Vannie pulled her new bedspread from the bag, Aggie stretched the sheets over the mattress and plumped her new pillows. Luke filled the upper shelves with Vannie's treasures as the girl pointed out where each thing went.

"Aghaooo!" Aggie looked up startled. Standing in the doorway, holding baby Ian, was William.

"I take it no one called me?" William looked both amused and irritated.

Luke glanced up and grimaced. "The phone? It was on the set; I know it because I put it on there myself. He couldn't *reach* it."

William said, "The call came in about two minutes ago, but I was nearby, so I volunteered. The dispatcher just said 'Another false alarm over at the old Ma—'" The officer clamped his mouth shut and looked suitably annoyed.

"Well, we're sorry, William. I have no idea how the baby could have called this time. I put that phone back on the set myself. It's become an obsession with me." Luke tried to be light hearted, but it was obvious that the deputy was no longer amused.

"Aggie, may I speak to you for a moment?" William's "request" was more like an order. Handing the babbling infant to Luke, William led Aggie downstairs and outside.

"Aggie, this has to stop. I may be forced to issue a citation regarding the inappropriate use of resources if you don't find a way to keep that child away from the telephone." He tried to keep his voice pleasant, but William knew that if the dispatcher mentioned it to the sheriff, he'd be in trouble.

"William, I don't know what you want from me. Where was the phone when you got here?" Aggie tried not to get upset. After all, he was just doing his job.

"Well, it appears to be back on the set, but the call was made, and we have to respond to *every* call."

"If it was on the set when Luke went upstairs, and it was on the set when you got here, then there is no way that the baby could possibly have called. *He can't reach it!*"

William was thoughtful. At last, he suggested that she keep the handset with her at all times. Someone was calling, and that had to stop. "Listen, Aggie, if some of the other guys get called out, they won't be as patient." He glanced around him at the mess in the kitchen, the unmade beds, and her mattress lying in the middle of the living room. "You might want to clean up a bit in here too. Not everyone has seen this room clean like I have."

Aggie's face fell. She started to reply, but William continued. "Look, I know it's hard, and you really are doing a good job. The children seem healthy and happy, and at least you haven't had accidents or anything. I just think you're in over your head with this and could use some help."

Weary, Aggie promised to try to do better. As she filled the kitchen sink with hot soapy water and loaded it with dishes, she told him about the work upstairs and invited him to see the progress. However, William refused, as if repulsed by the idea, and drove away. "I wonder what about me is so repugnant," she mused as she wiped the counter. "It's not like inheriting children is contagious or anything."

Aggie Says: TINA, COME HITHER!

Tina says: You rang?

Aggie says: He did it again.

Tina says: Who did what and to whom? My, that's an impressive sentence.

Aggie says: Ian. He called the sheriff again. William showed up very upset. He told me to clean the house up too.

Tina says: Ick. Tell him to mind his own business. Who does this creep think he is?

Aggie says: Oh, I think he's actually being kind — or trying to be. I just don't know where I am supposed to put things when there is nowhere to PUT IT.

Aggie says: We moved Vannie into her room and Laird's is almost done.

Tina says: WOOHOO!!! What birthday comes next?? Are you forgetting someone?

Aggie says: Let me look. Vannie said she put them all on the calendar for me. Next is Laird. Ian isn't until September.

Tina says: So what are you doing for Laird's birthday.

Aggie says: I have no clue.

Tina says: Boy you are a wealth of information today aren't you?

Aggie says: I am, aren't I? Did I tell you Kenzie and Ellie get their room next? They wanted pink and purple. Original aren't they?

Tina says: It'll make it easy to keep clean. Just let them have their fun.

Aggie says: I know. I just pictured dream bedrooms for everyone and somehow pink and purple doesn't seem very dreamy to me. It sounds like an explosion in a cotton candy machine.

Tina says: ROFLOL

Aggie says: I just have to figure out pictures and things. Furniture. What do I do for furniture?

Tina says: Is there room to cut bunks apart into two beds?

Aggie says: Ummm I think there would be room for two twin beds with the window between them, a bed table between the beds and the walls, and a small dresser on the wall by the door.

Tina says: They need a shelf, though. For their books, and special things.

Aggie says: What about between the beds?

Tina says: I saw a bookshelf in a catalog the other day. It had a peaked roof like a dollhouse. It was really cute!

Aggie says: OOOH!! I wonder if Luke could make that.

Tina says: I bet he could. He's done a lot around there so why not a simple shelf with a slanted roof! :)

Aggie says: True! I'll have to ask! Meanwhile, I'll do a Google search and see what I can find. Maybe I can order it.

Tina says: So, what about the twins' room... and Tavish and Ian... what are you doing in their rooms?

Aggie says: Oh, boy I'm so excited about the twins' rooms! Laird is making these headboards out of fence pickets. Luke showed him how to sand and paint them. I think he's going to do footboards out of the pickets too. I asked Luke to add shelves to the footboards so that they'd each have their own space within the room.

Tina says: Ok... so what are you doing with the colors?

Aggie says: Luke painted the room a light but bright sunny yellow and Vannie has been pounding a soaked rag with white paint all over it so it looks like sunshine through clouds. Then we're going to paint flowers growing up from the bottom. Big fat kindergarten retro type flowers are what I have in mind. Then, I bought bright pink, yellow, purple, green, blue, orange... etc plaid bedspreads and curtains. I saw the curtains and stuff first, and it gave us the idea for the room.

Tina says: OOH! I love this! And the boys?

Aggie says: No clue. Tavish doesn't care and Ian doesn't talk. I have to decide and I don't know. I was never a boy and didn't have brothers. The only reason Laird is getting a nautical look is because of the bed he wants with those big ropes.

Tina says: Baseball? Trains? Books? Travel? Jungle?

Aggie says: JUNGLE!!

Tina says: Just picture curtains and bedspreads with tigers on them, or just tiger skin looking fabric!

Aggie says: I like the tigers in the green leaves look. Oh, I can't wait to tell Tavish. I'll buy a safari hat to hang over the door. Oooh! And a big stuffed tiger for Ian!

Tina says: Well, it sounds like you figured that out easy enough!

Aggie says: Thanks to you! That covers everyone, doesn't it?

Tina says: Except for you. What are you doing for your room?

Aggie says: I have no clue. Maybe you can look when you get here and tell me what you think?

Tina says: You should have done yours first.

Aggie says: What would that teach the children when I tell them "you need put others first?"

Tina says: That's true. Oh, dear. Chinese is here. I have to go.

Aggie says: Ok, I need to get some sleep anyway.

Tina says: Poofs!

Aggie says: Poofs to you too!

DENTS & ACCIDENTS

Chapter Fifteen

Tuesday, June 25th

Aggie dropped the plate as the sound of breaking glass added percussion to the hymn she'd been singing. She scrubbed the dishes and sang "Whiter than Snow" at the top of her lungs as she worked, but the crash followed by tinkling came at just the wrong place. It seemed a bit incongruous to sing, "I see Thy blood flow," at the precise moment a window gave up its life for one child's pursuit of sling-shot excellence. Oh, Aggie knew what caused it, who was responsible, and her "give me patience, Lord" hymn was on her lips before she stepped into the broken glass at her feet.

"Um, Lord? Just want to put quick thanks in for prompting me to get the dishes done before I relaxed. I'd be needing some stitches right about now..." A new thought crossed her mind. "Then again, I might still be collapsed on the couch and would only have one glass mess to clean up. Couldn't you have let me be lazy this morning?"

The immense pile of washed dishes was only overshadowed by the even more enormous pile of unwashed ones. Aggie shrugged and grabbed the broom. "Ok, point taken."

"Talking to yourself again, Aunt Aggie?" Laird looked suitably penitent but tried to lighten the mood with a joke. It fell flat.

"Well, actually, I was asking the Lord how to deal with a kid who broke about thirteen rules in the space of about as many seconds."

With an expression that would one day melt the hearts of women, Laird shrugged. "Mom would have made me pay for the window. Does that help?"

"Well, somewhat. There's just one problem."

"What?" He no longer looked charming and irresistible. Now Laird looked positively nervous.

"You don't have any money. I haven't even started to consider allowances and things."

"Oh! Is that all? We have lots of money— in our bank accounts anyway. You could do an online transfer. That's what Mom always did."

Aggie passed Laird the broom and pointed to the plate fragments. "Clean that up. I need to sit."

"But, Aunt Aggie, I didn't break the plate—"

"By proxy, you did. Clean it up. I'll be back."

One day, Aggie would look back at her next move and shake her head. Today, however, it was all too much. She climbed the stairs and entered Laird's room, noting the irony of improving the room of the boy who had just destroyed part of another one. "Laird broke a window."

"Well, we were replacing the downstairs windows anyway." Luke wiped a drip from his roller onto his jeans and turned to Aggie. "I can do that when I'm done in here, if it's a standard size. Which one is it?"

"I don't know."

She looked lost, confused, and even a little helpless. It wasn't like her. "Well, I'll look at it soon and then see what has to be done. It'll be ok." He didn't know what else to say.

"What do I do about Laird?"

"What do you mean?"

Aggie tried again. "He knew he wasn't supposed to use that sling-shot near the house. I told him it had to be out in that field across the highway. He did it again. I can't let him get away with that, can I?" She almost sounded like she hoped Luke would say yes, and she knew it.

"I see. You're right. He can't get away with it."

"He says Allie would have made him pay for it."

A smirk appeared on Luke's face before he could turn to the wall and roll the paint on it. Aggie demanded to know what was so funny. "Well, not that I know anything about being a boy or anything, but it's been my experience that when a kid offers a consequence voluntarily, it's usually the one thing he doesn't care about." He loaded the roller again and then turned back to Aggie. "I'm not saying it's not true. I have no doubt that your sister was wise enough to require her children to make restitution when they ruined things. I'm just guessing there's more to it than that. I take it he has enough money to pay for a window? They can be expensive."

"I didn't know they had any, but apparently they have accounts in some bank. I have no idea *which* bank. I hope they know."

"I'm guessing it's the bank that you got about twelve statements from the other day. All were forwarded from your old address. You should change that with the bank, by the way." Luke rolled the last bit of the wall and stood away to examine his work.

"Oh. Yeah." She bit her lip. It wasn't the time to admit she had boxes of unopened mail, dating back to February. "So, if Laird was your son, what would you do?"

"How many times has this been a problem?"

She sank to the middle of the floor, pulled her knees to her chest, tucked her skirt around her ankles for modesty, laid her head on her knees, and sighed. "Since he found it in Doug's things."

Luke had decided what to suggest the moment he heard,

"found it," but Doug's name changed things. "Hmm. Do you want me to talk to him? I could tell him that he does have to pay for the window, as per your words, but maybe he needs a guy to talk to. Until you said Doug, I was going to suggest taking away the slingshot. Now I'm not so sure. I think maybe he needs that right now. I will tell him it goes if there's another problem, and I could require him to help me fix the window."

The tears still wet on her cheeks, Aggie's head slowly rose, and her eyes met Luke's. "Would you? Is that cheating?"

Silence was her only answer. Luke dropped the roller in the paint tray, pounded the lid back on the can of paint, and pocketed the funky hook-like thing he used to open the cans. Aggie's head dropped back to her knees. When a sniffle escaped before she could stop it, she cringed. How pathetic could she get?

Seconds later, she felt a hand on her head. "It's not cheating, Mibs. I'll go talk to him."

She sat there for several more minutes, until his words fully registered. "Mibs? What on earth are they, and what do they have to do with anything?" As she descended to the bottom of the stairs, she heard Luke talking to Laird on the porch. She leaned against the wall beside the door and listened, curious about what he would say.

"…needs your cooperation. She has enough to do, trying to keep the younger children in clothes, food, and out of trouble, to have to worry about something so easy to avoid. It's a two minute walk across an empty highway."

"I'm sorry, Luke. I didn't mean to shoot it. I was just check—"

"Laird. The rock didn't jump in the sling by itself. You may not have planned to release, but you made a foolish decision to risk that possibility. You're responsible for your actions."

Laird's defensiveness melted audibly. "You're right. I knew better. How much is that window going to cost me?"

"Which window is it?"

Misery crept into the boy's tone. "The dining room."

"Big or little?"

"Big." Misery melted into despair. "Expensive, huh?"

"Ca-ching."

Wednesday, June 26th

Aggie glanced around the downstairs, overwhelmed. Though the children's bedrooms were almost all completed, the furniture couldn't be carried upstairs until Sunday, at the earliest— assuming it didn't rain and keep the floor from curing properly. Aggie's room was also painted, and though she wanted to create a quiet hideaway, she decided that during the fall school days she'd have more time to work on it. For now, her new bed and an old highboy were all the furniture pieces that Aggie had to put in there anyway.

They planned to start the downstairs on Monday, as long as the weather stayed reasonably dry. It amazed her how much trouble rain outside could cause her inside. She stood in the doorway of the country kitchen and realized what Luke meant when he said it would have to be gutted. All food and dishes would have to be stored in another room, as well as prepared there. She was finally feeding the children real meals at regular times, and now it looked like they would be going back to frozen fare. The thought was depressing.

Luke had made himself quite indispensable. Aggie didn't know how she'd ever imagined that she could do all the work that had been accomplished by herself. Proverbs states that "Foolishness is bound up in the heart of a child," but Aggie wasn't sure that it didn't carry over to "no-longer-a-child-people" as well. Luke worked steadily on everything, and while Aggie was certain that he was being underpaid, her insecurity in spending money kept her from raising his bid prices.

"Luke?" Aggie stood in the living room after trying to find him. There was no way she could figure out where the man was. Aggie added another mental note to her endless list. *"Hook up the intercom."*

Luke sauntered into the room. "You need something?"

"Yep. I need you to tell me which room we're going to do first. I can't decide if we should save the kitchen for last, or do it first?"

Luke was frustratingly silent. What took the average person three seconds to say, took Luke thirty seconds to over a minute. It drove her crazy. Finally, he answered. "If you want to protect your furniture during the kitchen remodel, then I recommend that we get that out of the way first. It's a real bugaboo, but I think you'll be happiest with it finished."

Aggie waited. She had learned by now that if Luke's jaw clenched at the end of a sentence, he had more to say. Eventually, he continued. Just in time, too. Aggie was about to throttle the words out of him.

"I think that we need to set up a kitchen in the dining room. I can cut a hole in the wall and route the gas across to there, temporarily. That'll give you a stove. Then, we can put that big old desk you have out there, and cover it with some shower board to protect it and make it easy to clean. That'll give you a counter. You can use that nifty, built-in china cabinet for a pantry, and with the microwave there, all you have to worry about is washing dishes."

The silence came again. She could almost see the wheels turning. After a few more minutes, that seemed like hours, Aggie lost it. *"And?"* Hands on hips and eyes flashing, Aggie looked like Doris Day in *Calamity Jane.*

Poor Luke was confused. He looked at her, just before Aggie lost what was left of her patience, and asked, "Have I done something wrong?"

"Uh, no, I was just waiting for you to finish what you had to say." The sarcasm in her tone was unmistakable.

Before Luke could respond, a piercing scream came from the backyard. They ran outside in time to watch a goose egg swell to immense proportions on Tavish's head. Aggie's eyes registered fear, and her mouth went dry. She didn't know what to do. Vannie flew past her and into the house, only to dash back out with a bag of frozen peas and hand it to the boy. Tavish held the peas to his head very gingerly, as he sobbed in pain. Luke looked at the knot and turned to Kenzie. "Hey, Kenz, please go get us a dry washcloth."

After examining Tavish's eyes, and looking at the knot sticking out from the boy's temple, he turned to Aggie and said, "I think he needs to rest on the couch for a moment. Oh, and I have a suggestion for you."

Moments later, Aggie whizzed down the road with Tavish holding the peas against his head and moaning in pain. She was amazed. Luke had kept them calm and unaffected while he informed Aggie that he was concerned about a concussion. "I am sure you're fine, but let's have a doctor make that decision, ok, pal?" Tavish had smiled weakly at Luke and then climbed into his seat in the van.

Upon reaching the Urgent Care admittance desk, Aggie promptly passed out. All the stress and fear of the situation hit her hard, and down she went. The receptionist asked for Tavish's home number and called the house.

"May I speak to someone regarding," the woman glanced at the paper. "Um... Aggie Stuart." She read the paper more closely and corrected herself. "Oh, no... Milliken. Aggie Milliken? I need someone to give authorization for," She looked at the patient name slot and continued, "Tavish Stuart to be seen by a doctor."

Luke was confused. "Isn't Aggie there? How did Tavish get there if Aggie didn't make it?"

"Oh, she's here all right, but —"

Uncharacteristically, Luke interrupted. "May I speak to her please?"

"Just a moment; I'll wheel her over to the phone."

"*What!* Wait, what's going on?" Luke was past the point of calm and nearing panic. "What happened?"

"Miss Milliken had a moment of light headedness and

passed out, so we have her in a wheel chair. I'll get her."

"No. Never mind. I'll send my uncle over. Just make sure that she doesn't drive."

A cheerful and helpful nurse followed them into the cubicle, once Aggie became fully alert. "Well, hon, what happened to you?" Without the sincere expression on the nurse's face, her syrupy tone would have sounded contrived.

"I was walking past my brother, and he swung his bat and hit my head." The nurse looked concerned, and Aggie realized that she didn't know what happened.

"So, your brother hit you with his baseball bat? Was he mad at you?" The woman shot a disapproving look at Aggie.

"Oh, no! They were playing softball, and I was walking to the swing out back and didn't see them. Laird's probably pretty mad at himself." Embarrassment in Tavish's face and manner made him look dishonest.

"Didn't you see them playing? How could you just walk into the middle of a ball game?" Doubt and suspicion laced the nurse's words, and she surreptitiously pressed a buzzer on the wall. Aggie sighed. She knew they were in trouble now.

Tavish, unaware of the tension growing in the room, answered automatically. "Well, I wasn't watching where I was going. I was reading and looked up just in time to see the bat coming at me. I ducked, but I think that just kept me from getting it in the neck."

Aggie laughed. She couldn't help it. This was the boy's third accident stemming from walking while reading. "Tavish, I have to make it a rule now. You may *not* open your book if you are standing on your *feet*. Do you understand?"

Tavish sheepishly nodded. The nurse watched the exchange and then smiled. "Well, hon, I used to be real klutzy when I was your age, but it wasn't because I was reading. I didn't have a good excuse like that." She gave Aggie a knowing look. "I have to go stop the nurse from calling someone about the accident. You understand."

Relief washed Aggie's face, and she smiled. "I appreciate

it. Sorry to be a bother."

"I'll be right back. Happy to stop this one!" The nurse walked out of the room, and Aggie overheard her telling the receptionist to cancel the Social Services call. "I was premature— I remembered hearing about the house with all the kids and the 9-1-1 calls and jumped the gun. Tell Linda I am sorry for bothering her."

The doctor examined Tavish and determined that, while there was a concussion, there wasn't a reason to keep the boy overnight. With instructions to keep a close eye on the boy for the next couple of days, and a list of things to watch for, Zeke, a much stronger Aggie, and Tavish went home.

Deputy Markenson's cruiser drove up the driveway, and the children all raced out of the house and surrounded William, chattering about the day's excitement. Aggie's, "Oh, nooooo," sounded like a wail from a small child who found her favorite doll left out in the rain. "Who let the baby have the phone this time?"

Luke looked at Aggie and said, "Honestly, I had Ian with me the entire time you were gone. There is no way he could have called. The phone was in my tool belt."

Aggie sighed and followed the children outside, after instructing Tavish to stay on the couch and rest. Luke watched the little group for a few moments and then turned back to his project of converting the dining room into a makeshift kitchen. Had he known what was coming, he would have either followed the family out or jumped in his truck and driven home. Instead, he overheard Aggie talking to the deputy.

"How did that child call you *this* time?" William's face registered surprise, and Luke set his wrench back down and walked over to the window. "Ian was with Luke all afternoon, and Luke had the phone in his tool belt." Irritation was bubbling into fury. "Tell me how this happened. Is this just some joke you guys play on the new people? Are you going to tell me that he really hasn't been calling? I wouldn't sug—"

William held up his hand, and her words stopped mid-sentence. Aggie wondered how policemen did that. She couldn't stop a five year old for five seconds to hear herself think.

"No one called the station; I just heard about your accident when the clinic called—"

Aggie exploded. She wasn't prone to fits of temper, but even Aggie had her limits. The last four months had been difficult and stressful, and the idea that half the town knew her business was more than she could handle. She was used to the anonymity of larger towns, but this town was so small it seemed that they called a local officer to chitchat about their patients! "What happened to HIPPA anyway?" William, watching the storm brewing on Aggie's face, didn't understand the problem.

"That's it. This is an invasion of privacy. If you aren't here on official business, I think it is time that you go home. I don't need to offer you more fodder for your gossip mill, thank you very much!"

William held up his hand to silence her again, but Aggie erupted in a bigger ball of fury. "Your poor wife!" Confusion spread across William's face, and he started to speak, but Aggie continued her tirade. "Will you do this to your *wife* when you finally marry some unfortunate soul? Treat her like an errant car that must be stopped at your bidding? Boy, you have some nerve!"

Turning to the children, she ordered them back into the house to get ready for supper. She followed, but at the screen door, Aggie turned back to the shocked officer and pointed to his car. "Go make someone else miserable, and don't come back here, unless you have official business."

Luke was silent as Aggie ignored dinner and banged different things around trying to set up the pantry. Slowly, the thumps and bumps ceased, and Luke heard her humming

228

softly. He wasn't sure what song she was humming at first, but eventually she started singing the chorus softly. *"Love one another, thus saith the Savior. Children obey the Father's blest command..."* Luke heard her sniff and wondered what to do about it.

Minutes later, Aggie said in a very small voice, "I lost it, didn't I?"

Luke simply nodded. For once, his silence didn't annoy her. Aggie briefly wondered if it was because she was "all angered out," or if it was because she was grateful for not being lectured. They worked in companionable silence for a while, until Luke looked up at her and said, "Mibs, you need to apologize. I understand the strain you've been under, but it still doesn't make it right." Aggie's silent nod seemed to spur him on. "I think you'll feel better the sooner you take care of it. I was about to go home before this all happened, but if you need me to stay, I can." Aggie shook her head and went upstairs.

In Laird's room, she heard Luke's truck start up and pull away from the house. She spent the next thirty minutes getting herself right with her Lord. After calling her mother and getting advice on how to apologize, Aggie picked up the phone, and for the first time since Geraldine Stuart threatened her, Aggie called the sheriff's station and requested that Deputy William Markenson stop by her home. Having a few moments to herself, Aggie booted the computer and smiled as it logged into her messenger service.

Aggie says: You there? I really did it this time!
Tina says: Uh oh... what'd you do?
Aggie says: Well... You see... There was an accident and Tavish had to go to Urgent Care...
Tina says: What happened?
Aggie says: Well, the kid was reading and walking again...

Tina says: Hee hee… kid after my own heart.

Aggie says: Soooooo anyway, William heard about it from the clinic. Someone told him.

Tina says: And…

Aggie says: He came out here to see if everyone was ok.

Tina says: How kind of him! Makes you wonder who he really came to see!

Aggie says: Oh, PLEASE.

Tina says: So, why the histrionics?

Aggie says: I blew up at him. Badly.

Tina says: YOU?

Aggie says: We all have our limits.

Tina says: What I would have given to see that.

Aggie says: Hmmm. Well… it wasn't pretty.

Tina says: So… what happened.

Aggie says: Well, after I let him have it…

Tina says: For showing concern for you and your family…

Aggie says: More for my privacy being invaded and him playing traffic cop.

Tina says: Traffic cop?

Aggie says: He kept holding his hand in my face and trying to shut me up! I lost it.

Tina says: Uh oh…

Aggie says: You got it!

Tina says: You apologize?

Aggie says: I've got a call in now. Hopefully, he'll check his messages when he gets home. The girl at the desk was very helpful. :P

Aggie says: Whatever possessed me!?

Tina says: Hee hee… we all knew it'd happen someday. You never let anything ruffle you.

Aggie says: Yeah, well kids have unearthed many ruffled feathers in my house!

Tina says: Well, smooth them down, wash your face and put on your brightest smile and apologize. ASAP.

Aggie says: That's basically what Luke said.

Tina says: He's helping William? I've been picturing two testosterone-laden men fighting each other off like in that old Jane Wyman movie we liked about the three guys... remember?

Aggie says: Nope, far from it. I'm no Jane Wyman, that's for sure.

Tina says: Well, it's not a good time in your life for masculine interruptions.

Aggie says: AMEN to that one. I like having the support though. I can tell you that just knowing another pair of eyes is around helps.

Tina says: Well, I can understand that... Uh, oh!

Aggie says: What?

Tina says: Someone at the door, it's late, going to go. Love you, girl. Keep that upper lip nice and stiff! Hee hee.

Aggie says: Like it's coated in Julie's hairspray.

Tina says: Hee hee... nighters!

Aggie says: Nighters.

Getting the Point

Chapter Sixteen

Wednesday, June 26th

Wednesday, June 26th

William, still in a state of semi-shock, ducked back into his cruiser, and drove cautiously down the driveway, watching for darting children as he did. Mrs. Dyke was in clear view on her porch, and William sighed. He knew the grandmotherly woman could have overheard enough to provide a feast at whatever event the local gossips had planned. Should he assume "least said, soonest mended" or do damage control now? Slamming his fist on the steering wheel, he turned into her driveway. Damage control was necessary for Mrs. Dyke and her cronies.

The crunch of his tires on the gravel reminded him of his childhood. How many times had he run across the same gravel driveway as a boy? How often had his feet scattered the tiny rocks into the grass on his way to Mrs. Dyke's cookie jar and Mr. Dyke's stories from WWII? The memories were bittersweet, but William wouldn't trade them for anything.

"Hello, Mrs. Dyke. I thought I should stop in and say hi while I was in the vicinity." William's gaze always softened a tad when he saw the deepening lines on the woman's face. Winnie Dyke had seemed old when William was ten.

"William, you even talk like a policeman when you are *off* duty." Smiling, she patted the swing beside her. "Ok, son, its time you learned a few facts; you like facts. Not everyone appreciates being on the receiving end of your lawman stance." At William's bewildered look, she grinned and continued. "Son, being a policeman is so much a part of you, that you don't realize how often you treat people like they are wayward children caught toilet papering someone's house. It's time to learn to be an average Joe when you are off duty."

For what seemed like minutes, William stood in front of her and thought about her words. Understanding eventually dawned, and he sank wearily onto the swing's bench. They rocked in silence for a time, before William stood, gave the elderly woman a kiss on the forehead, and drove off into the night. He had much to think about and add to his prayer list.

Walking into his townhome, William began his nightly routine. He changed his clothes, fed his fish, gathered and sorted his mail, and then sat down at his computer. He paid the bills, checked his email, read the one blog he enjoyed, and shut off his laptop again.

That task done, William picked up his phone and activated his voice mail. He deleted three phone calls, making notes to return one from the station regarding Aggie and ignoring the other two. The last call startled him. The voice of Luke Sullivan filled his ear. "Uhh, William? This is Luke Sullivan. I've been working on Aggie's house—I'd— well, I'd like to talk to you for a few minutes if you have the time. Maybe coffee at Espresso Yourself? I'll be there at seven tomorrow morning, and— well— hope to see you, if you can make it. Well, thanks. Bye."

With the call to the station regarding Aggie forgotten, William sat in thought before flipping his phone shut. He turned out all the lights, crawled beneath the sheets of his perfectly made bed, and laying in the darkness, he prayed.

William's prayers were more formal and adult versions of his childhood, "Now I lay me down to sleep." With the blessings on everyone included, William ended his prayer and switched on his alarm. Remembering the coffee shop, he reset it for an hour earlier. Just before drifting off to sleep, William whispered his first spontaneous prayer in years. "Lord, help me know how to deal with Aggie. I am so lost."

Luke held the phone in hand a moment before hanging up. He'd considered making the call from the moment he heard the screen door slam shut and saw the pained look on William Markenson's face, but the decision hadn't been easy. He rarely interfered in other people's relationships; however, Markenson had asked that Luke tell him if the deputy could do anything to help make things easier for Aggie. He knew that William would not appreciate any interference, but it appeared to Luke that William was becoming more personally interested in Aggie. After an evening in deep prayer, he made the call.

Thursday, June 27th

Luke was at Espresso Yourself early the next morning, his worn Bible open to the book of James. He kept pondering the verse "he who knows the right thing to do, and does not do it, to him it is sin." By the time William arrived, Luke thought he knew what he wanted to say.

"Have a seat, Markenson. Can I order you anything? Juice, coffee?" William just looked over at the teenager behind the counter and nodded before turning to Luke.

"She'll take care of it, but thanks. I'd like you to tell me why we are here." William was not sure he wanted to hear what this handyman had to say, but the officer in him couldn't ignore the relational equivalent of a tip.

Luke was silent. With a steady gaze, he examined

William's face and then sighed. "Well, you aren't going to like what I have to say." The look on William's face almost stopped Luke before he could continue.

One of Luke's characteristic pauses drove William finally to say, "Spit it out, Sullivan," in a low but firm tone.

Luke smiled, and William decided to wait for Luke to get out whatever he had on his mind. "William, I am going to step out and tell you something. Aggie needs your friendship. She enjoys your friendship." Silence followed again, and William felt like shaking it out of him. "But, I have to tell you — well, I guess what I'm trying to say is, Aggie isn't a child. She doesn't appreciate being treated like one."

William started to speak, but Luke held up his hand. Shocked and indignant, he started to protest, but Luke continued. "Aggie felt exactly the same way, William. She didn't like being treated like a child any more than you did just now. And — well, you being filled in on her life probably didn't help. She's not used to a small town."

Lost in thought, William pushed his chair away from the table without a word. Before leaving, he started to speak, but Luke preempted him. "Look, Markenson, I know this was none of my business, but I had to say something, especially after you asked me to let you know if you could ever help. Aggie has a huge burden on her shoulders, and she's doing great. But, well, she can only handle so much, and I think it's our job, as Christian brothers, you know, to make sure we don't add to that burden." Luke sighed and then added, "Think what you will of me, but let's agree that Aggie needs our help. The only reason I called you was to try to help you see how you can help."

William grew increasingly angry at the thought of Luke interfering in his and Aggie's lives. The fact that he'd invited comment eluded him in his growing fury. He nodded curtly at Luke and pushed his way out the door, holding it for a businesswoman as he did. Unaccustomed to being corrected or advised, the officer didn't appreciate the interference. Deep down, however, William also suspected that he was bothered by the fact that Luke was probably right. What he couldn't decide, was why Luke was willing to help his friendship with Aggie. He'd been sure Luke had his own ideas about a so-called friendship with Aggie.

Aggie awoke wondering why William had never returned her call. It was after seven o'clock, but the house was silent, and everyone still slept soundly. Aggie climbed out of bed and wandered into the kitchen to make her favorite cup of coffee. She found the coffee open and spilled in the corner of the makeshift kitchen. With a weary sigh, Aggie poured a glass of iced tea and went out to sit on the porch. She wondered, yet again, if she'd ever have anything untouched and destroyed by meddling fingers.

As she drank in the beauty of the sunlight dancing across the lawn and reveled in the scent of alfalfa growing in the field across the road, visions of lovely wicker furniture and hanging plants for the porch flooded her mind with dreams of how things would be, and prayerfully soon. For now, she sat on a picnic bench that one of the children dragged out of the back shed. As she ran her fingers over the rough surface, she saw WJN carved into the wood and wondered who WJN had been. How long ago had he carved his, or was it her, initials in this bench, and why? Was it done idly and without thought, or was there purpose or perhaps rebellion in doing so? Did some little boy, long ago, carve his secret love's initials into the bench that now occupied a place on her porch?

Aggie heard the crunch of footsteps and saw Mrs. Dyke walking down her driveway toward her. It took the elderly woman some time to come, but Aggie sensed that she wouldn't want help. Not wanting to wake the children, Aggie just smiled and beckoned warmly. She dashed into the house and found a couch pillow to set down for the elderly woman.

"Good morning, Mrs. Dyke. So happy to see you today." Aggie hoped that she was telling the truth. She still hadn't decided if the elderly woman was friend or foe.

Mrs. Dyke looked at the glass of iced tea and smiled. "Out of coffee?"

Aggie laughed and nodded. "I would give anything for a real cup of French Crème, but this'll have to do." Mrs. Dyke smiled and then patted Aggie's knee.

"I am going to tell you something about young William. He feels bad about the way he acted yesterday, but he didn't know quite how to tell you. I am here to ask you to accept a dinner invitation with him next Friday night. Do you think you could forgive him enough to go?" The eager woman seemed impatient for an answer.

Aggie was flabbergasted. Opening her mouth and then closing it again, twice, Aggie answered. "I'd be happy to, I think. I just don't know who would watch the children... and, well, I guess I don't understand why he didn't ask me himself."

Mrs. Dyke smiled and appeared delighted. "Aggie, hon, it's hard for a man to say he's sorry. I think he just needs a bit of encouragement and help. Meanwhile, I'll watch the children if need be, but I bet old Zeke Sullivan would love to help that nephew of his watch them. I overheard him braggin' on those kids of yours just the other day."

Aggie hesitantly agreed and promised to let the older woman know if she needed sitting services. Looking down at her unsatisfactory iced tea, Aggie suddenly tossed it into the lilac bush and turned to her new friend. "Mrs. Dyke, were you serious when you said you would be willing to watch the children? I would really love some real coffee, and this just isn't cutting it." She paused to watch the older woman's face before continuing. "Would you mind if I ran to the store? Everyone is still asleep in there, and you'd likely just fall asleep from boredom, but I sure would appreciate it." She was almost holding her breath in anticipation. This was the first time in over four months that she might have a chance to do something *just* for her.

Shooed from the house, with instructions not to come back for a couple of hours, Aggie drove away, feeling both free and guilty at the same time. Mrs. Dyke sat on the sofa with a Jane Austen movie, snickering at the hidden jokes that so many of today's generation would miss. Aggie had the van windows down and the wind was doing a number on her hair, but she felt carefree and enjoyed the trip.

Driving toward the store, Aggie passed a little café. The name on the storefront made her smile. Interested, she turned back and parked out front. Someone had an imagination. Walking to the door, Aggie noticed Luke sitting at the corner window table, Bible laid out in front of him and intent on what he was reading. She watched him pause, take a couple of notes, and continue reading. A man tried coming out of the door and Aggie's startled "Pardon me," caused Luke to look up. He smiled and motioned her over, but Aggie ordered her coffee first.

"Morning, Luke. I am playing hooky!" Her bright smile and carefree expression were welcome changes from the past few weeks of strain and fatigue. She took a long drink of her coffee before continuing. "It's just eight, and I've already had a full day!"

Luke looked startled and checked his watch. The look of dismay on his face was comical. Beginning to apologize, Luke was silenced with Aggie's ringing laughter. "Luke, you are the first person I have ever heard of who lost track of time while reading the Bible as an excuse for being 'late' to work. Relax and enjoy yourself. The work'll wait. So, what are you reading?" She glanced around her, a look of blissful contentment on her face. "Oh, doesn't this place smell heavenly. I've missed writing college papers in my favorite coffee shop until all hours of the night."

The next thirty minutes were spent discussing James and contrasting his words with the Apostle Paul. They chatted over their very different styles of coffee like old friends. Luke saw a

239

deeper side to the sometimes-scatterbrained Aggie, and she saw his deep faith and struggles with accepting that he couldn't fix every problem that came along.

Luke seemed embarrassed to share his favorite verse with Aggie, but finally said, "I remember James chapter four where it says 'to him who knows the *right* thing to do and does not do it, to *him* it is sin' and I remind myself that if you know the *right* thing to do then it's ok to do something."

Aggie smiled and agreed. When nine o'clock rolled around, Aggie sighed. "I sure wish it was ten. I'd love to go have my hair washed and trimmed. It's looking so ratty these days. I just can't see expecting Mrs. Dyke to stay any longer."

Luke watched as Aggie looked critically at the ends of her hair. He couldn't see anything wrong with it but concluded that he'd never understood his sisters on this point, so why would Aggie be any different? Her sigh, combined the look of resignation and determination that set into her features, made him realize that she had probably not been able to do much of anything just for herself since assuming care of the children.

"Aggie, A Cut Above is open now. Go on over and then go get you some coffee for home. I'll go over and relieve Mrs. Dyke. I can do some work on the kitchen while the kids play." Silence followed. Aggie had learned to read Luke and realized that he wasn't finished. "Actually, maybe I'll scrape the outside trim while they play. It seems safer somehow. I'll take the phone with me too."

Aggie snickered inwardly but tried not to laugh. She couldn't tell if Luke was joking or not. His eyes were looking at the Bible in front of him, but he was almost too still. Finally, Aggie couldn't take any more suspense. She leaned way over the table and tried to peer at him. His head came up, and Aggie saw the twinkle in his eye. Trying not to spew her coffee into his face, Aggie choked it down, coughing and wheezing, until Luke pounded her back out of sheer desperation. The action, thoughtful though it was, didn't help, and Aggie finally begged him to stop.

Though she knew that she would have a *very* sore back the next day, Aggie laughed and joked with Luke all the way out to the curb. They parted company and went their own ways, each with a completely different project in mind. Aggie headed toward the hair salon, praying that they would have an opening for a walk-in. She reflected on her conversation with Luke and thanked the Lord again for friends who shared her faith.

Luke, on the other hand, drove away troubled, though unsure as to why. Shaking off the somber mood that threatened to overtake him, he stopped at the store, bought another jug of juice, drove to Aggie's place, and sent Mrs. Dyke home with profuse thanks. The woman had no doubt that she'd been a blessing when Luke was done thanking her for Aggie's sake.

Rounding up the children, he sent them all out back to play while he worked on scraping the trim. After a time, Luke noticed that Vannie was off by herself, swinging on the back porch swing. The poor girl looked exhausted. Wondering if he should do anything, Luke decided just to observe her for a while. The third time he heard Vannie snap at, and then send one of the twins away, Luke decided to talk to the girl.

"Vannie? Are you all right?" One of his characteristic pauses surfaced before Luke continued. "You don't seem to be quite yourself." He placed his hand on her shoulder and waited for her answer. The girl seemed near tears, but eventually she spoke.

"I'm ok, I guess. My stomach hurts— sort of. I have a headache too, and these guys won't leave me alone for even a second." Vannie's voice was irritated and tense.

Luke smiled down at the girl and gave her shoulder another squeeze. "Sweetheart, why don't you go lay down with a good book, and maybe take a Tylenol while you are at it." Vannie sniffed and nodded. Luke, noting how she seemed to walk slowly and listlessly, prayed.

Two hours later, Luke called the children in to wash up for lunch. Halfway through making sandwiches, he heard Vannie crying from upstairs and calling for Aggie. He started towards the stairs when Aggie came rushing in.

Aggie heard Vannie upstairs and ran up three steps at a time calling, "What's wrong? Where's Vannie? Why's she crying?" Luke smiled, despite his concern, and went back to praying and making sandwiches.

Aggie's cry brought him running to the stairs. "Luke, I'm taking her in. Something is terribly wrong." Sending Vannie out to the car, Aggie turned to Luke and whispered, "Please check the bathroom and make sure it's, well, clean. I don't want to frighten the children, but she has to be seen immediately. Something's wrong, Luke, the girl is—" Aggie's voice dropped to a low whisper in order to avoid frightening the nearby children, "she's bleeding!"

Turning away, Aggie grabbed her purse from the table where she'd dropped it and headed back out the door. Understanding dawned on Luke's face, and he called to Aggie. "Aggie, *think!*" but she just shook her head and rushed out the door. Luke's repetitive admonition to, "*Think, Aggie*" angered her, but she kept running. Just as she started to climb into the van, she looked up to see Luke shaking his head and calling again, "*Aggie, think!*"

Exasperation finally got the better of her, and she yelled as she tried to start the van, "I don't have *time* to *think!* I have to get her to the *clinic!*" With that, she started the van and tore down the driveway and onto the highway. Luke stood on the porch still shaking his head and wondering how long it would take for Aggie to realize the trouble.

Aggie tried to be calm and rational. Driving with one hand, she held Vannie's hand and prayed with the girl and then tried reassuring her. "I'm not a wise mother with lots of experience. You are probably just sick, and this is completely normal. For all I know, I have had some similar illness and just can't think of it right now. I just need to have you checked out in case it is serious, because...."

Sudden understanding hit Aggie like the proverbial ton of

bricks. "Ohhhhhhhh," was all that she managed to say. Vannie's silent sobs ceased, as she watched Aggie struggle between embarrassment and laughter.

"Vannie, honey, I think you are just fine. Um, well, this is pretty normal. Did your mother ever tell you about this happening sometime?"

The girl's clueless look answered Aggie before Vannie could speak. "Well, let's just go on to the clinic so that nurse that was so nice to Tavish can help me explain it. You'll be fine. Really."

Aggie's sudden calm manner seemed to reassure Vannie, and an hour later they enjoyed sundaes at the local ice cream shop, giggling like old friends. The nurse had been helpful, and Aggie showed her appreciation almost effusively. Vannie was just relieved to discover that she wasn't going to die of some horrible disease.

At the end of the day, Aggie realized that she and Vannie had broken some invisible barrier that had seemed to pervade their relationship from the beginning. They shared a secret, and it was a pretty special one. Vannie seemed to have forgotten that Luke was aware of it, and Aggie decided not to spoil things by reminding her.

She called her mother that night and recounted the story step-by-step. Mrs. Milliken laughed, until her husband had to take the phone, while she used her inhaler to breathe again. When she finally was able to come back to the phone, Aggie asked the one question that was on her mind. "Mom, Vannie's twelve, why didn't Allie tell her before now?"

"Well, honey, you and Allie were almost sixteen when you guys started, so Allie decided to make this a special turning thirteen kind of thing." Knowing Allie, Aggie knew this was not only likely but logical as well.

"What about school? I thought they taught this stuff in health classes!"

"It still requires parental consent. Allie preferred to handle these things herself."

Aggie said goodnight and decided to go have a chat with Tina. Before she could boot the computer, the phone rang. Aggie debated not answering. The idea that it could be William with exclusive details to Vannie's situation was discouraging. With a sigh, fear, and trepidation, Aggie answered.

"Aggie? It's Luke." Aggie said hello and waited. She knew he'd have to talk eventually. "How's Vannie? She doing all right? I just wanted to see how she's doing before I go to bed." Aggie smiled and sent a quick thank you via p-mail.

"She's sleeping well with ibuprofen and a heavy dose of chocolate. I told her that she could have all the chocolate she wants this week, and she didn't have to ask." Aggie smiled at the memory of Vannie's pleased face when she'd heard the news.

Luke sounded nervous as he spoke again. "Aggie, would you mind if I tell my mother what happened? With four daughters, somehow I think she'd relate." Aggie thought about it before agreeing.

"I just don't want it to get back to Vannie that you shared with anyone. She looks up to you, and I'd hate to break that trust. Please ask your mother to be discreet." Luke assured Aggie that his mother would understand and said goodnight.

Aggie says: Hey, you won't believe what I did today.
Tina says: Coming! Give me a second to pay the pizza guy.
Aggie says: Pizza again!
Aggie says: I'm talkin' to myself. How are you today, Aggie? Fine, Aggie, how are you? I'm doing great, thanks. Hey, did you hear what you did today, Aggie? No, I didn't. Well, your niece started her period, and you flipped out like she was dying and rushed her off to the clinic, praying that they could help her. No way, Aggie how could you be so blind. Oh, I don't know, maybe because I'm sleep deprived. Luke kept telling

you to think as if that does any good when you're in full panic mode. The good news is, she seems to have opened up a bit.*twiddles thumbs* *contemplates the meaning of life* *finds lint in her belly button* *gags*

Tina says: You didn't. Tell me you didn't. That poor girl!

Aggie says: I know. It was awful. I think I was so relieved that she was fine that I forgot to apologize too.

Tina says: Well, she'll understand even more, later.

Tina says: Did you say that she seemed to open up?

Aggie says: Not only that, but somehow, I think she almost likes it. That nurse said something right!

Tina says: Just think you only have to go through this, four more times.

Aggie says: :P Don't remind me.

Aggie says: I still have to apologize to William. He hasn't returned my call yet.

Tina says: Really? Hope he's not too upset!

Aggie says: I don't think so. He sent Mrs. Dyke over this morning to break the ice and invite me to dinner on Friday.

Tina says: REALLY? WOW. The FIRST DATE... oh, wait... it'll be your first date EVER won't it?

Aggie says: Yep. Hard to imagine going out at all, much less with someone you just gave a good old-fashioned tongue lashing to!

Tina says: Well, maybe you will get a chance to apologize Friday night. What are you going to wear?

Aggie says: Probably just a skirt and top. I didn't bring any of my good clothes when I came down here, and once I got here they seemed out of place. He'll just have to take me as I am.

Tina says: Well, be sure to wash your hair and dry it just before you go. It has such a great shine when you do that.

Aggie says: Well, I am not trying to impress him with how shiny my hair can be, but I am glad that Luke talked me into going to the salon this morning.

Tina says: Ohhhhhhhhhhh?

Aggie says: It's not as weird as it sounds, I simply mentioned how I wished I could get it cut... it was looking so raggedy... and he said that the place was open, so I should try it.

Tina says: uh huh. I see.

Aggie says: You know, today was a really good day when I look back on it. I got to see a deeper side of Luke, got an invitation to dinner, got to drink coffee in a café and have a hair wash, cut and style, got close to Vannie, and Luke doesn't seem to think I am a complete idiot, even after missing something so obvious!

Tina says: So, you have two men in your life. Which one do you like best?

Aggie says: Oh, they are both very good friends. I don't think either one has any real interest in me. Both are nice men though.

Tina says: Tell me about William.

Aggie says: Well, he's very tall.

Aggie says: He's pretty good looking. Kind of a modern version of Clark Gable meets a younger Harrison Ford.

Tina says: hee hee

Aggie says: Cari has him wrapped around her little pinky. He loves that child. Kenzie too.

Aggie says: He's a good officer, and I think, a Christian. That makes it nice. He sure can make me mad, though.

Aggie says: Have you ever seen me yell at anyone like I described?

Tina says: Nope, but there always has to be a first time.

Tina says: Tell me about Luke.

Aggie says: He's like the brother I always wanted. The children adore him. He knows so much about kids too.

Aggie says: He's done a great job on this house; he's working on the kitchen now.

Tina says: Did you figure out what he looks like?

Aggie says: Hmmmmmmm well…

Aggie says: I don't know! I think he's about, well I think he's shorter than William. Maybe dad's height?

Aggie says: That's probably it… He's pretty average I suppose.

Tina says: Eyes?

Aggie says: He can almost speak with his eyes. He has this habit though.

Tina says: oohhh???

Aggie says: Yeah, it takes him forever to spit out what he's trying to get at.

Aggie says: Honestly at first I was so insulting because I would say "and…" hoping to encourage him when he wasn't ready to talk. I just thought he was waiting for some kind of cue.

Tina says: eeeeekkkk…. That'd be frustrating!

Aggie says: Oh, it is!!!

Aggie says: All in all, they are both nice men.

Aggie says: Oh my, look it's after midnight! Ian will be up in like five hours! I have to get some sleep!

Tina says: Go to sleep, mama woman! And sleep well.

Aggie says: Thanks, you too.

Tina says: Nighters.

Aggie says: Night!

FIREWORKS

Chapter Seventeen

Saturday, June 29th

"Ok, guys, this is how it works. Laird, you scrape, Tavish you brush. For every board that you get done on each side of the house, I'll give you each two dollars. It's a lot of work, and it's worth more, but I don't expect you to do it perfectly. I just want the flakey parts scrubbed off so we can paint it again."

Aggie watched as Tavish started counting boards in his head. "What about the ones we can't reach?"

Aggie laughed at his exuberance. "Let's work on the ones you *can* reach right now, and then we'll see about the rest."

The boys, communicating silently with their eyes, grabbed the tools and attacked the house with gusto. While the other children played on the porch or in the yard, and Vannie read a book on the living room couch, Aggie washed the outside windows of the basement and first floor. Slowly, the "Shambles," as she affectionately named their house, was feeling like a home. Moving to Brant's Corners had created stability and added serenity to their lives. The children were happy and contented, and Aggie felt more confident in her role every day.

She'd often pictured her life as a single, maiden aunt, much as her mother's sisters had been, living alone in a little cottage, teaching history, and spoiling her nieces and nephews. She hadn't quite rejected the idea of marriage. She'd always hoped she'd find the right man, but she hadn't expected it either. Aggie had simply planned her life with what she thought she could predict. Inheriting Allie's children was most definitely not a part of her prescribed program, but she'd learned to enjoy it.

Splat! Aggie spun in place, looking for the culprit, just in time to see Laird dash around the side of the house. Grabbing the hose, Aggie took off in hot pursuit. She thought she heard a rustle as she reached the corner. Without looking, Aggie stuck her arm around the corner of the house and squeezed the pressure nozzle. The indignant roar that followed did *not* sound like Laird.

"What—" Aggie cautiously peeked out from her hiding place, her eyes wide with shock and dismay at the sight of William standing drenched next to a huge, overgrown lilac bush. "I um, well—" Aggie's apology was cut short almost before it began. With a stream of comments about "that Aggievating Aggie," William walked back to his car and drove away before she could follow.

Aggie clutched her sides and howled, unable to control her laughter. The picture of William standing in her yard with water dripping off of his hat brim and onto his nose was truly hilarious. From the corner of her eye, Aggie saw Luke laughing at her and realized that he'd witnessed the entire scene. Furthermore, Luke must have foreseen what was going to happen and just waited for it all to transpire! Without thinking twice, Aggie turned the hose on Luke and squeezed the nozzle.

A mammoth water fight ensued. To everyone's surprise, Ellie was the quickest and the sneakiest. Aggie made a mental note to remember to watch her when snowball season hit! That child would be dangerous with an arsenal of snow packed missiles.

Eventually, Aggie was surrounded. She stood smugly as seven children and an unrepentant Luke lined up in front of her holding water balloons, buckets, and glasses of water, ready to drench her. She raised her hose and squeezed while sweeping her arm in an arc to soak everyone at once. A tiny squirt spit from the nozzle, and then there was nothing.

Shock registered on her face— dismay. Slowly flattening herself against the house, Aggie began pleading for a drip-free outfit. First, she tried Luke. She wheedled and cajoled before finally trying to sound like a stern employer. Luke grinned as he tossed the entire bucket of water at her. Laird followed immediately with three balloons thrown in quick succession.

Aggie's tactics switched. Turning to Cari and Lorna, she tried to convince the girls to drown Luke, but failed. Cari triumphantly splattered her balloon on Aggie's knee, announcing that her shot was for William. Lorna followed suit. A barrage of balloons and buckets attacked her from every side. One balloon bounced off of Aggie's elbow and landed at her feet. She snatched it, and with a mischievous glint in her eye, stepped forward. The entire group dispersed in various directions, but Aggie had only one target in her sights.

Luke saw her determination and ducked behind the van. His goal was to leave her with the illusion of impending success without actually placing himself on the receiving end of her wrath. Carefully positioning himself, Luke stood with his back to Aggie's advances but watching every move reflected in the van's side mirror. As he saw her throw the balloon, he jumped aside and waited for the impending splat. Nothing happened. Puzzled, Luke turned to see where the balloon had fallen and almost immediately felt the sting of latex on his face and then the cool wetness of water soaking his shirt.

"Ha! Gotcha!" Aggie giggled and snorted gleefully.

"Well, this time. I demand a rematch!" Luke laughed so hard he could hardly breathe.

Aggie laughed again and then remembered something. "Did William just call me 'Aggievating?'"

Luke hesitated and then grinned. "Um, an appropriate term after the other night, wouldn't you say? With the Aggietude you had…"

"Aggietude!" Aggie pretended to be furious, while trying not to laugh.

"Yes, it was quite Agdorable…" Luke winked.

"Ok, ok, I get it. Enough is enough. Behave yourself!" Aggie chuckled again as Luke muttered something about being out of Aggieisms anyway.

Later that evening, Aggie picked up the phone and dialed William's phone number. Thanks to an eager-to-help Mrs. Dyke, Aggie now had his phone number and was able to call his home and apologize. When she reached his answering machine, Aggie was relieved. She left a short but heartfelt apology and replaced the phone in the charger.

William listened to the message just minutes later. "William, it's Aggie. I'm very sorry. Sorry for dousing you when I was trying to get Laird, but I'm even sorrier for losing my temper. Please forgive me. If I don't see you before, I'll see you Friday."

William racked his brains to remember why he would definitely see Aggie on Friday. With a shrug, he decided he'd show up Friday around noon and hope something would remind him why he was supposed to be there. For a few minutes, he pondered the damaging power of pride and then finally went to bed. It had been a very long, wet day.

Sunday, June 30th

"Now, before we pray for our upcoming meal, and in closing, I'd like to remind everyone that we have more than enough food; so please don't hesitate to stay for the picnic, even if you weren't prepared to share. We always take home leftovers; so stay and join the fun."

Marcus Vaughn smiled as he shook hands with the worshippers who filed out to the church's side lawn. "Aggie! How are you settling? I'm sorry we haven't made it out to your house yet to get to know you, but Myra made me promise that I'd get you to sit on our blanket, so we could become acquainted."

Aggie, shifting Ian from one hip to the other, accepted gratefully. She wasn't quite at home in the new congregation yet, and making friends would be a good start. She sent Vannie and Ellie to the van for the brownies and the huge salad they'd brought, Laird and Tavish walked over to the grocery store with William to buy sodas and ready-made potato salad, while the younger children hurried to the front lawn for games that the teenagers organized for them.

Myra Vaughn smiled and patted the blanket next to her. "Please, sit by me. I want to know all about you and your family. We've been so busy this summer, or we would have been over by now."

"Well, it's quite a mess anyway— Hey, William! Did you find the stuff? Do I owe you any money?"

"I found everything, and Laird has your change." William carried the bags of food and drinks over to the tables where a few of the women arranged them for him.

Myra watched the exchange and decided to try an experiment. "William, we have plenty of room here, would you like to join us?"

Laird coaxed Ian from the Vaughn's blanket to play with the other toddlers, and soon, the Vaughns, Aggie, and William were laughing and talking freely, while the children ate on tables nearby. Aggie learned that the Vaughns were fairly new to Brant's Corners themselves, and Marcus Vaughn still studied with Steven Connors of Christ Church in Rockland. "I've completed my basic seminary work, but I'm under Steven Connors for discipleship as a minister."

Aggie excitedly spoke of the services that she had participated in and the especially meaningful time of communion. "I loved how it wasn't rushed. It didn't drag or anything; we just really took our time and reveled in our fellowship with the Lord."

William listened intently, asked a few questions, and then grew thoughtful. As much as he loved the Lord and took his faith seriously, he'd never had the kind of intimate time with the Lord that Aggie had described. As he often did in circumstances like this, he wondered why he was consistently drawn to people who lived and felt things deeply. Personally, he never allowed himself to become intimately involved with anyone— including his Savior.

William pondered his spiritual and emotional deficiencies, heedless of the conversation around him, until he heard Myra say something to Aggie about her remodeling project and realized that he hadn't been paying attention. He watched as Aggie animatedly described her work on the house and the hours that Luke Sullivan was putting into it. Myra's next question unnerved him.

"Now, Mrs. Dyke said you bought the old Ma—"

William uncharacteristically interrupted the conversation. "Hey, is there any more of that potato salad left, Aggie? I'll go see. Would you like some?"

Myra and Marcus glanced at one another but said nothing. Aggie, distracted further as Vannie arrived at her side with a sleepy baby Ian, didn't even notice. By the time Aggie got him settled and sleeping in her lap, the conversation had shifted to the new family Bible study that Myra and Marcus were planning for Thursday nights.

"We'd start this Thursday, but we assume everyone will be at the lake to see the fireworks." Marcus pretended to be hurt, but the twinkle in his eyes gave him away.

"Are you going to the fireworks, Aggie?" Myra asked.

"I don't know. If I can manage to get everyone ready, and figure out how to get there before they're over, then I think so."

William smiled at sleeping Ian. "I'll come and drive you; you really should take the children. It's my year to have the day off, but I'll be half on duty when I'm there. We help out the Fairbury police force if we go. Carry radios, report problems, and things like that."

Neither Aggie nor William saw the look of interested curiosity pass between the minister and his wife. Aggie was enjoying the adult conversation, but Ian was heavy, and Cari and Lorna were showing a severe lack of afternoon rest. "I need to get these guys home. The twins need naps, and Ian is awfully heavy— dead weight, you know."

William stood and lifted Ian from Aggie's arms. Automatically, Aggie called for the rest of the children. She waved goodbye to the Vaughns and several other families before sauntering to the van. A few speculative glances were sent their way as William helped Aggie load up the children and followed them home.

Thursday, July 4ᵗʰ

William's alarm played its regularly scheduled and digitized rendition of *Taps* early the following Thursday morning. Not something the no-nonsense officer would buy himself, the clock was one of his prized possessions. A gift from a few of his fellow Marines upon the completion of boot camp, it had traveled all over the world with William and then back to Brant's Corners, where it faithfully bugled him out of bed each morning with its ironic tune of death.

After a restless night, of little sleep, William dragged himself from his bed and into the shower. Anyone watching would have assumed he was on autopilot as he moved mechanically through a morning routine. Bleary-eyed, he shaved and dressed, and though the ritual seemed set in stone, his routine was jumbled. He wasn't hungry and therefore, didn't eat, his coffee wasn't ready yet, so he'd have to pick some up at Espresso Yourself, and seven hours of tossing and turning would have to suffice for exercise. He was too exhausted to consider attempting his regular morning workout.

Mrs. Dyke had summoned him to her home, and he was curious enough to drive over there early and find out what the elderly woman had up her sleeve, or at least in her apron pocket.

The crunch of his wheels on the driveway brought Mrs. Dyke to the door, spatula in hand. "I have eggs, biscuits, and gravy all ready. The orange juice is still chilling in the icebox. Why don't you pour us some?"

William worked in relative silence with Mrs. Dyke, until time for grace. With bowed heads, William recited the oft-prayed meal blessing taught him by Mr. Dyke many years ago. "Heavenly Father, thank You for the food prepared for us. Sanctify it for our body's nourishment. In Jesus' name, amen."

Wise and wily, Mrs. Dyke waited until William had a full mouth before she spoke. "William, you have a date tomorrow evening. Seven o'clock sharp. Aggie'll be waiting; so don't be late. Gives a bad impression, you know." She smiled at him until she saw him swallow, then put a fork full of food in her mouth.

With more effort than he ever imagined possible, William managed not to choke on his food. Upon Mrs. Dyke's announcement, the man was ready to do battle. Had Aggie *really* asked him to go to dinner via *Mrs. Dyke?* Furthermore, had the traitorous old woman accepted for him? The idea was inconceivable. Wasn't it? This must be what Aggie meant by "see you Friday." The audacity!

William finally calmed himself enough to try to sort out the situation. "Mrs. Dyke, just when did Aggie suggest this?"

"Oh, son, *Aggie* didn't suggest it; I did. I asked her for you, and she accepted. By the way, if you stand her up out of anger at me, you'll really look like a fool. I suggest you just realize that I know what I'm doing and make the best of it."

He started to speak, but Mrs. Dyke cut him off with an afterthought. "Oh, and William, make sure you apologize. You really were quite imperious the other day. It's a wonder that she agreed to go. If she didn't feel so badly about losing her temper, I doubt that she would have accepted."

Again, William started to speak, but Mrs. Dyke preempted him. "I wonder why that girl hasn't been snapped up before now. William, if you aren't careful, that young man Luke will see what you seem too blind to see; and I think you might regret it."

William rose, rinsed his plate and glass in the sink as he'd been taught as a young boy, kissed Mrs. Dyke's cheek, and left without saying a word. The awkwardness of being with Aggie at the lake tonight with this deception hanging between them made him uncomfortable. As he contemplated his dilemma, a call came over his scanner, and when William heard the address, he quickly turned his car around and drove back to Aggie's. On duty or not, he had experience with this one.

It appeared to William as though Geraldine Stuart was determined to upstage the fireworks show. He stood back and allowed the on-duty deputies to try to reason with her but didn't expect much success. William looked everywhere for the children, but they and the van were nowhere in sight. When he finally spotted Aggie near the side of the house, he went to speak to her.

"Hey, Lisa." William greeted the officer talking with Aggie.

"Markenson, aren't you off today?" The young rookie, fresh from the academy, fought the temptation to flirt. Aggie would have found it comical in a normal situation. As it was, she was more concerned with controlling the nearly overwhelming urge to give the "GIL" a verbal thrashing.

"I know Aggie and have dealt with Mrs. Stuart in the past."

"Well, I don't know why the woman isn't taking the hint. Some guy was here, but he just packed up the kids and drove off. Creighton said it was ok."

William nodded. "She has full custody, and the grandmother doesn't have legal visitation. Actually, I thought you had a restraining order, Aggie."

"She doesn't. We asked." The young deputy was obviously disgusted.

"I didn't want the hassle of court, and I was afraid they'd drag the children into it." Her face drooped visibly. "I guess I hoped she would leave me alone." Aggie sighed.

When the deputies escorted Geraldine Stuart and her shadow of a husband off of the property, Aggie and William sat on the porch and waited for Luke to return with the children. "He wasn't even working today. He drove up just seconds after she did, packed them up, and left. I don't even know why he was here."

Her fingers lightly traced the edge of a bolt on the old picnic bench. William moved across from Aggie, leaning over the railing, watching her. After a while, he asked the question that seemed, in his professional opinion, to be the ultimate solution. "Have you considered that if you let her spend time with the children, this might not happen? Is it that important that you have them all to yourself?"

Aggie sighed and pulled a photocopied letter from her pocket, handing it to him. William read the letter carefully and then looked up at her. "I guess this answers that question."

"Do you think they were paranoid? She wasn't like this before I was awarded guardianship. Intense — oh yeah! But she wasn't out of control like she is when she's here. I don't understand the change. It's like she lost control of her world, so she lost control of herself or something." Aggie's heart felt tied in strangling, emotional knots.

"I think that Doug probably knew what is best regarding his mother. Most men don't decide that their mothers can't be around their children, unless it's necessary. We just don't rock boats that we can ignore." William's words were spoken intently — almost fiercely. "There are exceptions, of course. I know that. But, in my experience, women are more likely to create this kind of situation. Your brother-in-law had a childhood that some would consider abusive." Again, the words were nearly forced between clenched teeth.

Aggie wondered about his attitude but was too concerned about the situation at hand to question him. With a heavy heart, she decided to file the paperwork for the restraining order and questioned William about the particulars. As William explained the process, she saw him relax slowly but visibly.

After several minutes of silence, Aggie ran her fingers along the letters carved into the rough bench. "I wonder who WJN is? I wish I could just travel back to when they were here. It must have been such an innocent time. No ugly scenes with grandmothers—"

"Don't be so sure." William's harsh tone stunned her. She decided to change the subject and ask about the fireworks, but he pushed himself away from the porch, walked over to his midnight blue corvette, and climbed into the low seat. Driving up to the porch, he rolled down the passenger window and said, "I'll be here tomorrow at six. Does that sound ok with you?"

Aggie nodded absently and watched, confused, as he drove down the drive and onto the street. Did that mean he'd changed his mind about helping her find the fireworks display that evening? She considered William's attitude and words, but before she could give any serious thought to it, Luke drove in with a van full of laughing children. Aggie smiled from her perch on the porch as they all spilled from the van and shared the goofy stories and songs that they'd enjoyed with their impromptu chauffeur.

Laird sat next to her on the bench and waited for the right moment. "Is Grandmother ok?"

"I don't know, Laird. I'd love to be able to trust her enough to invite her to visit, but with the way she does things and what your father instructed—"

The boy seemed to lose interest in the conversation almost immediately. Aggie wondered if she'd hurt him by sending his grandmother away, but a few minutes later, he returned and laid his hand on her shoulder. "Aunt Aggie, I don't know if

Vannie or Mom told you, but Dad didn't let Grandmother visit us at the old house very often. I overheard him tell Mom once that they needed to keep visits to public places as often as possible. I didn't hear why, but if Dad said that about his own mother, then I think that's why he chose you to take care of us. He knew you'd do whatever he said was best."

Without waiting for a response, Laird raced down the steps and called, "Counting to fifty, anyone I see when I'm done is it!"

Luke sat beside her, holding a cup of iced coffee with a huge dollop of whipped cream on top out to her. Aggie laughed. "You hold that like it's a peace offering or something."

"It is. I offer you peace and quiet from overly intrusive grandparents, and you should know, we prayed that she'd relax and become reasonable."

"I'm not sure it's a good idea to put those ideas in the children's heads." Irritation grew slowly in Aggie's heart. The last thing she needed was a large crop of bad attitudes to harvest and burn.

"That came from Tavish. Vannie prayed that her grandparents would find Jesus and that Jesus would take away the anger and pain that makes her act so strangely."

Curious, Aggie asked about Kenzie. "Did she pray too? I think this is really hurting her the most."

"She prayed that God would take away all the mean grandmothers in the world and replace them with nice ones that have round squishy laps, bake cookies, and tell stories about the olden days when they were friends with Laura Ingalls." The smirk on Luke's face nearly sent Aggie over the edge.

"You're kidding."

"Not a bit. I don't know where that came from, but I wrote it down word for word so that I wouldn't forget it. My mother would insist it go in the child's scrapbook."

"Scrapbook! Who has time for scrapbooks! I've hardly

taken a picture in six months!"

"Well, I'd suggest you start now. Teach the older children how to use and care for your camera, but get pictures. You can't get these days back again."

"Since when," she questioned with just a hint of derision in her voice, "does a man care about pictures or a scrapbook?"

"Since he was brought up in a house with four sisters and a very feminine mother. She taught me that there is value in memories — and that it isn't specifically a feminine accomplishment."

Sighing, Aggie stood, brushed her hands together, and glanced around the yard where the children squealed as they raced to the largest oak tree for safety. "Why did you come this morning? I was just about to call Zeke when your truck rolled in."

"I realized you guys might want to go out to the lake for fireworks and thought I'd ask."

Her first inclination was to accept gratefully, and if William arrived, he'd just have to meet them there. From the way he'd acted, she was quite certain she didn't have an escort to the lake or the fireworks. However, the idea of going at all suddenly made her very weary. "You know, I really appreciate it. I was going to say yes, but I think I'll go into town and buy fireworks at one of those stands instead. The idea of a late night like that is just too much for me right now."

Luke pushed himself away from the porch railing and pulled the familiar notepad from his pocket. "Ok, what do you want? I'll go get them for you while you make the kids some brunch. They were complaining about missing breakfast while we were gone, but I didn't know if you had something fixed already or not, so I just got them apples to tide them over."

"I don't know what I want. Just buy one of those big packages and make sure there are lots of sparklers." She hurried inside for her purse and returned quickly. "Oh, by the way, would you mind grabbing some root beer and ice cream? We'll have floats for dessert. With the watermelon I got at that fruit stand, it'll feel very Fourth of July-ie."

"July-ie?"

She grinned. "Yes, that's right. July-ie."

Tina says: Happy Independence Day to you, Happy Independence Day to you...

Aggie says: Yeah, yeah. Stuff it.

Tina says: Thanks. I was getting tired of typing it already.

Aggie says: Did you see the fireworks?

Tina says: Yep. Saw your parents there.

Aggie says: How did Mom look?

Tina says: She stayed almost the whole time, so that's good, isn't it?

Aggie says: Hmmm... as long as she's not trying to be self-sacrificing, it's very good. I'll go for the hopeful approach.

Tina says: Did you guys go see anything spectacular? Didn't you say something about fireworks over a lake?

Aggie says: Nope. After the GIL showed up...

Tina says: Will that woman never learn?

Aggie says: You'd think. After that, I just didn't have the strength to think about it all, so I sent Luke for fireworks and decided to stay home.

Tina says: Not to add to your burden or anything, but you can't hole up in that house and never leave. Those kids need to have experiences outside their own four walls.

Aggie says: Well, I've got an idea. You come take them for these experiences. I'm doing good to give them the experience of food, clean clothes, and a roof over their head.

Tina says: And for now, that's good. Just don't let yourself become a recluse because it's easier.

Aggie says: I hardly think missing one outing qualifies me as a hermit.

Tina says: Don't get your panties all knotted. I'm just saying that it'd be easy to do, and I want you to think of it when

---

you're tempted.

Aggie says: Gotcha.

Tina says: You're taking offense when you know I'm not trying to attack you.

Aggie says: I'm sorry, Tina. I'm tired, I'm sick to death of this woman affecting our lives like this, and I haven't had more than two or three hours to myself in months. I can't go to the bathroom without someone asking if they can have or do something.

Tina says: I know. You're doing a great job, you know that?

Aggie says: I can't even take them anywhere without someone giving me advice on what I should do next. Get them into activities, they need music lessons, they need time with kids their own age, they need men in their lives...

Tina says: And then your friend gets on and gives it to you via cyber reproof.

Aggie says: Sigh. More like that faithful wound thingie that I never did like very much.

Tina says: Maybe one of the guys would volunteer to help. A zoo trip or the aquarium or something.

Aggie says: I'll wait and you can go with me. If it's so important to you. ;)

Tina says: You're typing very slowly. Go to bed.

Aggie says: I should. Ian will be up sooner than later.

Tina says: We're good?

Aggie says: Always good. Thanks, Tina.

Tina says: *poofs*

Aggie says: Poof!

DATE WITH DISASTER

Chapter Eighteen

Friday, July 5th

It was nearly five o'clock before William realized that he hadn't made reservations for dinner. After spending twenty minutes calling every decent restaurant in a thirty-mile radius, he finally decided to take Aggie to the local diner and forget trying to pretend that this was even remotely a real date. The evening wasn't his idea anyway, and William Markenson was *not* prepared to consider any kind of romantic entanglement. For that matter, he was clueless as to how one romanced a "mother" of eight, even if he was interested— which, he reminded himself, he was not.

Aggie spent the afternoon torn between anticipation of finally clearing the air and nervousness over the date aspect of the evening. Neither Aggie nor Allie dated in high school or college. They'd spent those years on group outings with friends but had always considered pairing off as shopping before you were prepared to commit to the purchase. It was a waste of time even if you did manage to find someone perfect. Allie met

Doug during her last college semester. Both of them were volunteers on a Spring Break mission with their respective churches, and by the end of the week, they were almost inseparable. At the close of the semester, wedding invitations were mailed to their friends and family, and a June wedding followed.

Over thirteen years later, Aggie dressed for what was, essentially, her first date. Vannie lay on her bed watching as she brushed her long hair until it shone. "Aunt Aggie, do you think someone like Luke, or Deputy Markenson will ever want to take *me* to dinner?"

Aggie looked amused, but asked seriously, "Why wouldn't they?"

"In every book I've ever read, no one likes red or frizzy hair. Mine is both. I'm not beautiful or brilliant, so why would anyone want to go out with me?"

Aggie paused and considered her reply before answering. "Vannie, honey, look at me. First, I've always loved your red curls. They are just beautiful, and you should be proud of them. Furthermore, I am not exactly what you'd call drop-dead gorgeous. To tell the truth, while some women need their beauty sleep— me, I need a coma. My hair is plain old brown, and while I certainly wasn't a dunce, I didn't manage the stellar grades that your mother did. This isn't the first time I've been asked out anywhere, but it is the first time I've accepted, and I still don't know if I am excited or dreading the whole thing." She prayed for wisdom in what to say before continuing. "But this I know; if God brings a man into your life someday, it wouldn't matter if you looked like a gnarled old witch from a children's fairy tale, for him, you'd seem perfect." Aggie paused before choking back tears and saying, "Well, that's what your mother told me while I laid on her bed not much younger than you are and wondered if anyone would ever want to marry me. She was trying on her veil and debating the wisdom of the hairstyle she'd chosen for her wedding the next morning. I think she'd want you to know that."

Aunt and niece sat and talked about relationships, attraction, and the wisdom in saving your love and affection for the man who will commit to love and cherish you as long as he lives. Another facet to their relationship was forged while Aggie debated between shoes, skirts, and blouses. At last, they heard Zeke and Luke come in. They raced downstairs and jumped into the bedlam that began as Zeke chased Cari and Lorna around the room snapping and growling. Aggie smiled as she realized that Mrs. Dyke had been absolutely correct; Zeke and Luke were the perfect pair to watch her children.

Shortly after Luke and "Uncle Zeke" arrived, the children all gathered around the large TV, waiting for the beginning of a musical and for Zeke's semi-famous stovetop-popped popcorn. Aggie hadn't even realized that people popped it that way anymore, but she snitched a handful from his bowl as she walked by on her way out to meet William on the steps. Somehow, the idea of his coming in with Luke and Zeke there seemed awkward.

The drive to Maizy's Diner was miserable. Aggie tried every topic of conversation she could imagine but to no avail. Her compliment of his car earned her a grunted, "Thanks." The story she tried to share about Cari's surprising horror of sparklers was met with a frown and a rebuke. "Those things are dangerous. They aren't for children." Root beer floats were disgusting, Mrs. Dyke was a busybody, and eventually, she quit trying.

William and Aggie sat in an awkward silence at the back corner of the half-empty diner. The friendly waitress tried to banter casually with them in the same way she did with all of her customers, until Aggie shook her head, signaling the middle-aged woman should leave. Taking a deep breath, Aggie spoke. "William? Have you had a bad day?"

William's eyes, if she looked closely, seemed a little cold — angry even. "I've had a pretty rough few days, thank you." His entire demeanor spoke volumes. He wasn't happy, he didn't want to talk, and furthermore, Aggie was to blame. Aggie had no doubt of the source of his misery, but she couldn't understand how she was to blame.

"Well, I am sorry. I guess there won't be a *good* time to apologize personally for my outburst the other day, so I'll say it now. I lost my temper. I know it was wrong, and I hope you'll forgive me." Misery etched itself in Aggie's face as she spoke. Had William not been so full of his own anger, he might have seen how painful the situation was for her. At the least, he would have accepted her apology. Instead, he flicked the carefully folded straw wrapper off the table and frowned as it landed on the floor several feet from them. Irritated, he jerked himself from the booth and retrieved it.

They ate in silence. Every bite of her chicken fried steak stuck in her throat and tasted like cardboard. People came from Rockland to eat Ernie's chicken fried steak, but Aggie hoped never to touch the stuff again. Dessert wasn't an option. Despite their waitress' urging to try the cherry pie a la mode, both of them snapped, "No, thank you," almost before she finished asking.

William paid for the meal, and then escorted her to the car, much like he would someone he'd just arrested, one hand steering her arm and putting the other on her head to prevent it from hitting the frame. She'd have laughed if she wasn't so miserable. On top of the nightmarish meal, his lack of acceptance of her apology left her frustrated and hurt— uncertain how to try to heal the breach between them.

Half-way home, William spoke. "Aggie, I guess I owe you an apology." He still sounded angry, not apologetic. "Mrs. Dyke instigated this whole dinner and then told me about it yesterday morning. I didn't appreciate her interference and took it out on you. I'm sorry." The tone of finality would have been comical if Aggie hadn't been so mortified.

"This wasn't your idea? Aggie was almost speechless. Almost. William nodded and started to speak, but Aggie continued. "I don't blame you for being irritated at her. She had no business sticking her nose in our problems. I was rude and offensive and had no business yelling like I did, but that doesn't give my neighbor license to interfere. I am *still* sorry. I am, but I am now almost as irritated with you as I was the other day." Aggie pulled a tissue out of her purse and emptied the contents of her overloaded nose into it.

William's face showed utter confusion. Aggie's irritation almost got the better of her, but she managed to keep her voice calm and her emotions in check. "William, you have spent this entire evening fuming at me, when I am not the one to blame. I did not invite you to this dinner against your will, and I don't appreciate being the one to take the brunt of your anger and frustration. Take it out on someone else next time."

The enormity of William's wrong hit him like a kick to the gut. For a man accustomed to being right or presumed right, in both his career and his personality, it was particularly difficult to accept fault and confess it. He later wondered how he'd managed at all, but somehow he choked out an apology and plea for forgiveness. His discomfort, and the obvious lack of apologetic experience, made the sincerity of it even more evident.

"Of course, you're forgiven. It's over. Let's just pretend tonight didn't happen, ok?" She prayed he'd agree readily.

William smiled for the first time all evening. "Definitely. We could retry the dinner too. This time I promise not to forget to make reservations." William's invitation was almost an order, but Aggie was beginning to understand how to read him better and realized how difficult it was for him to offer. He'd just made himself vulnerable when he had riled her so thoroughly and recently. Aggie didn't know how to respond. In the short time that they'd spent together, Aggie realized that she wasn't ready to consider a dating relationship. Maybe she wouldn't ever; she wasn't sure. Aggie just knew that at this point in her life, she wasn't ready.

"William, I appreciate the invitation, honestly. This has nothing to do with this evening or anything, but, well— I just don't think I am ready to date or anything like that. I don't have time to focus on anything but learning to be a mom right now." Aggie paused and took a deep breath. "I'd love to have you visit. Watch an old movie with us; help us paint a wall..." She winked and then hurried on before he could interject anything. "I would rather we became better friends, without the trappings of the whole going out thing. If something did happen to develop, then fine, but I'd like to become better friends first." Aggie prayed her words weren't offensive as the seconds ticked into minutes.

Thankfully, William seemed relieved. He smiled and released a very deep sigh. "Aggie, that's the best idea I've heard in days. I'd love to spend time with you and the children." He pulled into the driveway and parked in front of the porch.

Aggie smiled, but before she could speak, William asked wearily, "Is Sullivan *always* here? I think I'd rather make one new friend at a time."

Aggie laughed as she climbed out of the vehicle. Leaning back inside through the window, she winked at him again and said, "Luke leaves by six and usually isn't here on Sundays. He mentioned being gone for a week or two soon too." With that, she waved and skipped up the porch steps and into the house.

William watched her go inside and realized, despite her words, Aggie was upset. Putting the car in gear, William drove away as he mentally kicked himself into unconsciousness. He had taken an evening that could have been a wonderful time to get to know an unusual young woman and turned it into a sulk-fest. He thought of Marcus Vaughn's words on Sunday about intimate relationships with the Lord and turned his car around. He'd go have a talk with Marcus. It was time to start tearing down the walls he'd erected in his life.

Luke turned off the movie and started shooing children to bed, with orders for pajamas and clean teeth. Zeke, still seated on the couch, was deep in thought and absently playing with Ian. Luke scooped up the little tyke and smiled ruefully at his uncle. "Uncle Zeke, are you seeing what I see every day?"

Zeke nodded. "These children haven't grieved right. They are wound up tighter than an over-tuned fiddle. Any time now, one of them is gonna snap, and then there's gonna be trouble, son." The old man looked thoughtful. "For now, I think it's time that Aggie deals with her own grief. She had to jump in here so fast..." He rubbed his chin in the familiar manner that he had when he was thinking. "It's mighty strange, Luke. Children usually don't know how to stuff it down like this. I've never seen anything like it."

"I think their grandmother and her sense of propriety has something to do with it. I overheard Aggie talking to someone on the phone one day about how the first thing she heard when she arrived at the house for the funeral was the grandmother admonishing the children to be strong and brave and not give way to tears."

"I wonder why her parents don't help more. Why is she doing this all alone?"

Luke was hesitant to share private news. He knew why Aggie's parents had been in the background, and he also knew how hard it was on them. While Zeke waited for one of his characteristic silences to end, Luke wrestled with the delicate balance of helping Aggie and revealing what might be considered a confidence. At last, he spoke. "Well, Uncle Zeke, this I know. It isn't that they aren't willing to help. They didn't just abandon her and drive off into the sunset." Satisfied with his answer, he stood, grabbed the tote of dirty dishes, and carried them into the bathroom.

Scrubbing the dishes in that tub nearly killed Luke's back. When he thought of Aggie trying to clean dishes that way, he realized things had to change. The last thing that she needed was a regular chiropractic appointment, because she didn't have a sink for washing dishes. With dripping hands, he pulled out his notebook and made a note to install a laundry sink the next day. Meanwhile, he worked as quickly as possible to finish the job and stretch his kinked muscles.

Luke wondered for what seemed an infinite number of times, how Aggie managed to keep a cheerful attitude with the overwhelming amount of work allotted to her. Was she just in denial? Did the hymns she sang repeatedly, and at the oddest times of day or night, really give her strength for the next trial? *"Perhaps,"* he thought to himself, *"she has a faith that I need to learn, rather than sit here and doubt her."*

The screen door seemed to shut with a very decisive "whap." Luke peered around the corner of the dining room-turned-kitchen and saw Aggie listlessly walking across the room. Drying his hands on a nearby towel, Luke crossed the room and put his hand on her shoulder. "Did you have a nice time?"

Aggie sighed and then put on what she thought was a bright smile and said, "Well, that diner has a lot of local flavor, doesn't it?" Her chuckle was nervous, her smile wooden. Luke didn't have to be the perceptive person he was to realize something had gone terribly wrong.

Luke's voice showed concern and a hint of firmness when he finally spoke. "Aggie, your demeanor doesn't quite mesh with your words."

Aggie tried to be flippant. She really wasn't in the mood to talk about anything and was still mortified that she'd gone on a double-blind-but-know-the-guy, date. "Demeanor... My, we're quite the thesaurus tonight, aren't we? Got any other 'fifty dollar words' in your hip pocket?" Her joke was flat, and she knew it.

Luke led Aggie to the bench on the front porch where she received the detestable invitation in the first place. Grimacing at the irony of it, she sat down for what she knew would be a very painful talk. She half-listened as Luke attempted to drag what she considered a sordid tale from her. Leaves rustled in the evening breeze as the crickets chirped, and the lightning bugs danced across the lawn. Her heart just wanted to escape into their world for a time and forget the last couple of hours.

"Aggie." A sharper edge to Luke's voice broke her reverie. Aggie turned to him, emotionally and physically drained. "What happened? I can see that you didn't have a nice time. You are still upset and hurt by something." The silence was deafening to her, as Aggie waited for Luke to continue. "I think you'd feel better if you talked it out."

Aggie was thoughtful for a while and finally decided that Luke was right. She *would* feel better if she could say what she really thought. What would Luke think of her? Aggie shrugged off that thought. Who cared what anyone thought, and how much more humiliated could she be? "Well, I'll swallow my pride and tell you. William didn't invite me to dinner tonight. It was my first so-called date, and it was unequivocally a total wash. We spent the whole time in silence. Irritated. It was ridiculous."

Aggie gave a tentative glance in Luke's direction. She wasn't sure how to continue or even if she should. His face was a study in contrasting emotions. Relief, confusion, and anger flickered over his features. Aggie watched his brow furrow and his eyes harden, and yet she realized that she had never noticed how much compassion shone in Luke's brown eyes. Should she burden him with her problems? Well, if he didn't want to know about them, he shouldn't have asked. Shrugging off the questions that grew rapidly in her mind, Aggie plunged on.

"It appears that Mrs. Dyke is playing matchmaker. She invited me out to dinner with William. After I foolishly accepted, she then told William that he had a date with me and should consider not standing me up! Now, I thought I was really mad at her, but what really bugged me was the fact that William took his irritation at her, out on me. He sat there in this stony silence the whole time — like I am the one that put her up to it or something." Aggie would have been mortified to hear how incoherent her rant sounded. "Honestly, I am telling you, the last thing I need in my life right now is some elderly woman tricking me into a romance! I still don't know why I agreed to go in the first place. Wait until I tell Vannie. She's going to have her romantic illusions dashed into a healthy dose of reality."

Luke heard Aggie nearing her emotional edge. His mother always remarked on how he could hear more in a person's voice than most people could see in their actions. He knew it was a matter of moments before she would break down. Should he comfort her? Encourage her tears? It would be a perfect time to comment on how she and the children were still not dealing with their grief. Luke hated to see women cry. Most men do. But, unlike most men, he'd had a lifetime of helping girls and women through their tears. It was what he did best.

Aggie sniffled as the tears rose to the surface. In an odd moment of insightful personal introspection, she realized she'd been fighting tears for weeks— maybe months. Seconds later, heartbroken sobs drowned out the gentle sounds of nature at night.

The screen door opened, and Zeke stepped out onto the porch, his eyes searching Luke's for insight. Moments later, a sobbing, broken Aggie wept freely in the old farmer's arms. Her tears felt ridiculous, and she didn't understand why something as ordinary as a failed date, especially with someone she had no romantic interest in, would cause such an intense reaction. Between sobs, she tried to speak but could only stammer. Luke's "Shh... don't talk; just cry," sent her into fresh bouts of weeping.

An uncomplicated man, Zeke did things simply. He spoke little but usually had much to say. Until Aggie was in control of her emotions, the old farmer said nothing and held her, stroking her hair, much like he would a child or his favorite dog. When Aggie tried to speak and apologize for her outburst, Zeke interrupted.

"Aggie, honey, don't talk. Not yet. Luke and me, we've got something we want to talk to you about." The elderly man retrieved a wrinkled old bandana handkerchief from his overalls. Embarrassed, he quickly stuffed it back in his pocket and motioned for Luke to get Aggie something. "Honey, listen. You know you aren't just crying about a bad date. I've been talkin' with Luke here, and we think you all need to take time to grieve your loss."

Aggie's stammers were hushed when Luke came back with a box of Kleenex and held one up to her face. Zeke continued as if Aggie hadn't spoken. "Listen, hon, I know that it's simple, and a little overused, but when 'The Preacher' says, 'There's a time to mourn and a time to dance,' he knows what he's talkin' about."

Luke read Aggie's bewilderment over the reference to "The Preacher" and spoke softly. "Ecclesiastes, in the Old Testament, chapter three." He held a swift, for him, inward debate and continued. "You know, you also have more to grieve than the loss of your sister and her husband. You had dreams and plans that you'd expected to be a part of your near future, and those are gone now."

The concern and care, shown in the way the two men had taken her not-so-little family under their wings, was a balm to Aggie's spirit. "Thanks. I—"

Zeke stood and gave Aggie's shoulder one last pat. "It's gettin' too late for this old man to be gallivantin' around like this. I have to be at work in the mornin', so I'll be seeing you." Zeke turned to his favorite nephew. "Mrs. Jenkins is looking for someone to take out that old pine that's rubbing against her house. I think you might give her a call about it soon." Aggie jumped up and impulsively kissed the dear old man's cheek before he strolled to his truck and drove down the drive.

Aggie and Luke sat in a contented silence as Zeke's old truck rattled onto the highway and toward home. Time seemed to stand still as they semi-rocked the old picnic bench and listened to the cicadas and crickets nighttime symphony. "Aggie?" Luke's voice was regretful. She couldn't tell if it was because he didn't want to break the silence, or he didn't like what he was about to say.

"I know it's none of our business." Luke seemed to be

struggling more than usual to put his thoughts into words. "I wasn't going to say anything, really. But, honestly, when Uncle Zeke saw it too I—I—" He halted his train of thought abruptly. Moments later, Luke seemed more comfortable and tried again. "I guess what I am trying to say is, you need to help these kids grieve. They need the freedom to express the sorrow, anger, and pain from their loss. Everyone around here is walking like tightly strung and carefully orchestrated marionettes. If you don't do something, you will all begin acting out." He seemed finished but continued quickly with an afterthought. "It's not healthy, Mibs."

She nodded silently, acknowledging that she heard him. After a few minutes of thinking about how much the children needed her help, and realizing she had no clue where to begin, she sighed. Before she could ask Luke his opinion, he stood, helped her to her feet, and said goodnight. As he reached the bottom step of the porch, Luke turned. "Aggie, I can't be here next week and possibly the week after. I have a few jobs that have been scheduled for months. Even though I'll be busy, don't hesitate to call if you need me. I'm not far away." She tried to respond, but Luke continued. "Just encourage them to talk. The rest will take care of itself. See you in the morning." After giving her one last wan smile, he jumped into his truck and drove off into the night.

Aggie says: Ohhh Tiiiiiinaaaaaaaaaa… I'm hooooooommmeeee

Tina says: I've been waiting!!!!!! How'd it go?

Tina says: You going to go out again?

Tina says: Where did you go, what'd you eat, did you apologize?

Aggie says: WOOOOOOAAAAAAAH Do you want the story or not?

Tina says: Ok, tell it all, I won't speak. I'm just excited.

Aggie says: I'll give you the Reader's Digest version first then you can ask for details.

Tina says: Ok. But spit it out!!

Aggie says: Well he picked me up. We drove to the restaurant in silence. We ate in silence. I apologized for my outburst; he forgave me. Then, later, William tells me that he's sorry he's so mad. Then, he apologizes for being so weird. Said that Mrs. Dyke just invited me without telling him and then he either had to go or be a jerk.

Tina says: NO WAY

Aggie says: hee hee... Yep! That's exactly what he did.

Tina says: So, is everything ok?

Aggie says: Pretty much. I'm still kind of angry. I mean he treated me like the whole thing was my fault or something.

Tina says: Nah... I think he was just working through his own emotions, and you got caught in the middle.

Aggie says: I suppose. Zeke and Luke talked to me tonight. They think we aren't grieving enough.

Tina says: I've wondered about that. You don't talk about it much you know... You don't talk about the kids having problems or anything... Whatcha gonna do?

Aggie says: I love how you use words on the messenger you'd never use in person.

Tina says: Hee hee... if I'm gonna be a teacher, I gotta get my improprieties out somewhere!!

Aggie says: Yep! Anyway, Luke's going to be working somewhere else for the next week or two. I doubt I'll see much of him. This'll give us time to work on this grieving stuff though.

Tina says: You don't "work on grieving" like you do manners and things. You simply allow it. You talk about your loss, you ask questions... this isn't another item on the running "to do" list you keep filed in that one organized compartment of your brain.

Aggie says: Thanks... another Aggievating thing about me.

Tina says: Aggievating?? That's cute!

Aggie says: Compliments of Luke and William.

Tina says: Well, it's appropriate. Perhaps you should consider making a scrapbook with the children. They'll remember stories and things that meant a lot to them. It might help them grieve.

Aggie says: Luke suggested keeping up scrapbooks, but, like I told him, it's just one more thing for me to do. I don't need more to do, Tina.

Tina says: Well, not to imply you're a lousy scrapper or anything...

Aggie says: You know that sounds like I can't fight...

Tina says: Well, you can't and you know it. No, I thought it'd be healing for the kids to make the pages themselves. You know, put things on the pages that are important to them. Help them keep their memories contained and preserved.

Aggie says: GREAT idea. I love it. If they each do a page or three...

Tina says: That's the spirit.

Aggie says: Well... honestly, I'm going to go do some overhauling of my spirit. You go to bed.

Tina says: Good idea. Nighters

STAND OFF

Chapter Nineteen

Monday, July 8th

While William scraped the eaves and soffits, the boys worked on the planks on the east side of the house. Not to be left out of the fun, Aggie brushed the crevices of the porch railing with a steel wire brush until perspiration soaked her t-shirt in the summer heat. Vannie divided her time between supervising the Monday maintenance chores Aggie had instituted and matching socks from her bed. Ian played at her feet, as she directed the twins to put their stuffed animals back in the corner net, reassemble their dollhouse rooms, and called them back for the dozenth time to retrieve yet another shirt or dress that they hadn't worn but had dumped in the laundry pile outside Vannie's door.

"Aunt Aggie, I think they're ready for inspection," Vannie called from the window above the porch corner, where Aggie sanded and brushed a particularly difficult section of the railing.

"I'll be right up." She glanced down the side of the house where William stood on the ladder, his shirt soaked with sweat, hat covering his eyes, and face flecked with paint shavings.

He'd worked for two hours without even a quick break for water.

Inside, Aggie washed her hands and face, drying them as she climbed the stairs. The gate in Vannie's doorway kept Ian in, and the laundry-tossing twins and their various articles of clothing, out of the tidy room. Clipboard with checklist in hand, she stepped into Laird's room and surveyed it closely. The bed was stripped, fresh sheets were folded and waiting for him to remake his bed, trash emptied, laundry basket emptied, and his closet— "Ugh," she sighed. Well, she'd have him check that later. A thick layer of dust on the windowsill sent her pen scribbling across her checklist with a new task for the children— dusting. Would she ever remember it all?

Once the rooms were checked, with the detestable list she forced herself to use, despite the fact it made her feel more like a drill sergeant than a mother figure, Aggie jogged downstairs. The difference between floors was staggering. Now that the upstairs, with the exception of her bedroom, was completely refurbished with fresh coats of paint, appropriate furniture and décor, and refinished flooring, the downstairs looked even shabbier than ever. For the next week or two she'd be doing dishes in the odd laundry sink that Luke had installed, tearing off drywall, ripping up flooring, and, in general, preparing the kitchen for Luke's return. The result of her initial labors was a heavy layer of filth all over the furniture and floors on the first floor. Old sheets covered the couch and all other fabric covered furniture, but the table and chairs weren't safe to sit on, unless you liked the lighter-backside look to your clothing, and it would only get worse.

From the fridge that now blocked part of the entry to the kitchen, Aggie pulled a can of lemonade from the freezer compartment and dug through a plastic storage tote for the pitcher. She carefully replaced the lid and then growled under her breath to see both the plates and glasses totes with lids standing against their sides. Humming *Sweet Will of God* as she whisked the frozen glob of lemony goodness into the pitcher of water, Aggie prepared herself to find the culprits and make them return the lids to their rightful totes. She didn't have time to rewash dishes because children were too lazy to move a lid twelve inches.

"...*what power from Thee, my soul can sever? The center of God's will, my home. Sweet will of God, still fold me closer, 'til I am wholly lost in Thee...*"

When she came back, Aggie called for William, as she poured glasses of lemonade on the front porch. "You've been working too long without some fluids; come on down."

William gratefully accepted the glass she offered him and drained it in seconds. Undaunted, Aggie poured another glass and shoved it at him. "Drink. I'll be back in a minute. The boys probably need some too. Oh, and I have to see who was in the dish totes last."

Resting in the shade of the porch, Aggie and William sipped more lemonade and discussed their progress. She felt strange discussing her renovations with anyone but Luke. She'd spent the past month getting Luke's opinion and advice on everything from paint brands to designing her kitchen. William was the man who came out on 9-1-1 calls or to rescue her from Geraldine. Seeing him covered with paint chips seemed incongruous with the militaristic neatness he usually exuded.

"Have you decided on what color you are going to paint the house? I have vacation time on the books, so I talked to Frank, and he said I could take it now if I wanted."

"Oh, William, I appreciate that, but you can't use your vacation to work on my house. You work hard and need a vacation that lets you relax. Painting doesn't exactly qualify."

"Aggie, honestly, I would really like to do this for you. I am not handy with things like kitchens and wiring and stuff like that, but I can scrape and paint. I'm good with yard work too. Let me contribute. It'll also give us time to get to know each other better, and we did decide we wanted to try that."

Smiling, Aggie handed him another glass of lemonade.

"Ok then, it's a deal, but I get to feed you, and you have to stay for a movie now and then." She hesitated as though second-guessing herself, and then shook her head. "And, William, thanks."

"So about paint..." There was a wistfulness— almost an eagerness to his voice.

"Well, there was this house down the street from us in Yorktown. It was yellow with white trim and shutters and a green door— almost emerald green. It was such a cheerful and cozy house. I might do something similar."

Aggie was utterly unprepared for William's reaction— make that, overreaction. "No. I think that you should reconsider. Any other color or color combination would be preferable. Use *orange* if you must, but I think yellow and white is just tired. Besides, the green door would clash with your living room."

William's tone was adamant. She'd seen him act oddly about the house now and then, and this seemed to be another one of those times. Why should he care what color she chose for the house? He didn't have to live there! She'd paint it whatever color she liked— and that was yellow. To be fair, she knew that until that minute, she hadn't been sure. However, his imperious attitude irritated her into stubborn obstinacy. Aggie started to tell him as much, but Vannie dashed up the porch steps carrying the mail.

"Aunt Aggie! Look at the house on the cover of this magazine!" Vannie's face was alight with excitement.

Aggie looked at the house. It was striking, somewhat elegant even, but charming. The picture showed a very pale dove gray house, trimmed in glossy black paint, and boasted a cherry red door. Hanging from the eaves, red geraniums gave the house the homey look she'd tried so hard to achieve. The house style was nearly identical to their home, and Aggie felt as though the magazine challenged her to duplicate it. Instantly, without hesitation or a hint of doubt, Aggie changed her mind. Pointing to the cover, she passed the magazine to

William and insisted, "I want this."

Relief flooded William's face, and it puzzled Aggie, but she didn't have time to think about it. He didn't have a chance to comment before she called for the youngest four children to load up in the van. "We're going to run to Brunswick and get the paint. I'll leave Laird, Ellie, and Tavish with you and take the rest, ok?"

William nodded and poured the last of the lemonade from the pitcher into his glass. He watched them drive away and sighed at the glass he'd already drained. Oh, well, it was time to get back to work anyway. This was going to be an unusual vacation, but if he were honest with himself, he'd have to admit he was looking forward to it.

Thursday, July 11th

Just after six a.m., the "William Tell Overture" interrupted Aggie's fitful sleep. Groggy, she fumbled for the phone. "Hello?"

As though speaking to her from another universe, a voice gently broke through the fog into her consciousness. "Aggie? This is Luke. Did I wake you up?"

She struggled into a semi-sitting position, stretched while stifling a yawn, and tried to concentrate. "I didn't sleep well. It's Laird's birthday today, and I have no idea how to make it special." A yawn interrupted her jumbled explanation. "I wanted to make sure their birthdays this year were memorable. Something good to remember this year, you know?" Aggie was rambling, knew it, and frankly was too exhausted to care.

"Well, actually, that's why I'm calling. I had an idea for kind of a guy's night out type party for him." Luke hurried to share his plan. "We'll have cake and ice cream with everyone, and then Uncle Zeke, the boys, and I can pitch a tent in the front yard and camp out there. It wouldn't be the same as going to the lake or up by Little Vienna, but with a hibachi bonfire and a tent, it'll feel authentic enough." The eagerness in his voice made her wonder who would have more fun, Laird or Luke. "Oh, and I'd love to bring my nephew, Justus, if you're comfortable with that."

"I think that'd be fun. We could have a scavenger hunt!"

"Aggie, there aren't very many houses on your street..." Luke's voice was skeptical.

"I'll figure something out. Trust me. Oh, and I'll have to make him a cake— or buy one— and..."

"Aggie," Luke interrupted, "Mom wanted to do something for him too, and I know she'd be thrilled to bake the cake for you. She loves cake decorating and baking. Let her do it?"

Aggie agreed readily. Her cakes were fine if she used a box mix and a plastic can of frosting. Her only scratch cake had been a dismal failure, and her single attempt at decorating had been infinitely worse. Luke promised to arrive as close to four o'clock as possible, and Aggie promised to have dinner and a party ready by five.

Eagerly, she grabbed her Bible, made a cup of coffee, and crept out to the back swing for a little "closet time" with the Lord. Aggie's morning trysts with her Abba, as Tina always called the Lord, gave Aggie fuel for each day's trials and triumphs. She realized that since becoming guardian and ad-hock mother to the children, her relationship with the Lord was stronger and sweeter than it had ever been throughout her Christian walk. Continually amazed at the way things definitely did "work together for the good of those that love Him," Aggie thanked the Lord for the redirection she'd received that cold February morning.

The day passed in a whirlwind of chores, shopping, and secrets. While Laird tried to wheedle information about his gift from everyone in the house, Aggie and Vannie planned the party, decorated, and wrapped the pocketknife, canteen, backpack, and sleeping bag that Aggie purchased as a nod to the camping theme of the evening. Thus far, Laird was unenlightened about the upcoming evening and the true fun planned for him.

By four-thirty, Luke and Justus had arrived, bearing the tent, hibachi, and a huge ice chest full of flavored water and sodas. As Laird commented on his favorite, root beer, Luke winked at Aggie. "I just made sure I got stuff without caffeine. I need my sleep too!"

They grilled hot dogs and hamburgers and ate crisp sweet watermelon that dripped down their chins. Aggie's scavenger hunt sent them looking for items around the house and yard with which they traded for clues to find Laird's gifts. The twins, frustrated by their inability to read the clues, huddled under the tree, talking earnestly together and then raced into the house. Aggie didn't notice, or she would have rushed after them.

Not to be undone by the bigger children, the twins found the scissors, tape, and the leftover wrapping paper on Aggie's bed. They each grabbed their favorite stuffed animal and rolled it in paper, cutting—more like tearing— off excess here, and necessary paper there. With enough tape to supply Santa for a year, the girls secured their papered offerings and scrambled back down the porch steps. "We found them!"

Luke glanced at Aggie, who shrugged and asked, "What did you find, girls?"

"The pwesents! Look!" Cari's voice was indignant. Aggie noticed the earnestness in her tone but missed the challenge to defy the child's assertion. Luke, however, caught it.

"Is that a present Aunt Aggie wrapped?" Aggie started to answer, but Luke shook his head almost imperceptibly.

"Well—" Cari bit her lip. "It has the papew, see? It's Laiwd's gifts, and we found them fiwst! We win!"

Laird arrived just as Luke shook his head. "You're trying to deceive everyone, Cari. You know that those aren't the gifts that they're looking for."

Aggie's eyes narrowed. "May I talk to you, Luke?"

Without waiting for an answer, she waved Laird on to look for the clues and find his packages, while she mentally prepared to give Luke the tongue lashing of his life. "Just what do you think you're doing?"

"I am thwarting a child's attempt to deceive. You told me that if I ever caught them doing wrong, to put a stop to it."

"They just wanted to give him a present and be involved in the search too!" Hearing her voice rise with her indignation level, Aggie forced herself to speak more quietly. "Is it really necessary to squash them just because they created their own gift when they couldn't find the other ones?"

Luke's silence nearly sent Aggie to the edge of her wrath. At last, he spoke very quietly. "Well, they are your children, and you most definitely have the right to allow what you choose—"

"You're blasted-well right I do—"

He continued as though she hadn't said a word. "However, I want you to think like a child for a minute. If you got away with pretending you won a game that you really didn't, would you expect it to work again the next time? How would you react if it didn't? Those girls don't have malicious intent in their deception— selfish intent, yes, but not malicious. But, if they succeed in being allowed that selfishness, they'll try it again, and again. Eventually, selfish intent could even become malicious, and all because these things are so cute when the child is three or four. You wouldn't think it was so cute if Vannie got fed up and went and wrapped her own gift so she'd be able to try to claim the prize."

He'd never spoken so many words at once. Furthermore, he was right, and Aggie knew it. The last thing she felt like doing was admitting that he'd caught Cari in yet another situation. She glanced at the child a few feet away and watched the girl's little fists settle on her hips, trying not to smile at the glare on the girl's face.

"Did you see that?"

"Is she glaring at us? I think I saw her hands move to her hips, but I didn't want to give her the satisfaction of knowing I'm still watching her." Luke's voice sounded pained. It took

Aggie a moment to realize that it had been hard for him to speak up in the first place and she'd just undermined any authority that he'd established.

"Will you finish with her? I don't want her to think she can count on me to rescue her from you."

"Are you sure?" he hesitated.

"I'm definitely sure. I can see the look in her eye. She knew exactly what she was doing."

Luke missed most of the scavenger hunt and the unwrapping of presents, as did Cari. Lorna confessed quickly and was sent out to join the rest of the party, but Cari, in her characteristic stubbornness, refused to admit she'd tried to deceive. Had she not shown a clear defiance from the moment they brought the gifts out of the house, Luke might have been conned into believing the child didn't understand what she'd done wrong. However, Lorna's parting shot had been, "Vannie says cheaters never popper. I knew we shouldn't cheat."

"We won! We bwought gifts fiwst."

"The game was to find the gifts Aunt Aggie hid, and you knew it."

"We won."

For twenty minutes, Luke waited for the obstinate child to confess that she'd done wrong. Her countenance, her posture, and the hard glint of defiance in her eyes told him she knew it was wrong. She may not have fully understood why, but she'd known and done it anyway, and that was the problem.

Cari hadn't bargained for Luke's patience. She'd expected him to order, cajole, or even spank her in order to get her to say she'd done wrong, and she had no intention of obeying. She didn't know what the prize was, but she wanted it— badly. Luke's eyes never left her face, making her feel even more uncomfortable than she had the moment he asked if the gifts they'd brought out were Aunt Aggie's.

Finally, her little voice, anger seething beneath the surface, growled, "I sowwy I did wwong."

"No, you aren't. You are sorry that you got caught. If I

hear you say that pleasantly, I might believe you. But your eyes are angry, your voice is angry, and even your arms are folded across your chest — because you're angry."

"It's my pwize!" Defiance roared back to the surface when her lie failed.

"You will not get a prize for deception and defiance."

Ten more minutes passed. Aggie stood outside the door directing games and half-listening. She didn't want to start singing and serving cake without Luke and Cari, but it was growing late, and it didn't look like they'd ever be done at this rate. Just as she was about to step inside and ask, Luke's voice drifted through the door, making her realize that he knew she was listening; and he was answering her question without letting Cari know she'd hear.

"You know," Luke glanced at his watch. "I think it's just about time for them to have cake and ice cream. Then it'll be time for me to help Laird put up the tent. I can't do that now. Laird and Justus will have to sleep upstairs tonight after all. So, you and I won't get any cake or get to see Laird open his gifts, and he won't get to camp on the front lawn."

"Why?"

"Because I need to stay with you until you decide to confess that you did something wrong."

Cari's voice wavered slightly. "But it's Laiwd's pawty."

"And that is a special thing, but little girls and keeping their hearts from storing ugliness in them are much more important."

She tried a new tactic. "But Laiwd didn't do anyfing wong!"

"Did Cari do anything wrong?"

"No!" The defiance returned almost frighteningly quickly.

"I'm afraid rooting out that lie is more important than Laird's camping and party." Luke's voice never wavered.

Aggie wanted to listen to the conversation but knew he'd urged her to cut the cake. Perhaps there was more to it than simply moving along with the party. Maybe he had a plan.

With a sigh, she opened the living room door and hurried over to the table where the cake sat in a place of honor.

Libby's cake, decorated simply in her rush for time that morning, was missing a swipe of frosting, and Aggie chose to ignore it. Cari couldn't see that she'd noticed, and if Aggie said anything, none of them were going to get any sleep tonight. "We're going to sing Happy Birthday. I'll save you guys some cake for when you're done. Cari can have hers tomorrow if she waits past bed time."

"Sing extra loud for me," Luke insisted. He turned back to Cari and smiled. "So, do you have anything to tell me?"

"Laiwd should have his pawty. It's his biwfday."

"I agree. I hope you'll give him and yourself the one gift that will help you both enjoy the rest of the day."

"I twied." Her arms crossed again. "*You* didn't wike it."

"I loved the gift, Cari. I always think it's extra special when people give others something that is very personal. There's nothing more personal than your favorite stuffed animal—"

"How did you know—"

"I felt the package." Luke's smile was weak and sad. "I just don't like *how* you tried to give it. You tried to cheat in a game and deceive people to get a prize. That isn't a nice way to give a gift."

"But I couldn't find the 'nother ones. Worna and me twied." Tears formed.

"I know." Luke held out his arms and wrapped them around Cari as the little girl crawled in his lap. "It's hard being the little girls in a big kid's game, isn't it?"

"I wants to win."

"Would you have liked it if Vannie wrapped up some of her books or games and said *they* were the gifts, so she could win the prize?"

"That's not faiw!" As she said it, Cari burst into tears. "I want to win!"

"Even if you cheat?"

A sniffle broke the silence around them. "Noooo..."

"What you did was wrong— not because you gave a gift, but because you tried to steal a prize with a gift and a lie."

"That's bad." The adamant defiance was now replaced with certain insistence.

"It is bad. I'm glad you understand now."

Wiping away her tears, Cari jumped from his lap. Giving him a big hug, she grinned. "I unnerstood befow. I just don't wike getting in twouble. I'm always in twouble." Her matter-of-fact tone dwindled to a sigh as she confessed her propensity to misbehavior.

"Well, little troublemaker, let's go have cake and sing for Laird again."

"I can have cake?" Cari's eyes lit up excitedly.

"Of course. You didn't lie about the cake, or did you?"

"Well... I didn't lie 'zactly. But—" The temptation to hide her taste-testing was written all over the child's face.

"When you confess what you do wrong, you usually are in less trouble— it's when you try to hide it or make it a habit that adults have to try to teach you somehow not to do it again." Even as he spoke, Luke was sure the child wouldn't understand. He was trying to rephrase when Cari's voice interrupted his thoughts.

"Does that mean if I tell you I ate some fwosting fwom Laiwd's cake that I won't get in twouble?"

"I think, this time anyway, that's exactly what it means."

"I'm sowwy, Luke."

"I know, honey. Let's go eat cake and forget about trouble for tonight."

The relief on Aggie's face was mirrored in Luke's eyes. He hadn't bargained for nearly an hour of standoff between Cari and himself. As he helped himself to a piece of cake, he read the dread she'd felt and realized that she knew it could have been even longer. "Does she do that often?"

"Not if I can help it. I try to head her off at the pass, so she can't put me there. I almost never win once we get to that

290

point."

"That's why she does it."

"I don't have an hour or two every day, three or four times a day, to focus just on Cari and her stubbornness!"

"You don't have the time not to. Multiply her faults now by ten, and that is Cari as a teenager. Do you want her pretending to be going to a school field trip while she sneaks out to party with her friends? Those things start at age three when a mom lets them get away with pretending that they didn't *mean* to knock the eggs off the counter, even though the mom watched them deliberately push them off."

"Why do I get the feeling that one of your sisters had a mishap with some eggs?"

"Not them, me. Was mad at Mom, thought she wasn't looking, and pushed. I tried to convince her that it was an accident. Three hours and a sore bottom later, I confessed, and Mom told me what happens if you don't stop wrong behavior when it starts. I've never forgotten it."

"How old were you?"

"Around four or so. I don't think I was any younger, but I know I wasn't in school yet."

"Well, I'm glad you were here. I'd have taken it to be a cute thing for her to do. I didn't think of it as cheating."

"You also missed that she challenged you to defy her." Luke hated to mention it, but it was important.

"She did?"

"Yep. But, I'd say we've dealt with enough child-training for one night. How about I start the boys pitching the tent before it gets too much darker?"

Aggie decided to stay inside as the guys set up Luke's tent and dug a hole for the hibachi in the gravel driveway nearby. Between teeth checks, hair brushing, and goodnight kisses and stories, she watched as the campers sat around the fire, roasting marshmallows and singing the silly add-on songs that she hadn't sung since junior high camp. She'd offered to play a game with Vannie, but the girl had shaken her head and insisted she was too tired.

Just as she punched on the laptop's power button, Aggie heard tires crunch in the driveway. She met William at the door, surprised both to see him, and that they hadn't seen him earlier. He'd been over every day that week, but today he hadn't even called. "Hey, William!" She stepped outside and sniffed the air, catching the sweet scent of semi-burned marshmallows.

William lowered himself onto a porch step and rested his arms on his knees. With a jerk of his head in the direction of the tent, he sighed. "Mrs. Dyke saw the flames and decided that it was my duty to check it out. She's that way about things. I'm a one man volunteer fire department, paramedic, handyman, and law enforcer all wrapped up in one oversized package." A wink softened his words.

"She really thought a fire was over here?" Aggie glanced at the flames that barely rose a foot over the ground and shrugged. It seemed safe enough to her — especially half-buried in gravel.

"They lived over there when the first house burned over fifty years ago. Since then, she's been paranoid about fire. I'd say terrified of it too."

Aggie nodded. As they sat and talked, Luke watched from his seat by the fire. He never could decide what it was about William that made him feel so uneasy. Zeke's snores brought his attention back to the boys, and Luke decided that his comfort, or lack thereof, was most likely due to unfamiliarity. Regardless, the boys were trying to tell a continuing story, and it was nearly Luke's turn. There was no time for speculation about local law enforcement officers.

After a short conversation about the readiness of the house for painting, William stood and assured Aggie he'd let Mrs. Dyke know all was well on the Milliken-Stuart home front. She watched him tiptoe to the now-silent tent and poke his head in. Seconds later, a group of wild boys burst from the flaps, ready to pursue their invader. They chased him to his car, but the doors were shut and locked before the posse reached him. Laughing, William carefully backed out of the driveway and drove over to appease a curious and slightly frightened Mrs. Dyke.

Aggie smiled. It was wonderful to see William loosen up and have a little fun. As she climbed into bed a while later, Aggie was sorry she hadn't thought to invite him to stay. "Next time, Aggie. You can wait until next time."

Aggie says: Mornin' Tina!!

Tina says: Missed you last night.

Aggie says: They had a camp out for Laird's birthday on the front lawn.

Tina says: Who's they?

Aggie says: Luke, Zeke, Laird, Tavish and Luke's nephew Justus. He's such a cutie!

Tina says: Luke or Justus?

Aggie says: Justus you goof!

Tina says: Gotta make sure you answer quickly enough.

Aggie says: Aaaaaaahhhhhh, now I know how to protect myself.

Tina says: So, how come William wasn't there?

Aggie says: Don't know. He just didn't show at all yesterday. He must have been busy. Came by last night though. I saw an unusual side to him last night, though.

Tina says: Oh?

Aggie says: As he was leaving, he peeked into the tent and somehow got the boys to chase him to his car. It was so lighthearted and goofy. Not like the serious guy he keeps in the forefront.

Tina says: Hmm, what's he thinking? I can't wait to meet these guys!

Aggie says: I just can't wait for you to get here.

Tina says: We're going to shake up these kids and give them

---

some fun before school starts again.

Aggie says: Sounds fun! My troop is back inside. It started raining a few minutes ago and their breakfast looks really soggy. Guess I'll go make pancakes. I've gotten good at them. Did I tell you?

Tina says: No, but I am glad you can cook something!

Aggie says: Very funny!! Off to make blueberry pancakes... too bad you're not here to eat them.

Tina says: I'll take a "rain check." hee hee

Aggie says: ROFLOL... I'll do it. Bye!

Tina says: Bye!

ENTER MURPHY

Chapter Twenty

Friday, July 12th

After a week of scraping, sanding, and painting the massive house, William and Aggie were ready to paint the trim. William focused on the eaves and window trim, while Aggie laid out shutters over sawhorses and painted them the glossy black she'd chosen. Occasionally, one of them would take a swipe at the other as they worked. William wasn't used to the kind of playful silliness that Aggie displayed, but her antics seemed to inspire him. Naturally, Aggie took the first swipe at the back of William's knee as he walked past where she worked. Unwilling to let that slide without retaliation, William made a perfect x on the back of her t-shirt. All morning they dabbed at one another with their brushes, until they both were covered in black trim paint.

With an impish glint in her eye, Aggie handed the paintbrush to Cari and motioned for the girl to swipe William's ear. Giggling in delight, Cari tiptoed around the entire house and up the other side of the steps. Aggie thought the child was taking her role in the caper a bit too seriously, but she decided to let the child have her fun. With careful aim, Cari took a big swipe at William as he knelt to refill his paint tray and ran behind Aggie, thrusting the brush into her aunt's hand before William could look their way.

The result was bedlam. William reached up and felt the black paint on his ear, looked at Aggie with paintbrush in hand, and grinned. The usually stoic deputy thrust his index finger into the open can of paint, turned to her, and with slow deliberate strides, he advanced in her direction. Aggie took one look at the dripping finger and the determination in William's eyes and ran. William was in hot pursuit. Although he was faster, she was able to dart and dodge much more easily. He began to think it wasn't worth the exertion in the muggy heat, when Aggie foolishly darted behind a shed near the back of the property. It was apparent that she didn't realize that the shed butted up against the fence on one side, and she was trapped. He caught her arm just as Aggie tried to climb over the fence. If she hadn't been laughing as hard as she was, the look of abject terror on her face might have been alarming. Instead, she simply looked like a naughty elf.

"I— I— I didn't do it! Cari did it! Honestly!" Aggie pleaded as William pinned her arms behind her back and walked her back to the house.

"If you didn't do it, there was no reason to run, Aggie." William's deep voice was smothered with amusement.

"But you were coming at me! What was I supposed to do, wait until you painted Mickey Mouse ears on me before I convinced you that it wasn't my fault?" Aggie gave an unexpected wrench and broke free. Darting around the house, the fleeing woman didn't even think to check if William was pursuing her.

William ran the opposite direction. His side of the house was shorter, and he knew exactly where Aggie would run. He pressed himself against the side of the house and waited. Looking at his finger, William realized that the paint was dry and there was no way he could get her with it. Spying Cari, he motioned for her to bring him a paintbrush. The little girl grinned and darted across the porch for it. William thrust his finger deep into the bristles and recoated his finger. Hearing Aggie's footfalls and heavy breathing, William timed his catch perfectly. As Aggie darted around the corner, William reached out and briefly pulled Aggie against him. With his wet finger, he put a very large black blob of paint on her nose then released her.

Aggie collapsed on the ground in laughter. William's hearty guffaws rang across the yard and into Mrs. Dyke's kitchen, where the older woman was baking more Snickerdoodles for "her boy." The children giggled and made senseless jokes that amused everyone further. They combined the word black with everything imaginable until somehow even black grass was hilarious.

William and Aggie cleaned up as much as possible before dragging their laughter-laden selves inside to make sandwiches for the children's lunch. Aggie noticed a pile of rubbish near the base of the stairs and looked bemused. Winking at William, Aggie tiptoed to the door that led to the closet under the stairs and threw it open. There sat Tavish with a flashlight in one hand and a water bottle in the other. "Caught you! Now, it's time to help the little guys go clean up."

Tavish grinned, put his book, flashlight, and water back in the far corner of the closet and climbed out. Giving William a wave, Tavish raced out the door, shouting it was time to come in and wash for lunch. Laughing at his antics, Aggie turned to William, her amusement with Tavish more than evident. The look of pain, horror, and fury on his face startled her.

"William, what is the matter? What happened?" She watched him struggle to speak, then stared speechless as William opened the door and stormed out, letting it slam shut behind him. She took a step forward to follow and then jumped back again when William flung the door back open.

"Aggie, I don't know what you are thinking, locking that boy in there— and to *laugh* about it! I don't understand you!"

297

He turned to push the door open again, but Aggie jumped forward and grabbed his arm.

"Hey! Don't just walk out like that! Why are you so angry? Tavish always reads under the stairs— has for years from what I understand. What is wrong with it?" A range of indiscernible emotions flickered over William's face like a movie projector in a theater. Aggie wasn't used to seeing him show *any* emotion. Their date was the first time she'd seen anything but a calm, serious, and professional demeanor.

"William? Come on, talk to me. I'm new to this parenting thing. Is it not safe? Is it too anti-social for him to do that? What?"

William sighed. A look of utter dejection washed over him, and he looked at Aggie with pain-filled eyes. "Aggie, it's just me. I have this hang up about it. I guess I'm not rational about the idea. Let the boy play, it won't hurt him. Not with an aunt like you."

Releasing another deep sigh, William stepped toward Aggie again. With his thumb, he rubbed a bit of black from the corner of her eye and pushed her bangs away from her face. She could see the deep suffering in his eyes and wanted to comfort him. He wanted something from her, she could see it, but what it was, she couldn't tell. His hand on her shoulder, William whispered in a voice filled with pain, "You'd never hurt anyone, would you, Aggie?"

A lump that felt the size of Alaska filled her throat. Aggie wanted to qualify her response. Of course, she wouldn't hurt anyone— deliberately. Unable to share her heart, she shook her head and tried to make her eyes relay the truth she wanted to speak. Satisfied, William pushed the screen door and let himself outside again, closing it quietly behind him this time. She watched as he picked up a fresh paintbrush, opened the can of paint he'd been using, and went back to work painting the eaves. The raw pain that seemed to hold him captive slowly melted away as he worked, but Aggie still had one question. What prompted his outburst?

Unease tried to invade her heart, but hungry children tramped into the kitchen asking for sandwiches, popsicles, and chips. Crumbs in the bottoms of four separate bags of chips removed chips from the menu, but she created an assembly line with mayonnaise, mustard, turkey slices, cheese slices, and a strip of lettuce, then slapped another piece of bread on top and cut them in half. The children began chanting in unison from the moment she opened the bread bag and stopped as she finished. At one hundred eighty-four, the tenth sandwich landed, cut diagonally, on the last paper plate.

"You did it in one sixty-two the other day. You're slowing down," Laird teased.

"William is here. That's another sandwich."

"Luke was here that day. Same number. You're schluffing off, as Dad used to say." A quiver hovered in Laird's voice.

The next thing she knew, Laird and Vannie clung awkwardly to one another weeping. Elspeth pulled Kenzie to her, and Tavish sniffled. The twins stared at everyone in confusion, until Lorna started crying as if by osmosis. Cari, not to be outdone by everyone around her, sent up a wail that would have brought the house down and ran outside seeking comfort from William. It was several minutes before Aggie could pull out the cantaloupe, chop it into cubes, and push the bowl across the makeshift counter for the children.

Half an hour later, tears dried, paper plates piled into the huge dumpster, food gone, and another gallon of milk drained, she shook her head in wonder. At the rate her children drank it, Aggie was concerned that she'd need to invest in a herd of cows. She wiped her own tears from her eyes once the room emptied and grabbed the counter for support. "Lord, Luke wasn't joking, was he?"

"It Is Well with My Soul," flooded her heart and soul, and immediately, she began humming. It was instinctive, the hymn. She wasn't aware that her mind had switched to hymn comfort mode, until she found herself singing, *"Though Satan should buffet, though trials should come..."*

As she stepped outside to go back to the sawhorses and her shutters, childish giggles and squeals caught her attention. On the side of the yard, a sprinkler shot water high into the air, creating rainbows in the sunbeams. Amid the delighted sounds that pierced the afternoon air, her children— Aggie's thoughts froze for a moment. *Her* children— they really were *her* children— danced under the falling drops.

That evening William drove down her driveway so deep in thought he almost didn't notice a light in the house next door to Aggie's. The sight concerned him. No one had lived in that house since the Nesbit family moved last fall. He wondered if local kids were messing around in there, or perhaps a vagrant had taken up residence. The electricity shouldn't be on, though. That seemed odd. Pulling into the driveway, William noted the for sale sign still in the front yard and out of state plates on the car parked in the open garage.

Unaware, although he wouldn't have been surprised, that Mrs. Dyke was watching every move he made from behind her binoculars, he knocked on the door and waited for an answer. The woman who opened the door surprised him. "Ellene?"

"William! How'd you know I was here?"

Hugging her, William jerked his thumb toward Aggie's house. "I was helping a friend next door and saw your lights as I left—"

"You still answer a question as if you were on the witness stand."

"That doesn't answer the obvious but unstated question. What are you doing in Brant's Corners?" William followed her inside the house and noted the perfectly neat stacks of boxes along walls of every room visible from his vantage point. The difference between this house and Aggie's was extreme.

"I took a job with the Rockland County Social Services. They were going to put me in the city, but I convinced them to start me out here first."

Ellene Tuttle, a fellow Marine from Camp Pendleton, started to offer him coffee and then shrugged. "I don't have any food in the house at all. My furniture arrives tomorrow; I was just bringing more boxes over and organizing them tonight."

"Let's go to Maizy's. I want to hear what's been happening in your life since you left here."

They talked into the wee hours. William learned that Ellene remembered him talking about how close-knit Brant's Corners and the surrounding towns were and decided to apply for a job in the county. Her first assignment was Brant's Corners/Brunswick. Though he tried to disguise it, William was a little dismayed to think of any social worker, especially Ellene Tuttle, living next door to Aggie and her eight children. Would she understand about baby Ian calling 9-1-1 and the screams and squeals that seemed to characterize Aggie's home? Would she and Aggie be friends? Would she remember late night confessions of William's childhood and keep them confidential? William's questions bothered him long after he dropped his friend off at her new house and went home to his own bed.

Saturday, July 13th

Laird unintentionally arranged a hasty meeting with the new neighbor late the next morning. While Aggie and Luke stripped wallpaper from the walls and tried to keep Ian from eating the scraps off of the floor, Aggie heard the faint tinkling of glass. Moments later, a dejected Laird and excited Kenzie burst through the back door. "Aunt Aggie, Laird hit a *great* home run. We think that we broke the window next door and guess what?" Not waiting for an answer, the child continued. *"A lady came out of the house when it happened!"*

Aggie sighed and looked at Laird. The boy was miserable. Despair settled around him like a cloak, especially in his expressive eyes. For the first time, Aggie realized that she could read his thoughts much in the same manner that others often read hers. "Laird, let's go talk to whomever is over there and get this straightened out."

As she turned to leave, Vannie handed Aggie a plate of cookies she'd pulled out of the oven just minutes before and covered them with a clean kitchen towel. "Sometimes people aren't as upset if you bring a peace offering."

She smiled and thanked the girl. Sometimes Aggie thought that all the children had really needed was Vannie. The young girl's practical knowledge far exceeded Aggie's, and while Aggie had a degree in education, she often felt that Vannie was the teacher and she the student.

The doorbell rang almost simultaneously with the opening of the massive front door. A well-dressed woman, with perfectly styled hair, holding a note pad, wore a pasted-on smile. "I see you've heard about the incident. I'm pleased to see you taking responsibility for it."

Aggie was somewhat taken aback. She wasn't quite sure if the woman was speaking to her or to Laird, but she gave a weak smile and offered the plate of cookies. "Our eldest, Vannie, just baked these cookies. Please have some as our apology. Oh," she added quickly, "I am prepared to pay for the window, of course."

Aggie had intended to require that Laird do the talking. This woman, however, was not the understanding, sympathetic woman that she'd prayed she'd be. Not knowing exactly how to handle herself, Aggie plowed ahead. "I have a handyman who is working on my home. Would you like me to ask him to come give you an estimate of the damages?" Aggie added another note to her p-mail, asking the Lord to ensure that Luke would be willing.

After a few moments of uncomfortable silence, the woman spoke. "That isn't necessary. My insurance will cover it. I'm just relieved to see that you are not going to let your children run wild and destroy property. Too many parents just simply don't care." The woman gave another of her artificial and rehearsed-looking smiles and shut the door in their faces.

Aggie, still holding the plate of warm cookies, was dumfounded. Laird looked at her with questions racing across his eyes, but she shrugged helplessly. Nodding, Laird and took the plate from her, resignation replacing the misery in his eyes. While he mentally calculated what a window that size might cost, Aggie realized that she and Laird were enough alike to almost communicate by facial expression. How fascinating!

Vannie took personal offense at the apparent rejection of her cookies. While Luke and Laird grabbed handfuls, Vannie went in search of Ian, who no longer played at her feet. Aggie heard her frantically calling the crawler's name, and soon, the entire family was searching for the boy. When minutes passed, and there was no sight of the baby anywhere, Aggie, with shaking hands, picked up the phone and deliberately dialed 9-1-1.

Seeing the line of sheriff's cars in the Stuart driveway, the new neighbor came across the lawn and joined in the search. The children scouted everywhere, from behind rosebushes, to beneath beds, while Aggie, still shaking, sent each one looking in a new direction as they arrived empty handed. If a lost baby wasn't enough stress for Aggie, it was quite apparent that Ellene Tuttle found a large family like hers very distasteful.

She broke down, weeping, as the new neighbor asked difficult questions—ones Aggie couldn't answer. She felt like a prisoner being interrogated about a crime and soon became defensive, refusing to talk to the woman. Visibly frustrated, Ellene strode across the road to ask Mrs. Dyke if she'd seen a baby crawl past the house. Aggie, hearing Ellene's intentions and nearing the point of hysteria, giggled. "I can see her now, 'Mrs. Dyke, have you happened to see a nine month old baby hitchhiking around here?'"

Aggie's property was large, full of bushes and tall, un-mowed grass in the very back. The house itself had plenty of places a baby could crawl and hide. Deputy Megan had immediately gone to check all buckets, toilets, bathtubs, and the wading pool on the side of the house. Luke crawled under the porch with his flashlight, and another deputy went to search the attic. They combed the entire property, as well as side streets, and even the highway. After two hours of intense searching, the sheriffs suggested instituting an Amber Alert.

However, before William could radio in the call, Tavish raced around the corner of the house shouting, "I hear Ian whimpering, but I can't find him!"

Everyone followed the excited boy to the playhouse where they could hear Ian's whimpers evolving into frantic wails, but they couldn't see him. Beside the playhouse, an attached carport protected Laird's Jaguar from the elements. "Did anyone check by the Jag?" William's voice boomed from near the tailpipe as he looked under it.

One of the other officers assured them that he'd swept the entire carport with his flashlight. "Nothing— I checked under the car, behind those boxes, everywhere."

"I see a foot."

Before William could get to the front of the car, Aggie found Ian, his overalls impaled by an old nail that refused to let him crawl to freedom. "He must have been asleep in here or something."

"I don't know how he could have been in here, I checked everywhere."

Aggie carried him to daylight and shook her head at his sleepy eyes. "You're right, he was asleep— maybe under the car?"

"Probably," William agreed. "Did the nail scratch him? He's keeping that side away from you."

She unbuttoned the denim short-alls and saw an angry scratch. "Yep. Poor guy."

"Is he up to date on his tetanus shots?" Ellene's voice was all business.

"I —" Aggie frowned. "I don't know. I assume he was as of four months, but that's been a few months ago."

Aggie cradled the now grinning boy and carried him inside to wash the welt and bandage it. Ellene dragged William aside and ranted about her perception of the situation. While no one could decipher William's deep rumbles, the woman's whispers were loud enough for everyone to hear. Aggie had once heard someone describe such communication as learning to whisper in a sawmill. It seemed a fitting description, and from the angry accusations audible to all, it was evident that Ellene considered the entire episode bordering on the criminal.

In an attempt at discretion, William steered Ellene toward her house. Though no one could hear what he had to say, or her response, everyone saw his hands fly up in the air in exasperation and heard him exclaim, "Man, Ellene, children have done things like this for centuries. Usually when we're sent out on these kinds of calls, the child is asleep under some piece of furniture in a corner somewhere. It happens."

"I just think that it's impossible to keep your eyes on so many—"

"It's just as easy, maybe easier, to lose track of one child as it is one of a dozen. Where did you lose the common sense you used to have?" The tirade continued as they walked away from Aggie's house.

Everyone left behind appeared to be at a loss for words. Eventually, Aggie turned to Meg and said "Is it really that serious? Am I going to be investigated or something because somehow he crawled across the yard and under a car?"

Megan gave a wry grin. "From what I hear, Ellene is just over zealous sometimes. Being the new gal over at social services, she probably wants to make her mark, and you were a prime target. William will win her over. She has had her eye on him since the first time they met."

Aggie sighed, and Megan mistakenly concluded that Aggie viewed Ellene as a rival. Minutes later, she said, "I wish Murphy and William would leave."

"Murphy?" Megan was confused, but Aggie's explanation just confirmed the woman's suspicions. The young deputy would have been surprised to see how wrong she really was.

"As in Murphy's law. If anything can go wrong, it will. This woman just seems to personify that. I'm calling her Murphy. It'll help me keep my sense of humor." Aggie sighed, thanked the officers for their help, and led the children inside for dinner.

Tina says: Aggie...oh, Aaaaaaagggggggieeeeeeeee...
Aggie says: At last... a REST!
Tina says: Well... how is the kitchen coming?
Aggie says: It's at a standstill.
Tina says: How come?
Aggie says: Luke has been busy with some properties and with some other prearranged jobs.
Tina says: Miss having a man around the house?
Aggie says: NOPE!
Tina says: I thought you liked him.
Aggie says: I do!
Tina says: But with no man around how are you getting things done?
Aggie says: Who said no man? You said LUKE and assumed no man!
Tina says: William!
Aggie says: You should see the outside of this place. The shrubs are pruned and the whole thing is mowed and weeded... there are flowers growing, half the trim is painted, and the door is a beautiful RED.
Tina says: WOW! Why didn't you guys finish the kitchen?
Aggie says: Oh, Tina... he just hates this house. He won't come inside.
Tina says: HE WONT COME INSIDE?
Aggie says: Not for more than a minute or two. He's been in this house for a grand total of 20 minutes. MAX.

Tina says: What's up with that?

Aggie says: Dunno! I have more news though

Tina says: Ohh?

Aggie says: Yep… we have a new neighbor.

Tina says: Oh, yeah?

Aggie says: Yep, I've christened her Murphy.

Tina says: Hmm as in "if anything can go wrong it will?"

Aggie says: You got it!

Tina says: So what's wrong with Murphy?

Aggie says: Well… besides the fact that she's an overzealous social worker, and appears to want her talons in William (not that he seems to notice, mind you), she doesn't like me.

Tina says: What's not to like!

Aggie says: Yeah, you tell me! Hee hee

Tina says: Well… sounds like your date with William paid off anyway. He appears to be coming around more.

Aggie says: I think he's more comfy without Luke around. Too much testosterone or something.

Tina says: Hee hee… that's for sure.

Aggie says: Well, Luke had one day to work on things today, and it was a good thing.

Tina says: Why?

Aggie says: Well, it has to do with a broken window, a crawling baby, and a near Amber Alert.

Tina says: I think it's a good thing I'm sitting down.

Aggie says: Got aspirin?

Tina says: Do I need it?

Aggie says: If you don't, I do. No seriously, Ian…

Tina says: Ian. 9-1-1. Again?

Aggie says: No, I called this time. Ian went missing.

Tina says: No! That's my worst nightmare for you.

Aggie says: Don't I know it. We looked for two hours! Based upon Ian's lack of interest in an afternoon nap, apparently he slept the whole time he was hiding.

Tina says: Do I want to ask where?

Aggie says: Can you say under the Jag?

Tina says: *thud* You have to be kidding me. How did he get way out there? I've seen the pictures. It looks a long way from the house!

Aggie says: Your guess is better than mine. By the way, that place stinks to high heaven. It took a lot of soap to get the old oil and rotted wood smell out of him. Blech.

Tina says: Really? Amazing that an old house that has been empty for decades would have a carport that stinks and is oily. I'm just stunned.

Aggie says: It's a mystery — kind of like how he fell asleep in that filth and stench.

Tina says: And no one bothered to check the Jag for over two hours?

Aggie says: Um, Tina, they looked — the entire sheriff's office. With flashlights even.

Tina says: Are you writing this stuff down?

Aggie says: Scrapbook?

Tina says: I was thinking more like Reader's Digest or maybe fodder for Calvin and Hobbes or something.

Aggie says: Calvin's mother flashes back to babyhood when she dreamed of the old days and then shudders?

Tina says: Something like that.

Aggie says: There's the phone… better go… poof

Tina says: Poofs!

GooD GRIEF

Chapter Twenty-One

Sunday, July 14th

The soothing sounds of four-part a cappella harmony drifted out the windows of the Stuart-Milliken home Sunday morning. Ellie lay curled on the couch, a bucket on the floor next to her, the victim of overindulgence on chocolate syrup over ice cream. The children had neglected to tell Aggie of Ellie's weak stomach for chocolate syrup, and Ellie had managed to wheedle a second bowl out of an exhausted Aggie. The result was a long night of retching and whimpering. Motherhood was a messy job sometimes. Aggie was extremely thankful that they had ditched carpets and kept the hardwood floors.

The youngest three children chased a balloon all through the first floor, their squeals drowning out the a cappella quartet. Lost in the story of Joshua and Jericho, Aggie occasionally grumbled for them to, "keep it down." Ellie, sipping on 7-UP, didn't have the energy to read, watch a movie, or even play with her paper dolls. Instead, she lay on the couch, with her eyes closed, listening to the music.

"Aunt Aggie?"

"Hmm?"

"Can I have a cracker? I think I'm better. I'm hungry."

By the time William and the rest of the children arrived after church, Ellie was hiding one of Ian's toys and watching the twins search for it, Ian crawling behind as if trying to participate. Aggie made grilled cheese sandwiches and sliced a watermelon, while William heated a can of chicken noodle soup for Ellie, and everyone changed into play clothes. Seeing the wistful look on Ellie's face as everyone else thundered outside for a game of tag, William swallowed his discomfort and nudged Aggie.

"What about charades after lunch. Something to keep her interested but resting most of the time?"

Her eyes traveled to where Ellie sat, arms laying across the back of the couch, head resting on her arms, gazing outside quite pitifully. "That would be great."

It took several tries to explain and demonstrate the concept of charades to most of the children, but once they got the hang of it, everyone got into the spirit of the game. Aggie, amused at the silly antics and elaborate acting, almost gave away her charade the moment she unfolded it. Her slip read, "Be a school dunce," and as she read it, her face immediately contorted into an idiotic expression. Laird howled and in quick succession, tossed out idiot, fool, and finally, dunce.

"You win."

Ellie had a surprising talent for the game and guessed one out of every three charades on the first try. By the time everyone acted out their third charade, she was obviously quite well and started a killer game of hide and seek by simply covering her face and counting. Aggie shrugged and stepped outside to survey the work accomplished on the house. After two more pairs of shutters, the paint on the front porch floor, and the eaves on the "Murphy side" of the house, the outside work would be done — well, once the screens were replaced.

Several hours later, Aggie pulled a bag of hamburger

patties from the freezer. William, his hands covered in black paint, came into the living room and washed his brush in the laundry sink. "I have to go home, Aggie. There is a homeowners association meeting tonight, and I'm the ad-hock secretary, since the regular is on vacation."

"Can you stay for dinner?"

William shook his head. "Thanks for including me in your day today; it was really a lot of fun, and we're down to reattaching the shutters and painting the porch floor. I have to start work on Tuesday, but I'll be over tomorrow if you want."

Aggie assumed a regal air and said in her snootiest English accent, "Ohhh, I think that would be lovely. Do come, William, m'dear. It'll be such fun! What?"

Aggie giggled as William took her hand, making a courtly bow. His earnest look as he kissed the back of her hand was unsettling; she hadn't intended for him to play along with her. Luke entered the room in the middle of their game but darted back outside before she could welcome him. What had seemed funny was now awkward.

William winked at Aggie before walking out the door. "Hey, Sullivan, we haven't seen you around here much lately." William's voice carried across the yard as he hopped in his car and drove home— just as he'd intended. Mrs. Dyke could make of his words what she would.

The burgers were half-grilled before Aggie realized she hadn't expected Luke to come by that day. She carried the lightly buttered buns to him, as he flipped the meat, and then she attempted a nonchalant inquiry. "Did you manage to finish up the work you had to do?"

"House is ready to put on the market," Luke's mouth twitched, but Aggie didn't notice.

"And the woman with the tree leaning over her house?"

"Tomorrow's job. I knew William was here through tomorrow, so I took Friday off and spent it with Mom and Corinne."

"You didn't have to stay away, Luke. I mean, I know

311

you've got your own things to do, and you need a break now and then too. But, if you needed to do something around here, you could have come." She bit her lip and tried to rephrase. "Wait; that sounded as if I expect your life to revolve around me. I just mean that I know you have worked out a schedule, and I didn't want you to feel obligated to stay away just because William was helping me outside. He only came because—"

She swallowed hard, and Luke finished for her. "Because I wasn't going to be here. I think William is just an introvert in an extroverted job. I was one less person to have to interact with on his vacation."

"Should I have refused his offer?" Uncertainty tinged her voice. The last thing Aggie wanted to do was impose on anyone.

"I think he would have been insulted." Several minutes passed as Luke removed the burgers, toasted the buns, and piled everything on the platter in Aggie's hands. Just as she'd decided he didn't have anything else to add, Luke finally said, "In William's job, he's had to interact with your family, mostly in a professional capacity. I think, especially after Mrs. Dyke's double-blind date, he needed time with everyone as a person rather than an officer."

The contrast, between Luke's ease in her home and William's avoidance of the interior whenever possible, was marked during and after dinner. While Aggie washed dishes in the laundry sink, Vannie and Laird scrubbed the walls and wiped down the new drywall with a tack cloth. Aggie planned to paint the first coat of primer that night when the kids were in bed, so no little fingers could mar it before it dried.

Luke, having missed the little ones, chased them on hands and knees and then retreated as quickly as possible before they piled on him in a fit of giggles and tickles. As much as she tried not to, Aggie couldn't help but compare the stark differences between how each man related to her, her home, and her children. Some of it, she assumed, was William's job. He was instinctively more protective, seeing things through eyes that likely had witnessed great suffering in his profession. Luke, from a stable and loving home with siblings, nieces, and nephews, was naturally more comfortable.

As another burst of giggles erupted at Luke's crazy antics, Aggie decided that she needed to talk to Mrs. Dyke. If anyone could explain William's behavior, she could. "Hey, I was wondering if you could stay a while. I really would love to go next door and visit with Mrs. Dyke."

Luke assured her he'd be happy to stay. "I'm glad I stopped by. I've missed these little guys." He paused and then with a teasing glint in his eyes added, "Well, ok, ok, I've missed the older kids too." Aggie stood, hands on hips, pretending to glare at him. "Ok, so maybe I've thought of you now and then."

Something in Luke's tone unsettled her. Being on a mission, she didn't have time to dissect her reaction. Instead, Aggie smiled at him and mouthed a thank-you before marching down her steps and across the road. Her shoulders were squared, her footsteps firm, and her hands clasped behind her back to hide her fidgeting. She succeeded only in advertising it to Luke and Vannie, watching from the screen door.

Mrs. Dyke stepped out onto her porch as Aggie reached the steps. "I've been wondering when you'd come to visit."

Somehow, Aggie knew that Mrs. Dyke had been expecting her to come for more than just a neighborly chat. She considered exchanging pleasantries but decided that directness was probably wisest. "Mrs. Dyke, I know you've known William for years. Please tell me what is hurting him. Is it me? The house? My kids? What is bothering him?"

Mrs. Dyke was surprisingly silent. As she waited, Aggie determined that she wouldn't ask twice. If the woman didn't feel comfortable sharing, then Aggie was not going to pressure her. After a time, Aggie realized the woman was praying. Hesitantly, Aggie took the old wrinkled hand in hers and prayed aloud. "Father, we are here... together... hurting. William is in such pain, and I don't know how to help him. Please give Mrs. Dyke a peace about speaking to me. If my understanding isn't in Your will, please help me accept that, and show me how I can help him. In Jesus' name, we pray, amen."

The two women sat in the darkness on the antique porch swing and rocked— a study in contrasts. Young and old, lithe and arthritic, slender and plump, they couldn't be more opposite. The only thing they knew they shared was a concern for one man. Aggie decided to tell her neighbor what was on her mind and see if it helped the woman decide how to respond.

"Mrs. Dyke, William has been acting strangely."

"I noticed that. Chasing you around the other day— what got into the boy?" Mrs. Dyke's eyes twinkled at the blushing young woman.

"Well, I guess I started it. We sort of had a paint fight..." She shrugged. "—then Cari swiped his ears with my paintbrush. I don't know how she got that..." Aggie winked at the elderly woman, and they both chuckled.

"What I don't understand, is William's aversion to my house. I know that must sound harsh, but honestly, the man has hardly spent more than five minutes inside! Well, until this morning, and even then, it was obviously sheer torture. The other day, Tavish was under the stairs, and William came unglued. First, he was angry, and then he was so sad. How can I help him if I don't know why he's so upset?" Aggie's frustration was evident.

"The stairs? Oh, my." A long silence followed. After what seemed to be several minutes, Mrs. Dyke continued. "Aggie, I'd love, more than anything, to be able to tell you what I know. It'd be nice to have someone else help carry the burden. But, this isn't my story to tell. I've always had a hard time not sharing things I shouldn't, but this one... no matter how much I want to, I've never been able to speak of it." She looked at her

314

gnarled hands and then back up at Aggie. "Talk to him. Make him talk to you. Win his trust. He needs someone to confide in. What he doesn't need is that spit and polish woman that has moved in over there." Mrs. Dyke's disdain for Ellene warmed Aggie's heart.

"Murphy is enough to drive any man to drink. I don't think you need to worry about him. He was quite angry with her the other day when Ian disappeared. I thought he was really going to let her have it."

"Murphy?" Mrs. Dyke looked very confused.

Blushing, she said, "I christened her that on a bad day. She kind of got under my skin, so I named her Murphy. As in Murphy's Law..." Mrs. Dyke still looked confused, so Aggie continued. "If it can go wrong it will?"

Luke's trademark smirk twisted at the corners of his mouth, when he heard gales of laughter from across the way. The children were all in bed, he had the first coat of primer painted, and the brushes and rollers washed. Not knowing what else to do, he opened the armoire and flipped through the DVDs on the bottom shelf. Finding an old Fred Astaire and Audrey Hepburn movie that he'd never seen, he eased his tired body into the recliner and tried to focus on the movie. If it was a good one, he could surprise his mother by bringing it home for a mother-son video night.

As a crazy woman demanded that American consumers "think pink" on the TV screen, Luke realized that Aggie had been gone for hours. Furthermore, he sensed that she probably had no clue how much time had passed; it would likely feel good to be out and carefree. She carried such a heavy burden, and that thought weighed on his heart. She was doing a job that most married women would find overwhelming, and Aggie did it alone. He thought of the time he'd spent there, the days Iris Landry or his uncle visited, and the two weeks of William's help and amended that thought. She did it nearly alone. Luke wondered if she'd ever considered marriage or if she just hadn't found the right man. Did she give up a relationship to become mother to the children? She didn't act as if she was heart-sore.

Audrey Hepburn arrived at Orly airport in Paris when Aggie finally came home. She kicked off her shoes, plumped the couch cushions, and settled in without a word. While they watched the rest of the movie in a companionable silence, Luke popped microwave popcorn, the sounds of crunching corn blending in with the songs and quips of the movie. As Fred Astaire searched for Audrey Hepburn in the little garden behind the chapel, Aggie sighed.

"Romantic at heart, Aggie?" Luke's voice held a discernible trace of amusement. "I had you pegged as more practical than romantic."

"Well, I've never been accused of being romantic, but there is something enchanting about someone who knows you well enough to go to all of that trouble for you."

After a few more frames of the movie, Luke spoke thoughtfully. "Well, then, I'd say that you are one of the most enchanting people I've ever met."

Aggie tilted her head backwards over the arm of the couch, nearly hitting her head on the recliner she often thought of as "Luke's chair." He grinned down at her. Eventually, he decided to be merciful. "Aggie, you go to a lot of trouble for a lot of people, every single day. Every. Day. You even keep my favorite soda and chips nearby when I'm working. If enchanting means going to a lot of trouble for someone, I'd say you are definitely enchanting." He hesitated, as if unsure if he should continue, and said, "Then again, you've enchanted me for a long time."

Luke rose, gathered his things and with a final, "See you later, Mibs," he pushed open the screen door. His voice, barely audible with the door shut behind him, reached her ears as almost a whisper. "Sleep well."

Monday, July 15th

316

William was working on the yard before Aggie was awake the next morning. When she came out to the front steps, she was surprised to see that he had planted four new rosebushes, two of them with blooms. "I'm going to call you *Quiet Man*."

William looked at her and raised his eyebrows. "Am I supposed to understand that?"

Aggie quirked one of her own eyebrows and shrugged. "John Wayne and Maureen O'Hara. Old movie. She teases him that he is planting roses when they need potatoes or cabbage — or something like that."

William forced a polite smile onto his face but added honestly, "I've never been a John Wayne fan."

Aggie agreed. "Me either. I just like this one. Stay tonight. We can watch it, and you'll see."

William nodded and went back to his planting. Once finished, he began working on a watering system that involved odd sounding components like bubblers, drippers, and soakers. Aggie, with a hungry crew of children who would inhale every box of cereal they owned if she let them, left him to play with his big boy toys and went inside to cut apple slices and boil eggs to go with the cold cereal. She'd learned the hard way that a bowl of cold cereal did not keep her children satisfied for long.

Once they washed, dried, and put away the breakfast dishes, a fierce game of freeze tag broke out on the front lawn. William and Aggie watched several switches in chasers before Aggie developed a glint in her eyes and yelled, "I'm in! Gotcha, William; you're it!" and darted behind the tree.

Aggie and Laird joined forces in distracting the other it players and managed to avoid being tagged. William, with careful maneuvering, tagged a few others, with what appeared to be serious attempts to get Aggie and Laird. However, he was bluffing, as he bided his time. He knew that if they were on their guard, Aggie and her nephew would be able to elude him.

William moved in for the kill. He pretended to attempt to tag Vannie but deliberately tripped over his own feet. Aggie,

317

who was sneaking behind him, tripped and fell over him. William laughed. "Gotcha. You're it."

Ellene heard the squeals and laughter, while watching glimpses of the game from her window. She wondered what was so fascinating about Aggie and all those children that William chose to spend so much time there. *"I thought he'd love to stay as far away from that place as possible,"* the woman thought to herself, before picking up the phone to make another call.

As Aggie helped the twins brush their teeth on their way to bed that night, she heard odd sounds coming from downstairs. She arrived at the bottom of the stairs to find the TV and the DVD player gone. "Hey, William, I thought officers were supposed to stop thieves— not become them!"

"I thought we could watch that movie you were telling me about. Come see; I've got it all set up on the porch."

Aggie found it odd, but she had to admit to herself that it was fun sitting in beanbag chairs on the front porch and watching *The Quiet Man,* accompanied by a chorus of crickets. It occurred to her, as they munched on microwave popcorn and laughed at the funny courting practices, that perhaps William's discomfort with being in her home had more to do with propriety than anything too disturbing.

William paused the movie. "You know what, Aggie? This is fun. I just realized how much I've enjoyed being here these past couple of weeks. Thanks for letting me into your lives."

Before Aggie could reply, he punched the play button on the remote, and the priests on screen sang hysterical songs at the wedding reception about not wanting to get married. "Can you imagine such an arrogant boob?" Aggie always became indignant when the brother swept the dowry on the floor.

William smiled at her. "Aggie, champion of the underdog. What about this guy? He's like Jacob. He got tricked into giving his sister in marriage."

Aggie laughed. "He took it personally. He had no real objection to Sean; he just objected to losing a housekeeper. He didn't like Sean, no, but there was no rational reason not to. It's just ludicrous."

"Well, personally, I objected to the deception, but no, you're right. He was just being selfish. It's the deception that irritates me."

"Ooooh, look! I love this part." Aggie settled back into watching as the scene with the roses unfolded.

William roared with laughter. "What part did you like? The part where she joshes him for planting the flowers, the part where he gives her a flower, or the part where he swats her?"

William watched Aggie's face and wondered if she knew how easily he could read her thoughts. Rolling sideways, he reached between the porch railing and plucked a rose from his newly planted bushes. Settling back into his chair, he handed the rose to Aggie. "I planted the roses. I'll even give you the flower, but I stop there!"

Aggie laughed. "I'll say you better! My father would have your hide!"

Mrs. Dyke watched them from her second story guest room and found them charming. "Giving her a rose. Smart move, Billy Boy." Poor William never knew how often the elderly woman called him that when he couldn't hear her.

Aggie noticed a change in William's posture and glanced at him. Slowly, he tensed as he sat up straighter, leaning further forward as each second passed. Aggie smiled to herself. The fight scene began, and William became completely engrossed in the scene. Before long, he dodged blows and leaned even closer, jabbing his fists in a perfect imitation of the priest on screen.

She tried not to laugh when he jumped to his feet and yelled, "Deck that water guy!"

Embarrassed by his outburst, William sheepishly settled back into the beanbag and watched as the movie ended. "I liked the movie, Aggie. It proves that John Wayne can act—given the right part."

In her freezer, were several pieces of cheesecake she'd squirreled away for an escape after a bad day. Aggie dug through the cavernous recesses of the appliance, retrieved the contraband, and cut slices for each of them. William had the electronics replaced and working before Aggie could get them forks out of the totes. Taking his plate, William led her back to the front porch. Somehow, even though it still bothered her to see further evidence of his discomfort in her home, the evening seemed to solidify their friendship, and that feeling remained long after the tail lights of his Corvette faded into the moonless night.

Tuesday, July 16th

Tavish, working hard all weekend, despite the summer heat, cleared the storage area underneath the stairs, painted it, and cleaned up his mess from the previous Friday. Tuesday, he began moving in. After watching him for quite a while, Aggie pulled him aside for a little chat. "Tavish, why did you go to all this work? What is wrong with your room upstairs?"

The boy ducked his head and was quiet. He didn't answer until Aggie, obviously concerned, urged him again. "Aunt Aggie, I just like to be alone. The noise bothers me, and I can't think. I like to read and think, and try to figure things out, and it's just a lot easier when I don't have anyone around. Our room isn't just my room, it's Ian's too. I can't tell him to be quiet or go away when it's not all mine, and he has to take naps in there and stuff." With that, he turned back to making his little corner of the house "home."

Determined to get back on track with the kitchen renovation, Aggie decided to ask Luke if another coat of paint was necessary, or if she should carry in the flooring now. "Ok, Luke..."

Aggie looked around for him, and eventually she saw him through the picture window in the living room. He was out front, guiding a large truck, as it backed up the driveway. Curious as to who was backing in, Aggie dashed out the door and tripped down the steps, fortunately unseen by teasing children or an over-protective Luke. When she saw Luke and a man she didn't recognize unloading cabinets from the truck, she gasped. "Luke, where did you find them? They are exactly what I wanted!"

Her squeals of excitement brought children from every corner of the house. Even Tavish the hermit stepped from his own little world to see what made Aggie squeal with such obvious delight. Luke and Laird helped unload each cabinet from the truck and carry them to the back step. Once finished, Luke thanked the driver for bringing them, as he handed the man a check. The burly man jumped into the truck, and as he put it in gear, he stuck his head out the window and said, "Hey, Luke. Anytime you feel like building more cabinets like those, let me know. My wife is green right now. I'd love to see her natural color again." With that, the truck slowly drove down the driveway and pulled onto the road.

Luke arranged the pieces in the proper position for the new kitchen while Aggie watched. His frown over a ding on the corner of one cabinet amused her. Although she was eager to inspect the cabinets closely, she felt awkward; custom cabinets were completely unexpected. They'd decided, weeks ago, to purchase prefabricated, boxed cabinetry for the new kitchen, as a cost-saving measure.

No wonder he'd been so scarce. With all of his other commitments, he must have been working late into his evenings to build them. If the walls were done, they could install the floor! "Do I need to do another coat of paint in the kitchen or—"

Luke shook his head and called for Laird and Tavish to help him carry in the flooring from the corner of the living room. While they pulled box after box of her new oak flooring into the house, Aggie inspected the cabinets. She'd considered making her kitchen out of old antiques. She thought that, with a little work, a Hoosier, a few desks, and a few sideboards could be combined, raised, and connected to make the room look like it was created out of antiques. The resulting kitchen would have looked like it grew into the house after years of use. Aggie loved the eclectic feel of her idea, although Allie had always found that side of her irritating.

Luke, trying to evoke that same feeling Aggie had described, had created false fronts on the cabinets. Perfectly crafted to resemble furniture, each piece had all the best components of an eclectic mixture of furniture and the convenience of real cabinets. Aggie didn't know how to cook, but she was going to have her dream kitchen! She wondered, as she absently ran one finger over a carefully turned leg where the sink would go, if perhaps she and Vannie should take a cooking class together.

Luke startled Aggie from her reverie by covering her eyes with his hands in the age-old "guess who" manner. "Do you like them? Do you think they'll look right when you are done?"

Aggie turned, grinning. "They're perfect! I can't believe you — all that time — and where did you learn to do this? You are more than just a handyman; you are an artist!" Her admiration for his skills was a little effusive but understandably so. His craftsmanship was impeccable, the quality far beyond anything she could have imagined, and she felt inadequate in fully expressing her appreciation.

Luke blushed. After a few stammers and false starts, he said simply, "Thank you. Do you think you can help? We're going to need a third pair of hands."

After a hasty lunch, four bumped heads, a couple of dirty diapers, and several unfortunate bruises, the floor was laid, and the base cabinets were screwed to studs in the wall. Aggie was exhausted, Laird was near tears, but Luke seemed as fresh as he'd been when he started that morning. She watched, fascinated, as Luke installed her favorite cabinet.

Along one wall, Luke had carefully measured a spot to put in a mock Hoosier. Looking as if it'd been rescued from an old farmhouse and refinished, the piece of furniture was the last piece Luke had created. The corners were dinged, and there were random gouges that Aggie learned were made with a hammer and screwdriver. Punched tinwork gleamed on the upper cupboard doors, and the stain was darker in one corner as if it had been repaired many years ago.

"Aunt Aggie, is it time for dinner? I'm hungwy." Lorna munched on a cracker, crumbs dropping on the new floor. Aggie surveyed the unfinished kitchen, the hungry child, and the mess strewn across the living room, and decided that she was too tired to consider cooking.

"Ok, guys, pack it up! Faces, hands, shoes, socks, and hair done now! March. March. Left, left, left, right, left. Move 'em out! We're having pizza!" Squeals of delight followed. The stairs sounded like thunder in Arizona's monsoon season.

Luke grinned at Aggie and said, "If only all drill sergeants were that popular, huh?"

Aggie smiled, realizing fully, and for the first time, she liked this mothering thing. She enjoyed the trust the children placed in her and the way that they all interacted with each other. In college, she'd specifically planned her studies to focus on high school rather than elementary. She could now see that her decision would have been a huge mistake. She loved the wonder of it all. Their discovery of the simplest things delighted and stimulated the smaller children, while the older children felt full of wisdom with their "years of experience." Aggie knew that most people would think she was crazy, but she now hoped that she'd get to experience pregnancy, birth, and those first days of infancy as well.

Shaking herself out of her musings, Aggie invited Luke to join them. She wasn't surprised when he declined without looking up from his work, but she was disappointed. The children would love eating out with Luke. "Well, we'll bring you some, ok? Want anything else? Soda, dessert... Ben Gay?" Luke chuckled, as he helped her load the children into the van. He didn't know he'd regret not going that night.

The drive into town was accompanied by impromptu parodies of We're Marching to Zion by Laird. He sang lustily down the road and all while Aggie struggled to parallel park a fifteen-passenger van, "We're going for pizza, wonderful, cheesy pizza..."

"Ok, ok, move 'em out! Pizza and soda pitchers, coming up!" Aggie continued her drill sergeant fun as the group moved into the pizza place. The usual stares of those already seated made Aggie want to scream. She led the children to the last two tables in the restaurant, inconveniently placed in the middle of the room, and seated everyone. With the younger children coloring on the line-drawn tablecloths, and older ones supervising, Aggie went to order.

"Welcome to the 'ria. I'm Cissy; may I take your order?" The petite blonde had a voice that only a cheerleader would use.

Aggie considered for a moment. It was awfully late for soda. Throwing caution to the wind, Aggie ordered two pitchers of root beer and three large pizzas. The girl eyed her cautiously before asking, "Are those kids a group from The Church or something?"

Aggie grinned. "Nope. All mine."

"All yours! Really? You don't look a day over twenty-nine!"

Aggie hesitated and then spoke. "I'm twenty two." She considered letting the girl live in abject confusion then sighed and added, "Their mother was my sister. She died. I inherited. Can we get some breadsticks for right now?"

Flustered, the girl turned to the warmer behind her and pulled out two baskets. Dumping two more orders into them, she turned back to Aggie and handed her the breadsticks. "Here you go! Enjoy!"

Aggie enjoyed all right— she enjoyed the girl's discomfiture. In the past six months, Aggie had heard every remark imaginable. From "Are they all yours?" to "Are you having any more?" Aggie was thoroughly sick of the constant assumption that the number of children in her family was open to discussion with strangers. Then there was the extra attention over the twins. Lorna and Cari received even more comments and exclamations regarding their adorability. Sometimes she and the children made up goofy responses to the questions as they rode in the van or sitting around the dinner table. Aggie's personal favorite was to the often heard, "Oh, my, you have eight children!" Laird's brilliant masterpiece of a response was, "Uh oh, who are we missing?" One evening, as she was feeling especially ornery, Aggie had come up with "Well, for now, but you never know when God'll surprise me with three or four more!"

Once at the table with the baskets of breadsticks, Aggie sent Vannie and Laird for the drinks. Cups full of root beer were distributed, but before everyone got theirs, Cari knocked over Lorna's in her eagerness to reach hers. Sighing, Aggie went to the counter and asked for a roll of paper towels. Bouncy Cissy gave her a small handful of napkins, but Aggie shook her head. "No, I need a full roll of paper towels, please. I'm sure you have one somewhere; please get me a roll. We're going to need them; I can guarantee it."

By the time that the pizza arrived, five out of the eight children had spilled their sodas, three breadsticks landed on the floor for much longer than a five-second rule could cover, and Ian was chewing on one of the ones retrieved from under the table. Aggie hadn't figured that part out yet, much to Laird's relief. The pizza was piping hot, and three children burned their tongues before she could caution anyone. Ian whined for his bites as she frantically tried to cool it. She was mortified and felt as though everyone in the restaurant would consider her incompetent. Aggie knew she was but didn't want the rest of the world to know it. Taking a deep breath, she glanced out the window to mentally regroup and saw William exiting his vehicle.

She wanted to crawl under the table. Great. With all that was happening, the last thing she needed was more proof for William that she couldn't handle her children. Resigned to her fate, she cheerily waved across the restaurant. William, nodding at a few of the guests, joined the lively crew. Cari squealed and jumped up, knocking over her chair. Kenzie sat and stared adoringly at him, while Laird tried to catch the deputy's eye.

In an attempt to divert attention from the bedlam, Aggie dragged two pieces of pizza onto a plate for William. As if things couldn't get worse, William backed into her as she stepped toward him, and the result was a beautiful grease glob on the back of the officer's shirt. The restaurant erupted in laughter, proving, to her mortification, that she was the entertainment du jour.

William's ears turned red as he looked behind him. "You sure know how to welcome a guy, don't you, Aggie?"

Either angry or mortified, William glanced over his shoulder and sighed. Armed with paper towels, Aggie tried to undo some of the damage to his shirt. "I think you're going to need some stain remover. Sorry."

Aggie gathered all the trash that they'd accumulated and tossed everything in the over-sized garbage can near the door. She filled another plate with food for William and set it at the one empty chair. Indicating her peace offering, Aggie sat back down and tried to get the children to eat quietly again.

As if by example, William ate in relative silence. Laird chattered about the events of the day, the "awesome" cabinets that Luke had made, and their amazing kitchen floor. This all piqued William's interest. A kitchen would mean that the worst of the house renovation was nearing completion, and this would get Ellene off of Aggie's back and make life easier for Aggie. Watching her wash dishes in the bathtub, had been hard to stomach, and the laundry sink wasn't much better. He'd seen her walk gingerly for a while afterward, and he knew if it bothered someone as young and active as Aggie, it couldn't be easy.

As he finished his pizza, William watched Aggie trying to clean up the baby, toss even more trash, and corral everyone in their seats. An elderly couple stopped by the table on their way out the door, and the man put a twenty-dollar bill into her hand. Several people in the room overheard the man say, "They're fine children, very well behaved. You're doing a great job with them. Take this and get them some ice cream, ok?" William beamed at Aggie's obvious surprise.

"Thank you. I'm sorry we were so noisy. I've never taken them all out to a restaurant and didn't know how messy things get—"

"Young woman, you are doing a great job. I'm sure their parents have no idea what a treasure they have in you." Turning to the children, the elderly man playfully shook his finger at them. "You tell your mama and daddy that you guys were very good tonight, you hear?"

The children erupted into a chaotic explosion of emotions. Vannie burst into tears, rushed out of the building, and ran down the street. Laird, ready to cry, glanced at Aggie, and rushed after her. Tavish and Elspeth clung to each other and sobbed, while Kenzie threw herself at William, wailing. Cari and Lorna didn't understand the situation but began sobbing and crying along with everyone else. Ian whimpered and fussed, as Aggie stood helpless, in complete despair, and unsure what to do.

William, however, was in his element. He was very good at restoring order to difficult situations. While he escorted the couple out the door, he explained the situation. With a quick glance around him, he saw Vannie and Laird turn into the park, and instantly understood where he'd find them. Soothing the toddlers, and taking the baby, William gathered Kenzie onto his lap with Ian and helped calm her. "Shhh, baby, it's ok. Why don't you, Tavish, and Ellie go sit in the van and buckle yourself into your car seat? I'll help your aunt. "Come on, Aggie; let's go get the others."

Aggie nodded dejectedly as she fought her own tears. Since actively talking about Allie and Doug, their loss, and the hole it left in their lives, Aggie had noticed that the children seemed to fall apart at the most unexpected times. It was as though their parents had just died all over again. Everyone was touchy, and though the little children weren't as affected, they did react to the pain of everyone else.

"Where could they have gone? I can't believe I'm sitting here failing again. I can't do this, William! I should let Geraldine Stuart try it, 'cause I am just blowing it." Aggie now joined the chorus of weeping, pain-riddled Stuart-Millikens.

While Aggie cried, William drove to the nearby park and went to find Laird and Vannie. Before long, he spotted them sitting on the old merry-go-round, their arms wrapped around each other's shoulders, and swaying with the gentle motion created by Laird's restless feet. William heard Vannie's sobs from three hundred yards, and though Laird, wiping his own eyes intermittently, tried to comfort his distraught sister, he wasn't succeeding. William motioned for Laird to go back to the van and took his place.

"I haven't sat on this merry-go-round since I was about your age or a little younger. It's odd; I was crying too."

Choking out the words, Vannie asked, "Why were—" she sniffled, "you crying?"

"My father left us that morning."

"He just left?" Vannie was stunned enough to stop crying.

"Yep. I thought my world had ended." William's voice still held a trace of pain.

"Wow. That's even worse than him dying, isn't it?" Vannie started crying again but more softly this time.

"How do you figure that?" William had often thought death would be preferable, but people had been quick to assure him that, as long as his father was alive, there was hope that he'd come home.

"Well, Momma and Daddy left, but they didn't want to. They had to go. You know, they had no choice. But, your dad chose to leave. That would be terrible."

William nodded. "That's what I always thought." He cleared his thick throat and continued. "Vannie, your aunt is really worried about you. We need to go back. Are you ok? You ready to go home?"

Vannie sniffed and nodded. They walked slowly back to the van where Aggie sat sobbing, her head in her hands. "Mr. Markenson? Is it ok to be glad that home isn't where Momma and Daddy lived? Is it wrong to be glad we're gone from there?"

William smiled and gave the girl a quick squeeze. "It's just fine, honey. I understand. Really."

Vannie glanced up at him curiously. "You don't like our house though, do you?"

William was visibly startled. "What makes you say that?"

"I don't know, really. I just noticed that you don't seem to like to be inside, is all. You seem nervous. Well, not the first time you came. You sure showed Grandmother who was boss." The girl giggled as she got into the van. "I think Grandmother is a little scared of you."

Aggie's eyes questioned William through her tears, but he just smiled. The drive home was swift and punctuated with sniffs and sobs, and William began to worry. He was used to people pulling it together after an initial burst of grief. He'd never been around long enough to see the aftermath of the misery that a bereavement call created. As he turned into the driveway, William visibly sagged with relief when he saw Luke's truck still parked in its usual place on the side of the house.

Luke sauntered out onto the porch, looking quite pleased with himself, but when he saw William driving Aggie's van, he rushed down the steps to help. "Aggie, are you ok?" It was one of those unnecessary questions that people ask and then kick themselves for later.

The temptation to throw herself at Luke and sob out her troubles on his understanding shoulders nearly overrode her last shred of self-control. Luke had that something, she never could define it, that understood women, or at least understood how to respond to them, even if lost as to who they were or what they wanted. However, it wouldn't be right to take advantage of him like that. Clinging to a single man, one who

329

spent most of his days and many of his evenings at her house might just qualify as inappropriate behavior for an equally single Christian woman and mother of eight. Instead, she ran upstairs and threw herself on her bed, in the same manner that she had done the night that her sister told the family that she was getting married. It seemed to her that not much had changed in fourteen years.

William helped Luke get everyone inside, and though it was nearing bedtime, Luke turned on a movie and popped popcorn for everyone. William seemed surprised. "You don't think that they should go to bed? I was going to put everyone down."

"I think they'll need reassurance that Aggie's ok before they can sleep. Do you think Mrs. Dyke would come over and talk with her? Can you tell me what happened?" For once, Luke didn't struggle for words.

William gave him a brief recap of the evening's turmoil and then headed down the driveway. Luke was surprised to see him turn toward Murphy's house. Knowing Aggie's dislike for the woman, Luke dragged himself upstairs. He hesitated outside Aggie's door. Should he knock or just go in? Knock and go in? He doubted she'd answer, but Luke knew that Aggie would not want to be caught unaware by Murphy. Taking a deep breath, Luke knocked and then entered her room.

The scene was heartbreaking. Out of habit, Luke started to close the door and realized that this wasn't a good idea. Instead, Luke pushed the door wide open and sat on the edge of Aggie's bed. "Aggie? Mibs, you need to cry, really. Cry it out. Let it all go. I'm so sorry."

Vannie appeared at the doorway. With a weak smile in Vannie's direction, Luke pulled Aggie's hair away from her face. "I wanted to let you alone to cry it out, but William seems to have gone after Murphy, and I knew you'd want to know."

What had been sobs, turned into gut-wrenching wails loud enough to reach the neighboring houses. It seemed like the world was against her. As she gained a little control, she looked tentatively toward the door, as if expecting to see Ellene standing there already. Seeing Vannie made her smile through her tears. Luke nodded at Vannie's silent question and watched as she ran and threw herself into Aggie's arms. A moment later, he left the room, closing the door quietly behind him. When he arrived downstairs, William and Murphy were rushing up the steps to the front door. "Mur— um, Ellene, I think she's going to be ok, but—"

"I'll go up. I'm used to dealing with situations like this. It'll be ok. Really. She'll see that I'm not a threat soon enough. I'm just here to help." Ellene gave Luke a reassuring smile and climbed the stairs. It was easy for her to find the correct room. The sounds of sniffles and sobs were audible down the hall. Ellene wondered, irrelevantly, if that little round room she passed was the one William had talked about so long ago. She shivered. Turning her focus back to where it belonged, Ellene knocked on Aggie's door and then entered.

Luke and William stood and stared at one another, neither knowing what to say or do. Cari, unaware that things had changed, tugged on William's pant leg. "The man said we could have ice cweam, but we didn't get any. Can we have ice cweam?" Luke looked questioningly at William.

"Of course, we can, Cari. We'll get it right now." Following Luke into the new kitchen, William whistled. "This is looking sharp!" His second thought, almost on the heels of the first, as his mind registered what his eyes saw, was indicative of the question Aggie would probably hear for years. "Why don't any of the cabinets match?"

Luke shrugged, as he pulled dishes out of one of the cabinets that he'd tried to fill just minutes before they arrived home. "Aggie wanted the kitchen to look like it'd been created with old furniture. She thought about buying stuff at garage sales and thrift or antique stores but decided it was too much work, time, and effort. Instead of the prefabricated ones she settled for, I made custom cabinets with a furniture façade. This way, she has the kitchen she really wanted, but they're easier to use and keep clean." He passed spoons to William before changing the subject. "Now, can you elaborate a bit on what happened?"

William explained further regarding the scene at the restaurant, while Luke scooped ice cream into bowls. Once every bowl had a generous scoop, Luke grabbed for the phone on his tool belt. "I'm calling my uncle; he's good with Aggie. Can you pass out the bowls?"

As Zeke's pick-up bounced up the driveway, Ellene, Vannie and Aggie came downstairs. Almost like universal cure-all, the ice cream, served with generous toppings of love, understanding, and compassion, slowly melted the fresh layer of grief that had stolen over the hearts of the Stuart-Milliken family that night. Assured that the situation was well in hand, William called Ellene aside and whispered something to her. The woman nodded and left with a wave and instructions to call at any time of day or night if Aggie needed help.

William then whispered to Aggie as she prevented Ellie from taking a second helping, "I'm actually on duty tonight, and I left the cruiser at the 'ria. Ellene is going to drive me back to work now that everyone is ok. I hope you understand."

While Luke cleaned up the ice cream mess and marked holes for the placement of upper cabinets, Zeke played with the twins, rocked the baby, and comforted Kenzie. Once the youngest four children were tucked into their beds with fresh pajamas, teeth brushed and faces washed, Zeke led Tavish and Elspeth out back to the swing. Though they were outside for a long time, both children returned with genuine smiles, although a bit weak, on their faces and went up to bed. Laird was next. With one arm around his shoulder, Zeke walked down the road talking with Aggie's oldest nephew, and though Aggie never learned exactly what Luke's uncle said that night, Laird returned looking more peaceful than he'd ever seemed. Later, Vannie and Zeke sat on the bench on the front porch as Vannie sobbed out the ache and loss she felt over the death of her parents. Without a word, the old man stroked her hair and wiped her tears, wisely allowing her the freedom to express herself without feeling the need to instruct.

Aggie watched it all with mixed emotions. Although he clearly helped each child that night, would it make the children emotionally dependent on Zeke too? What would happen to them if he died? How would the children cope with another loss? Aggie shook herself and sighed. This was no time to become paranoid. At Luke's quizzical look, Aggie confessed, "Faith and obedience are so interlocked that they are pretty easy at times. Trust— now trust is a whole 'nother ball game."

By ten o'clock, all the children were in bed, and Aggie sat next to Zeke on the couch, Luke in his favorite recliner. Zeke held one of Aggie's hands and listened to her ramble about all sorts of incomprehensible subjects. While Zeke comforted and advised, Luke, while appearing to be resting, prayed more fervently than he'd ever prayed in his life.

Once Aggie seemed at peace again, Zeke prayed for her and promised to bring his wife over sometime in the next week or two. "She's back from that mission trip she took for six weeks. They did sewing for families in Haiti, but she's coming home tomorrow."

"I'd like that. I've only met her that once. I'm sorry you had to come rescue me again."

Waving her apologies aside, Zeke opened the screen and called out goodnight, as he climbed down the steps. Luke followed, intending to leave himself, but Zeke stopped him. "Son, you need to go back in there and talk a spell. Don't leave here without speaking about this. It'll build a wall in your friendship. Things'll get awkward, and that little lassie needs all the friends she can get.

"I saw what you did with the kitchen in there. I bet she hasn't noticed some of it yet. Ask her if it's ok or if there is anything she wants changed. That'll do the job. Trust me." Zeke hesitated, as if he wanted to say more, but the wise old man kept his counsel and ambled slowly to his ancient truck.

A strange feeling of awkwardness washed over Luke as he

considered his uncle's words. The realization of that awkwardness proved his uncle's insight to be true, and he opened the screen door once more. "Aggie, I know it's not a convenient time, but can you tell me if everything in the kitchen is ok? The counter guy called while you were gone and said he has an opening tomorrow — got a cancellation. So, if everything is all right…" He looked around the living room and saw that she wasn't there.

Movement in the kitchen told him where he'd find her. As he watched from the kitchen doorway, Aggie opened and closed every cupboard and ran her fingers along the details he'd added to each piece. For a moment, Luke was concerned that he'd done everything wrong. Perhaps what looked right as an individual piece, didn't work once assembled. Her expression, while unreadable, didn't have the ecstatic overjoyed look he'd hoped to see. "Aggie? Are they ok? I can change things around or make new ones if these aren't right. You don't have —"

She spun in place, a huge grin lighting her face. "It's better than I ever imagined! Luke, I love it!" Impulsively, she threw her arms around him, hugging him fiercely. Embarrassed at her outburst, Aggie moved to the other side of the room, trying to hide her pink cheeks.

In order to avoid yet another set of walls from forming, Luke chose to ignore her embarrassment. "I take it that means this is ok? I can call Chet and have him bring the counters?"

Aggie nodded. Biting her lip, she tried hard not to overreact to her overreaction. "I think it's perfect. This island is just so amazing! I thought we decided I couldn't afford one."

"Well, buying the cabinets you were going to, you decided you didn't want to spend the extra money. Since you're only paying for the wood, this kitchen is actually costing less than you'd budgeted."

"Oh, no! I intend to find out exactly what the going rate for this kind of custom work is, and I intend to pay it. You've already given me a huge break on your labor; I'm not going to take advantage of it now!"

"But—"

Unwilling to start the argument she knew would ensue, Aggie interrupted with another question. "Why is the island so much shorter on that side?"

"Well, that was Mom's idea. She gave her input on almost every piece, and when I got to the island, she drew it and told me exactly how big to make everything." Scrunching down on his heels, he demonstrated. "Mom said when we were little she always wished that she had a part of the counter area that we could work at comfortably without a stool." He shrugged. "I just thought I should listen to Mom, or we'd both regret it."

Laughing at Luke's wink, Aggie ran another appreciative hand across the shorter side of the island and murmured absently, "What a wise mother; I wish I knew her. She could probably teach me so much."

"Would you really like to meet Mom?" Luke beamed. The love and respect he felt for his mother were etched in his eyes and his smile. "She's been anxious to meet you, but I didn't want to impose..."

Aggie stood in the middle of her new kitchen in thoughtful contemplation. If all went according to plan, her kitchen would be complete by Friday, at the latest. Could she get the dining room cleaned up by Sunday? Throwing caution to the wind, she issued her first official invitation. "Luke, would you and your mother like to come to church with us on Sunday and then here for dinner? I was planning a large roast. There'll be plenty, but..." She winked at him. "You might not have as many sandwiches next week!"

Without hesitating, Luke grabbed the phone off his work belt for the second time that night and dialed a family member. "Mom— no, I'm not home. Aggie has invited us to church with her on Sunday and over for lunch." He listened for a minute, and then, covering the phone with his hand, turned to Aggie. "Mom has my nephew, Rodney, this weekend. She'd have to bring him..."

"The kids will love it. Someone to play with. I can't wait to meet them both."

Luke relayed the message to his mother, promised to call soon, and disconnected the call. "We'll be here. Mom wants to know if she can bring something."

Ignoring Luke's question, Aggie asked, "How did you know that she'd still be awake? It must be after eleven by now!"

He shrugged with an obvious deliberate air of nonchalance. "Well, I may be almost thirty, but mom still worries about me. I call every night before I go to bed, so she can sleep well. I've offered to move back home, but Mom thinks I need to live near my duplexes so that the tenants will take me seriously."

Thanking him again for all the extra work he'd put into her cabinetry, Aggie walked Luke to the door, waved goodbye, and then climbed the stairs to her room, toting the laptop with her. She hummed "Burdens Are Lifted at Calvary" as she scrubbed her teeth, washed her face, and brushed her hair. Her characteristic lilt on the word lifted made its way into her humming, as she donned her favorite pajamas and crawled under the covers. Jesus was most definitely near.

Aggie says: Whew, what a night!
Tina says: How so? And howdy to you too!
Aggie says: hee hee... I took the kids to the local pizza place
Tina says: ALL OF THEM? Alone? You are a brave woman!
Aggie says: It was mayhem. Spilled drinks, I dumped pizza on William, and then this older couple gave us ice cream money and told the kids to tell their parents that they'd been good.
Tina says: uh, oh!
Aggie says: Yep, everyone fell apart right there in public. It would have been hysterical, if I hadn't joined the sob-fest.

Tina says: Everyone ok now? Are YOU ok now?

Aggie says: Yep, William brought us home and went for Murphy.

Tina says: Ugh!

Aggie says: Well, I have to admit she was very comforting.

Tina says: Really? What'd she say?

Aggie says: She said what Luke is always saying. "Cry it out, honey. It's not good to hold it in. I'll hold you, and you just cry."

Tina says: Luke offers to hold you, huh?

Aggie says: Ok, ok, so she was nice! And no, Luke doesn't offer to hold me, thank you very much!

Tina says: Gotcha! Did she say anything else?

Aggie says: She thinks maybe we need grief counseling. I told her no.

Tina says: Uh, oh, how did that go over.

Aggie says: Well, surprisingly she didn't argue. She said that counseling doesn't do any good if you don't want to be there.

Tina says: Sounds like I'd like her.

Aggie says: Well, you like her, and I'll avoid her, and we'll all be one big happy family.

Tina says: Hee hee… so you ready for the invasion?

Aggie says: You're coming!! REALLY? WHEN!?

Tina says: Sunday.

Aggie says: No way!

Tina says: WAY!!!!!

Aggie says: I thought you weren't coming until next month!

Tina says: I decided I wanted a longer visit. Do you mind?

Aggie says: NO!!! OOOH!!!! Luke is coming with his mother to church and lunch! You'll get to meet her with me.

Tina says: Nope, sorry not leaving until after lunch myself. I have to substitute for the 4th and 5th grade Sunday school teacher.

Aggie says: Rats. Well, maybe I can get Luke to watch the kids one day and you and I can go out and meet his mom at Espresso Yourself for coffee.

Tina says: So… still having fun having William around?

Aggie says: Well, he left kind of oddly last night and then didn't come back today like he said he would, but I figured he was just busy.

Tina says: Think he's getting interested?

Aggie says: You should have watched Quiet Man with us the other night. It was so funny. He gave me a rose.

Tina says: What color?

Aggie says: Red. Why?

Tina says: Just curious. Interesting that he chose red.

Aggie says: You silly. There are only red roses planted out front. He couldn't pick any other color if he wanted.

Tina says: But who PLANTED the red roses? Why didn't he plant yellow?

Aggie says: Because with the red door, red is more striking.

Tina says: uh huh

Aggie says: Look, I won't pretend that I don't know that he's interested in something, I'm just not sure it's me.

Tina says: Then WHAT?

Aggie says: I don't know. He still doesn't like to be in the house. I wonder if it's some propriety thing.

Tina says: Like eight chaperones of varying ages and sizes aren't enough.

Aggie says: Yeah. Something like that. But, then again, I talked to Mrs. Dyke and I think it's something more. I think he's more interested in the house… or rather NOT interested in the house. I think if I lived anywhere else, he'd be both happier and less interested in me.

Tina says: that's ridiculous.

Aggie says: Well, you'll have to see when you get here.

Tina says: Ok. I guess I'll go pack the rest of my boxes.

Aggie says: Ok… no matchmaking when you're here. I have

very good friends in Luke and William, and I don't want to ruin that.

Tina says: Fine then, I'll leave my Yente shawl at home.

Aggie says: Silly. Goodnight! Poofs!

Tina says: Poof.

FRIENDS

Chapter Twenty-Two

Saturday, July 20th

Luke, William, and Laird half-dragged, half-carried a huge farmhouse trestle table into the dining room. It needed to be refinished, but with a good scrubbing and a large tablecloth, it'd work for dinner. Vannie pawed through boxes, trying to find tablecloths and napkins to run through the washing machine. When the table was in place, scrubbed, and ready for the linens, Aggie looked around the house. The living room, library, downstairs bathroom, mudroom, and dining room were the only rooms that remained to be completed. As soon as the children went back to school, Aggie hoped to work on her bedroom and more on the yard.

For the first time ever, Aggie knew why mothers looked forward to their children going back to school. She also knew that she would miss them. The idea of home schooling flitted across her mind again, but Aggie had enough to do without adding in more work. She decided to think about it again next summer when the house would be done and she had at least a year of mothering under her belt.

"Luke, where did you find this great table? I love it!"

Aggie watched, as the men hefted a huge lazy Susan onto the top of the table and fitted it into the hole provided.

"There was an auction in Ferndale a few weeks ago, and I went looking for pieces for a couple of my rentals. When I saw this, I knew it was exactly what you needed, so I nabbed it."

Luke was like a child in a toyshop with the table. He reached down and picked up Ian. "Here, bud, try this for size." Luke sat the baby in the middle of the lazy Susan and slowly spun him in circles. The children all begged to try, but Luke, realizing the example he'd set wasn't optimal, shook his head.

"Sorry, guys, I shouldn't have done that. Don't ever sit on this. The baby doesn't weigh much more than a dressed turkey, but you are all too big."

"That's right, guys. It's an instant twenty minutes of work to anyone who attempts it. We have to take care of things, so they'll last." Cari and Lorna exchanged glances, but Aggie saw them and stopped their mental shenanigans. "And that goes for you girls, too. You can scrub walls until your fingers pucker if anyone sees you on that table." Her tone was firm, but she winked at the girls to soften the disappointment, leaving William amazed at how successful her interaction with them was. Things that would make many mothers lash out at the children, never seemed to faze her.

Sunday, July 21st

Sunday morning dawned bright and surprisingly cool. Rain was forecast for the evening, and it was keeping the day much cooler than the previous weeks had been. Aggie dressed carefully. For reasons she couldn't identify, making the best impression possible on Luke's mother was very important to her. Knocking on Vannie's door, Aggie called to her and told her to get ready for church. Down one side of the hallway, and up the other, Aggie went and awakened the family.

After six months of Sundays, Aggie had learned that, for everyone but Ian, granola bars were the most filling and cleanest foods she could feed them. She fed Ian and set him in the makeshift playroom, with Tavish keeping watch from a nearby couch. She wondered as she left them, if she called on him too often for that job. Brushing the twins' pixies, Aggie sighed over their lost curls. A real mother would have known to take pictures of the crazy events surrounding those cuts; Aggie hadn't. With a million things to do before leaving for church, Aggie forced herself to let the guilt go.

Her family was ready and at church on time, much to Aggie's delight. It was one of those rare and magnificent days, where everything rolled smoothly without any hiccoughs. She had learned to treasure days like those— they were too few and far between. She was so amazed how much more quickly things could be done when the house wasn't in a constant state of emergency.

Once by their usual pew, Aggie placed the children in their seats in order of whom she was likely to have to correct most. Since becoming a fulltime Mother-Aunt, Aggie had spent most of her Sunday mornings training children to sit quietly, whisper, go to the bathroom before they left for church, and similarly exciting things. She had begun to wonder if the Apostle Paul was referring to Sunday mornings when he said that women would be "saved through childbearing if they continued to persevere."

Aggie spied Luke escorting his mother into the church. The middle-aged woman, dressed in a classic summer dress, walked beside him with her arm tucked in his in the quaint way of days gone by. Luke led his mother to Aggie, who stood to welcome her. "I'm so pleased to meet you, Mrs. Sullivan. Thank you for coming."

Libby Sullivan smiled at Aggie. Luke's mother had wondered what kind of young woman "Mibs" was. Her son spoke of the Stuart-Milliken family so often, that Libby had been concerned for him. A compassionate man like Luke could become emotionally entangled with the wrong woman if that woman knew how to play her cards right. One look at Aggie, as her eyes slid sideways and she shook her head at a little girl swinging her feet and kicking the pew in front of her, and Mrs. Sullivan knew that she didn't need to worry. This young woman seemed more focused on her children than trying to entice Luke's emotions.

"Thank you for your invitation. Luke speaks of you and your family so often that you feel like a friend already." Mrs. Sullivan turned her attention to Luke. "Will you go help Zeke get Rodney out of his seat? He always has trouble trying to figure those things out, but he insists on trying."

Libby seated herself between Luke and Aggie. Zeke, next to his wife Martha on the other side of Luke, held a little redheaded boy with big blue eyes and tried to help the child sign the song *Jesus Loves the Little Children*. Aggie hadn't thought to teach such a little one sign language, but she held Ian's hands and made the signs with him.

What had begun as a smooth and cooperative morning, slowly dissolved into reminders of proper behavior and consideration for others. Ian sat peacefully on Luke's lap and fell asleep mid-service, but Kenzie and Cari both found themselves outside and in trouble for their antics. The end of the service couldn't come soon enough.

Aggie was relieved when, as she stood outside the door supervising her troublesome children, she heard the final hymn swell in the auditorium. Cari's nose popped out of the corner she'd been facing, but Aggie's narrowed gaze sent her face back to the corner where a crack in the mortar piqued her curiosity. The first person out the doors was Ellene, with William following quickly. It was evident that Aggie's neighbor was not happy to be at the service.

She wanted to talk and enjoy a little fellowship with her church family, but Aggie knew she needed to get the children home, where she could more easily deal with them if they got out of line. So, with a wave and enough apologies to show her friends how embarrassed she was, Aggie ordered her clan into the van and drove home, the Sullivans following behind in

Luke's truck. The temptation to drill them on proper behavior was nearly overwhelming, but Aggie knew it was wrong to demand that they perform to make her look good.

At home, Vannie took the little girls to change into play clothes, while Luke changed Ian. Watching her son tickle the baby as he swapped a dress shirt and pants for shorts and a onesie, Libby squeezed Aggie's hand affectionately. "Aggie, I can see why my Luke is always talking about your family; he seems right at home. I thank you for allowing him to get his kid fix while he's working."

Aggie smiled. "You'd think, with as much time as these children seem to steal from him, that he'd not get anything done at all, but you should see everything he's accomplished!" Aggie hesitated and then asked, "Would you like to see the house? I took before and after pictures, but I don't have them printed yet. The rooms might be a little messy, though. I haven't learned the art of everything staying neat on Saturday nights and Sundays."

The tour was short but fun. Libby seemed to love what they had all done to decorate and make the rooms special, but when they reached Aggie's room, the woman shook her head and said, "Don't neglect your private space, Aggie. This room will be a sanctuary when days are hard. Make it one that will help refresh you."

Aggie took her words to heart and led her guest to the kitchen. Libby Sullivan exclaimed over the island. "Luke! You did it! How marvelous! Oh, son, you will have to make me one when you have the time. I just love it. Rodney and the girls would have such fun working with me at a spot like this." She raved about the style of the room, her son's workmanship, and even the paint on the walls. Aggie noticed how genuine the woman sounded, in spite of her profusions. She began to suspect that Luke must be the apple of his mother's lovely blue eyes.

"Mrs. Sullivan, I love this kitchen, but I need to brighten it up. I chose that milk white for the walls, and I'm thinking about adding some stripes or something, but I don't know much about decorating. I want something cheery, with some green and red, but I don't want it to look like a Christmas kitchen. Do you have any suggestions?"

Libby Sullivan looked around the room for a moment before speaking. "I have one idea. Why don't you find a lovely geranium print for curtains and then maybe you can add baskets or red speckled graniteware or something? It would be so pretty and bright in here!"

Aggie, seeing a spot over the large side window that could hold a plate rail for graniteware, nodded her head in agreement. Red geraniums would be perfect for her new kitchen, and, doing things that way, when the curtains faded or wore out, she could change the entire look for relatively little expense. She mentally decorated her kitchen as they placed the platters of food on the dining room table and called everyone in to eat just as Zeke and Martha arrived.

Zeke said a simple heartfelt grace, and everyone ate and chatted. The meal was merry and full of laughter and mishaps. After the third glass of milk spilled, Mrs. Sullivan went into the kitchen in search of different glasses. Finding a few pint-sized canning jars, she came back and poured the children's drinks in them. "These are the same width on the bottom as on top. It makes it harder to knock over. You might consider buying more, or finding different glasses."

Aggie murmured her thanks. She realized how much someone with Mrs. Sullivan's experience could teach her. As she loaded the dishwasher, she pulled Luke aside and asked what he thought of his mother giving her homemaking lessons. "Do you think she'd think that was weird? I could really use some help, and she seems to know all the things I want and need to learn."

Luke swallowed hard. Tears threatened, but he managed to hide his emotions. Something about Aggie asking for his mother's help touched a very tender spot in his heart. He smiled. Knowing he wasn't speaking prematurely, Luke said,

"I am certain that she would be thrilled to do it. Say the word, and I'll ask."

Nodding eagerly, she went back to her dishes. She wondered at how Luke hadn't needed to search for words, but a smiling Mrs. Sullivan interrupted her thoughts. "My Luke tells me you would like me to help you simplify housekeeping. I think that would be lovely. Why don't I call you in a few days and see when would be convenient?"

Aggie remembered Tina's impending visit and said, "Well, I couldn't start immediately; my friend Tina is coming this evening, and I am hoping to get to spend as much time as possible with her." Raising her voice dramatically, so Luke could hear her, she continued. "I'm also planning on begging Luke to *watch the children a few times…*"

Luke turned and smiled his yes. Zeke boomed out a hearty, "Martha and I'd be glad to help too, wouldn't we, Martha?" while the children squealed with delight.

Aggie led Mrs. Sullivan out to the porch and tried to describe what she hoped do with it. The porch floor was slated to be the last thing painted, but Mrs. Sullivan suggested painting it immediately. "I can tell how much you want to use the porch as living space, and if you wait for the rest to be done, you won't get to use it this year. As a matter of fact, I'd even bring out your wicker things now. They can be moved onto the lawn and covered with tarps while the boards dry."

Aggie blushed and confessed that she hadn't bought any yet. "I keep meaning to look for them, but I haven't had time. I can just picture coming out here before the children wake up, reading my Bible, praying, and sipping on my favorite coffee…"

While Libby, Martha, and Zeke explored the changes outside, Aggie dashed upstairs and changed her clothes. She'd eaten and cleaned up in her nicer clothes without creating a stain, but she was tempting Providence to wear them any longer. For the second time since becoming a mother of eight, Aggie wondered what she should wear. She didn't want to throw on her work clothes; they were looking a little ratty these days. She finally pulled out her favorite denim skirt that she'd reserved for after renovations were over. The skirt had been expensive. It was butter soft and draped beautifully. Knowing it was her most flattering color, Aggie pulled out a thin green plaid top, raced into her bathroom, and dressed quickly.

Aggie had no illusions about her beauty. She'd always considered her looks average enough to keep her from being remarkably ugly or gorgeous. However, she also knew that she looked best with her hair hanging around her face. After debating a few moments, Aggie sighed, picked up the brush, and pulled her hair into a ponytail. In a fit of whimsy, Aggie divided her ponytail in half. With her hair pulled out, side-to-side, she looked like Pippi Longstocking. She did a silly little head dance and sang, "I am Aggie-Millie-Mommy how I love my happy game—" An indiscernible movement in the mirror froze her mid-song. Turning slowly, she found Luke leaning against her bedroom doorjamb, grinning.

"Well, Aggie-Millie-Mommy, would you like some blackberry cobbler?"

Aggie tried to act affronted; she even tried to convince herself she should be offended, but her sense of humor demanded that she see the amusing side of the situation. Unconsciously, she gave her hair one last smoothing and straightened her skirt. As she walked out of her room, she stuck her tongue out at Luke in a most unladylike fashion.

If she thought she would distract him, she was wrong. Luke, still leaning on the door jam, waited until she was halfway down the hallway and said, "Aggie, you look very nice. Then again, you always do."

She glanced back at him, but Luke didn't move, and he didn't say anything more. Unsure how to respond, Aggie settled for a simple thank you and hoped that he wouldn't be offended by her lack of enthusiasm. "What's gotten into him?" she muttered to herself, thinking she wouldn't be overheard.

"Can't imagine." This time, his voice was near her ear.

Aggie jumped. How did he move so quickly and quietly? "Well, I can't either!"

"Can't what, Aunt Aggie?" Kenzie looked up the stairs expectantly.

"Can't wait to try this cobbler. Blackberry is my favorite." Aggie grinned at the little girl and accepted the plate Libby offered her.

Halfway through dessert, Libby spoke. "How selfish can I be? I've been struggling within myself since you shared your ideas for the porch."

"Why? Do you have a different idea?" Aggie took another bite and tried to decide how to show Libby that she wouldn't take offense at alternate suggestions.

"No, I was thinking about my mother-in-law's wicker furniture. It would look so lovely on your wide porch, but I was hesitant to offer it. It's all been covered in sheets up in my attic for years, because I have no room for it all, whatsoever. If you'd like them, I'll send them out with Luke tomorrow."

"I can't take your mother-in-law's things! They belong in your family. Surely one of your daughters—"

"Mom's right. They've been up there since I was in high school. If any of the girls wanted them, they'd have asked by now." He waved his hands at her objections and motioned for Laird to follow him. "I'm going to go get them now."

An hour later, Luke and Laird unloaded the loveliest wicker settee, chairs, and table that she'd ever seen. There was even a matching hammock chair to hang from the porch roof. Aggie had always wanted one of those hanging chairs. The weaving pattern looked ripped from the pages of Southern Living magazine, and Aggie gasped as Luke set them down in the curved section of the porch in exactly the places she'd hoped to put them. "They're so beautiful! Are you sure you want to part with them?"

Libby nodded. "I'm happy to see them loved by someone who appreciates them like Mama Sullivan did."

"I just can't imagine anything more per—" Aggie's words

caught in her throat, as Luke pulled the cushions from behind the seat of his truck. " —fect." The cushions were hideous.

Before Aggie could find a way to ignore the atrocious print on the cushions, Libby shook her head in disgust. "Now, I know the cushions are horrible. I mean, I still can't understand how Mama Sullivan tolerated something so vile. But, you can get some new ones on clearance this time of year." Libby Sullivan's eyes twinkled. "I considered raving about them to see what you'd do, but honestly, what can you say about them that isn't awful? My daughter, Corinne, says that Grammie was into Shabby Chic, without the chic."

While discussing the merits of different fabrics and colors, Aggie noticed a familiar car pass her road and continue down the highway. "Oh, my, I think that was Tina. She missed the street. I think I'll go down to the corner at the highway and flag her down."

When she reached the corner, Aggie saw her friend's car returning. She waved to get Tina's attention, and then laughed as her friend exclaimed, "Well, lookie me... I got myself a pretty little hitchhiker!"

"You came early!"

"Yeah, well, I found someone else to sub for me. I thought maybe I'd make it in time for lunch, but I had a flat and my spare was flat too."

"I'll reheat you a plate. Mrs. Sullivan brought the most amazing blackberry cobbler you've ever had in your life." Aggie pointed to her driveway and then laughed when Tina said she'd been looking for Aggie's Beetle convertible. "I haven't had that for months."

"Well, I kind of forgot about your new monster van. I took one look and kept going."

Libby appeared with a hot tray of food just as Aggie finished making the introductions. "And this is Luke's mother, Libby Sullivan."

Sometime later, Ellene crossed the lawns through a gate Aggie hadn't ever noticed. Aggie rose to greet her, and trying hard to keep distrust out of her face and voice, she introduced her to her guests. Flustered, her greeting came out all wrong. "Murphy! Welcome! You've come at a great time."

Ellene's face was a picture of confusion, but Aggie continued with her introductions. "You've met Luke. This lady is Luke's dear mother, and that is my friend Tina over there. She's visiting me for a few weeks before classes start again."

The odd looks that Ellene sent her way made no sense to Aggie at first, but when Luke jumped up and said, "Here, Ellene, take my seat," she turned red and excused herself. Luke followed close behind her. At the bottom step of the stairs, he caught her arm before she could go up to her room. With a sympathetic grin, he said, "Your thoughts will always catch up with you, Aggie. Just go out there and make a clean breast of it. If you mention losing Ian and the run in with the nurse over at the clinic, everyone will find it funny, and she won't be upset."

She sighed and nodded. Luke was right. Again. Aggie forced herself to return to the porch and sat on the floor across from Ellene. Laird started to offer his chair, but she shook her head. "I'm fine here, Laird, but thank you." She smiled up at Luke leaning against a post before turning to her newest guest. "Ellene, I owe you an apology. When you came over, the day we lost Ian, I was so upset about the baby and everything, that I wasn't rational. When you were questioning William, my mind saw you dragging the children away, and it killed me to think of it when they've lost so much already. I took an instant dislike to you, and in my anger, I christened you Murphy." Ellene just looked at her as if she'd grown two heads. Trying to clarify, Aggie added, "You know, Murphy's Law? 'If anything can go wrong it will...'"

Laughter erupted as the two women tried to build a bridge between them. Good-natured teasing flew back and forth between everyone until the walls that Aggie had started to build were demolished. They might never be dear friends, but Aggie no longer felt that Ellene was an enemy.

The evening passed pleasantly. Luke fired up the grill,

while Aggie set up a croquet court on the lawn. William arrived, much to the delight of Ellene, the curiosity of Tina, and the amusement of Libby. The children sang silly songs, and Vannie recited a poem. Rodney and Ian fell asleep, side-by-side, on a blanket under the biggest oak tree, while the youngest twins cuddled on the couch.

Long after sundown, Luke and William cleaned up after the evening meal, while Mrs. Sullivan and Aggie put the children to bed. Tina and Ellene chatted while they washed the dishes and then sat back on the porch getting to know each other. Ellene learned a whole new side to Aggie through Tina's eyes, and with a broader picture of the circumstances, the new neighbor developed a genuine admiration for the inexperienced aunt-turned-mother.

When everyone had gone, Aggie and Tina chatted. After an afternoon of observing Aggie in her new home, with her new friends and neighbors, Tina thought that she had a realistic picture of how things were in Brant's Corners. She also realized that everyone in Aggie's life was too close to the situation to see how things stood. She'd watched Ellene relate with Aggie, Luke, and William. She watched the foursome interact and knew that things would be getting interesting, and unfortunately, she also realized someone was bound to get hurt.

The long conversation that Tina and Ellene had enjoyed turned into an even longer one with William. Tina discovered, contrary to Aggie's description, that William was a charming and fascinating conversationalist. They hit it off quite well, but Tina also saw that William seemed to keep a protective eye over Aggie. All of these things whirled in her mind as she talked with Aggie. "So, which of the two men would you see yourself with, oh, say in ten years?"

Tina's directness and lack of hesitation was refreshing for Aggie after weeks of Luke's slow and deliberate words. "Tina, when did you become such a matchmaker? I picture myself as good friends with both of them for years to come! What did you think of them?"

Tina was thoughtful. "Well, William is by far the handsomest, but there is a certain charm about Luke, isn't there?"

Aggie laughed. "Today Luke caught me being downright goofy a couple of times. I was so embarrassed."

"I can see that they both look out for you, but Luke is much more subtle, and as a result, it seems more— something."

"Mrs. Sullivan says it's because he grew up protecting his sisters. Anyway, she says he always finds someone to help in some way." That conversation with Libby had meant a lot to Aggie. Changing the subject, she asked, "Did you see the cabinets he built me? I am in love with them."

Tina laughed. "Wouldn't Allie flip? I remember the way she reacted to your idea for her bridesmaid dresses!"

Laughing, Aggie thought of something else and changed the subject again. "Do you think that the kids are adjusting ok?"

It was well past eleven o'clock when Tina finally dragged herself into the library and curled up on the air mattress Aggie provided. Accustomed to those few minutes of silence after the end of a long day, Aggie powered up her laptop once she'd climbed into bed and went to check her email. To her surprise, Mrs. Landry was added to her messenger contact list.

Aggie says: Iris!!! Hello!

Landry's Lady says: I'm excited to see you. You gave me your name, but I never remembered to add you. How are you doing in that big old house?

Aggie says: I love it. We've just finished the kitchen. In a week or three, we'll be done with the rest and my little haven will be complete.

Landry's Lady says: Haven. I like that. With all of the turmoil

---

your family has been through, you need one don't you?

Aggie says: And how. I've met a woman I think you'd like. She lives fairly close to you, I think. I'd like to introduce you.

Landry's Lady says: What is her name?

Aggie says: Libby Sullivan. Do you know her?

Landry's Lady says: No, but anyone you want to introduce me to, I'd be happy to meet. Can we all go to lunch soon? Mark was hired back on at work again.

Aggie says: Oh, I am so glad! May I bring my friend Tina? Do you remember the one who insisted that I hire someone? If it weren't for her, I wouldn't have met you!

Landry's Lady says: Please do! I heard all about her from Vannie.

Aggie says: You did?

Landry's Lady says: Yes. She's small and pretty and filthy rich. That about sums up Vannie's perceptions!

Aggie says: She forgot to mention pushy and too smart for her own good. Oh yes, and she's also my best friend!

Landry's Lady says: That sounds like the best kind of best friend to have.

Aggie says: So, when are you going to come see my house? Why don't you bring Jonathan out, and you can help Tina and I go through the furniture up in the attic and set up the rest of the house! I'd be happy to pay you.

Landry's Lady says: And I'd be happy to do it just because I am your friend. How about Wednesday? I have a Bible study early, but we can drive over right afterwards if you'd like.

Aggie says: Oh, that would be wonderful! I'll fix us lunch and we can dream this house into perfection.

Landry's Lady says: Or at least into Aggie's haven.

Aggie says: Isn't that a wonderful thought. It's really becoming that, too. I feel peaceful and at home, even when things are going wrong and everything is "sixes and sevens."

Landry's Lady says: God has blessed you beyond measure.

Eight children, a beautiful home, the ability to stay home with those children and serve them. You are becoming a veritable Proverbs 31 woman!

Aggie says: Except that she sewed, had a business, and a husband!

Landry's Lady says: One thing at a time dear. Those will come, you'll see!

Aggie says: I never pictured myself married... even as a little girl— not that I was against it or anything. Maybe it's because God knew I was going to be so busy with these children that I wouldn't have time for being a wife too.

Landry's Lady says: That is possible, but don't count on it.

Aggie says: You think that I'm out there on this one?

Landry's Lady says: No... it's possible that you're called to singleness. I just think that marriage is the rule, rather than the exception.

Aggie says: Well, that is true, but then I'm already an exception. There aren't many twenty-two year old mothers of eight.

Landry's Lady says: Oh my, Jonathan has a finger gushing blood and Mark can't get it to stop. I have to go. Bye.

Aggie says: Bye... Praying.

ODDLY ENOUGH

Chapter Twenty-Three

Wednesday, July 24ᵗʰ

"Aggie... where do you want these clothes? They're all over the couch!" Tina sounded almost as exasperated as she looked. Aggie danced down the stairs. The sight of all the day's laundry still piled on the couch touched a sore spot. Tina watched as she walked over to the kitchen and splashed water in her face.

"Front and center," Aggie's voice was loud and clear. The children came from all directions and in all states of dress and undress. Aggie rolled her eyes and took a deep breath.

"What do I see on that couch? Anyone?"

Kenzie piped up with the obvious. "Clothes!"

Aggie looked pointedly at the older four children and raised the question again with her eyes. The younger children seemed clueless, but the older children had the grace to look ashamed. Eventually, Vannie spoke up. "I'm sorry, Aunt Aggie."

Tina listened and then turned to Aggie. "May I?"

Aggie nodded and picked up Ian. "Break a leg."

"Ok, guys. Here's how it works. Each of you older four children will have a "sheep" who is one of the younger four. It'll work oldest takes youngest and on up, so that middle children aren't working with the least trained. So, Vannie, your job is to help Ian, when he learns to walk that is, get his things upstairs and in his drawers. Laird, you help Lorna. Gather all of Lorna's clothes and help her fold them. Ellie, you help Cari, and Tavish, you help Kenzie. You guys have thirty minutes to have this room ship shape and your drawers filled but not overflowing."

Aggie giggled as she watched the younger children excitedly rush to get the clothes folded, hung, and put away quickly. Vannie talked to Ian, as she folded his clothes and ticked his feet with his socks. Tina folded towels and sheets, while Aggie put them and her own clothing where it belonged.

Iris and Libby arrived at exactly the same time and introduced themselves to each other as they came up the steps. "Aggie! The paint is magnificent! How did you get it painted so quickly?"

Aggie giggled. "William, a friend, painted it during his vacation. It was a lot of hard work, but Laird and Tavish were an enormous help. They each earned about fifty dollars in the process!"

"Hi, Mrs. Landry; where is Jonathan?" Laird seemed very disappointed.

"His father had to take him to the doctor to get his stitches checked, and then they'll be by."

Without a thought to saying hi, welcome, or in any other way acknowledging Libby Sullivan, Laird dashed off to tell the others. Aggie shook her head. "I'll figure out how to instill basic etiquette eventually!"

The four women joked, laughed, and talked as if they'd known each other for years. Libby and Iris knew many of the same people and spoke regretfully of the years that they could have spent together. Iris, in particular, seemed blessed to have new friends at that time in her life. Smiling as she glanced around her, Iris grabbed Aggie's arm and said, "So, Aggie, show me your house! I want to see everything. The dining room looks like it's really coming along!"

Aggie led the women into the kitchen with their eyes closed and described her dream kitchen. At her word, all three women opened their eyes, and Libby spoke. "He did it, didn't he? I knew it was what you wanted, but I didn't realize how closely he came!"

Iris was enthralled. "I love the graniteware!"

Aggie laughed. "I took Mrs. Sullivan's advice and accented with it. Thanks to Tina's shopping skills, it's here already, but I haven't found curtains. There must be some geranium curtains somewhere!"

Iris raved over each room and its décor. Aggie and Tina showed the other ladies plans that were not yet executed and described how each room would look when the final pieces of furniture and the accents were added. The jungle room, with its huge tiger draped over the boys' dresser, made everyone chuckle.

"Aggie." Iris frowned as she stood in the doorway of Aggie's room. "What about your room? Aren't you going to do something in here? Oh— look at those windows!"

Everyone looked at the two half circle topped windows that flanked each side of the fireplace. "Stained glass! How wonderful! What do you plan to do in here?" Iris waited anxiously to her the plans.

Aggie grinned. "Tina and I have been talking. We think we know what we're doing. Tell 'em, Tina."

Her friend nearly beamed, becoming extremely animated. "Well, that fireplace has to go. The brick is all wrong."

Aggie looked confused. "And when did we decide this?"

"Just give me the chance to explain. Luke doesn't know it, but he's going to cover all of this with stone. That ugly brick is stained, chipped, and garish."

Aggie pondered the potential transformation of her fireplace, as Tina described the white and tan color scheme.

"It'll have Windsor green accents here and there but not too many. I'm trying to talk her into a four-poster bed with sheer canopy type curtains just kind of looped over it. Ohhh, and over the windows too."

Aggie laughed. "Ok, but if I don't like it, you can come redo it."

"What kind of furniture do you have for the room, Aggie?" Iris was intrigued by Tina's ideas.

"None. But, we're taking you guys up to the attic, and maybe you can help us find some! That place is just stuffed with antiques." Aggie was obviously very excited.

"Aggie?" Mrs. Sullivan stood in the bathroom doorway. "Are you going to carry the colors in here?"

"Well, I want to keep the colors the same but add more of the green. It's such a ridiculously large bathroom. Especially for one person."

"Are you sure you want green in a room where you're getting ready every morning? It might give you sort of a Martian look." Libby frowned as she tried to picture Aggie's plans.

Tina nodded in agreement. "She's right. You want something more neutral in there. Maybe go with a lighter tan and add another color accent."

"What color?"

"I don't know," Tina demurred. "Maybe blue or something. We'll figure it out."

The ladies excitedly planned Aggie's rooms in the most incredible detail. After a long time of debating different options, Aggie dashed downstairs to retrieve the baby, so Vannie could read her book in peace. The children's squeals announced the arrival of Jonathan and his father before Aggie could go back upstairs.

"Come on up, Mark. I'm showing your wife my room and what we're doing, but you'll survive, I'm sure!"

"There's nothing Iris loves more than to see a room get a face lift." Mark Landry tickled the baby's chin and reached for him. Aggie handed the baby over willingly. He seemed extra heavy lately, and Aggie personally thought that Solomon must have been talking about carrying babies when he commented on how the ideal woman "makes her arms strong."

When Mark heard the ideas for the bathroom, he pulled his wife aside. Iris was obviously excited about what her husband had to say. She squealed like a teenager and hugged her husband, which seemed ridiculously out of character. Taking Ian, she sent Mark back home and turned to share with her friends.

"Mark just reminded me. Last weekend we were at this garage sale over in Marshfield and found these hand-painted tiles. They're leaves— oak, maple, ash— all kinds of leaves in various shades of green on buff colored backgrounds. I think there were twenty-five of them. You could use them here and there in the backsplash, maybe around the shower surround— something like that."

With Tina talking a mile a minute, Aggie led the group up to the attic and listened as Tina and Iris planned her bathroom. Though she'd always loved rearranging her bedroom as a girl, and had created a very home-like space in her dorm room at college, Aggie was somewhat insecure about making such detailed decorating decisions. To date, anything she'd tried had cost little to no money and was easily changed. In this house, she needed to make a good plan the first time, because she didn't have time for redecorating if the idea failed.

As the women reached the top of the attic stairs, the dank scent of age and decay assaulted them. She'd opened the windows a few times, but after forgetting them and discovering destroyed books from rain, she didn't trust herself to try it again. Aggie pointed to the wall in front of her. "I thought I'd use that mirror and paint it the Windsor green. What does everyone think?" The consensus was a unanimous affirmative, so Aggie leaned the mirror against the stair railing.

Iris found an old battered trunk. The cloth was torn in places, but it was sturdy. "What about this for your bedside

361

table? You could put a lamp on it and an alarm clock."

Aggie readily agreed and pushed the trunk toward the door. Behind the trunk, she found a piano stool lying on its side. "Oh, look! This might work for a desk if I find one."

"Hey, Aggie, look at this!" Tina carefully folded a dusty sheet away from what looked like a bed frame. As the dust cleared, the women saw a beautiful antique wrought iron bed frame, headboard, and footboard with verdigris antiquing.

"Oh, wow! I love it, but how are we going to get this out of here?" Aggie was frustrated. When she got excited about a project, she didn't like to have to stop. Unfortunately, she knew that there was no way the four women could move all the heavy pieces downstairs.

Libby Sullivan smiled. "I'll go get Luke. He'll know how to take it apart."

"Have him call and see if William has a moment to come help." Aggie found different things here and there that she wanted in different rooms of the house. The attic was full of amazing treasures and boat loads of junk. Finding what she wanted wasn't quick or easy, but it was a lot of fun.

"Aggie, look at this neat desk! I thought it was a bookshelf, but it's a desk! Look at the front of it!"

The women moved the old bicycles and the dress form that blocked the way to the desk and turned the filthy piece of furniture around for a better look. The desk was beautiful in its simplicity.

"Wow. I think it's perfect!" Aggie was excited.

Libby Sullivan spoke from the doorway. "I think that's a Hitchcock. The color is wrong... and I think they always had stenciling or decals or something, but the style looks just like my mother's."

Aggie looked carefully at the back and sides. Pulling out the drawer, she saw the stain inside was much darker than the exterior. "Look... do you think it was refinished?"

Libby looked carefully before nodding. "Yep. It's a shame, I think these can be quite valuable, but honestly, and you didn't hear this from me, I think it's nicer without the pictures on it. It's beautiful."

Aggie heard William's voice downstairs and called for him to come see what they wanted. As she led him to the bed and showed him the desk across the room, William stiffened and grew and visibly nervous the closer she got to the bed. Aggie didn't notice, but Tina and Libby grew concerned.

William shouted a warning, as Aggie reached to pull the bedstead away from the wall. "Aggie, watch—"

She yelped. William's shout startled her, and she stumbled into one of the studs in the wall. A wave of pain washed over her as she saw a nail embedded in her upper arm. She wrenched free, the blood pooling against the surface of her skin.

The blood covered nail appeared to be holding something on the other side. Despite her pain, Aggie was curious. She reached for what appeared to be fabric of some kind, but the pressure ripped the pieces, and they fell to a heap on the floor.

"Aggie! Let me see your arm." Panic filled William's voice, and when he saw the large bubble of blood, he practically pushed her out of the room and down the stairs. Despite her protests, he insisted that she climb into his car. In the attic, the women heard a siren wailing as he tore out of the driveway, unaware that he left several terrified children gawking after him.

"What was that all about?" Tina spoke first. The other ladies shrugged.

"It was almost like he knew where the nail was, wasn't it?" Iris was thoughtful. "Not to mention, he sort of overreacted with that siren, don't you think?"

The deflated group retreated from the attic, its treasures forgotten. Downstairs, they made lunch for the children, reassured them that Aggie would be fine, and dreamed up more ideas for the other rooms. Tina hardly participated in the discussions; her mind was occupied with all the things Aggie had shared about William and his reactions to her home. She wanted to get the other women's input but realized it wasn't her story to share.

Aggie was frightened but not because of her arm. The pain was almost gone, and there was very little blood, but William was completely distraught, and it unnerved her. She didn't understand what was wrong, and he wasn't talking.

At the clinic, he escorted her inside, and his mere presence seemed to command immediate attention. As Dr. Schuler inspected the wound, he gave William an odd look. Pulling William outside the examination cubicle, Aggie heard the doctor questioning her friend. "William. Pull it together. What's with you? This is a simple puncture." The doctor's voice trailed off, and Aggie heard sobs. Surely, they couldn't be William's!

"William, come into my office; she'll be fine. I'll get Linda to give her a tetanus shot, just in case."

Aggie fired off one p-mail after another, in rapid succession. She didn't notice the pinch of the needle as Linda gave her a long overdue tetanus shot. She also didn't notice the sting of the cleanser used to clean her wound. The only thing on Aggie's mind was the obvious pain William felt and how she could help.

Sooner than she expected, William returned to the cubicle, led her out the door, and to his cruiser. Dr. Schuler followed them outside and hollered after William about paperwork, but William waved him off and drove toward town. At the park, William pulled over and parked under a large shady tree.

"I watched you all here one Sunday. Did you know that?" William's tone was broken and weak.

Aggie shook her head. "William, what's wrong?"

He sighed and hung his arms over the steering wheel. She recognized the sigh as the same one she'd heard after one too many 9-1-1 calls and the episode with Tavish and the stair cupboard. Absently, she rubbed her thumb over a scratch on her hand. They sat in complete silence for quite a while before William looked over at her. "Are you ok?" His voice was ragged — husky with pain she didn't understand.

Aggie nodded. "Are you? What's going on, William?"

"Aggie, I don't know how to tell you about it. I will sometime; I will. But, you triggered a memory today, and I wasn't prepared for what it would do to me."

Aggie started to reply, but William shook his head. "Aggie, I know I owe you an explanation, not to mention an apology." He shook his head as she began to protest. "No, I do. But please, can you give me time until I'm ready to explain? I will soon, but I want to talk to the Vaughns first."

He sounded as though he was pleading with her. Unable to refuse, Aggie nodded. She wanted to talk, ask questions, but a heavy wave of exhaustion crashed over her unexpectedly. Between the adrenaline rush and the emotional upheaval, Aggie suddenly needed a nap.

"What happened? Why is she unconscious?" Tina's panicked voice grew louder as she saw William's unsuccessful attempts to rouse Aggie.

Lifting her, as difficult as it was to extract her from the car, William grunted, "I don't know. She got drowsier and drowsier as we drove home. I think she's just exhausted from the whole ordeal. She should be fine after a nap."

William carried Aggie upstairs and carefully laid her on her bed. Luke and Mark Landry, working in Aggie's bathroom, put down their tools and silently agreed to work on it later. As Luke left the room, he glanced at sleeping Aggie. William had laid her on the bed and rushed away, but Luke was concerned. He looked at her arm and wondered why she was so exhausted from a simple nail puncture.

When Luke arrived downstairs, Tina was still questioning

William about Aggie's condition. William started over for the third time, telling exactly what had happened. "I think Linda gave her a tetanus shot while we were talking, and then—"

"That's it." Tina's voice was flat. She took note of the time on her watch and thanked him for taking Aggie to the doctor. Then, as if nothing happened, she turned and asked Iris about window treatments for the library.

"What! That's it? What's it?" William vocalized Luke's thoughts.

Without looking over her shoulder, Tina explained. "It's this thing with Aggie. She's had at least two tetanus shots since I've known her, and both times, it put her to sleep for a few days. It's some kind of unusual reaction, from what I understand, and it seems to start earlier and last longer each time. The doctors have some other protocol for punctures for her. I bet she forgot."

Tina was quite matter of fact about it, but William looked worried. Luke watched Tina's expression and visibly relaxed, as she appeared to be unconcerned. William, on the other hand, still bothered by something, left without another word, and strode across the lawn to Murphy's house. There was still something not quite right with the situation, but Luke didn't know what it was or if it was any of his business.

"Aggie, come on. Wake up, Mibs." Luke's voice was gentle but firm. Tina and the children were off at the park, but he'd stayed behind to work on the bathroom. He'd been reticent to work on it, but after Tina banged two cooking pans together next to her head without a stir on her part, he'd agreed the noise probably wouldn't bother her, and the finished bathroom would be a nice surprise when she was conscious again.

"Aggie," Luke shook her again. According to Tina, after the last shot, the doctors had suggested trying to wake her every few hours for a little water, but if he couldn't get her to wake up, how was he supposed to get her to drink?

The house was silent. Everyone was gone, and Luke was frustrated. He felt helpless, alone in the house with an unconscious Aggie. How was he supposed to know if she was getting worse? Luke tried again. "Come on, Mibs, you gotta wake up. Just open your eyes, say howdy, and I'll let you sleep."

Aggie stirred but didn't open her eyes. Luke disappeared down the hallway and returned with a cold wet washcloth. Rubbing it on the back of her neck, Luke then held her up in a sitting position and began wiping her face. She moaned, and her eyes struggled to open. Luke saw slits of iris as she tried to speak.

"Wh— what's going on?" Aggie's speech was groggy and slightly slurred. She sounded drunk.

"Tina said to make you wake up now and then. You scared me for a minute; I couldn't wake you."

Aggie's eyelids drooped, but willpower forced them open again. "Why am I so tired?"

"Tina said it was the tetanus shot." Luke watched her reaction.

"They gave me a shot? I don't remember that. They shouldn't have done that. Tetanus shots make me sleepy." Aggie tried to focus on Luke's face but was too tired. "I gotta lie down again."

"Take a drink of water first." He thrust the water at her and nodded with satisfaction as she swallowed a few sips.

"Nice water. Thanks."

Luke chuckled and settled her against the pillows again. He noticed her shoes were still on her feet and removed them, setting them at the foot of the bed. A storm was coming, and a cool breeze blew through the open window. He hated to close it, but Aggie shivered in her sleep. Feeling quite pleased with himself, he grabbed the corner of her comforter and pulled it over her. Luke smiled. Aggie looked like a small child with her hands tucked under her cheek and her hair spilling over the pillow.

Aggie says: Hey, Iris... you there?

Landry's Lady says: Yep, how are you feeling?

Aggie says: Awake. Weird, huh.

Landry's Lady says: Well, I've never heard of someone getting sleepy from a shot!

Aggie says: I do. Sigh. Sorry I ruined our lunch...

Landry's Lady says: It's not like you jabbed yourself to get out of it deliberately, you know.

Aggie says: Yeah, wasn't that whole thing, well, a bit odd?

Landry's Lady says: It was VERY odd. I am not exactly sure what happened, but something wasn't right.

Aggie says: William said he'd explain later.

Landry's Lady says: Hmm... Regardless, you've got some amazing things in that attic. We found a chifforobe behind the bedstead. It's really cute. Tina thinks you'll want it for the girls' room. It's very distressed, almost like an original shabby chic piece, but it looks cute!

Aggie says: OOOOOOHhhhhhh I love the sound of it. The twins don't have enough drawer space, and there's that spot on the wall by the door... Well, unless it's too big.

Landry's Lady says: Ask Tina. She'll know. So, what's this I hear about a housewarming?

Aggie says: I don't know! What IS this you've heard about a house warming?

Landry's Lady says: Oops, I hope I haven't ruined a surprise!

Aggie says: I doubt it. They probably haven't mentioned it due to some misapprehension that I'll fall apart from the stress of my most terrible ordeal.

Landry's Lady says: Giggle. You were funny. William carried you upstairs, and you should have seen Tina's expression.

Aggie says: Do tell. He really carried me up there?

Landry's Lady says: Yep. It was like out of an old movie. Tina looked like she would swoon.

Aggie says: Sounds like she needed hoop skirts and smelling salts!

Landry's Lady says: LOL. Well, according to reliable sources, next Saturday is your house warming. Should I put bugs in some ears that they should give you another week or two?

Aggie says: Nah. I can't wait to show off the house. The guys have done such a GOOD job! Who'll be there?

Landry's Lady says: Sounds like your old and new churches are coming, and of course, your neighbors, and Libby and her son.

Aggie says: Sounds good.

Landry's Lady says: Well... I really appreciate you inviting me over. It was definitely the most exciting lunch date I've ever been to!

Aggie says: You have to get a life Iris...

Landry's Lady says: LOL. I just keep my excitement for after dinner. Too much to do during the day.

Aggie says: Well, I'm going to go play Monopoly with the kids. They've been asking all day. I'll see you Saturday, I guess.

Landry's Lady says: Have fun. Don't land on Boardwalk!

Aggie says: I'm gonna OWN Boardwalk. Just watch me.

Landry's Lady says: I prefer the greens... they always get hit... those and the oranges.

Aggie says: I'll strive for at least one of those! See you Saturday

Landry's Lady says: Saturday it is!

Aggie says: Bye!

Landry's Lady says: Bye, Aggie.

The Home Stretch

Chapter Twenty-Four

Saturday, July 27th

For the first time in a long time, Aggie awoke after a full night's sleep, completely refreshed, and without the aid of an alarm clock or a child posing as one. The recent rains had cooled the temperature, as she'd slept through her reaction, but now the heat combined with the increased moisture meant long, hot, muggy days. Feeling sinfully decadent, Aggie lay in bed and considered her wardrobe options. As much as she wanted to wear her tiered gauze skirt and coordinating blouse for comfort's sake, they were tackling the living room, and that meant sturdy clothes. She was thoroughly sick of her faded, ugly, old clothes.

On a brighter note, Tina's help would mean they finished the room that much quicker. She tugged on an old cargo skirt and a faded Rockland Warriors t-shirt, pulled her hair into a ponytail, and tied tennis shoes onto her feet. Oh, how she wanted to wear flip-flops, sandals, or go barefooted and free. However, the last thing she needed right now was another nail puncture.

The house was too quiet for comfort. No children's squeals

of pain, delight, or impishness filled the air; there were no hammer or drill sounds. She didn't even hear the clackety-clack and squish of the paint roller. The dishwasher, however, hummed merrily as if to announce that something was doing its job, even if she wasn't.

"Come out; come out, wherever you are!"

Luke's head peeked around the corner of the downstairs bathroom and he grinned. "Mornin', Mibs. I was just taking some measurements."

"Where are the children? Where's Tina?"

"She took them to town for breakfast."

Aggie didn't bother to comment. "Want some coffee?"

Taking Luke's nod as a yes, Aggie went into the kitchen to make her morning cup of coffee. She poured a cup for Luke from the little coffee pot that was set on a timer each night and then scooped French Vanilla coffee mix into her cup. The process took a fraction of the time it once had, and as she stood stirring her cup, Aggie realized that the difference was a clean, orderly kitchen with enough room for everything she needed. Her hands slid over the cool, stone countertops, and her heart swelled as she marveled, once again, that they were hers. One finger traced the pattern in the wood around a drawer front, as she stood there lost in thought.

"You ok, Aggie?"

She nodded, blinking back tears. "It's—" Well, talking wasn't going to work. Aggie felt ridiculous standing in her kitchen almost crying over how wonderful it was.

"You don't look ok. Is something wrong?" She shook her head. "Are you still tired? You could rest on the couch if—"

"I'm fine." Her words were punctuated with two tears splashing on the countertop.

"Tears usually don't equal fine." He took her cup, grabbed his, and nudged her toward the living room. "Let's get you out of here."

Hands gripping the countertop, Aggie refused to budge. "I don't want out of here."

"Ok, you don't want to leave. What do you want?"

With a quick brush to erase the tears, Aggie looked up at him. "To say thank you again. I love this kitchen. I love coming in here and trying to make something edible. Even if I fail, it isn't a chore to clean it up like it used to be. I like cleaning the cabinet faces and feeling the different designs you put into them." She swallowed hard as her voice broke again. "I still can't believe it's mine sometimes."

After a minute or two, Luke put down his half-empty coffee cup and leaned across the island to meet her eyes. "That is one of the, if not *the* best thing anyone has ever said to me. I'm glad you like it, Aggie. I w—" He cut himself off and paused for a moment. "Now, let's see if we can do the same for that bathroom."

"I thought we were doing the living room next."

"Well, I keep thinking it should be last, so we don't scratch the floor dragging stuff through the house."

"Bathroom it is. Lead on, John Henry." Aggie shrugged at his questioning look. "It's something my dad always says."

As she glanced around the dingy and dilapidated bathroom, Aggie saw herself in the mirror and frowned at her reflection in the cracked and smudged glass. Luke stepped outside the door, and Aggie, thinking he'd gone, grumbled at her reflection. "I look about as drab and ratty as this bathroom."

A moment later, Luke filled the doorway, pointing to the corner next to the toilet. "There's room there for a shower. I don't know why they have all those cupboards there when there is a large linen closet outside the door. I'd run a counter along that wall," he pointed to their right, "with a nice sink and cabinet, a new mirror above it, and," he jerked his thumb to the opposite wall, "tear out the cupboards for a shower. It'd be nice to have a shower downstairs for when the children come in covered in mud."

"Great idea. I've always wondered why there wasn't a shower in here."

Luke offered to drive Aggie to the home improvement warehouse to choose cabinetry, shower stall, new toilet, and flooring, but she shook her head. "I think I'll start stripping wallpaper from the library. You know what'll match in here. Just choose something appropriate."

With list in hand, Luke fished his keys out of his pocket and sauntered through the front door. Seconds later, Aggie heard the door slam again and peeked around the corner. There, just a few feet inside the small foyer, he stood, hands settled loosely on his hips and with something to say. She leaned against the doorjamb, waiting for him to speak, wondering if she shouldn't just agree to go along for the ride. As she stepped from the bathroom to grab her purse and insist they go, Luke raised his eyes to meet hers.

"For what it's worth, I've never seen you looking drab or ratty." He turned as if to leave and then added almost inaudibly, "I wouldn't change a thing."

As his truck rolled down the street and onto the highway, Aggie jogged upstairs for another look at herself. Her latent insecure side mocked her with accusations of vanity and pride, while her practical side nodded with satisfaction. Luke was right. Her face was clean and unblemished, her hair healthy, and she was in the best physical shape of her life. So, her clothes were a bit worn and faded; why shouldn't they be? She'd been wearing them, doing hard work, for weeks. It'd end soon and then she'd be able to wear something a little more attractive.

Sometime later, Luke found her singing as she peeled several layers of hideous flocked wallpaper from the library walls. He stood in the bathroom, sledgehammer ready, and listened to the words of the hymn before he took the first swing. "'– *Lay your gifts at His feet; ever strive to keep sweet. Let the beauty of Jesus be seen in you.*'"

Tina's presence cut Aggie's workload in half. While Aggie stripped wallpaper, scrubbed and primed said walls, and then drove to the store to choose paint, Tina and the children played games, made lunch, cleaned upstairs, took a walk, and finally made dinner and cleaned up the mess. With the upcoming housewarming party, Luke and Aggie felt the pressure to work long hours, and as quickly as possible, to finish as much of the house as they could. The children, Tina, Ellene, and William were roasting marshmallows over the grill and singing campfire songs by the time Aggie returned with the paint for the library.

The paint she'd chosen concerned her. Despite her original intention of going bold in the library, she couldn't bring herself to do it. All the rich wood accents around the fireplace, the doorframes, and the beautiful pocket doors with their frosted glass demanded the foreground. She'd hesitated over a camel color but finally decided it was too bland. Her next choice, the color of pale pumpkin pulp, seemed a bit daring. With just the wrong lighting, it would scream, "this is an orange room," and that was not the feeling Aggie wished to evoke. At last, she'd found a very pale sage named "Heathered Laurel," but now that she was home, she doubted herself.

"Luke? Do you have a minute?" Aggie pried the lid off the paint as she called for input.

"Hmm?" He paused near the doorway, unwilling to bring dust near the paint can.

"What do you think of this color?"

"Looks good from here. Is the wall next to that window dry?"

Careful not to mark up the primer if it wasn't, Aggie brushed the back of her hand along the wall. "Nothing comes off on my hand, it's not tacky at all, but it's still cool to the touch."

He hesitated and then disappeared around the corner. "I'll be back. Let me dust myself off."

In the meantime, Aggie threw on every light in the room

and felt the walls to find the least conspicuous and driest place to test the paint. By the time Luke returned, she'd wiped a wide swatch of paint down a short space of wall behind the door. "It was drier over here."

They both stood back and surveyed the effect. The color wasn't too dark, and it blended perfectly with the wood. "Well," Luke admitted, "I wasn't sure about it when you held it up. I mean, it looked fine and everything, but I didn't think it was anything special. Now I'm thinking it might be the perfect color. Why don't you go get Tina and get her opinion while I put the lid back on the can? You can't paint tonight anyway."

"You don't think so?"

"The wall is still too cool. It's better to let it cure until morning."

"Well then," Aggie muttered on her way out the door. "I'm glad I bought the one-coat stuff. Maybe it'll really only take one coat."

Tina pronounced the color perfect, Ellene nodded her own approval, and William managed not to wince when Aggie mentioned she'd almost purchased pumpkin, a fact that only Ellene seemed to notice. With an arm draped over one of Aggie's shoulders, William pointed out a few places where the wood needed to be sanded on the walnut molding. "That one spot is pretty deep, though. I'm not sure you can fix it, and putty would ruin it."

"I'm not sanding any of it. I'll refinish spots that absolutely need new sealant, but since none of it is broken or missing, I'm leaving it as it is, for the most part."

"But with a brand new room—" William's protest seemed excessive to Luke, but he kept his opinions to himself and listened.

"This isn't a young house. We're fixing what needs to be fixed, but I don't want to redo every inch of it like an older woman filling her face with collagen and overdosing on cosmetic surgery. It has lines and wrinkles. Where appropriate, I want them to show."

Once the children were in bed, Tina, Ellene, and William tried to get Luke and Aggie to play a game or watch a movie, but neither of them was willing to stop working. Luke had the bathroom gutted. The fixtures, floor, drywall— everything was removed, and new plumbing was in the works for the shower. Aggie, unable to work in the library until the paint dried, sanded, stripped, patched, and prepared every inch of the living room for paint.

A heated game of hearts ensued on the front porch, while the work inside continued. William and Ellene stayed until past ten o'clock, before they gave up on Aggie and Luke and went home. As much as she wanted to stay up and help, Tina was exhausted. Instead, she dragged her air mattress into the mud room and closed the door. A fan, as loud as a turbine engine, dulled the sounds of Luke's occasional thumps and thuds, but he and Aggie kept working.

The need for another length of drainpipe halted Luke's progress midstream. His watch mocked him with a time of one fourteen, which told him it was time to go home. To his surprise, Aggie was in the living room, half the furniture gone, and marking off different places with blue painter's tape. "Um, Aggie?"

She jumped. "Oh! I forgot you were here."

He walked around the squares and rectangles on her floor, trying to get a feel for what she was doing. "It's after one. I need pipe, and church is in eight hours." She groaned, but before she could respond, he pointed to the rectangle closest to him. "Coffee table?"

"Yep."

"I think there's one in the attic just about that size."

Her face lit up, erasing all signs of exhaustion. "Really? I was sure I'd have to buy one."

"Chairs?" Luke pointed to two squares, one on each side of the fireplace.

"Mmm hmm. I'm not sure about those. I can't put a table between them— not with that fireplace there— and I don't

377

think there's room for a table on each side of the chairs." She pointed to the walk space it'd clutter. "I just think the kids would be bumping them all the time."

"Why do you need tables?"

"Something to hold reading lamps and a coffee cup or glass."

"Well," Luke yawned. "Let me sleep on it. I might come up with something. That's the couch?" He pointed to a long, deep, L shaped rectangle.

"Two of them. I want to keep it versatile. I was thinking maybe I'd get a table for the corner, so I just marked it all off as one piece."

"There's one of those old drum tables up in the attic. The pedestal is broken, but I'll bet we can find another pedestal easy enough. The tops are the hard parts to find."

Aggie yawned and picked at the edge of the tape, ready to peel off another strip, but Luke took it from her. "Go to bed, Aggie. Tomorrow will be here before you're ready for it." He turned her shoulders and gently pushed her toward the stairs. "I'll be back after church. I think I can get that shower in place before dinner, if I don't run into any more problems. After that, only the floor will take any real time. You can paint the walls as soon as the shower is in place. The primer is about dry now, but I'd rather wait until morning."

"I didn't buy paint for it. I don't know what color —"

"Did you get enough of that green for the library?"

"You think it'd work in the bathroom?" Aggie looked hopeful. Tired, but hopeful.

"The cabinet I bought is almost the same shade of wood. It's a little darker, but it'll look good, I think."

"That's good enough for me." She placed one foot on the bottom stair and then turned her head. "Thanks for earlier. It's horribly vain of me, but I needed to hear that."

Luke started to respond, but Aggie disappeared up the stairs. As he pulled the door shut behind him, he heard the shower come on in her bathroom. All the way to his truck, the faint sound of her voice followed him. *"... Let the beauty of Jesus be seen in me..."*

Sunday, July 28th

Luke's cell phone rang as Aggie was starting the last wall of the library. Tina had the children outdoors and away from the living room, except for Ian, who slept soundly in his crib. Luke left the bathroom with its completed shower and went to find Aggie.

"That was my cousin Chad. He has a friend — it's a long story — but anyway, she made something for Cari and Lorna, and they want to bring it out this afternoon."

"Sure! I can't understand why someone would make something for the girls, though. That seems a little strange."

"When I took them to see Uncle Zeke's puppies the other week, Willow was there, and Chad said something about her having leftover fabric, so she made something for the girls to use it up. I don't quite get it, but I don't always get Chad."

"He seemed normal enough when he came out the day I got hurt."

Luke's brow furrowed trying to remember. "Was he here that day?"

"Not for long. He came, made the comment about gravestones, you got irritated, and dragged him inside."

"Oh, right. I'd forgotten. I think his visit was overshadowed by your accident." Luke nodded thoughtfully. "That was the day Cari informed me that she doesn't 'wike me sometimes.'"

"Doesn't like you?" Aggie's eyebrows narrowed, and she took another swipe at the wall with the roller.

"She was running, I told her to stop, she didn't want to, so I made her sit on the step until I was done with Chad."

"She told me about that."

Nodding again, Luke smiled. "I'm glad to hear it. I forgot to follow through and see that she did. You must have gone

379

upstairs after that."

"So, what did you say to her when she said she doesn't like you sometimes?" This was a new one for Aggie. She didn't know how to handle something like that.

"Well, I think her exact words were, 'Luke, sometimes I don't wike you vewy much,' so I just told her that I'd always love her *very* much."

"You don't think she should have been reprimanded for being rude?"

Luke took the roller from her and ran it over the paint tray before it dried. Handing it back to her, he shrugged. "I thought she needed a little reassurance that no matter what she did, she was loved. That child gets in trouble five times for every once that any other of the children do."

"Tell me about it," Aggie muttered as she rolled the paint onto the wall, taking care to overlap the edges where Luke had cut in the paint for her already. "Will the bathroom be ready for me when I'm done?"

"It's ready now. I think I'll grab another roller and do it while you finish that wall."

"I can finish—"

With a paint tray and roller in hand, Luke shook his head. "No, just finish that wall and then go change. You'll want to relax while Chad and Willow are here, and you won't relax if you're covered in paint and thinking about the bathroom."

For just a brief moment, Aggie was irritated. Who did Luke think he was, deciding she didn't have time to do something? Just as she was about to stalk down the hall and blast him, Aggie saw her paint-splattered skirt and her sweat soaked t-shirt reflected in the window. He'd overheard her complain about her appearance and then, when someone was coming to visit, took over so she could change clothes and feel more comfortable. All along the rest of the wall, she hummed an unintentional medley of half a dozen unrelated hymns, before dumping the roller in the water bucket, removing her shoes on the tarp, and tiptoeing upstairs to change.

"Libby!" Aggie rose from her wicker hammock chair and went to greet her guests. Luke was still rinsing the paint rollers by the side of the house, but with Libby there, Aggie didn't feel quite as self-conscious.

"Aggie, you know Chad, of course, and this is his friend, Willow Finley."

Willow stepped forward and handed a bundle of fabric tied with a string to Aggie. "It's good to meet a friend of Chad's."

Luke rounded the corner, drying his hands on his jeans, and hugged his mother. "See, I told you I'd get you out here today."

"Chad did, you ornery boy."

"And I will take you home." He looked around the group and asked, "Does anyone want cookies? I think Tina is baking in the kitchen."

While Luke left to retrieve the cookies, and presumably Tina, Aggie unwrapped the bundle and unfolded the jumpers. "I can't believe you made dresses for little girls you saw once for such a short time! They're so cute too. Thank you!" Aggie hugged Willow impulsively.

"You're welcome. I had fabric left over and wanted to use it up, so—"

"She hand painted that paisley fabric. Can you believe that?"

Libby and Luke, returning with the cookies, exchanged amused glances. Clueless to the silent debate raging around her regarding Chad's true interest in Willow, Aggie went into new ecstasies over the fabric. "I can't believe— I mean, I see it now that I look, but it's so perfect..."

"Except for the spot where Chad made me mess up. It's under—" Willow showed a streak of paint under one corner of the overskirt and pretended deep offense at his goof.

Luke led Chad into the house to show him the progress on

the bathroom, while the women discussed the nuances of sewing and fabric. When they returned, Willow was trying to take pictures of the girls wearing their new dresses but finding it difficult to capture them with her 35mm camera. Everyone watched, slightly shocked, as Chad explained how to use Luke's digital camera and assured her that she could take five hundred pictures and simply delete the ones she didn't like. It seemed that the woman hadn't ever seen or used a digital camera.

The screen door banged shut as Vannie brought Ian outside after his nap. Sitting him on the floor near Aggie's feet, she nodded at Chad and Willow before sauntering around the side of the house, calling for a game of Mother-May-I. Ian started to crawl to Libby, but at the sight of Willow, crawled to her side as fast as his chubby legs would allow and tried to climb her leg.

"May I pick him up?" Anyone could see that Willow was as nervous as someone around an unfamiliar puppy.

"Sure." Aggie and Libby spoke simultaneously.

As she fumbled, Willow sent an apologetic look in Aggie's direction. "I don't know how to support his head. Aren't you supposed to support their heads?"

Assured that he could support his own head just fine, Willow played with Ian. A few minutes later, she asked, "What is his name?"

"Ian. He likes you. You seem very good with children. Do you have siblings?" Aggie knew Luke and Libby were curious about the young woman and decided to see if she could draw Willow out a bit.

"I've never been around children before that Sunday I got the pup."

"She was a natural then too; wasn't she, Luke. She handled Cari like—"

Aggie's head whipped up, and her eyes sought Luke. "What? You didn't tell me she was a problem."

Willow interrupted quickly. "Oh, she wasn't a problem.

She was tempted to do wrong, and I encouraged her to reconsider. It wasn't anything serious; was it, Luke?"

"Not at all. You were great though. Not everyone—" Luke paused and gave Chad a meaningful look. "Not everyone knows how to handle a childlike Cari."

Chad and Willow stayed, played schoolyard games with the children, and then left. Aggie raised an eyebrow at Libby, as Chad's truck turned the corner onto the highway and asked, "Ok, what was that all about?"

"I'm thinking Chad has himself a girlfriend and doesn't even know it." Luke's smirk grew into a smile as Libby nudged the back of his knees, making them buckle. "Mom, did you not see what I just saw? He spent the whole time singing her praises."

"And I think, in his position, you wouldn't want your family speculating about your romantic entanglements."

"If I ever have any, you speculate all you want." Luke put his feet up on the wicker coffee table and leaned his head back in his hands.

Tina and Libby exchanged amused glances, but Aggie's question changed the subject. "Did she really say she's never been around children? She seemed quite natural with them. I was certainly much more awkward when I took over at Allie's, and I'd been around them before that."

Luke nodded. "According to Chad, it was just her and her mother."

"Why didn't he bring her mother? I would have liked to meet her."

Luke untangled his feet and leaned forward, arms on his knees. "That's what the gravestones comment was about the other day. Chad was here asking for help in making one for her mother's grave."

"Oh." Aggie's deflated voice killed the conversation. For quite some time, they all sat on the porch listening to the children's laughter as they played.

Minutes later, Aggie stood and quietly walked into the

living room, wiping tears from her eyes as went. Libby's heart jumped into her throat, and she looked helplessly at Luke. "I don't know how to help at times like this."

Luke rose and offered a hand to his mother. "Mama, does anyone know how to help someone else through their own grief?"

As practical as he sounded, that single word, Mama, told Libby that her Luke wasn't as unmoved as he seemed. "I guess that is why we're supposed to lean on the Lord, son. He is the only one who can, isn't He?"

Aggie says: Mom? Wooohoo... Mom?

Martha says: How are you tonight?

Aggie says: We're getting a lot done. Luke almost finished the bathroom today, and we're going to sand the library and hallway floors tomorrow when he's done.

Martha says: How are the children?

Aggie says: I think they're doing really well here. There's a lady at church that is planning a young women's group and wants Vannie to join. I think it'll be good for her. She does so much around here as it is. I think she needs the break.

Martha says: *nods* Well, what about Laird? I've been worried about him missing his father's influence.

Aggie says: No one can replace Doug, Mom. I don't want to pretend they can, but between Luke being here all day every day, William here often, and Zeke coming by from time to time, I don't think Laird is suffering for male companionship or influence. Luke is really good with him, and I think Laird likes William's job. They talk a lot about what it means to be a deputy and the good and hard parts of the job.

Martha says: Oh, that's good. What about your new neighbor? Have you had any more run-ins with her?

Aggie says: Nope. She's actually becoming a friend, I think.

Tina seems to like her.

Martha says: Tina! Really?

Aggie says: Yep!

Aggie says: I think we just misunderstood each other at first. I seem to have a habit of making dramatic first impressions on people.

Martha says: Well, that hasn't changed, has it?

Aggie says: I'm WOUNDED!

Martha says: *giggling* You are who you are, Aggie. What about Cari? Is she still giving you problems?

Aggie says: All the time. She told Luke the other day that she doesn't "wike him vewy much sometimes."

Martha says: She got in trouble?

Aggie says: How DID you guess?

Martha says: Kenzie used to try to say that when she got in trouble. Allie had a time stopping that one! Geraldine was on a "you must let them express themselves" kick. Fortunately, it didn't last.

Aggie says: Well, I don't know if it's going to be a recurring problem or not, but I'm afraid it is. Luke didn't reprimand her.

Martha says: Oh.

Aggie says: I asked him about it.

Martha says: And did he say why he let her get away with it? If you give that child an inch…

Aggie says: He said he told her he'd always LOVE her and sent her out to play. He said that she needed to know that she's always going to be loved. That a child who is always in trouble like her needs that reassurance, but I think we're just going to confuse her when we don't let her get away with it over and over.

Martha says: He has a point. So do you. I guess time will tell. Maybe it's worth some extra work with her to reassure her like that. He's really been firm about things in the past, hasn't he?

Aggie says: I guess. Hey, is Dad around? I wanted to say hi, but we've got an early morning tomorrow. I've got to get to bed.

Martha says: He's right here. I'll go get ready for bed myself. We're coming next weekend. Tina called and your dad says we can make the trip.

Aggie says: See you then. Night, Mom. I love you.

Martha says: Night, Aggie. Here's Dad.

Martha says: I'd change this thing, but I don't know how.

Aggie says: That's ok. I know you're not Mom.

Martha says: How do you know I'm not Mom?

Aggie says: Because Mom would never admit she didn't know how to do something on the computer. ESPECIALLY if she didn't know.

Martha says: Touché. How is everything?

Aggie says: Dad, I don't know what I'm doing. This whole thing is just insane.

Martha says: Top problem of the moment.

Aggie says: I have a house full of grieving children who are afraid to grieve.

Martha says: And how are you grieving?

Aggie says: I don't have TIME to grieve, Dad! I have a house to get in decent order so the social worker next door doesn't decide I'm an incompetent parent, children to feed, clothe, and register for school. Need to make a note of that one too. Then there's the whole "what happened to my life" thing when I look around me and think, "I like this. This is good." And then I remember that it better be because I have eighteen years of it to go.

Martha says: I know what you mean, Aggie, but if you don't take the time to grieve, it's going to hit all at once and hard. And, those children don't know how to grieve without you. You need to show them how.

Aggie says: I don't KNOW how, Dad. If it was just me or a child or two, that'd be one thing, but the minute one of us crumbles for even a second, everyone falls apart and it's hours of recuperation. If I'm gone too long, the kids worry. Tina says my reaction to the tetanus shot the other day had Vannie snapping at everyone and Tavish hiding under the stairs. He didn't even come out for dinner.

Martha says: I think it's going to be like that for a while until they realize that they can cry or get angry about their loss anytime they want or need to. But if you don't set the example, they're just going to start acting out, and you don't want that.

Aggie says: It's been five months…

Martha says: It can take five years… or longer.

Aggie says: Suck it up and do the right thing?

Martha says: And I'll see how I can help on Friday when we get there. Mom reserved a room at a local bed and breakfast. She's so excited about seeing your house. I'll probably have her coming and going half the day, so she will get some rest.

Aggie says: You know, there's that back room I was planning for a storage room, but I think I need to reconsider it as a guest room. I want you guys to be able to stay here when you come.

Martha says: Well, your Mom can't handle the stairs, but if there was a sofa bed even…

Aggie says: I don't like the idea of mom on a sleeper sofa. I'll make a guest room. I don't know what I was thinking. I kept assuming you could take my room. I forgot about the stairs.

Martha says: We'll see you Friday and don't worry about the children. They're more resilient than you think. We'll get through this.

Aggie says: Night, Dad. Thanks.

Martha says: Night, Aggie-girl.

READY. SET. GO.

Chapter Twenty-Five

Saturday, August 2nd

The sun shone on their housewarming party, and the house and yard swelled with guests. Aggie's attention was diverted from her guests as she heard Mrs. Dyke's voice through the kitchen window exclaim, "Just tell her, William!"

"I will— I just can't get comfortable. This house!" William's voice almost sounded distraught.

"Aggie isn't like her, William. She would never put you or anyone else through what she did." Aggie had trouble following Mrs. Dyke's pronouns. Who was the other "she?" "I know, Mrs. Dyke; I'm just not rational when it comes to her, and this house—" he sighed. "— and the memories. I just don't think—"

Exasperation was evident in every inflection of Winnie Dyke's voice. Few people had the confidence to be so direct and show irritation toward him. "Not every woman is like Mona, William. Most women would be appalled at what she put you through. Just talk to Aggie. She'll understand. I think you've put her through enough with your bizarre behavior."

"I know. I have. I just can't get past the stupid house, but the kids— Aggie…"

"You're getting attached, aren't you?" Aggie couldn't miss the note of triumph in her neighbor's voice.

"I don't know. Sometimes I think I am; other times, I think that it's just this house and the awful hold it has on me."

"Not all women are out to hurt you, William. Aggie wouldn't."

Mortified, Aggie realized that she wasn't just an innocent observer any longer and moved away from the window. William might have a genuine interest in her, though, which was a fascinating thought. Aggie wanted to ponder about how she felt about what that meant to her but didn't have time. Then again, if she didn't have time to think about it, did she have time to do anything about it if he was? The thoughts were dizzying.

Guests mulled about the house, while the children darted in and out of doors. Tina, the unofficial tour guide, led everyone through the rooms, showing before and after pictures that she'd mounted on poster boards in each one. Once assured that they'd be added to scrapbooks and photo albums, Aggie had ordered half a dozen pictures of each room and let Tina and the children go to town with their collages.

The coffee table, dining room table, and kitchen island were overflowing with housewarming gifts. Fruit baskets, snack tins, houseplants, gift bags, and a few wrapped boxes teetered precariously, like wooden blocks stacked by a baby. One gift wouldn't be allowed near the kitchen, much less on her island. William, with Tina's help, had cajoled Aggie into allowing him to bring a kitten as his gift. The last thing she thought she needed was a pet, but William promised that the animal was box trained, weaned, and would probably spend most of its life outdoors, chasing field mice and chipmunks. Now that she'd warmed up to the idea, Aggie couldn't wait to see the children's faces when he brought it in the house.

Iris picked up a unique lamp sitting on the kitchen island.

"Aggie… wouldn't this look incredible on that old trunk next to your bed?"

"It'd look wonderful, but you couldn't really use it. The light would be too low; wouldn't it?"

"Well, not if you turned the trunk on its end and let it stand half open…"

"Oh, Iris! What a great idea! I've never seen those old bobbins made into a lamp, but it's really amazing."

William let the screen door bang behind him. The kitten, terrified by all of the noise, the ride, and the unfamiliar surroundings, clawed his arms in a frantic attempt to escape. "Aggie, can you come get this thing?"

Aggie laughed and extricated the kitten from William's arms. "He's cute!"

"She. I got a girl so you wouldn't have spraying issues. Even neutered toms spray sometimes."

Aggie cuddled with the kitten in one of the chairs by the fireplace, gifts from her parents and delivered early that morning. "I love the orange and white. She looks like sourdough toast with marmalade."

Before long, the children surrounded her, each vying for a chance to pet, hold, or squish the poor creature. Squeals of excitement made the kitten shake with fright, until Aggie sent Vannie upstairs to put the kitten in her room. "There's a basket under my bed for her."

"What's her name, Aunt Aggie?" Vannie walked toward the stairs petting the kitten's soft fur.

"She doesn't have one yet. You be thinking of one, and we'll talk about it after dinner."

"So, Aggie. Did you have a nice time?" William and Aggie sat on the back swing, watching the fireflies and dodging the June bugs.

"I can't believe how many people came. It was wonderful.

391

I really got to know some of the members of The Church, and that was really important to me. I've felt like such an outsider."

William nodded. "I felt that way when I moved back here too."

"Moved back? Oh, right, you grew up here, didn't you?" Aggie had forgotten.

William talked of summer days working with Mr. Dyke. "He was like a second father to me when my dad took off."

"That must have been so hard. I can't imagine what would possess a man to leave his family like that. Are you sure something terrible didn't happen to him?"

"I checked, when I was in the academy, as part of an assignment. He's alive and living down in Florida."

Aggie was silent. She rocked the swing and eventually picked up the kitten when she walked by. "Are you ever sorry you came back here? I mean this town must have sad memories for you and everything."

"It's been hard at times, but I love Brant's Corners, and well, Mrs. Dyke doesn't have anyone anymore. I'm all she has left."

"I thought she had several children." Aggie was confused.

"Four. All boys. Three died in Vietnam, and the youngest was shot in the line of duty seven years ago. He left behind his mother and a fiancée that committed suicide a year later."

Aggie noticed the difference in talking to William and Luke. William thought quickly and spoke decisively. Luke was more prone to listen and think before saying anything. Aggie wondered why William's quicker conversation was grating on her, when she usually found the delays in conversation with Luke so frustrating.

"You've done a good job with this place, Aggie. It was such an eyesore for so long."

Aggie nodded. "I have hardly done anything, but Luke has been worth his weight in gold."

"You have become pretty good friends, haven't you?" William's voice seemed too tense.

Aggie nodded again. "And his mother. She's such a special woman. How about your mom, does she live here?"

William startled visibly. "No, I think Mom is in Virginia. She's in pretty poor health."

Aggie recalled the earlier conversation between William and her neighbor. Who was Mona? Did William have an ex that had hurt him terribly? Did he have a wife in the past? Had they lived in this house? Aggie gathered the courage to ask a few questions.

"William? Have you ever been married?" He shook his head, and Aggie considered dropping the subject, but she had to try once more. "Ever wanted to?"

William was uncharacteristically thoughtful. Then, as though he realized that he had been silent for too long, answered quickly. "Not until recently. I'll have to wait and see if God agrees, I guess."

Aggie shrugged, as awkwardness stole over the conversation. "Well, you're so uncomfortable in this house; I wondered if maybe you'd been married or loved someone who lived here or something. It sounds pretty silly, now that I say it." Aggie was almost embarrassed.

"It's closer to the truth than you'd think, Naggie Aggie, but it's not what you assume."

William glanced at Aggie and wondered what was wrong with him. Most men sitting outside with an eligible woman that they found intriguing would focus the conversation on the woman. Why did personal situations always make him act so socially backward?

"What about you? Did you leave someone special when your sister passed away?" William hoped she'd say no. She had given up so much; it would hurt to think that she'd given up yet another dream for her family.

"No, I've never had anyone special to me like that, and obviously I've never been married!" Aggie laughed. "Were you and Mur— Ellene close at one time? She kind of hinted at it once, but you don't act like exes or anything like that."

393

William was frustrated. Mrs. Dyke had warned him that Ellene had hopes for a deeper relationship, but until now he hadn't taken it too seriously. She was right, however. Ellene was definitely making herself readily available. "No. I helped her get over a bad relationship, and we became good friends. Mrs. Dyke thinks she's here for other reasons, but we'll see. I can't see that ever working out for us. We'd be miserable together."

As William and Aggie continued to talk, Ellene overheard heard more than she wanted. She'd seen them out talking and planned to join them, but hearing the obvious lack of interest in William's voice hurt. Mrs. Dyke was right. She came to Brant's Corners to see if there was a chance that she and William were compatible, and apparently, William was certain they weren't. As Aggie discussed a myriad of topics with him, Ellene went inside her home to take inventory of her life.

Aggie stopped talking mid-sentence. "What is that?" She walked over to something under the tree and found a scrapbook lying in the dew-dampened grass. "Would you look at this? They all worked hard on this, and now look at it. Half of this thing is ruined!"

William's eyes widened as Aggie, furious, marched into the house holding the scrapbook. He jumped up and followed, ready to try to calm her down. Aggie mopped up the damage, trying to flatten the pages. "I'll have to figure out who took this out there tomorrow. They've got some fixing to do."

William seemed surprised. "You're not going to wake them up?"

"Are you nuts? Have you not heard the old saying 'let sleeping dogs lie?' I'll deal with the culprit after we've all had a good night's sleep." Aggie was utterly bewildered.

William shook his head and headed for the door. "It's getting late. I'd better go."

A broken William rushed out the door. Aggie considered letting him go but couldn't. She raced after him, calling his name. "William? Come on, William, talk to me." As she reached his side, Aggie grabbed his arm and turned him, so she could see his face. Moist eyes confused her further. "What is going on with you? Every time you are at my house, you are agitated; right now, you're almost distraught. What's going on?"

William visibly sagged. He led Aggie to a very large oak tree in a field across the highway. Sitting down, William breathed the deepest, most pain filled sigh Aggie had ever heard. Moments later, he began to sob. It was heart wrenching. She'd seen men cry so seldom that, by contrast, his cries seemed wrung from him by force. Shocked, Aggie, unsure what else to do, wrapped her arm around him and tried to hold him. Being so much smaller, it seemed an exercise in futility.

"Cry it out, William. You've held in whatever this is way too long. Everyone keeps telling me that we need to cry when we're hurting." She hoped it was the right thing to say. The grief tormenting him overwhelmed both of them— William as he tried to gain control and Aggie as she struggled to console him.

After what seemed to be hours, William was dry. He couldn't have cried another tear. A long silence followed before William said, with a voice ragged and soaked in pain, "Thank you, Aggie. I—"

Aggie listened. Everyone opened up to her in ways they wouldn't with others, and William was no exception. Once started, the story seemed to gush forth as if unstoppable. "You know, Aggie, how you call that house the 'Shambles?' It's almost ironic. That is exactly what that house represents to me; the shambles that my parents made of my life." He sighed. "We moved into that house when I was four. I couldn't wait to leave."

When William spoke of his father, Aggie noticed a strange dichotomy. One minute, he sounded as if he held a hero-like worship for the man, and the next, his anger flared again. "Why would a man leave three helpless children with a woman like my mother? Why didn't he take us with him? He just went to work one day and never came home." Unsure of what to say, she waited for him to continue but her heart dropped at his next words. "Mom blamed me, you know."

"Oh, no! I'm sure—"

"No, Aggie. She really did. Anything she could blame on one of us children, she did. She blamed us for being born. It was insane!"

William seemed on the verge of tears again. As concerned as she was for him, she was human enough to be curious as to the end of William's story. She didn't have to worry. Once William began talking, it seemed as though he couldn't stop. He spoke of beatings that he, his little sister, and baby brother endured. His mother's rages, while unpredictable, had often seemed to punctuate almost any event, which invariably meant a beating for one of her three children. However, when Mona Markenson left her eighteen-month-old child unconscious, ten-year old William made a decision. He determined she would never hurt either of his siblings again.

"I remember being confused as to why my brother and sister wouldn't have anything to do with me. For some reason, Social Services left me with my mother. I had no evidence of broken bones from the x-rays, but Pam and Mike did. They believed Mom when she said my father caused the breaks. They took Pam and Mike from us because Mom didn't get them proper medical attention when our father supposedly beat them, but they left me because she wasn't a danger to me. Isn't that pathetic?"

Aggie nodded. She was speechless. The raw pain in William's eyes was hard to swallow. She wanted to say something, anything, but was speechless. "I'm sorry." She meant it, but it sounded so trite.

"I'm sorry too. I overreacted with Tavish that day with the stairs. My mother used to lock me under those stairs. It was dusty and often filthy. She'd forget about me until I'd give in and beg for her to let me out. Then I'd get a beating again, but at least I was out. It was worth it at that point." He was silent for a moment before going on.

"And Vannie's room." He swallowed hard. "I found my baby brother beaten and half-unconscious in there. I found out later that she broke two ribs that time. I had to take him over to Mrs. Dyke for most of the day so that Mom wouldn't get angry and hurt him when he cried with the pain of it all. She tried once." He pointed to a small half-moon near his temple. "I have this scar from it. I stepped between her and Mikey, so she threw the fireplace shovel at me. She would have killed him, I know it."

Aggie remembered something and asked William what he meant when he said that his brother and sister hadn't forgiven him. "For what? What did you do?"

William sighed. "I didn't go too. They thought I defended Mom and said she didn't hurt us. They had no idea that my staying behind made it worse for me. I guess I can see why they thought what they did. I hoped that when we were all adults we could reconnect, but we never did. They still won't speak to me. They stayed with the same older couple for their whole childhood. They didn't move around like some kids have to. I'm glad for that."

"Why didn't Mrs. Dyke do something? Couldn't she have called the authorities?"

He shrugged. "I never asked. I think they are the ones who finally got the little kids out of here, though. I just didn't want to know, you know?"

"Afraid to damage the only solid relationship you had?"

"Well," he admitted, "questioning them like that seemed to be a poor way to thank them for all their support over the years."

William seemed calmer. He was silent for a long time and then looked at Aggie. Her face, always expressive of her heart, showed the concern and empathy she felt for him. He seemed to get the burden off his chest, but now she felt an awkwardness come over him. "William?"

"Hmm?"

"Thanks for trusting me with your story. I guess I see why you didn't want to talk about it before. It's not the kind of thing you share with someone you hardly know, is it?"

"It's never been something I shared easily with anyone. It always feels like it's not real if I don't acknowledge it."

That statement produced an unexpected reaction. "I think you're wrong. I think you keep stuffing it down until you're ready to burst with it. It might be time to accept the reality of it when memories arise and then move on, instead of trying to pretend they don't exist." She shrugged, sheepishly. "That's what I keep trying to remember with the children anyway."

He looked down at Aggie. "You're really good with them. I mean, you've had quite a few mishaps, but they aren't afraid of you, and they're coping with the loss of their parents. That's pretty incredible from my viewpoint."

William sighed. "You need help though, Aggie. It's too much work for one person. God didn't intend for children to be raised with only an extremely young mother."

She started to answer, but William didn't seem to notice. "Aggie, I wonder…" His expression looked expectant, but he said nothing more.

"I think that maybe you should finish before I can respond." She tried to interject a little lightheartedness.

"Do you think that we could try again? That date we had— it was such a disaster." The indignation that appeared on her face sent him scrambling to clarify. "I know it was my fault! I'm not trying to make excuses, but let's face it; I ruined it."

"I don't know…" Aggie was a little surprised. She knew they had become much closer friends, but she thought they'd had an unspoken understanding that neither of them was interested in that sort of relationship. "Why?"

"Well, Naggie Aggie, I'm not sure, but with the last wall between us torn down, it seemed reasonable to consider it."

Aggie was thoughtful. After their disastrous attempt at a date, she was certain that she was through with dating all together, and she wasn't interested in trying it again. Then again, if they both hadn't wanted to consider a relationship, and now William did, perhaps the Lord had other plans for her. "I guess the worst thing that would happen is we'd find out this isn't what the Lord wants for us…"

"Well, if that isn't the most unenthusiastic "yes" I've ever heard…"

"You know, I won't have much time for this. Between my responsibilities with the kids, the work still left on the house…"

"We'll take it as it comes, if it comes, then. I just thought," William seemed to struggle for words, in an almost Luke-like manner, "it made sense for us to see. Meanwhile, I'm on duty in the morning. Wade's grandmother died, and I took his shift."

They walked back to her house, where William climbed into his car and backed out of the driveway. Aggie smiled to herself as she climbed the steps to her newly refurbished home. "Lord, it's a good thing that life isn't supposed to be like a Hollywood movie. This one would have flopped big time. There wasn't any music swelling into a crescendo, we didn't have those nauseating long, lingering glances at one another, and thankfully, there was no passionate kiss," she whispered, relieved. "You know, Lord, there has to be more to living than Hollywood's shallow imitation of life."

As she crawled into bed, the irony struck her. The Shambles represented pain and rejection to William; however, as Iris had said during the toast of lemonade to her family, this house had most definitely become Aggie's and her family's haven. Almost six months before, ready or not, the Lord had thrust her into the most unfamiliar life she could have imagined. Chaos often characterized her days. She rarely knew what she should do, but thanks to an unlimited p-mail account, a generous supply of hymns, the comfort of the Bible, and dear friends and family to bolster her, Aggie's life was as imperfectly perfect as she could desire. She wasn't ready yet, but she'd come a long way.

The End

Libby's Blackberry Cobbler

<u>Ingredients</u>

1 ½ sticks butter (Forget margarine, eat the real thing!)

2 cups all-purpose flour (If you want whole wheat, fine… but it won't be as good)

1 ½ cups sugar (Yes, the lovely white refined kind)

4 tsp baking powder (Stephen always said was a housewife's gunpowder!)

1 tsp salt (Zeke, it won't raise your blood pressure if you eat just one piece!)

1 tsp Lavender blossoms (optional)

1 cup milk, half & half, or whipping cream (I recommend whipping cream)

2 tsp vanilla extract (Everything is better with vanilla)

2 TBS tapioca pearls

4 ½ cups (2 average-sized packages) frozen blackberries, thawed and drained (You can have the taste of summer all year round thanks to the lovely invention — the deep freeze!)

<u>Directions</u>

Bake in a 13" x 9" pan (Think of it as dessert casserole!)

Preheat oven to 375 degrees. As the oven preheats, add the butter to the baking dish and place in the oven. Remove pan from oven when butter has melted. (Hint: You really do want to keep an eye on it… burned butter just isn't the flavor you're trying to achieve.)

Meanwhile, mix flour, sugar (reserve half a cup), baking powder, lavender blossoms and salt into a large mixing bowl. Next add milk (or if you want an exceptional product, cream!), and vanilla extract to the dry mixture, and mix well. As you mix, remember to thank the Lord for creating berries!

Spread the batter evenly over the butter in the baking dish. Next, arrange the blackberries over the batter, and then sprinkle the tapioca and half cup of sugar over the berries. Place the baking dish in the oven (DON'T forget to use potholders! That pan is just out of the oven, and if you'd been in the oven at 375 degrees you'd be hot too! You can burn your hands so fast it'll take prescription strength salve to soothe them— not that I'd know anything about that) and bake for 45 minutes to 1 hour (until the crust is golden brown). To test doneness, insert a toothpick into the batter. A "clean" toothpick indicates a done dish (which in cooking is a done deal)!

Serve with whipped cream or vanilla ice cream.

For Keeps

Chautona Havig

CPSIA information can be obtained
at www.ICGtesting.com
Printed in the USA
LVHW011710210121
677114LV00015B/2047